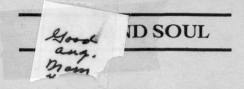

ND SOUL

Good aug. Mom

Clothes fell away as heartbeats accelerated. And when Diamond stood before him clothed in nothing but the truth, Jesse started to shake.

"My God, woman, but you're beautiful," he whispered.

She moved against him and moaned softly when his lips found the wild, pounding pulse at the base of her throat.

"Mine," Jesse said. The harshness of his voice was evidence of the passion about to overwhelm him. "You're mine."

He pushed her onto the leather couch, pausing above her so that the desire on her face would be forever etched on his mind. He wanted never to forget her.

Also by Sharon Sala

Chance McCall

Available from HarperPaperbacks

DIAMOND

Sharon Sala

HarperPaperbacks
A Division of HarperCollinsPublishers

HarperPaperbacks   *A Division of* HarperCollins*Publishers*
10 East 53rd Street, New York, N.Y. 10022

Cover photograph by Herman Estevez

First printing: February 1994

Printed in the United States of America

HarperPaperbacks, HarperMonogram, and colophon are
trademarks of HarperCollins*Publishers*

❖ 10 9 8 7 6 5 4 3 2 1

This book is dedicated to sisters.

To my birth sister, Diane, who I wish with all my heart had lived to see my dreams come true.

To my sister of the heart, Loretta Broyles Sawyer, who's been my best friend since we were five years old.

And to my sisters in writing, all the members of Oklahoma Romance Writers of America, especially Nancy Berland, Charlene Buerger, Olga Button, June Calvin, Debbie Cowan, Elizabeth Dew, Connie Feddersen, Janis Reams Hudson, Kathy Ishcomer, Patsy Klingstedt, Merline Lovelace, Curtiss Ann Matlock, Peggy Morse, Julia Mozingo, Lynne Murphy, Sara Orwig, Maggie Price, Karren Radko, Wendy Rego, Amy Sandrin, Willena Shales, Pat Shaver, Mary Jo Springer, and Ruth Wender.

Prologue

Prologue

The room smelled mousey. Like old clothes and unwashed floors and walls. A place where sunshine rarely ventured.

Twelve-year-old Queen Houston stared up at the dusty, narrow window high above the principal's desk and then back at the woman behind it.

Her younger sister, Diamond, grabbed at her hand and clenched it as the principal shifted in her chair.

Their baby sister, Lucky, was unconcerned with the ominous silence. This was her first year in school, yet already the second school during that year.

Queen and Di were veterans at this process and knew to give nothing away. They volunteered no smiles, no information.

"So," Mrs. Willis began, "you girls have just moved to Cradle Creek, have you? Let's see, the first thing we need is an address. Where do you live?"

"403 Front Street," Queen answered, and watched

the principal's eyebrows arch. She knew what the woman was thinking. She'd seen that look . . . on other faces . . . in other places.

"Front Street," Mrs. Willis repeated, and entered the information on the correct line on the form in front of her.

Jedda Willis tried not to frown. Poverty was a way of life for many in Cradle Creek, Tennessee, but ill repute was not. 403 Front Street was next door to an all-night bar and across the street from the residence of the town's one and only prostitute.

"Parents' names?" she asked next.

"Johnny Houston," Queen answered, and once again Mrs. Willis noticed that only the elder girl spoke. The others seemed frozen in silence.

Mrs. Willis looked up, pen poised above the paper, and waited. But it was in vain. Nothing more was said. She persisted. "Mother's name?"

Tears welled up in the eyes of the skinny blonde child sitting on the left, but otherwise nothing revealed the depth of the pain the woman's question had elicited.

"Mine's dead," Queen said. She smoothed back a stray lock of her unruly red hair and glared, almost daring the woman to continue. She did.

"What about theirs?" she asked, pointing to the two younger children.

Queen gripped Di's fingers tighter, then pulled Lucky into her lap. "She ran off. Been gone more than three years. Don't know where she is and we don't care . . . do we, girls?"

Lucky ducked her head, and her straight, dark hair fell across her face and eyes. She barely remembered anyone in her life other than her Queenie . . . and Di. But it was to be expected. She was only seven.

She slipped her thumb into her mouth, closed her eyes, and began to rock against her sister's budding bosom.

Jedda Willis had seen a lot of life in her fifty-nine years. But something about their defiance made her sick at heart.

"All right," she continued, as if their answers were commonplace. "Let's see . . . what's next? Oh yes! Father's occupation?"

The girls grew still. There was a subtle shift in their posture as they began to press against each other, nearly melding into one entity as Queen answered.

"Johnny gambles."

It was an unexpected statement. Jedda Willis repeated the word without thinking. "Gambles?"

The oldest girl nodded once, and her mouth thinned perceptibly, giving her an impish quality. But the impression was as far removed from fact as night from day. There was no whimsy in Queen Houston's life. Nor financial security, social standing, or respect . . . for themselves or anyone else. They were simply the gambler's daughters.

Three pairs of wide green eyes stared at Jedda Willis, waiting. She had an instinctive notion to apologize, but for what, she didn't know. Instead she stood.

"Come along, girls. Let's get you in class."

They followed. Quietly. Resigned to their fate.

1

Johnny Houston was a gambler. He'd always said it would take an act of Congress to make him quit. He'd been wrong. It was an act of God.

An itinerant breeze lifted the heavy blonde hair from Diamond's neck. She shifted her weight from one hip to the other and squinted against the sun's glare.

The minister was sweating. Diamond resisted the urge to smile. It wasn't a time for levity, although Johnny would have been the first to laugh. It had taken death to get Johnny Houston before a preacher.

Tears suddenly rushed to her eyes, blurring her vision. She blinked and looked down at the grass beneath her feet, trying to ignore the deep hole just to her right. It was as close to a pauper's grave as Cradle Creek could manage and was about to become the final resting place of her father, John Jacob Houston.

Queen's gaze was fixed. Her chin jutted in stubborn defiance, daring the reluctant minister to say one derogatory word about her father or his life-style. She'd hated it and resented him for it. But if anyone was going to pass judgment on Johnny Houston, it would be her—or God. At twenty-nine, and as the eldest daughter, it would be her right.

She saw Di's tears. They were as familiar to her as Di's wide, generous mouth and surprising beauty. No matter how many times in their lives Johnny had gambled away every cent they had, Diamond was the one quickest to forgive. It was Queen's opinion that Di had too much compassion for her own good.

Lucky stared blindly at the deep, shady hole on the side of the hill and tried to envision her fun-loving father beneath six feet of Tennessee dirt . . . forever. She shuddered and swallowed a sob. It was unthinkable.

The minister began to repeat the Lord's Prayer. Lucky's fingers twitched. And then each of her sisters reached out to her. Their palms touched. Fingers intertwined. But she didn't look up. She didn't have to. As always, her sisters were beside her.

They stood, three abreast at the foot of their father's empty grave, bound by the touch of their hands and the bonds of birth. Marked by a man they'd called father and the life that he'd led.

Brother Joseph Chatham breathed a quiet sigh of relief as his sermon came to an end. From the moment he'd stepped onto the hillside until now, he'd felt the fire from three pairs of sharp green eyes. He knew that Cradle Creek had not been kind to Johnny Houston's girls. But fate had. In all his years of ministering he'd never seen three more striking women. He flushed with guilt as he realized that he'd been thinking covetous thoughts about a family in mourning.

At the minister's nod, the gravediggers began to slowly lower the plain pine casket into the ground.

Queen gritted her teeth and stared, refusing to show weakness or emotion. Lucky closed her eyes as a single tear finally slid down her face. But it was Diamond who broke the silence of the moment. She stepped forward, lifted her face to the sun, took a long deep breath, and began to sing.

It had been good to go home, even if only for overnight, and regardless of the fact that Tommy Thomas, his manager, had thrown a fit the size of Dallas Stadium when Jesse had announced his intentions. The familiarity of family and high school football, not to mention hunting and fishing, had slowly taken a backseat in his life. It was something he missed and had decided last week to reclaim. When his dream of success had become reality, *ordinary* had disappeared from his vocabulary.

Jesse Eagle of Rocky Flat, Kentucky, was one of the hottest, if not *the* hottest, country singers in the nation. His career had been five years in the making, but the fast track he was on showed no signs of slowing down.

He geared down as a sharp curve on the narrow mountain road appeared, and grimaced as his tired muscles pulled across his shoulders. It was an unwelcome reminder of how long he'd been driving. He tried to stretch his long legs beneath the dash of the sports car, but his knee hit the steering column.

The car was a culmination of several childhood fantasies, but Jesse's tall, lanky build would have been better suited to an eighteen-wheeler than the interior of a Maserati.

A warning light came on, reminding him that fuel was running low. He looked up in time to read the small green sign at the side of the road. He was less than three miles from someplace called Cradle Creek, Tennessee.

"If I'm lucky," he muttered, "they'll have a gas station. If I'm real lucky, they'll even have a cafe."

He looked in the rearview mirror and then laughed at himself. It was the first time in almost three years that he'd had a chance to be alone, and here he was talking to his reflection.

Cradle Creek was larger than he'd expected. Signs of a worked-out mine at the edge of town and another farther off the road suggested coal, as did the telltale smoke columns rising into the atmosphere. Obviously when the first had played out, they'd simply moved the mining farther up the mountain.

Sunshine glared across the hood of his car and into his eyes as he entered the outskirts of town. He slowed to accommodate a gaggle of half-dressed, half-grown boys carrying fishing poles. As one of the braver ones flipped him off and then laughed, Jesse honked playfully in return. In his youth, he would have done the same. This low-slung car said money, and in this town, it would be like waving a red flag in front of an angry bull.

Tin-roofed, unpainted houses occupied every nook and cranny of the hills surrounding the single, two-lane road that ran through Cradle Creek. Some boasted porches that barely hung onto the residences on which they belonged. Others were bare-faced and open-doored, allowing freedom to any dog, chicken, or child who happened to be coming through.

A sign to the left caught his eye. *GAS.* Short and to the point. Jesse grinned. He smiled a lot these days. It was to be expected. Jesse Eagle had plenty to smile about.

He pulled up and parked between two outdated gas pumps at the front of the store. One wore an enormous cardboard box over its top that informed whoever cared to know that it was "BROKE." The last person to use the other had neglected to replace the hose back in the cradle. Jesse stepped over it before dragging it out of the dirt. He frowned at the grit and grime clinging to the nozzle and looked toward the station's open doorway. He had no intention of sticking it into his fuel tank until it had been cleaned.

He blinked and pulled his black Stetson lower across his forehead as the fierce glare of the sun glanced across his vision. The smoky tinted windows on his car had protected him from this intense blast of July heat. He was eager to crawl back inside his car and head toward Nashville and the ranch on the outskirts that he called home.

And then he heard her singing.

"Fill 'er up?" a man asked as he sauntered from the station.

Jesse didn't answer. He was dumbstruck by the clear, almost crystal quality of her voice. Hair stood on the back of his neck as the pain in her voice pulled at his heart. It was the first time he'd ever contemplated the true meaning of "Amazing Grace." For just a moment, following the pitch of her voice, he felt as if he'd just received grace . . . straight from God himself.

"*. . . that saved a wretch like me . . .*"

"Who's that?" Jesse asked, turning slowly around in place, trying to locate the owner of that voice.

The man hitched at his pants and spit. "Just one of them Houston girls," he drawled. "You want I should fill 'er up?" he asked again.

Jesse nodded as he continued to search for the voice's owner. "But clean the damned nozzle before you put it in my car," he remembered to add.

The man hastily did as he was ordered. It wasn't every day he got a chance to fill anything up. Usually all he sold was a few dollars' worth at a time.

"Where is she?" Jesse asked. Something vast was expanding inside his chest. An understanding . . . a need to find this woman and see what kind of a person had been blessed with such a voice.

The man spit again, aiming for the same spot as before, superstitiously telling himself that if it landed close, what he revealed wouldn't matter.

"Up yonder," he answered, pointing with his chin toward a sloping hill beyond the station. "At the cemetery."

Jesse stared. Cemetery? The man answered his unspoken question.

"Yep, cemetery. They're havin' a funeral . . . if you can call a preacher and three family members a funeral." And then he snickered. "Hell, I plumb forgot the gravediggers. That makes two more. And they're more than that sorry som'bitch deserves. He cheated me out of my honest wages more than oncet."

Jesse frowned. It was his opinion that a man couldn't be cheated out of money he never bet.

"Where?" he persisted as her voice pulled him toward the hill.

". . . once was lost . . . but now am found . . . was blind . . . but now . . ."

"I see," Jesse whispered, unconsciously saying the words he knew came next.

"Ifen you see, what the hell did you ask me for?" the man whined. And then he laughed, anxious that his customer not take offense and leave before the fill-up could be completed.

Jesse walked away. Drawn by the haunting voice and its message, he hurried toward the trees below the cemetery, his long, jean-clad legs quickly covering the distance. Coming to a halt beneath the shade of a sickly pine, he looked up at the thin but telltale covering of coal dust on the needles. Nothing grew healthy around places like this, including people.

". . . when we've been there, ten thousand years . . ."

Jesse looked past the trees toward the grassy hillside. A staggering number of makeshift tombstones dotted the area. Miners were a strange lot. Men who were willing to work beneath the ground their entire lives also spent eternity in the same location. It was a juxtaposition of logic.

And then he saw them. Standing side by side, not touching. But in the moment he looked, he felt their togetherness as strongly as if they'd been bound. It was the one in the middle who was singing. The unconscious sway of her body gave her away. Lost in the song and its words, she moved to a silent rhythm that only a true singer would recognize. Jesse felt her emotion . . . and her pain. And he wondered if everything she sang came from her heart as this had. If it did . . .

"*. . . than when we've first begun . . .*"

The song ended, as did Jesse's reverie. He stared long and hard, willing them to turn. He had an overwhelming need to look at her face.

They were tall. All three were dressed in faded blue jeans and shirts that looked as if they'd first been bought to fit someone smaller. But that was where their similarities ended. One had lush curves and a mane of wild red hair. Another was almost boyishly slender with a rope of hair hanging down her back that was nearly as black as the coal dug from these hills.

It was the one in the middle, the one who'd been singing, who caught his eye. Somewhere between the other sisters in build, her distinction lay in a swath of wild honey hair catching the heat of the overhead sun. And then she turned, and it moved across her neck and shoulders like melted butter.

Jesse grunted. He hadn't expected her beauty to match her build. "Sweet Jesus," he muttered, and leaned against the tree trunk as they came off the hill toward him.

No tears. No emotion whatsoever showed on their faces. They neither touched nor looked at each other or at him as they walked by. But he saw their eyes, all vividly green and bright with unshed tears. He shuddered and knew that what he'd considered moments ago was suddenly foolish and useless as hell.

He watched until they turned a street corner and

disappeared. Feeling strangely bereft that he'd been unable to touch what had touched him so deeply, he cursed beneath his breath and stomped back to his car.

"Twenty-two fifty," the man said, and then added, "Don't take no checks or plastic."

Jesse fanned the bills in his wallet, pulled out a twenty and three ones, slapped them in the man's hand and then slammed his backside into the driver's seat, suddenly eager to get away.

"Thanks, mister," the man said. "Say . . . you know what? You look awful familiar."

Jesse frowned. He'd wondered how long it would take for this to happen.

The man persisted. "Did anyone ever tell you that you're a dead ringer for that country singer fella . . . what's his name . . . Hawk? . . . or some bird name like that."

"Eagle."

"Yeah! That's it! You look just like Jesse Eagle. Did anyone ever tell you that?"

"No," Jesse said shortly, and shot out onto the road, leaving Cradle Creek and that voice behind him where they belonged.

"Well, hell!" the man said, turning away from the rising dust. "He wadn't none too friendly." And then he felt in his pocket for the money and hustled into the station. It was his opinion that when a man had money, he had no need of friends.

"What are we going to do now?" Diamond asked. "I don't want to stay here." She closed the door to her father's room, unwilling to look at that empty bed against the wall. "I *can't* stay here." The words burned in her throat.

Queen nodded in agreement. There was no longer anything—or anyone—to stay for. "I don't want to either," she said, "but where would we go? And more important, with what? We can hardly take our inheritance and jet off to see the world." As always, bitterness hovered just below the surface of her voice.

She, more than the others, had resented the hell out of her father and his lackadaisical life. He'd cheated her out of her childhood by leaving her to raise her two younger sisters. Even when they were old enough to take care of themselves, she'd still been unable to break the ties of responsibility that life had ingrained into her personality.

Lucky sighed and sank down onto the couch, avoiding the cracked leather in the middle cushion. "Morton Whitelaw repeated his offer to buy this house," she said softly.

They turned and stared at her, shocked by the announcement.

"When?" Queen asked.

"Yesterday, before you got home from cleaning the Abercrombie house."

Diamond frowned. In a small way she felt betrayed. There was no love lost between Morton Whitelaw and herself, but she *did* work for the man.

The first time she'd crossed the alley and walked into the bar to ask for a job, tall and well developed beyond her eighteen years, she'd known he would hire her. Even though he was older than her father, she'd seen that look of wanting in his eyes. She'd asked if he wanted a singer, and he'd hired her as a waitress. On busy nights he let her sing for tips.

He'd never crossed the line she'd drawn, and in return she'd given him seven years of hard work for little pay. Anger flared in her now. So this was how he repaid her loyalty.

She leaned against the window and stared at the fading daylight. Night came swiftly in the mountains, even in summer.

"It's okay, Queenie," Lucky said. "It's not like it was the first time he'd asked."

Queen frowned. First at the childish usage of her name that she hated and only allowed her baby sister to use, and second at the fact that Whitelaw hadn't had the decency to wait until their father had been buried.

She sighed, dropped down on the other end of the couch, and stared at the buckled and peeling wallpaper, the faded linoleum, and the limp curtains hanging at the windows. What did it matter when he asked? She should be thankful that he still wanted the place. They didn't.

Cradle Creek had little to offer in the way of employment for women. Lucky didn't work, and never had. She'd simply hovered at her father's side all of her life. Her sisters knew of her skill with cards and of the fascination they held for her. Wagering was no secret either. Her slim, nimble fingers could shuffle and deal with the best of players. But she didn't have the fever. Just a secret desire to go to one of the shiny places, maybe Vegas or Reno, and display her skill and expertise. Thanks to Johnny Houston, it was all she knew.

Lucky frowned, remembering Whitelaw's knowing stare and the way his hands had twitched as he watched her breasts instead of her face when he'd made the offer. If Johnny'd been alive, Whitelaw wouldn't have dared behave in such a manner. But he wasn't. Her lip trembled. She had a horrible suspicion that their bad luck had taken an unbelievable turn for the worse.

To sell or not to sell had been a bone of contention between the Houstons and the owner of the bar next door for over ten years. Whitelaw had wanted to expand. Johnny had laughingly refused.

Oddly, it was the one and only thing that Johnny Houston had refused to wager. Every time Whitelaw had asked, Johnny had responded with a cryptic "I lost my luck, but I'll be damned if I lose my home." It had infuriated Whitelaw, but he'd had no choice but to accept.

The news Lucky had just given them made Queen livid. Obviously Whitelaw had been unable to contain his greed until Johnny was decently buried.

"What did he offer?" Queen asked, expecting to hear the usual amount quoted.

"Five thousand," Lucky whispered, knowing the eruption that would ensue.

She was right. Queen came off the couch in a flash of red hair and anger. Diamond turned away from the window and grabbed her older sister just as she started through the door.

"Don't," she begged her. "It'll only make things worse. He doesn't have to give us a thing. If he wanted, all he has to do is wait until it's time to pay taxes and then buy it for nothing, and you know it."

Queen slumped. It was one of the few times in her life that truth had stopped her fury. That and the fact that today they'd buried Johnny. Memories overwhelmed her. Di was nearly twenty-six, and Lucky, twenty-four. It didn't seem possible. Where did the time go?

Tears began to form in her eyes, a rare event. She'd done all she could to hold this family together, and now they were going to lose what little they had.

"It's half what he offered last month," Lucky muttered, refusing to give in to panic. She waited. Queenie would have an answer. She always did. But the answer to their dilemma came from an unexpected source.

"I'll deal with him," Diamond said. The fierce glint in her eyes was a warning of how deeply this had affected her.

"I don't know . . ." Queen began.

"No!" Diamond interrupted her. "Leave it to me. I said I'll handle it—and him, okay?"

Silence was their agreement.

Jesse tossed his hat on a table and set his suitcase down beside the bureau. He dropped onto the bed and stared at the ceiling. It was nearly midnight, and he was still a couple of hours out of Nashville. Too weary to attempt the drive in the dark, he'd opted for the next Motel 6 he'd seen. He'd registered and then made a quick getaway from the desk before he was recognized. He was beginning to appreciate what his manager usually did for him.

His stomach grumbled, reminding him that he hadn't eaten since breakfast. He'd been going to get a bottle of pop and some chips at that gas station back in . . . what was that town? Cradle something. Creek! Cradle Creek. But that was before he'd heard her. And seen her. And then run like the scared dog that he was.

He flung an arm across his eyes, trying to block out her image. It was no use. He'd driven the last hundred miles with her face staring back at him through his windshield as plainly as if she'd been a hood ornament.

"Godammit to hell," Jesse muttered, rolling to a sitting position and grabbing for the phone. It didn't take long to punch a series of buttons, nor for the raspy voice at the other end of the line to berate him once he'd identified himself.

"Hell yes, I'm alive," he said, as his manager shrieked in his ear. "No, nothing's wrong. I'm just tired and decided to spend the night in a motel."

Another set of shrieks erupted, and for the first time that day, Jesse began to smile. "Yes, Mother, I'm alone," he teased, knowing that nothing panicked his manager more than the thought of groupies and paternity suits. "Calm down, Tommy. I'm tired but fine. The visit home was worth it." A sense of peace enveloped him as he lay back on the bed and closed his eyes, remembering the voice . . . and the song. "Everything was worth it. I'll talk to you tomorrow. Sleep tight, buddy," he said quietly, and disconnected.

For one long moment, silence reigned. Then he leaned down and pulled off his boots. In a few minutes the only sounds in the room were running water and Jesse singing a wet rendition of "All Shook Up."

2

Diamond hefted the tray of drinks and started across the floor, competently weaving her way through the tightly packed tables in the smoke-filled room. Most of the normal banter she would receive on a night like this was absent, as was the man who always sat in the corner chair at the last table. She'd known that coming back to work would be hard, but she'd had no idea how empty that spindle-back chair would look without her father in it. Nor how much she would miss the occasional wink he used to give her as she passed his way.

"Hey, blondie," a regular yelled. "Bring another round. It's thirsty work in the hole." His reference to the mines was as well used as the bills he slapped on the table to punctuate his order.

She nodded and headed back toward the bar.

Grit crunched beneath her scuffed ropers as she scooted to a halt. "Five more at Murph's table," she said shortly, knowing that Morton Whitelaw kept a mental running tab on every table in the place.

He filled the mugs and slid them toward her. The overflowing brews left a wet trail along the counter as she quickly refilled her tray.

"Real sorry about Johnny," Morton finally muttered.

It had taken him three hours to get up the nerve to say it. The comment had been on the tip of his tongue when she came to work, but the look on her face had put him off. If he didn't know better, he'd have sworn she'd glared. He'd expected sadness from her, even depression, but not anger.

Diamond watched his mottled complexion turn a deeper shade of red as she ignored his condolence and silently walked away with the order.

Morton frowned. She was obviously angry, and he would bet a month's receipts he knew why. But what the hell did they expect? A man had to make a dollar when the opportunity arose, even if someone else suffered in the process. Besides, he told himself, if those three sisters weren't so damned uppity, they'd do what any self-respecting woman in these parts did, and that was get themselves married. They needed to let someone else take care of them. Maybe then they wouldn't be so high and mighty.

"Hey, shiny girl," Crockett Tolly yelled, "sing us a song."

She smiled. Crockett was her favorite customer. And his teasing nickname was old business between them. He'd always told Johnny that giving her the name Diamond was probably smart because no one would ever have the money to give her real ones. She decided she might feel better if she fell into a routine, as if nothing had changed. She turned to Morton for the okay.

He nodded. It wouldn't hurt to give her some leeway

tonight. It wasn't Saturday, but what the hell, if they wanted her to sing, she could sing. He didn't care as long as they kept drinking.

Diamond retrieved the old guitar from a closet in the hall. One of the men relinquished his stool at the bar and dragged it into the small, empty space in the center of the room. She sat down and wound her long legs around the rungs of the stool, absently locking herself in place as she strummed keys and chords while tightening the strings to the proper pitch.

"Sing us your favorite," one of the men called out.

The murmurs of agreement swept through Whitelaw's Bar as the men settled down. They knew well the depth of emotion that Johnny Houston's middle daughter could wring from a song, and having her sing her "favorite" was the only way they knew how to express regret for her loss without voicing the sentiment.

Diamond smiled as she bent over the instrument. Her thick, honey-colored hair fell forward, half hiding her face from the men's knowing eyes. Her fingers strummed across the strings, touching tentative chords as she relaxed. And then as always, she took them unaware.

The song burst forth in the middle of a chord, her fingers catching up with the melody as the words filled the smoky room. And one by one the men fell silent and listened—until she reached the chorus.

"Did you ever know that you're my hero . . ."

At that moment, every man in the room, including Morton Whitelaw, would have given a year of his life to have been the man in her song.

". . . and everything I'd like to be . . ."

Her voice rang out—one clear, pure note after another, without any struggle for breath or timing, without pause for effect. Diamond Houston had forgotten everything but the song filling her heart and her soul.

Guided by the flashing red Christmas lights strung across the porch, Jesse pulled into the parking lot and leaned his forehead on the steering wheel. Only a dive like this would use Christmas lights in the middle of July.

He still couldn't believe he was here. He'd awakened a little after noon, eaten, filled up the car with gas, and backtracked to Cradle Creek without conscious thought.

She'd haunted him the night before. He'd tossed and turned, dreaming of green eyes and tall women and a voice that kept calling him home. When he'd finally slept, it had been out of exhaustion. And when he'd awoke, he'd known what he needed to do.

"Well, dumb ass," he told himself, "you're here. Now get out of the car and go find her. What you do after that is your own damn worry."

He didn't have far to go. It had been his intention to go into the bar and casually ask the locals for an address. But the moment he emerged from his car, he knew his search was over before it had really begun. That voice filled the night air . . . and his heart. His legs began to shake. It took all his strength to walk onto the porch and push his way inside. His sense of survival told him this might be the stupidest thing he'd ever done, but instinct told him he'd be sorry the rest of his life if he didn't.

As Jesse entered, he dreaded the impact his appearance

might make. He could have spared himself the worry. The place was packed, yet not a man turned at his entrance. They were locked in place by a woman and a song—and dreams of something better than what life had dealt them.

Jesse Eagle leaned against the back wall and let himself be drawn into her world and her music. And when her voice soared, he felt unexpected tears beneath his lashes. He swallowed and stared as the sound vibrated through the air.

"*. . . fly higher than an eagle . . .*"

His stomach tilted. With a voice like that, she very well could fly higher than eagles, even one called Jesse. And yet he stayed, his gaze pinned to the curtain of hair hiding her features, anxiously awaiting the moment when she'd straighten. Then he could see her face, and those eyes, and know whether or not he was a fool.

Diamond sighed as the last note faded. It was habit that made her stand and turn toward the chair at the back of the room. The shock on her face was apparent. A soft gasp swept through the bar as the men realized what she'd done.

It had been Johnny's practice to pass his hat after her song, collecting her tips as he coerced the younger men to pitch in extra, teasing them with promises Diamond had no intention of keeping.

But no one stood and started the applause that normally followed. Shock froze the assembly in place.

Jesse sensed the drama but was unaware of its cause.

"Hell!" one of the men muttered, then shoved back his chair and bolted toward the door. He'd rather face a cave-in at the mine than let these men see him cry.

"What's going on?" Jesse asked quietly as the man walked past him.

The man looked back at Diamond. "Her old man always used to pass the hat after she sang. I guess she forgot he ain't here." He shook his head and walked away, unable to continue his explanation.

But Jesse needed no further explanation. Yesterday they'd buried the man who passed the hat.

He never knew what made him do it. Possibly it was the look of pain that came over her face as she turned and walked from the room. That and the fact that she never looked back.

He pushed himself away from the wall, yanked off his trademark black Stetson with the gold eagle emblem on the band, and started weaving his way through the tables.

"Come on now, boys," he chided. "Cough it up for the lady."

At first they were stunned. Some even scooted back in their seats, half expecting to see Johnny Houston's ghost. But it wasn't a ghost—it was a shooting star.

"Hey!" Morton Whitelaw shouted. "Aren't you Jesse Eagle?"

Jesse put on what Tommy called his "famous face" and started working the crowd like a pro.

"Hell yes, I'm Jesse Eagle," he said, and laughed aloud. "And I've just heard an angel sing. Come on boys, ante up. She deserves everything in your pockets, but I'll settle for half."

The room erupted. Everyone crowded around, trying to outdo his neighbor and stuff the most money into Jesse's hat. They'd forgotten that the money was only going to one of the Houston girls. They were in the presence of fame, and for just a moment they felt the glory as if it were their own.

Unaware of the turmoil she had left behind, Diamond leaned against the wall outside as she fought down her rising nausea. Whitelaw saw her exit and followed. "Now, honey," he said as he walked up behind her. "Don't let it get you down. I'll do all I can to help you." His hands slid across her shoulders and started down toward her breasts. "If you'd just let me, I could . . ."

She slapped his hands away and pivoted toward him.

"Help? You want to help?"

The tremor in her voice should have alerted him, but it didn't. He nodded when he should have run.

"Let's see," she said, choking on her words as fury enveloped her. "By help, you mean lowering the price you've been offering on our house for the past ten years. By help, you mean cheating three women who've just lost their father. By help you mean—"

"Now, Di, baby," he began, "you've got to understand my position."

"No I don't," she said, jabbing her forefinger into his paunch. "You're the one who's got to understand. And don't call me baby!"

She leaned closer until all he could see was the green fire in her eyes.

"Our asking price has gone up, not down. You make out a separate cashier's check to each of us in the amount of five thousand dollars, or I swear to God we'll give the damned property to that Holiness Church in the next hollow. Then you can spend the next five years with a nest of holy rollers and their snakes in your backyard. They'll preach the wages of sin to your customers until they're blue in the face and you're broke."

Morton blanched. She was serious. He could just picture those cages of rattlers and the men who believed that snake handling went hand in hand with faith. He started to argue and then realized that the less he said, the better. Mad as she was, it would be just like her to up the price again.

"Okay now, girlie," he growled, grabbing her by the arm. "You win, okay? But you can't blame a man for trying."

"I want the money by Saturday," she said, unable to believe that he'd folded so easily. She'd pictured having to go home and tell her sisters that they weren't getting five thousand dollars after all and that, instead, they had to give their house away to a religious congregation that had publicly reviled them and their father's ways.

"Sonofabitch," Morton mumbled. "That's day after tomorrow."

"Before noon," she said. "The bank closes at 1:00. Oh," she added, as Morton started inside, "I quit."

He spit, glared, and stomped back into the bar, shoving his way past a man with a hat full of money.

Jesse hesitated outside the doorway and stared into the darkness, trying to find the owner of that voice.

"Are you there?" he finally asked.

"Depends on who you're looking for," Diamond answered, and drew back a little farther into the shadows.

She didn't recognize him, but he had her money. That much she did recognize. And yet the longer she stared at the tall, dark-haired stranger, the more familiar he became. In fact, if she didn't know better, she'd swear that he was—

"You're Jesse Eagle, aren't you?"

Her question was expected. The lack of excitement in her voice was not. It wasn't the usual female reaction. Jesse was uncertain what came next. If she'd have asked for an autograph, or giggled, or thrown herself at him, he'd have known. But she did none of the above. She simply waited for his answer.

"I have your money," he said. "Heard about your father. I'm sorry."

Diamond's stomach tilted. She stepped out of the shadows and onto the porch. "Thanks," she said. "He died like he lived. Fast."

"I'm really sorry," Jesse repeated. "Accident?"

"Shock—I think," she said, and then started to laugh. "He'd just drawn a full house." Tears of laughter mixed with those of sorrow as she leaned against the wall and buried her face in her hands. "He had the rottenest luck of any fool gambler I ever knew."

It was the laughter that did it. When she widened that beautiful mouth and smiled through her tears, Jesse felt his belly sliding toward his boot tops. He didn't want to feel this attraction. He'd come to see a woman about her voice, not the rest of her life.

Diamond dropped her hands and let her head tilt backward. It hit the wall with a thump. She winced but relished the pain. She needed a good jolt of something to get her out of this funk.

"So, Jesse Eagle, what in God's name are you doing in a dump like this?" Then she started to laugh again.

"Excuse me, I think that should have been your line. You know the routine," she added, catching the puzzled look on his face. "What's a beautiful girl like you doing in a place like this?"

He looked down at his hat, brimming with wads of bills and heavy with coins, then back up at her. "I came for you," he said, and handed her the Stetson.

Diamond took the hat and two steps backward, sliding along the wall of the porch toward the darker shadows. It wasn't far to the house. Lucky was probably inside, and Queen had to be home, too. If she yelled as she jumped they'd surely hear her. He wouldn't have time to—

He saw her fear, and it made him angry that he'd been so completely misunderstood. He stepped forward and grabbed her by the arm just as she started to run.

"Dammit, lady, I didn't backtrack across a hundred and seventy miles of pissant mountain roads to attack a total stranger. Who in blazes do you think I am, anyway?"

"I know who you are, but not why you're here."

Her answer silenced him. It was as good as a slap, any day. He ran his hands through his hair, but it only made it more unruly.

"Will you at least listen to what I have to say? Please?"

She shrugged.

He persisted. "Where do you live?"

For one long moment they stared, assessing each other. Diamond was the first to speak, and when she did, she was rewarded with one of the most beautiful smiles she'd ever seen a fully dressed man wear.

"Next door. I guess you can come over, but I won't be alone. My sisters are home."

He sighed with relief as he followed her retreat. "Good," he muttered quietly. "The way I feel right now, we both need referees."

His gut twisted as her hips swayed seductively with each long stride she took toward home. Her body was a study in rhythm and motion, and he wondered if she made love as slowly as she walked. The thought elicited a groan that made Diamond turn and glare, thinking he'd bumped into something in the dark.

"Watch your step," she cautioned. "We don't have homeowner's insurance, you know. You fall and bust that pretty face of yours, you fix it yourself."

He laughed.

Diamond frowned again. This was a man to be wary of. It didn't seem to matter how rude she got. He never seemed to mind. In fact, if she didn't know better, she'd swear he liked it. She opened the door and walked into the house, leaving him to follow at will.

"Queenie, look!" Lucky's squeal at the sight of all that money in the hat was nothing compared to the glare Queen sent toward the tall, dark-haired man who followed Diamond through the door.

"Who's he?" she asked.

Lucky's second squeal was answer enough. "Ohmigosh! Jesse Eagle!" She tugged at her T-shirt and then shoved her hands into the pockets of her cutoffs, trying desperately not to giggle.

Queen stood up, willing herself not to overreact to the fact that a very famous man had just walked into their home. But she had an awful feeling about this man and his arrival. She knew what he did for a living. And she knew what a gift her sister had. Please God, not that—not now, she thought. She couldn't face losing a sister, not this soon after Johnny. And then he spoke.

"Ladies. I'm really sorry to intrude into your family during your time of grief."

"But you did it anyway," Queen said. "Just what we need, another man intruding when our defenses are down."

Diamond interrupted. "Our defenses aren't quite as down as they were, Queenie." She grinned as her older sister glared at the use of that nickname. "It seems that Morton Whitelaw had a change of heart. By Saturday noon, we're each going to be in possession of a cashier's check for five thousand dollars."

"Each?" Lucky staggered backward and landed on the sofa. She didn't even wince when the curling edges of the middle cushion snagged the tender insides of her bare legs. "Why did he change his mind?"

"Because I told him if he didn't, we were going to give the property to the Holiness Church across the hollow."

"Those snake handlers? My God, Di! Did he faint or what?" Lucky asked, then started to smile. Just the thought of Whitelaw side by side with Bible thumpers was priceless.

Lucky jumped up from the sofa and threw her arms around her sisters. They laughed and shouted and did a little dance of jubilation in the center of the room.

Jesse was forgotten in the tumult, and it was just as well. He wouldn't have wanted them to see how dumbstruck he'd been by their abandon. Over the years he'd seen a lot of women. Some more beautiful than others. But he'd never seen anything like these three sisters.

Their height was unusual and as striking as the high Slavic cheekbones shaping their faces. And those matching sets of eyes, as clear and pure a green as new spring grass. But there the similarities seemed to end. A redhead, a blonde, and one with hair as black as coal. Each sister also seemed to have a distinct personality. He stared at them.

Diamond sighed as she dropped onto the couch and dumped her tips from the hat. "I was scared to death the entire time," she said. "I just knew I'd have to come back and tell you I'd failed."

"Are you ready to listen now?" Jesse asked, interrupting their moment. His eyes never left Diamond's face.

His voice was like a splash of cold water. The sisters looked at him with wary interest. All except for Queen, who closed her eyes and waited for the bullet.

"I don't even know your name," Jesse said to Diamond, "but I heard you sing yesterday at your father's grave— and then I drove away. It was a mistake. I don't often make them. That's why I came back. Lady, if you're willing, I'll take you with me to Nashville. I can guarantee you a record. I can guarantee you a manager. The rest will be up to you. If you want the career, it's yours."

"Diamond."

He frowned. His heart sank. He couldn't have misjudged her so badly. He'd promised her a shot at stardom, and she was already asking for diamonds?

"My name is Diamond Houston," she repeated.

"Hell, I thought you were . . ." He shrugged. "Never mind. Is that the name you use when you sing at the—"

She laughed. "I'd hardly assume a stage name for that

dump. It's real. And you may as well meet the rest of us, Mr. Eagle."

"Jesse," he corrected.

She shrugged. "This is Queen. She's the oldest. And Lucky is the baby. My father had a propensity for gambling and all that went with it. We know that they're rather unusual names, but we've grown to love them, right girls?"

They looked at one another and then burst into laughter.

"I suppose that's an inside joke," he drawled.

"I don't suppose you were just blowing smoke about Di's singing?" Queen asked. Anxiety was evident in the taut lines around her mouth.

Jesse shook his head. "I've never been more serious in my life."

For one long moment the girls stared at him, and then they stared at Diamond, absorbing the implications of his offer.

Diamond looked up at the man in their doorway. This had to be a dream—or a nightmare. Yesterday they'd buried Johnny, and today they'd sold their house for more than it was worth while someone offered her a chance at stardom as icing on the cake.

"Take it, Di," Lucky said quickly. "Don't waste luck. Johnny would turn over in his grave."

Queen swallowed once. "Go if you want," she said. "But I'm not following on your coat tail. I've always had a yearning to see New Mexico . . . or maybe Arizona. Somewhere that doesn't have a permanent pall of black coating the air I breathe."

Lucky's eyes widened. The fear of being on her own was almost overwhelming, but the excitement overshadowed it. "I'll go west," she whispered, her fingers curling in her lap at the thought of Vegas . . . and Reno . . . and all the shiny places that Johnny had spoken of.

Jesse felt their fear and, in a way, felt responsible. If he hadn't come back and been the one to separate them, they might never have done it on their own.

"Will you wait?" Diamond asked him.

Jesse nodded. Right then he would have waited forever.

She disappeared into a room off the hallway.

Queen walked toward him. When they were inches apart she spoke. Once again the hair crawled on the back of his neck. Jesse realized that these women were capable of eliciting great emotion, even fear.

"Don't hurt her," she said softly, her eyes never wavering from his face. "If you do, somehow I'll know. And I'll find you, Jesse Eagle. I'll find you."

The pain was tearing her apart. He could feel it. Without conscious thought his hand cupped her face.

"You won't have to look far, lady. I'll be standing in the shadow of your sister's glory."

He dropped his hand from her face and stepped back, sensing her discomfort. It was obvious that men and touching were not common commodities in this house. He dug through his pocket and then handed her a card.

"Here," he said. "This is my private number. And you can write to your sister at this address."

She nodded, took the card, and stuffed it in her jeans as Diamond came back into the room.

Jesse stared. One small bag. The woman was carrying

a single, small duffle bag. He'd dated women who carried larger purses. When you didn't have much, it didn't take a lot to pack it.

"I'm ready," she said, trying not to cry.

"I'll wait outside," he said quietly, suddenly realizing their need for privacy. The sound of one quiet sob followed him off the porch and into the night.

He'd never seen sunrise from this side of night. His eyes were dry and burning, his shoulders stiff from the long hours behind the wheel. Last night he'd simply loaded her up, bag and all, and headed west. Stopping at a motel with her had been unthinkable. He'd sensed her panic and known that one more shock would have been her undoing. And so he'd driven . . . and finally she'd slept.

A familiar curve in the road and the cattle guard they bumped across was warning enough that he'd just driven onto his property.

"Thank God," Jesse muttered, and pinched the bridge of his nose with his thumb and forefinger.

He glanced over at his passenger and tried to ignore the fact that the two top buttons on her shirt were missing. A generous amount of ivory skin showed beneath the faded plaid shirt she wore tucked into a pair of very worn, very tight jeans. Sometime during their drive she'd shed her boots, and he noticed that she wore no socks. Something about the small red blister on the side of her big toe made him want to curse. Instead he pulled beneath the split-log roof of his carport, shoved the stick shift into park, and turned off the engine, welcoming the silence.

He leaned wearily against the headrest and closed his eyes as he inhaled. A faint scent wafted across the interior of the car. He inhaled again, trying to identify the smell. And then he opened his eyes and turned to look at his sleeping passenger.

Her hands were curled into loose fists, lying limply in her lap. There, poking out the side of her hand, was a half-eaten roll of Lifesavers. Cinnamon.

Guilt overwhelmed him. He'd never even seen her put one in her mouth. He didn't want to guess when she'd eaten last. But he hadn't offered, and she hadn't asked.

"Come on, sweetheart," he said, shaking her gently. "Let's go inside and find you a bed. You can stretch out those long, pretty legs and sleep till you wake. We'll talk later."

Diamond didn't hear the endearment. She was too sleep-muddled. And if she had, she wouldn't have trusted him. She'd been dreaming. Of a tall, dark-haired man with laughing eyes who kept promising her heaven. And she'd cried because she hadn't believed him.

She crawled stiffly out of the small, low-slung car, her boots in one hand, her bag in the other, and staggered into the house behind him, thinking that maybe she wasn't so different from her father after all. She'd just gambled her life and her future on a stranger's promises.

3

A door banged in another part of the house. Diamond sat straight up in bed and looked around wildly, wondering why the wallpaper wasn't still peeling off the walls around her and why she smelled coffee instead of smoke from the mines.

Then she remembered.

What had she done? she wondered, looking down in dismay. Her nudity was as obvious as the room's opulence. Vague memories surfaced of Jesse's touch, and his voice, and something about promises. She'd undressed alone, of that she was almost certain. But the thought of food and coffee superseded any other worries that might have surfaced.

The corner of a bathtub was visible through the half-open doorway at the end of the room. She staggered toward it and into the shower, unable to appreciate the unexpected luxuries she was experiencing due to the deep growl her stomach was making. More than twenty-four hours had passed since she'd eaten anything substantial.

The hot water helped, as did the shampoo and blow-dryer conveniently placed on the vanity. And it didn't take long to dress. There wasn't that much in her bag from which to choose.

She stomped her foot to slide a boot into place and then headed for the door. She heard men's voices near-by and followed them and the smells of breakfast to what she supposed was the kitchen.

"It's the middle of the goddamned afternoon, you asshole," a man was saying to Jesse. "If your car hadn't been in the driveway when I arrived, I was calling the state police."

"Bull," Jesse muttered, rolling off the side of the bed. He headed for the bathroom, ignoring his nudity and his manager as he stepped beneath the shower head and turned on the water full force. ". . . worse than . . . if I'd . . . old mother hen."

Jesse may just as well have just shut up and saved his breath. Tommy had been near hysterics. He'd expected Jesse to arrive a full day earlier. As far as he was con-cerned, one phone call in the middle of the night over twenty-four hours ago did not constitute "checking in." And he was nobody's mother, least of all this man's. If he had been, he would have beat the hell out of him years ago.

Minutes later they headed toward the kitchen, with Jesse in the lead. "I made you some coffee," Tommy said. "There wasn't any ready. I suppose Henley's still gone?"

Jesse didn't answer, refusing to acknowledge

Tommy's thoughtfulness as well as his reference to the missing houseman.

"Goddammit, Jesse, you had me worried," Tommy went on, relenting just the least bit as he realized that his heavy hand was about to undo the uneasy truce they'd come to a few days earlier.

Jesse shrugged and poured himself a cup of coffee. Tommy's anger was justified, and he knew it. He just couldn't bring himself to admit why he'd been delayed. Even in the daylight, he could hardly believe it himself.

And then she walked into the room.

Tommy spun around, his bootheels leaving small black scuff marks on the ivory floor tile.

"Well, that explains everything," he said, waving his finger in Jesse's face. "Just what we need, some dumb blonde groupie hanging around when you've got that new album to cut. What happened? Couldn't you get enough without bringing her with you?"

Jesse saw red—and Diamond. But he didn't react quickly enough to stop her. From the corner of his eye he saw her swing, and then Tommy was flat on his back against the cabinet, holding his hand against his mouth as a thin stream of blood seeped between his fingers.

"Hell! You busted my damned mouth."

"I missed," Diamond said. "I was aiming for your nose."

She turned to Jesse, her coffee and her hunger forgotten in the fury that overwhelmed her. The words the little man had said were nothing she hadn't heard before, but their injustice was the last straw in a week of hell.

"Which way to Nashville?" she asked Jesse. "I want out."

Jesse staggered. Her reaction to Tommy's words had been unexpected but justified. But this took him unaware. He panicked.

"Diamond, no," he pleaded. "He didn't mean—"

"Let the bitch go," Tommy muttered.

Jesse pulled him up from the floor by his collar. The words he whispered in Tommy's face were all the more ominous by their lack of emotion.

"If you call her one more indecent name, so help me God, I'll bust your nose myself. Now shut the hell up. You don't know what you're talking about."

Tommy sat on a bar stool and bled quietly.

"He meant what he said, and we both know it," Diamond said. The pain in her eyes didn't reach her voice. "It doesn't matter," she continued, and turned her back. "You don't owe me anything."

She started for the door.

Jesse grabbed her by the shoulder and then let go the moment she turned. He took two steps backward just for good measure and held up his hands. He'd learned his first lesson about Diamond Houston. She, like her sister Queen, didn't like to be touched.

"Just listen to me," he said. "Tommy was upset. I didn't call him, and I should have. He thought something had happened to me. It's my fault for worrying him."

She crossed her arms and braced her feet, trying to ignore the quake in her belly and the tremble in her legs. Coffee drifted back across her senses, and her stomach growled again, reminding her once more how long it had been since she'd eaten.

"If this was worry, I'd hate to see him mad," she snapped, then closed her eyes as the room tilted.

"You're right," Jesse said. "And Tommy is going to apologize. Aren't you, Tommy?" He turned and glared at his manager.

If he hadn't turned, he might have caught her. As it was, he only heard the thump when she hit the floor. The sight of her lying sprawled at his feet with her hair spilling across his boots made him sick.

He dropped to his knees, his fingers frantically searching her wrists for a pulse. Fear for a woman he didn't even know nearly overwhelmed him. Then he leaned back on his bootheels and sighed with relief as he discovered her lifeblood ran strong beneath his fingertips.

Her face was pale and cool. She had thick lashes, several shades darker than the honey-colored hair falling through his palms. Her lower lip trembled and she moaned. Her stomach growled. It was then that he remembered the Lifesavers. It hurt him to think of her hunger when he had so much to share and hadn't offered.

"Here," Tommy said quickly as he knelt, "let me help."

"No!" Jesse said softly. He scooped her up in his arms and stood. For one long moment he stared at her face. "I'll do it," he finally said. "I promised."

Her eyes opened slowly, and with the movement came memory. Jesse grimaced as he watched her expression turn generic. He'd never met a woman who kept everything inside herself as Diamond Houston did. He had no idea how to deal with her, so he waited for her to make the first move.

"I never faint," she said, and swung her long legs off the edge of the sofa, wincing as another wave of dizziness overwhelmed her.

"So I see," he said. "I realize we didn't share any personal information with each other. I hope this is not a sign of things to come—like babies, for instance?"

She flushed angrily. "I'm not pregnant, I'm hungry."

It was Jesse's turn to flush. "I'm sorry I gave my cook the week off," he said. "But when backed against the wall, I can manage a pretty fair omelet. Come with me?" He held out his hand.

She stared at the hand, then up at the man. "Seems to me you're about as far back as a man can get and still walk, mister," she said, and then smiled. She reached toward him. Their hands touched and then clasped. Jesse pulled.

Then they were inches apart, staring nearly eye to eye. She inhaled slowly, and Jesse tried not to look at the way her breasts moved beneath her shirt as she breathed. Once again, he felt himself losing touch with reality. What was there about her that fascinated him so? She was prickly as hell and as close to a man-hater as he'd ever seen.

"Well done," she said.

"What?" He kept losing his place with this woman.

Diamond smiled and walked past him toward the kitchen and the alluring scent of coffee. "I like my eggs well done."

"Oh." There was nothing left to say. Jesse followed.

She looked around the area suspiciously, noting that the blood on the floor was missing, as was the man who'd shed it.

"I sent him to Nashville," Jesse said. "I explained the situation, as I should have done before we ever arrived. The misunderstanding was my fault, the rudeness was his. When you see him again, he will apologize."

She nodded and poured herself a cup of coffee, inhaling appreciatively before taking the first long sip. "Who is he?"

Jesse grinned. "He's my manager—and the man who's going to make you a star."

She turned and stared at him, the cup halfway to her lips. And then she grinned. Just once, and only from the left corner of her mouth. "Does he know that?" she asked.

"He does now, in spades," Jesse said. "Now quit worrying about the small stuff. Sit! You're about to eat food fit for a king."

"You don't have to fuss," she said. "I could do this myself if you'd—"

"No!" Jesse pointed at the table. She took her coffee with her and sat down. "That's better," he said. "Now stay where I can see you. It makes a man nervous to cook for a woman whose right hook is better than his."

Her face was frozen in shock. And then the small smile that had been hovering around her lips erupted into a full-blown laugh.

Jesse had the strangest urge to brush her hair away from her face and kiss her until laughing was the farthest thought from her mind.

His hand shook as he turned away and began digging

in a drawer for a spatula. He cracked eggs and diced ham, grated cheese and chopped onions. And tried not to think of how she'd feel lying beneath him as they made love. Over. And over. And over.

Feeding her had been difficult. What to do with her afterward had been impossible. He had phone calls to answer and people to see. But if he tended to business, who would tend to Diamond Houston?

A very unhealthy but obviously possessive streak had begun to assert itself. Jesse realized it for what it was: lust. He pulled himself together. Shuffling through a stack of sheet music in his office, he gathered some that he thought would be of interest to her and headed back to the living room.

It had to be lust, he kept telling himself. Either that or a simple fascination with a woman who sang like an angel. He didn't believe in love, not at first sight or even forever after. It was a highly overrated emotion that did not fit into his life.

But when he walked into the room and she looked up, he forgot everything he believed in except fate.

"Here," he said. "Why don't you look these over? See if there's anything in here that interests you. Maybe find something you could do for Tommy. If you don't find anything, don't worry. I've got a man who stays on the lookout for new material for me. All he needs to do is hear you sing, and then he can do the same for you."

She took the stack of music and dropped it into her lap without giving it a glance.

"What?" he asked. "So now you aren't interested?" She made him nervous, but he gave nothing away as to how desperately he awaited her answer.

"Oh, I'm interested," she drawled. "I'm just trying to figure out how much of what you're doing you already regret, and how much you wish you'd never stopped in Cradle Creek."

Blood drained from his face. He'd never had so many of his actions questioned in all his life. He placed a hand on either arm of the chair in which she was sitting and leaned forward until he could see his own reflection in those clear, green eyes.

"Don't even try to second-guess me, lady," he whispered. "I never regret anything that comes from my heart. I heard you sing. I liked it. I think you have more than a good shot in this business if you'll quit trying to defend something that isn't in danger. I won't hurt you, Diamond. I promised, remember?"

The urge to taste her lower lip was overwhelming. But it trembled once beneath his gaze. He pushed himself away as if he'd just been burned, then stomped from the room in a fit of injured dignity. Something made him stop just outside the hall, and he stood, holding his breath as he listened.

For a few minutes he heard nothing. He closed his eyes and swallowed, almost willing her to move . . . or curse, or do something to give him an indication of her true feelings. Then he heard the sounds of paper shuffling, knew that she was riffling through the sheet music, and sighed with relief.

"Thank God for small favors," he muttered softly, and went back to his office.

* * *

Diamond looked up from the stack of music and tried not to stare at the man who'd just entered the room. The fat lip she'd given him had gotten fatter since last they'd met. She cocked an eyebrow and waited. It was all the invitation that he was going to get. What he'd called her, with no provocation other than her presence, still rankled.

Tommy wanted to swagger. It was part of his personal intimidation process and usually worked wonders when negotiating deals for clients. He'd spent the better part of his forty-two years perfecting the art. But it was hard to work up the initiative to do so in front of a woman who, hours earlier, had knocked him on his ass. Instead, he shoved his hands into his pockets, pulled himself up to his full height of five feet, nine inches, and leaned against the door frame.

"Miss Houston."

"Yes?"

"It seems I owe you an apology."

Diamond dropped the stack of music onto a table and rose. "Seemed like that to me, too," she said quietly.

Tommy's toes curled at the ends of his boots. He resisted the urge to duck as she walked toward him. He hated to look up at anyone, especially a woman.

"Sorry." He shrugged, unwilling to waste anymore time on the subject. "I'm Tommy Thomas, Jesse's personal manager. He tells me you sing."

She stopped in midstep, assessing how much of this man's behavior was bravado and how much was his true personality. If he really was a son of a bitch, she'd already decided to cut her losses and leave. But if he'd only acted out of frustration and anger at Jesse, she could live with that—as long as she didn't have to live with him.

"Everyone sings, Mr. Thomas," she answered.

He flushed. His ears were still ringing from the dressing down Jesse had given him. It had never happened before, and he was ready to place blame entirely on this woman who'd entered their lives out of the blue.

"Okay," he drawled, and grinned, realizing that he'd probably met his match. "He said you had a hell of a voice and that if I had anything between my ears besides a fat lip, I'd listen."

"Apology accepted," she said quietly, and held out her hand.

Surprised by the gesture, he shook her hand before he realized it. When she turned and walked back to her music, he didn't know what to say. Like Jesse, Tommy had come in contact with all kinds of women, many who'd try anything to get in the business, or into the pants of a man already there. But this woman didn't seem to play by any rules he knew.

"So," he continued, "Jesse says he promised to make you a star."

"Those were his words, Mr. Thomas, not mine. I believe at the time he said them, I thought he was trying to steal my money."

"Steal your money?" He shoved himself away from the door frame and stomped away in search of Jesse. There had to be more to this story than he'd been told, and it was obvious that she wasn't going to tell him a thing.

"Damned closemouthed woman, anyway," he muttered. "Jesse! Where the hell are you?"

Her baptism by fire had come and gone with Tommy's departure. Diamond had gone to bed at the end of the day as weary as if she'd never slept the night before. This war of words was getting her down. Losing Johnny and her sisters in the space of a week was nearly more than she could bear. And she didn't know how much longer she could evade the issue that she was going to be living beneath the same roof with Jesse Eagle.

He fascinated her. Unlike any man she'd ever known, he seemed to sense when she needed her space. He never overstepped the unspoken boundaries she erected or resented the fact that they were there. And yet she knew to the second when he entered a room. He was full of energy and opinions, positive about the things he knew best—himself and music. And it seemed he was hell-bent on drawing her into his world whether she liked it or not.

Diamond flopped onto her stomach and doubled the pillow beneath her chin. The sheet slipped across her back and then down, coming to a halt just above her waist. Her breasts pressed into her body as she shifted on the mattress, and then her long legs scissored angrily as she struggled to free herself from a tangle of covers. If this was any indication of the rest she was about to get, it was going to be a long night.

Muttering to herself about the futility of trying to fit in where she didn't belong, she reached out to turn off the bedside lamp. A knock at her door startled her, so that when Jesse asked if he could come in, she told him yes before she thought.

He walked into the room and forgot why he was there.

She reached down and pulled up the sheet as she rolled over onto her back. In one smooth motion she'd covered herself.

"The next time I come in, for God's sake wear a nightgown," he muttered, trying to suppress the urge that surfaced below his belt.

"I wasn't expecting company," she said. "And I don't own one. Never did, never will. Don't like restrictions. Never have, never—"

"I get the picture," he said, and leaned against the wall, trying not to grin. *And you certainly are one*, he thought. He stood and stared, lost in imagination of what her long legs, high breasts, and narrow waist must look like beneath that thin covering of sheet.

"You knocked?" she reminded him.

"Oh!" He shoved himself away from the wall. "Yeah, right. I just wanted to tell you that early tomorrow morning we'll be driving into Nashville. I have my first rehearsal for the new album. I want you to just sit in and get an idea of how this process works. I won't pressure you into anything you're not ready for, okay? Tomorrow you just watch and learn. Later on, when I think you're ready, I'll give you a shot at a recording session just to see how you sound on tape."

Diamond tried to still the shiver of nerves and excitement that threaded through her system. But it was no use. She nodded and pulled the sheet just a tiny bit higher.

Discomfort was a mild word for what she felt to be

stark naked in this bed with a man like Jesse Eagle only feet away. And she was no fool. She could see the want in his eyes. But wanting wasn't what she needed. Diamond wasn't like Johnny. She wouldn't take a chance on anything except herself. If it wasn't a sure bet, she wanted no part of it. That included men and their infamous ability to mouth empty promises just to get what they wanted.

Jesse watched her shiver and cover herself more completely. He mistook the motion for one of fear. It angered him that in spite of everything he'd said and done, she still didn't trust him one bit.

"See you in the morning," he said, and stomped out, slamming the door behind him to make a statement.

He was halfway down the hall when he heard her turn the lock, making a statement of her own.

The air was clear and pure. Many scents were identifiable there on Jesse's ranch, but none of them spelled coal. For the first time since her adventure had begun, Diamond let herself imagine what life might be like away from the mines and the poverty.

She turned and stared at the panorama of the Tennessee hills, then back at Jesse's two-story home, admiring the cedar siding and the shake shingles on the steeply pitched roof. The massive rock chimney at the north side of the house blended perfectly with the flagstone walkway that led to the deep porch running the length of the house. To Diamond, it was all too perfect to be believed.

A horse neighed beyond a cluster of outbuildings, and she looked with interest, hoping for another glimpse of the foal she'd seen from her bedroom window the previous day.

"You ready?"

She hadn't heard Jesse approach. He startled her, as did the look in his eyes. But he pulled a pair of dark glasses from his pocket and slipped them up his nose, hiding whatever had been lurking before she had time to interpret it.

She nodded. "I've been ready for hours," she said. "I'm sorry, I don't have anything else to wear."

What he'd been about to say stuck in his throat. He could tell that her nervous excitement warred with her anxiety over not fitting in.

"Honey, don't ever apologize for what you are," he said softly, and slid his hand up her arm, ignoring the flinch of her muscles beneath his fingers. "This is the home of country music, remember? What you have on is standard fare. Besides, I know of at least three women who call themselves stars that would kill to fill out a pair of jeans like you do, okay?"

She blushed and turned away, unwilling for him to see the pleasure his words had given her.

"Let's get this show on the road," she said, and headed for the car.

"Wanna drive?" he asked, thinking the offer would please her. But once again, he'd opened another door into her life that Diamond would rather have left shut.

"No thanks," she said, and began to fumble with the seat belt.

Jesse slid in behind the wheel and shoved the key in the ignition. "I'm insured," he teased.

"I don't know how."

Motion ceased. The words hung between them and lengthened into a very uncomfortable silence. Finally it was Jesse who broke it.

"I guess you didn't have much need to drive, did you? After all, you lived next door to your job. It's not everyone who can claim that convenience." He was trying to minimize the importance of what she'd admitted. But it was useless; the damage had been done.

Diamond's hands knotted in her lap. She rubbed the tip of her finger across an old scar on her knuckle as she began to explain.

"Queen learned. That was before Johnny lost the pickup in an all-night poker game. Lucky learned when she was in high school. Boyfriend taught her. I guess I kind of fell through the cracks." She laughed and shrugged, but this time there was no joy in the sound, only bitterness.

Jesse didn't know what to say. Every time he opened his mouth around this woman, he said the wrong thing.

"It doesn't matter," she said. "I'll learn someday."

"I could teach you."

She leaned back. Laughter rang out, and this time it was sincere. "You? Teach me to drive?" Another spate of laughter deflated his ego.

"I'd like to know why that's so damned funny," he said as he started out the driveway.

She chuckled and leaned forward to adjust the volume of music coming from his tape deck.

"You always have to be in control, Jesse. How could you do that if I'm behind the wheel?"

The car swerved. It was slight, but enough to tell her she'd hit home with her comment. For her own safety and peace of mind, she'd had to say it. She stared out the window, absorbing the sound of his music as the view blurred before her eyes.

Confusion warred with frustration as he turned onto the road leading toward the city. How did this woman, whom he'd known only three short days, know so damn much about him and his personality? Where did she get off constantly refusing every offer of kindness he made? For two cents he'd take her back where he'd found her and—

His thoughts stopped short. He was lying to himself, and he knew it. There was no way in hell he would take Diamond Houston back to Cradle Creek. Not if Tommy threatened to quit tomorrow. Not if she begged. Not if she made him mad as hell at least once a day. Not if his life depended on it.

Whether it was a feeling of portent or a silent admission of honesty, he had the strangest sensation that his last thought was nothing more than fact.

Nashville was more than Diamond had expected and yet not as frightening as she'd imagined. She gawked and fidgeted as Jesse drove along the streets, unable to believe that she was actually there. Jesse turned off Broadway onto Fifth Street, and she took a deep breath as they drove past the Ryman Auditorium, the original home of the Grand Ole Opry. She imagined she could feel the lingering presence of music stars long gone and shivered in response to her fantasy.

Jesse watched Diamond's eyes widen and saw her fingers tighten on the seat as they passed one landmark after another. Just seeing her excitement made him remember his own emotions years earlier—how much he'd wanted to succeed as a singer, though he knew that the odds were highly stacked against him. It had left him hovering somewhere between awe and despair. But that was before Tommy Thomas came into his life.

Diamond turned toward Jesse, her eyes shining, the

corners of her lips tilted in a rare show of joy. Jesse inhaled sharply. The sudden vision of her lying beneath him with that same expression on her face made him swerve, barely missing a parked van on the street.

"Hell," he muttered softly.

This kind of thinking would get him nowhere. He'd seen the touch-me-not look in her eyes often enough to get the message. Besides, he told himself, he hadn't dragged her out of Cradle Creek just so he could sleep with her. He wanted to help her build a career. End of story.

But this thought did little to stem the heat simmering in him as he drove down Music Row toward the recording studio and parked his car. He watched her swing out one long leg and then the other before levering herself into a standing position.

"I wasn't built for cars that small," she said.

His grin was more like a grimace as he tried not to think of what she *had* been built for. A vivid image of her sensuous body and long legs made sweat break out on his forehead.

"Me neither," he said, trying to forget his earlier fantasy as he settled his black Stetson firmly onto his head. "But I hadn't yet outgrown my teenage fantasies when I had my first hit song. That car was the result."

Diamond grinned at his confession, her eyes dancing with merriment as she tried to imagine a younger, more naive Jesse Eagle. It was impossible. She could see him younger, but naive? That took more imagination than she could muster.

As he led her across the parking lot, Diamond let the excitement she was feeling overflow. In a few moments she was actually going to see the inside of a recording studio. And, before the day was over, she'd see firsthand what it took to cut an album. There was also the satisfaction that she'd have an excuse to sit and look at Jesse Eagle while it happened. Although she was sleeping in the same house with him and eating at the same table, it was a luxury she had not allowed herself.

They entered the studio to find that most of the members of Muddy Road, Jesse's band, had already arrived.

"Hey, hey, hey, Jess, old boy. I don't know where you went for vacation, but I want the address. If there's any more back there like her, I quit."

Jesse's gut jerked. It was an unexpected reaction to his bass guitar player's remark. For some reason, he took instant offense at the idea of Diamond being the butt of anyone's joke, no matter how innocent.

Mack Martin had a reputation with women that the guys in the band often joked about. Jesse didn't need to see Diamond's face to know that she was probably angry. He remembered Whitelaw's Bar and knew that Diamond had certainly heard worse, but that didn't change what he was feeling. His ability to appreciate the humor in Mack's attitude had just disappeared.

A faint blush swept across Diamond's cheeks, but her expression never wavered as she stared straight into the bearded man's eyes.

His long, lank hair was streaked with gray, as was the bushy beard that framed his wide face. His mouth was smiling, but his eyes were hard.

Diamond watched the guitar bounce against his leg as

he rose from a stool and started toward them. The name *Mack* was woven into the guitar strap. It fit him, she decided. He was as big as a Mack truck and about as ugly.

He slipped the guitar off his shoulder and enveloped Jesse in a boisterous hug. When Jesse wasn't watching, he looked Diamond up and down in a suggestive manner, winked, and blew her a kiss.

"Damn, Mack! I haven't had a greeting like this since my mother visited. If I'd known you cared, I would have written." Jesse let the sarcasm in his words substitute for the spurt of anger he felt.

Mack laughed loudly, as did the rest of the band, and gave Jesse a firm slap on the back.

Jesse quickly introduced Diamond to the other men, started to explain why she was there, then stopped when he saw their smirks. They didn't believe him, but he didn't care. He knew when the time was right, Diamond would prove herself all on her own without any help from him. Her talent was proof enough.

Diamond's smile never quite bloomed as she politely shook hands with each of the band members. Besides Mack, there was Jake, Monty, Al, and Dave. They all gave her varying looks of interest, none of which had anything to do with singing talent. And when Jesse's manager arrived, she got another, more calculating look. But this time, it was not unexpected. Tommy Thomas didn't like her, and considering their brief history, it was no wonder.

Tommy glared and then slid a practiced smile in place. He shook hands with Jesse and gave Diamond an offhand slap on the back as he swept past.

Diamond wisely ignored Tommy's locker-room

greeting and refused to respond to the antics of the men in the band. As the session got under way, they seemed to forget she was there. It was just the way she liked it. And so was Jesse's music.

Five hours later, Jesse's voice faded on the last note of the song he'd been singing, as strong and clear as when they'd begun. His broad hand splayed across the guitar strings and pressed gently, stilling them into silence.

Diamond shivered and leaned her head against the wall. Listening to him make love with his voice was almost too much for her to endure. And that was exactly what Jesse Eagle did with a song. He seduced and compelled, enticed and begged. And in the end, when the song was over, it was easy to believe that he'd been singing it just for her.

It was a singer's magic and the trap that often caught his female listeners. Diamond was aware of his magnetism but determined not to believe in the magic his songs created. She knew he sang them for himself as much as for everyone else's enjoyment. There was no one special woman in his life, but she suspected there was a long line of many who'd come and gone. She had no intention of falling for that line or into that trap, and it might have been possible to avoid doing so if she hadn't seen what happened next.

Jesse leaned across the stand holding his sheet music and pointed toward a passage he intended to rearrange. His guitar lay across his lap, held firmly in place with one hand as he gestured with the other. And all the while he was talking, he unconsciously stroked the warm, golden wood with his fingertips, letting them run along the curve in the instrument as a man follows the shape of his woman's body with his hands.

The strokes were long, slow, steady, and unceasing. She could see the moisture from his fingertips leaving small, almost invisible tracks across the wood.

Diamond jerked up, overturning her chair as she stalked out of the room.

The men looked up, surprised by the noise. She'd been so quiet, they'd almost forgotten she was present.

But not Jesse. He'd felt her presence throughout the day. He knew, to the moment, when she'd shifted in her chair and had seen her swing one long leg over the other as she changed position. He'd also heard her humming softly to herself through song after song. But her exit was unexpected, as was the expression he saw on her face. It was pain.

Jesse slid the guitar from his lap and called for a break.

The men smirked, allowing a few off-color remarks to surface as Jesse quickly followed Diamond out of the studio. Mack stared, mentally calculating the time it would take for Jesse to tire of her before he could make his move. Just looking at that woman made him hard.

The room she'd just left wasn't hot, but Diamond was. Watching Jesse's hands on that guitar had set a dream in motion that she'd been trying to deny existed. Try as she might, the feelings inside her were too strong to ignore. She knew the signs. They were rare, but it had happened once before when she was younger. Before she knew that all men lied and women cried. She was falling in love with a man who was already a legend in country music. It was probably the stupidest, most futile thing she'd ever done.

"Diamond, honey . . . are you all right?"

The concern in Jesse's voice was unmistakable. So was the icy look she gave him when she turned and answered.

"I'm not your honey. I'm just tired and hungry. And I'm sorry I ruined whatever was going on."

Jesse reacted to her anger, but not as she'd expected.

"I'm sorry, Diamond," he said quietly. "It's just a habit I have, calling women 'honey.'"

"Figures."

She was sick inside. She'd just come to the conclusion that she was falling in love with Jesse, and the first thing she did was lash out at his kindness. But she couldn't stop it from happening. It was the only form of self-protection she had. If he never knew how she felt, he could never use it against her.

Jesse sighed and ran his fingers through his hair, shuffling it into disarray. He didn't know what had prompted this latest outburst, but he knew what he wanted to do. He wanted to put his arms around her and hug away the pain he saw in those wide, green eyes. Instead, he dug a wad of bills from his pocket, stuffed them into her hand and pointed toward the small sandwich shop across the street.

"Food's good. The roast beef sandwiches are the best. Take your time, eat all you want. But when you're through, would you mind bringing back a dozen burgers? I'd really appreciate it, hon—"

Jesse sighed with frustration. He'd done it again. Honey! How had such a sweet word gotten him into so much trouble so quickly?

Diamond looked down at the wad of money in her hand and resisted the urge to throw it in his face. Her lips thinned as she bit the inside of her cheek to keep from shouting.

"My pleasure," she drawled, as she turned and walked away.

Jesse watched her until she entered the sandwich shop and knew that he'd taken two steps backward in an already tenuous relationship.

"Well goddammit it all to hell," he muttered, and stomped back into the studio.

The drive home that evening was long and uncomfortable, the conversation stilted. Diamond refused to look at Jesse when she spoke. She was afraid to. What was in her heart was too obvious to hide from his all-seeing gaze.

Jesse didn't force the issue. He wasn't certain what had prompted her reticence, but he knew enough about women to leave them alone sometimes, especially when one balled up like a fighting cat. He'd seen what she could do with a right hook and had no intention of starting something he didn't want to finish.

"Good," Jesse said as he pulled into the garage and parked. "Henley's back."

It was the first thing he'd said that had gotten her attention. Henley? This was something . . . and someone

new. She was out of the car before Jesse had unbuckled
his seat belt.

Diamond's mouth watered as the smell of chicken
and dumplings drifted from the open kitchen window.
An unladylike growl rumbled around her midsection.
She frowned as Jesse's mouth twitched with suppressed
mirth.

"Who's Henley?" she asked, determined not to
respond to his teasing grin.

"That would be me, miss," a man answered, his deep
voice echoing within the garage walls. "And you're just
in time. Supper is served," he announced before disappearing back into the house.

"Supper? . . . is served?" she echoed.

Jesse grinned. "Henley is big on ceremony. But the
evening meal has been supper all my life. Just because I
can pay all my bills on time doesn't mean I'm all of a
sudden eating 'dinner.' However, Henley insists on
announcing something, so 'supper' is served."

"Good," Diamond said as she headed toward the
door. "I'm starved."

"I heard," Jesse said.

Diamond stuck out her tongue and then beat him to
the door. "A gentleman wouldn't have called attention
to the fact that my stomach growled."

"I'm no gentleman," he said quietly, so close behind
her that tendrils of her hair brushed across his face. He
inhaled and then closed his eyes.

His breath feathered across the back of her neck,
sending a shiver of desire through her. But Diamond
refused to let her imagination take hold. With food in

front of her and Jesse behind her, there was only one way to run.

"Give me five minutes to wash up," Diamond said on her way up the stairs. "And don't start without me. I'm—"

"I know, I know. You're starving. Right?"

She left muttered comments lingering in her wake. There were none he felt warranted deciphering, as the tone of her voice told him enough.

He smiled, and then began to laugh. He'd distinctly heard her stomach grumble one last time just before she'd left.

Joe Henley's eyebrows arched into two perfect angles that pointed toward his sparse red hair and receding hairline. His mouth twitched with undisguised mirth as he gave his employer the once-over.

"Houseguest, sir?"

Jesse grinned. Henley was a master of understatement and tact.

"Sort of, but not what you're thinking. That lady has a near-perfect singing voice. I found her singing in one of the most god-awful places I've ever seen. All I did was offer her a chance out and a shot at a career she richly deserves. No strings attached."

"Of course," Henley agreed. "No strings at all, sir."

Jesse frowned. "And I thought I told you to quit calling me 'Sir,' dammit."

"I didn't call you 'Sir Dammit.' I simply called you 'Sir,'" Henley said. "If you wish to change your title, Mr. Eagle, all you need to do is let me know. I'd be more than happy to—"

Jesse started to smile. Sarcasm was thick in his voice

as he sauntered toward the kitchen. "Just shut the hell
up, Henley. You win. You always do. And that chicken
and dumplings is making my mouth water. Hope you
made plenty. The lady is—"

"Yes sir. I believe she's starving."

Henley retied the bib apron he wore over his dress
pants and white short-sleeved shirt and adjusted his bow
tie, readying for the meal he was about to serve. He knew
people. From the bit that he'd seen of her, the lady *was*
starving—but not necessarily for food, more likely acceptance. He'd seen the look in her eyes, and he'd seen similar
looks on women's faces a lifetime ago, half a world away.
In Saigon, and again in the jungles of Cambodia. And
they'd all meant one thing. A complete and encompassing
distrust of the human race, with men at the top of the list.

Henley pushed aside these thoughts as he began to
carry the food to the table. What happened between that
woman and his employer was none of his business . . .
absolutely none at all. And he kept his vow to remain
neutral up to the time she asked for seconds. By the time
he'd served her a third helping of his cooking, his opinion
of Jesse's guest had changed. She at least trusted his
cooking.

Diamond smiled to herself, remembering the rich
chicken and dumplings and the look of surprise that had
swept Henley's face when she'd asked for more.
Sparring with the short, stocky man had taken the edge
off having to converse solely with Jesse. In fact, now that
she thought about it, she'd almost ignored him.

Diamond leaned against the porch post and stared across the meadow, grinning at the young foal's foolish antics as he raced along the fences that held him at bay. His mother, the mare, grazed quietly on the thick green grass, always keeping her youngster in sight as she ate her fill.

Diamond stretched, stepped off the porch, and started walking toward the corrals. An evening breeze had sprung up only moments ago but was already well on its way to cooling off the heat of the day. A crow cawed loudly beyond the thick band of trees surrounding the house, while another answered from a distance away. She shaded her eyes against the setting sun and watched as it circled the skies before coming in to roost.

Even the crow had a tree to call home. Everyone and everything seemed to belong there but her.

She reached the fence and leaned over the top rail, gazing across it to the verdant beauty beyond, and watched the little horse play. "And you, pretty baby, you have someone who cares about you, too, don't you?"

Diamond's voice carried across the evening air. It startled the colt and stopped his play. He tossed his head and nickered, kicking his spindly legs out behind him as he headed toward his mother and security.

Jesse watched from the doorway as Diamond walked toward the pasture. The evening breeze lifted and tossed her long hair. He saw her twist it into a rope and then pull it over one shoulder as she folded her arms across the top rail of the fence.

He stepped off the porch and followed. It was instinctive. But the way he was feeling, it might also be a mistake.

"Have you forgiven me yet?"

Diamond jerked. Her heart thumped twice in rapid succession before settling back down into a constant rhythm. Darn him. She hadn't even heard his approach.

"There's nothing to forgive," she said, unwilling to admit that he could hurt her in any way.

Jesse put his hands on her shoulders and turned her around.

"I hurt you. It was unintentional, but nevertheless it happened. I don't like how it makes me feel, Diamond Houston. I need to hear you say you forgive me. I need to hear the words. If you don't, I know I'll lose sleep over it. And if I do, the boys will just think we've been carryin' on together . . . if you get my drift."

His slow smile and warm hands did things to her heart they had no business doing, but she couldn't speak.

"You wouldn't want me to go into the studio tomorrow with dark circles beneath my eyes and—"

Diamond ducked her head and punched him playfully on the shoulder. "Okay, okay! I get the idea. You don't need to keep drawing me a picture of what the band thinks I'm doing at your house. It's painfully obvious, even to a country girl like me."

"Do you mind what they think?" he asked. "Even when we know it's not true?"

Diamond shrugged. "I can't help what they think. It's what I think about myself that matters."

Jesse slipped his hand beneath her chin and tilted her face up to meet his gaze. "And what do you think about yourself, shiny girl?"

Tears came in profusion without warning.

Jesse's arms enveloped her before she could run, then tightened around her shoulders as she buried her face in her hands.

"My God, darlin'. What did I say? I didn't mean to make you cry." The soft, almost undetectable sound of her sobs made him sick to his stomach.

"It wasn't you," she said, unsuccessfully trying to regain her composure as a fresh set of tears began to roll. "It was what you called me, 'shiny girl.' It's a name Johnny used to tease me with. I didn't think hearing it again . . . from someone else . . . would hurt. But it does."

Jesse rested his chin on the top of her head and stared blankly across the meadow. Something he hadn't expected was happening here, and it had nothing to do with lust. He'd seen plenty of women cry. Sometimes in fury. Sometimes over him. But the knowledge that this woman hurt and he couldn't fix it made him angry. He didn't know why her happiness was becoming so important to him, but he had a suspicion that if he asked himself, he'd get an answer he wasn't ready for.

"So," he sighed, "I came out here to apologize for one thing, and it seems now I should apologize for two."

"Oh hell," Diamond said softly, allowing herself a moment's weakness. "Forget the apologies and just hold me. I'm too tired of pretending."

Jesse did as he was asked. It was his pleasure. He did some pretending of his own as he let himself enjoy the feeling of holding her against his body. He pretended that it was only the beginning for them. And when darkness chased them into the house, he forgot he'd been pretending.

He walked her to the foot of the stairs and leaned close. "'Night, darlin'," he said, and kissed her gently on the cheek.

Long after she'd crawled into bed, Diamond could still feel the imprint of his lips on her cheek and the pressure of their bodies as they'd touched and then melded into each other. She rolled over on her stomach, wishing for the first time in her life that she owned a nightgown. Her bare skin burned, her body ached, and the tears she'd buried began to fall once again. Only this time she wasn't crying for Johnny. She was crying for herself.

When Jesse walked into the studio with Diamond the next morning, the members of Muddy Road were already tuning up. Tommy glared. Some of the others whistled or called out gentle, teasing welcomes.

Mack Martin watched, silently assessing the fact that the same woman had shown up with the boss two days running. He couldn't ever remember that happening. Either she was hell on wheels in bed, or Jesse hadn't been shuckin' them yesterday, after all. Maybe she *could* sing.

He turned away so that they wouldn't see his grin. Just what he liked, little girls with stars in their eyes. They were the kind who'd do anything for a chance at the bright lights. Mack adjusted the strings on his guitar and readied for the session that was about to begin. He could wait until Jesse was through with her. He was a patient man.

Hours later, his wasn't the only patience running thin as Jesse started a new rendition of the same song they'd been working on all day.

Don't tell me lies, just say you love me.
Don't try so hard to make me believe.
It's not too late, if you really mean it.
But you can't stay just to watch me grieve.
But the smiles and lies of a lying lover
go hand in hand like kisses and wine.
I've had my share of one or the other.
But like the fool I am, can't get you out of my mind.

Jesse ended the song with a frustrated curse and dropped his guitar onto a chair.

"Dammit, Tommy, it doesn't work. It just doesn't work."

"That's not what you said when we bought the damned thing," Tommy said, resisting the urge to shout.

Jesse shoved his hands through his hair and then turned to face his band. "Sorry, guys," he said, "but let's try it once more from the top, and this time when we get to the second stanza, I want to hear more fiddle on the melody. You got that, Al?"

Al nodded and cracked his neck to alleviate the pain beneath his shirt collar. The boss wasn't near as pissed-off as *he* felt. He and his wife, Rita, had been trying to celebrate their anniversary all week. If something didn't break on this song arrangement soon, he envisioned an all-night session that would have Rita fuming.

Diamond leaned against the wall just out of Jesse's

line of vision and watched him flex his arms as he worked out the kinks from sitting too long in one spot. The muscles rippled beneath his shirt, as did the ones in his thighs as he bent down to retrieve his guitar. She shivered, wondering what he looked like beneath the fabric, and then closed her eyes against the thought.

"One more time from the top," Jesse said, weariness heavy in his voice, "and then we'll call it a day. Maybe all I need to do is sleep on it."

"Maybe that's what's wrong, Jesse. Maybe you ain't gettin' enough sleep. Maybe what you're sleepin' on—or with—is keepin' you from—"

"Shut the hell up, Mack," Jesse said.

The sharpness in his voice matched the look in his eyes. Mack got the message loud and clear and didn't like it. He didn't like it one bit that some easy fuck was coming between Jesse and the band. He wondered what Jesse was thinking, letting a woman like her matter, especially when there were a hundred just like her waiting to be had.

Diamond gritted her teeth and resisted the urge to shove Mack's words down his throat. And she didn't have to look at Jesse's manager to know that he was smiling. She'd already heard his satisfied chuckle when Mack had started in.

Her presence was resulting in exactly what Tommy had hoped for. If Jesse saw for himself what trouble she could cause, he'd dump her himself and save Tommy the trouble of having to do it for him.

Diamond never knew what prompted her to do what she did next. Maybe it was frustration at being an unwelcome

outsider, or the exhaustion she saw weighing heavily on
Jesse's face. But when the band started to play, she walked
over to the table where Jesse had tossed his hat, slapped it
on her head, and took the words of the song right out of
Jesse's mouth.

Her voice filled the studio, blending perfectly with his
deep, husky sound until it seemed as if it were no longer
a song. Every stanza Jesse sang, Diamond echoed right
after him, in her soft, crystal-clear voice. Every plea he
made in the song she repeated with heartbreaking
pathos.

Al slid his bow across his fiddle and blinked back
tears. He didn't know who to believe was telling lies,
the man or the woman. And then he caught himself and
almost laughed aloud as he realized he'd been pulled
right into the emotion of the moment. It wasn't really
happening, they were just singing a song. But hot
damn, he thought, what a song. This was what had been
missing.

Tommy wanted to kill. She *was* good . . . and he
wanted no part of her. Her presence in their lives was
the first wedge between him and total control over Jesse
Eagle, and that was something he wouldn't allow.

And then Diamond's voice ended the song on a whisper
as she sang, ". . . *can't get you out of my mind.*"

Jesse stared. He couldn't speak past the lump in his
throat. Instead, he took his hat off her head, tossed it into
the air, and yanked her off her feet and into his arms.

Laughter bubbled out of him, overflowing into
Diamond's ears as he swung her around and around.
The shocked silence of the men in the room began to

lessen as, one by one, the members of the band joined in. Jesse's excitement was impossible to ignore.

"My sweet Lord," Jesse said as he finally stopped spinning and set Diamond's feet back on firm ground. He did not, however, turn her loose. "That was fantastic, lady." He wrapped his hand in the tangle he'd made of her hair and tugged gently as he growled in her ear, "But what the hell kept you? If you knew you could do that earlier in the day, why did you let us suffer through six hours of rearranging that damned song?"

Diamond flushed but had nothing to say. She only shrugged. What she'd done had been on impulse. She'd had no intention of trying to make herself part of the song.

Jesse grabbed her by an arm as he turned to his manager. "Do you believe me now? I told you she could sing."

Tommy shrugged and grinned. There was nothing else he could do, but inside he was furious.

"I want this on the album," Jesse said. "I want her singing with me, just like she did a minute ago. She'll have equal billing on the song and her credits listed on the album cover. Now . . . Tommy, don't get that look on your face now. I'm right, and you know it."

Diamond was in shock. "But Jesse, I didn't intend for you to think—"

"I don't care what was intended. I know what's good, and so does the band. Right, boys?"

Smiles and a scattering of "You bet, boss" came and went. But the men were in shock. Granted the woman could sing. But equal billing for a complete unknown on one of Jesse Eagle's albums? That was a bit much, even for a good song. To a man, they began to eye her differently. This Diamond Houston must be heaven in bed for Jesse to be so eager to share billing with her.

"Let's call it a day," Jesse said. "But tomorrow when we come in, it's going to be down to serious business. 'Lies' was the last song on the album that hadn't been arranged." He grinned and tugged at Diamond's hair again. "But thanks to her, that's over. Tomorrow we start recording. Our schedule says this album has to be out before Christmas. Tommy, set it up."

Tommy shoved his hand in his shirt pocket for a cigarette and then cursed as he remembered he'd given that habit up nearly a year earlier. He stifled the urge to break something and managed to nod in agreement to Jesse's order.

Diamond was lost somewhere between elation and embarrassment. Her intention had been to lighten the moment. Instead she'd made the tension worse. Even she could feel the men's disapproval, but she had no way of undoing what had already been done. And, truth be told, she had little desire to do so. After all, wasn't this why she'd left Cradle Creek? Wasn't this why she'd trusted a stranger?

She smiled back at Jesse and then went to retrieve his hat. Standing in front of Jesse's band and his manager made her feel a bit like standing before a firing squad while she waited for someone to yell *fire!*

5

Jesse's elation lasted until they walked through the door and Henley handed Diamond an envelope postmarked from Cradle Creek, Tennessee.

"My money!" she said, tearing it open and waving the cashier's check in the air. She unfolded the accompanying letter and leaned against the wall, avidly scanning the page for news of her sisters.

Jesse watched the expression changing on her face and knew that he should leave her alone to read in private, but he couldn't bring himself to do so.

"Should I postpone serving supper, sir?" Henley asked.

Jesse nodded. It was obvious that for once, food was the farthest thing from Diamond's mind.

"Lucky left." The words came out in a whisper. "Queen's leaving in a couple of days." Diamond looked at the date on the postmark and then back at the letter, trying not to cry. "I suppose by now she's gone, too." She looked up at Jesse, her chin quivering.

"Honey, don't cry," Jesse said, and then winced at himself as he realized he'd called her "honey" again. But this time she didn't notice, or if she did must not have cared.

"I'm not." Unaware of the tears running down her cheeks, she continued. "I knew they were going. I don't know why I'm making such a fuss. After all, I was the one who left first. I didn't expect them to sit there in that hellhole and wait for me to come straggling back."

But in her heart that's exactly what she'd expected, and now her last link with her family was gone. Johnny was dead. Lucky was on a bus heading west, and Queen was right behind her. Diamond had never felt so alone in all her life. The breath she took turned into a sob.

Jesse frowned and gathered her into his arms. He needed to take away her pain.

"It will be okay. They know where you are, remember? You may have lost momentary track of them, but they know where you are. They know you're with me."

She nodded, for the moment relishing the comfort of being held, but she wouldn't allow herself the pleasure of prolonging it.

"At least my money came." Embarrassed by her behavior, she shrugged out of his arms. "Now I can get a place of my own in Nashville, and whenever it fits into your schedule I could meet you at—"

"No!"

It was hard to tell who was more startled at the vehemence with which he grabbed and shook her. He stared at his hands on her arms and turned her loose as if he'd just burned himself.

"I'm sorry," he said, unable to look at her face. "But it wouldn't be a good idea."

"Why?"

"Because," he began, fishing for a reason that wouldn't make him look any more foolish than he already did. "Because . . . we've just made plans for the album. Helping you find a place and moving you right now when we need to be recording would mess up the schedule."

Diamond stared at the flush across his cheeks. His eyes darkened, almost daring her to argue. Wisely, she did not. In a way, what he had said made sense. In another way, he'd given her what she'd wanted, a reason to stay. She didn't want to leave Jesse any more than he wanted her to.

"Well . . . okay," she said. "But just for now, until you have time to help me find something else."

"Right," he said, feeling relieved. "Just for now." He cupped her face with his hands and swept his thumbs across the tear tracks on her cheeks. "Go wash your face and then come right back," he said quietly. "Henley will skin us both if we let supper ruin."

She clasped her letter and money to her breast and walked away. There would be time enough later to decipher how she'd felt when he'd touched her mouth with his fingers. Time enough later to remember that she'd distinctly felt his body harden as he'd held her against him. But there would never be enough time to face how she'd feel when it came time to leave his home. Leaving Jesse Eagle was going to be nearly as painful as leaving her sisters had been. But it was inevitable, because Jesse didn't belong to her. He belonged to his music and his fans.

*   *   *

Three days had come and gone since the day of the letter. That was how Diamond had categorized the second phase of her life with Jesse. There was *the day after the funeral*. That was when he'd taken her away from Cradle Creek. And then had come *the day of the letter*. The previous day had been *the day of the song*.

She still had a difficult time convincing herself that she'd really sung a song with Jesse Eagle that was going to be on his new album.

She wished everyone else wasn't so uptight about it. She walked past the stores in the shopping center without noticing the displays, remembering instead Tommy's air of practiced martyrdom concerning her part in the new album. Even the band members seemed to have reservations about the way Jesse had thrust her upon them.

She knew they'd been with Jesse a long time, and she'd come out of nowhere and was getting special treatment right away. It was as if she hadn't quite earned the rights that had been given to her.

But earned or not, she was there, by the grace of God and the voice he'd given her. Try as she might, Diamond could think of no place else she'd rather be.

She glanced down at her watch, noticed the time, and then shifted the packages she was holding to a firmer position. Her shopping spree had taken longer than she'd expected.

The outfit on the mannequin in the store window was

enticing, but the weight of her purchases convinced her that she would be wise to leave more shopping for another day.

The tall, elegant woman she saw reflected in the store window did not resemble the Diamond Houston from Cradle Creek. This one wore soft gray slacks and a pink cotton sweater, not hand-me-down plaid and worn-out denim. The slim gray slippers on her feet were nothing like her old scuffed Ropers. But the face was still the same, and the look in her eyes was still wary. It was going to take more than a few regular meals and some money in her pocket to convince her that her luck had changed. In fact, Diamond didn't trust anything to luck. It had been the elusive love of Johnny's life, and it had gotten him nowhere.

However, the knowledge that she had a substantial bank account and the possibility of adding to it soon made her feel a little better.

Tommy kept promising her that they'd cut her demo tape just as soon as Jesse's album was finished. When he had her demo in hand, he said, then it would be time to start pitching her to the major recording studios.

The fact that Tommy repeated that promise without looking her in the face did not convince her of his undying sincerity. But Jesse was insistent, and she knew that in the end Tommy would capitulate.

Diamond hailed a cab and crawled into the back seat, sighing with relief as the driver headed for the studio. She'd walked as far as she could go today, especially in new shoes. Jesse and the band should be about ready to call it a day. She was ready to go home and sort out her new purchases. It would be a treat to have something to hang in her closet other than someone else's throwaways.

Jesse paced the floor in front of the sound booth, alternately frowning at Tommy and staring at the door. The recording session had gone better than expected, and they'd called it quits for the day nearly half an hour ago.

The engineer had given him a thumbs-up sign as they'd begun the mix, combining the prerecorded tracks into one digital copy that would be the finished product. It should have reassured him. But the only thing that was going to help Jesse relax was if that door opened and Diamond came walking through it.

"She's not lost," Tommy said. "You couldn't run her off if you tried, so quit worrying. Hell, she's right where she wants to be, Jesse my man, and you know it. She's in the lap of luxury."

Jesse glared. He was getting sick of Tommy's attitude. "You just can't face it, can you?" he said. "You heard us yesterday when we cut the first song for the album. Singing with her is pure magic, and the song was perfect. Even though we sang it three times, we could have used the first damned take, and you know it. She's good, Tommy. And either you're stupid as hell or you're less of a man than I thought. I never took you for the kind who holds a grudge."

"Thank you for your vote of confidence," Tommy said sarcastically. "And just for the record, I'm not holding a grudge against anyone."

Anger swept through Tommy and he had to restrain himself from screaming. He resented like hell the fact that Jesse was becoming so attached to a woman who had put him on his butt.

It was the principle of the thing. He wouldn't deny that women had their place in a man's life, all right. He liked a good fuck as well as the next man. But Jesse didn't realize that he could ruin his reputation and lose his star status in a heartbeat by becoming attached to some two-bit singer.

If Jesse up and moved some blonde into his life, Tommy knew what the millions of women who dreamed of wedding and bedding Jesse Eagle would do. They'd move on to the next male hunk with tight buns and a pretty face, and that would leave Tommy Thomas representing a has-been. That wasn't in Tommy's plan. And neither was Diamond Houston.

Jesse didn't like the look on his manager's face, but there was nothing he could do to change Tommy's opinion. He could, however, fulfill the promise he'd made to Diamond's sister. Diamond was going to have her chance at stardom, or he'd know the reason why. A promise was a promise, and Jesse was a man of his word.

"Don't forget what I said about giving her billing on the album," Jesse said.

Tommy rolled his eyes, wished again that he hadn't quit smoking, and slid a smile into position.

"As if I could," he said. "You're a goddamned broken record about the issue."

❊   ❊   ❊

Mack Martin leaned against his pickup truck and took a long drag on his cigarette. The smoke curled around his eyes and then spiraled upward into the air as the nicotine leveled off in his system and pulled his ragged nerves back into gear. Recording sessions always made him edgy. He'd choose the spontaneity of a live performance any day.

A cab pulled up at the studio gate. A slow smile parted the brush of whiskers on his face as he watched the passenger emerge from the back seat. It was Diamond!

He flipped the cigarette butt onto the pavement, ground it into the concrete with the toe of his boot, and wiped his hands on his thighs.

"Hey, hey, darlin'," he called, and met her as she came across the lot. "If you spend all of Jesse's money, then you just come to me. I've got plenty of that . . . and anything else you might need."

Diamond flushed but said nothing. His implication was obvious. The last thing she needed was what Mack was offering.

"Here now, let me help you with some of those bags," Mack said, purposely sliding his hands across her breasts as he took the packages from her arms. The look in his eyes dared Jesse's latest woman to ignore what he was offering.

He was being rude and pushy, but Diamond was used to men like Mack. Whitelaw's Bar had been full of them. She knew exactly how to handle a man with too much on his mind.

"Thanks," she said, letting him have her bags. "Here's another one." She piled a package on top of the armful she'd relinquished. "Follow me. I'm going to tell Jesse I'm back."

She walked away, leaving Mack literally holding the bag.

Mack's eyes narrowed as his lips thinned. That hadn't gone exactly as he'd planned. This one was cool, he'd give her that. But he could wait. And when he got hold of her he'd warm her up good.

The *In Session* light was off over the door. That meant they'd finished for the day. It hadn't taken Diamond long to catch on to the ins and outs of how an album was cut. There were rules governing everything, and she was good at following rules.

"Did anyone miss me?" she asked as she breezed through the door.

As Jesse turned, he knew that the smile he was wearing was inches too wide for his face, but he couldn't help it. He'd never been so relieved to see anyone in his life.

"Didn't know you were gone," he said, and then watched her smile. He was lying, and she knew it. He didn't care.

"Guess what?" she said.

Jesse started to hug her, felt her body stiffen with unconscious resistance, and then stepped away, giving her the space she so obviously needed.

"You're hungry?"

She punched him on the arm and then motioned toward Mack, who'd entered the studio carrying her packages.

"No, smart aleck," she said. "Well, actually I am, but that's not what I was about to say."

Jesse stuffed his hands into his pockets and rocked on

the heels of his boots as he waited for her to continue. She was so damned pretty that he was having a hard time concentrating on what she was saying. All he could do was watch how those wide green eyes caught and reflected the light, and how the pink on her cheeks matched that soft pink sweater cupping her body.

"Are you listening to me?" Diamond asked.

"No," he said. "I was looking at your sweater. It fits you good . . . real good." He wiggled his eyebrows and gave her a practiced leer.

"You're such a . . . such a *man*, Jesse Eagle."

It was meant to be denigrating. Men didn't rate high on her list of trustworthy people. But Jesse took what she said and turned it into a compliment that made her blush.

"Yes I am, lady," he said softly. "And don't you forget it. I haven't."

Diamond did completely forget that she'd been about to tell him she'd spent some of her money. She forgot to tell him that she'd also opened a bank account and had looked around at some apartments. She forgot everything but the fact that this evening when she left the studio, she'd be going home with a man who was driving her crazy.

"Where ya' want me to put this stuff?" Mack asked. He wasn't any too happy about being a pack mule for this love-struck pair. In fact, he was getting pissed off about the whole deal.

Jesse dug in his pocket, pulled out some keys, and tossed them to Mack, who managed to catch them without dropping his armload of bags.

"Just put them in the trunk of my car," he ordered.

Mack swallowed a curse, turned around, and headed back out the door with Diamond's new clothes. He needed to work on his strategy. He wasn't putting up with this shit again.

"Give me a minute to firm up tomorrow's schedule with Tommy, and then we'll go home, okay?" Jesse said.

Diamond nodded and tried not to feel sorry for herself. If only home and Jesse were synonymous.

Henley hovered in the background, quietly refolding and repacking everything that Jesse was stuffing into his bags. Jesse's muttered curses and complaints went in one ear and out the other. Henley knew what was wrong. He just didn't know if Jesse knew.

It wasn't the first time he'd helped Jesse pack to leave, but it was the first time that Jesse would be leaving someone other than Henley behind.

"Is that everything?" Jesse asked. "Don't forget to pack my silver jacket. And for God's sake get my hatbox. The last time I went without it, someone slept on my Stetson. Took the hatter a week to get the damned thing back in shape."

"Yes sir," Henley said. "It's all here. Don't worry." And then he added—as if in afterthought, although he knew it was the excuse that Jesse needed to make an exit and tell Diamond good-bye—"Miss Houston is in your music room, sir, if you want to give her any . . . instructions." The hesitance on the word *instructions* was pointed, and they both knew it.

Jesse whirled and stomped from the room. He moved through the house and down the hallway as tension snaked itself inside his belly. It wasn't as if he didn't trust her alone in his house. It wasn't as if he didn't want to go sing, either. Hell, he told himself, performing was the other half of himself. He'd die without it.

But this was the first time he could ever remember being reluctant to leave, regardless of the fact that he would only be gone three or four days. Denver wasn't all that far from Nashville. He knew it would be a good gig. The performance had been sold out for months.

"What the hell are you doing?" he asked. The door slammed against the wall as he shoved it open and stomped into the music room.

The stack of sheet music fell from her hands as Diamond turned around in fright. The look on his face matched the sound of his voice, and she wondered what she'd done wrong.

"You told me to—"

"I'll be leaving soon," he said. "I don't mind you being in here, but be sure and put everything back where you found it when you're through."

His anger was so unexpected, she didn't have time to suppress her reaction. A swift set of tears came to her eyes, but she blinked them away. She was well practiced at hiding her emotions.

"I will," she said. "You forget, I'm only following orders, Jesse. In fact, that's all I've done since I got here—follow orders." The censure in her voice was thick.

Jesse's fingers curled into fists as he closed his eyes

and wished he could rewind the last few minutes and do it over again. But there were no retakes in life, and he knew it. There was nowhere to go but forward.

"Sorry I snapped," he said. "I always get edgy before a road trip. I'll get over it."

"And that's supposed to pass for an apology?" Diamond muttered.

"What did you say?"

"Nothing of importance," she said. "Just have a safe trip."

She picked up the scattered music, placed it carefully on the desk, and walked past him without saying anything further.

Jesse reached out, but he was too late to stop her, and the words wouldn't come to say he was sorry. All she left behind was the scent of her perfume and the sound of her heels tapping sharply on the floor as she walked away.

"Your ride is here!" Henley called.

"Hell," Jesse said. It was a combination of how he felt and where he supposed he should go.

"Jesse! Jesse! Jesse!"

The auditorium rocked from the sound of his name as the fans screamed for him to make just one more curtain call. But three was his limit, and they had come and gone.

"Let's wrap it up, boys," he said, and headed offstage with the members of his band close behind.

As always, it was like running a gauntlet to get from the stage to the dressing room and not be taken apart at

the seams. It was the only part of his public life that
made him uneasy. No matter how tight the security or
how intricately they planned an exit, a swarm of fans
always managed to get past the guards. In the back of
Jesse's mind there was always the knowledge that someone could be deranged enough to kill.

"Ooowee," Mack shouted, still on an adrenaline high
from the rowdy crowd. The louder and wilder they got,
the better he liked it. "That was one fine show, Jesse. I
saw good pickins on the front row, too. Al, did you see
that redhead? The one wearing red Rockies and that little
bitty bandana she was passin' off as a blouse? Hot damn!
She bounced more than my mattress on a good night."

Any other night Jesse would have laughed and joked
with his band, throwing in his own observations about
the female fans. The groupies were always the ones who
dared to be different, willing to try anything to get an
entertainer's attention, certain that this time his reaction
would be different. Certain that this time their hero, the
entertainer, would fall hopelessly and madly in love with
them.

Only they never did. The only place the entertainers
fell was in and out of bed. The groupie was just another
notch on someone's bedpost. Another girl without a
name. After a while, they didn't even ask . . . they didn't
even care.

During the concert Jesse had gotten lost in the music
and pushed the guilt he'd carried with him to the back
of his mind. But the music was over. The night was just
beginning for the band, only this time, Jesse had other
plans.

He pushed his way through the crowded dressing room, past the boys in the band and the string of women who were straggling inside. They were the chosen few with backstage passes. In less than an hour, the pairing would have taken place, and Jesse wanted no part of it. He wanted a phone. And he wanted it now. Before he closed his eyes on another day he had to hear Diamond's voice. He had to say *I'm sorry* and let her know he meant it.

"Jesse, there's someone I want you to meet," Tommy said. "This is Bobbie Lee. Isn't she a honey?"

Jesse looked. The woman hanging onto his manager's arm was smiling. It was a smile he'd seen before. It said *yes* to whatever he wanted. Long black hair framed her plump, pretty face. Her eyes were big, and bright, and lost somewhere beneath several layers of makeup. Her ample figure underneath her western shirt and tight jeans gave new meaning to the word *filled*.

"Ma'am," Jesse said, smiled, tipped his hat, and headed toward the phone at the back of the room.

The woman pouted, smiled up at Tommy, and knew that he was going to be all she got for the evening. It was her policy not to play favorites. Bobbie Lee's favorite was always the man she was with.

Tommy frowned, and then she squeezed his elbow and leaned her breasts against his shoulder just enough to set his blood to racing. He swore beneath his breath, angry that he'd been unable to swerve Jesse's attention from that damned woman back home, and took what was offered.

Jesse took the phone and carried it into the only place in the dressing room that had a modicum of privacy, the bathroom.

He shut and locked the door then dialed the phone. The closed lid of the commode served as a chair as he plopped down and began peeling off his hot, sweaty clothes. Finally he was shirtless, hatless, and nervous as hell, had counted thirteen rings, and still no one had answered. And then he remembered the time. He looked down at his watch. Back home in Nashville it was two o'clock in the morning. He'd be apologizing for more than being an ass. Then she answered.

"Hello?"

"Mornin', honey," he said softly.

"Morning? Is it?" Her sleep-befuddled manner made him smile.

"Yes, it's morning. A little early, but morning nonetheless."

"Are you all right?" she asked.

"I'm fine."

"Are you drunk?"

He laughed. "No, Mother, I'm not drunk. I'm just on a concert high. One of these days you'll know what I mean."

Diamond stood in the darkened hallway of Jesse's home and stared at the shadows on the walls, wishing he was there but afraid to say so.

"Sorry I woke you," Jesse said, "but there's something I need to say, and I knew that I'd never rest until I said it."

She waited, hoping, uncertain of what it was that she hoped for.

"Honey . . . about the way I acted the day I left. I'm sorry, really sorry. I don't know what made me act like such an ass. I wish it hadn't happened."

Diamond sighed. She heard the regret in his voice.

And she'd known when he yelled that he wasn't angry about her going through his music.

"It's okay," she said, wishing she had the right to say more, like how much she missed him, and to come home soon. But she didn't have any rights where Jesse was concerned. So her remark came out sounding offhand and disinterested.

Jesse's stomach turned. She sounded too distant. He had a sudden urge to go home that moment. He needed to see her face, reassure himself that his "shiny girl" would be waiting for him when he returned.

"I'll be home day after tomorrow," he said.

"I'll tell Henley."

Mack's voice boomed through the thin paneled door. "Hey, Jesse, either get out or move over. Someone else wants in, old buddy, and she's a hell of a lot prettier than you are—and a lot more willing!"

He laughed raucously at his own wit. Jesse winced, knowing that Diamond would hear everything that was going on and misunderstand his part in the levity.

"I've got to go," he said. "It's so noisy in the dressing room that I had to come in the bathroom to be able to use the phone. Unfortunately, it's the only one, and it seems there's a line forming to use it."

She smiled, but he didn't see it. All he heard was her swift intake of breath as a moth fluttered across her line of vision.

"Are you all right?" he asked.

"Yes. It was just a moth. It flew in my face."

"Just looking for some light, like the rest of us," he said, grinning.

"Oh, there's no light," she said. "I wouldn't dare turn it on. That's what took me so long to answer the phone. I couldn't find it in the dark."

"Why in hell didn't you turn on the light?" he asked.

"Because I sleep in the nude, remember? I can't be running all over the house with the lights on. Someone might see."

Oh hell, Jesse thought. *I had to ask.* But all he could say was, "Oh." His ability to speak had suddenly disappeared. And walking was going to be damned near impossible with this growing ache behind his zipper.

"Thanks for calling," Diamond said.

The line went dead and Jesse's mind went blank. It was either that or burst from the wanting she'd created in him.

6

Diamond put down Jesse's guitar and looked around the music room in frustration. Spending the better part of two days in there had gotten her nowhere. She knew the words and music to every song he had and some besides, and she was as ready for Tommy and her demo as she'd ever be. She needed a diversion, not more practice.

Trying to forget Jesse's call the previous night had been impossible. She'd read all sorts of importance into the fact that he'd called and then read herself the riot act for imagining that he actually cared about her.

Footsteps echoed in the hallway and then ceased outside the room. Diamond turned toward the open door.

"Is there anything special you'd be wanting, Miss Houston?" Henley asked.

Diamond took a good long look at the aging ex-marine who'd turned himself into Jesse Eagle's other right arm. As usual his attire was casual but immaculate. Neat brown slacks just a shade too tight emphasized his short, stocky legs. His white short-sleeved shirt was neatly pressed, and the ever-present plaid bow tie was tucked beneath his second chin.

Henley's sparse reddish hair was parted neatly and hairsprayed to his head. His face stayed in quiet repose, but his little round eyes seemed to be in a constant state of emotion. It was in those hazel eyes that Joe Henley revealed his true self, that of a caring and compassionate man.

For a long moment, neither spoke. And then Diamond surprised them both when she answered.

"Yes there is, Henley. I want you to stop calling me 'Miss Houston,' and I want you to teach me how to drive."

His jaw dropped, but the fact that he made no comment other than to close his mouth said much for the control he maintained over his emotions.

"Yes, Miss Diamond," Henley said. "Will there be anything else?"

Diamond grinned. The concession he'd made with her name was as far as he'd go, and she knew it. "Not today." She pinned him with a hard stare. "When can we start?"

"At your convenience," Henley said.

"What about now?"

"Very good, Miss Diamond. Please follow me."

She did, with alacrity.

Jesse's touring bus was empty save for Jesse and the driver. Tommy and the members of Muddy Road had disembarked in Nashville and headed for their respective homes. They had exactly one day of rest before recording on the new album would resume, and Jesse knew exactly what he'd do with that day. He didn't intend to move from his premises for at least twenty-four hours. As always, traveling to and from concerts left him drained, not to mention the performance itself.

When the driver turned down the dirt road leading to his home, a kick of excitement surfaced as he realized that in minutes he would see Diamond. It was a strange, almost comforting feeling to know that someone was waiting for him. He wasn't certain how he felt about Diamond Houston except that he didn't want to lose her. He had yet to decide whether that added up to selfishness, lust, or something else. It was the *something else* that was making him nervous.

"Hey, Jesse!" the driver shouted aloud. "Look out there!"

Jesse looked toward the direction in which his driver was pointing, expecting to see almost anything but what came into view as they turned the curve in his drive.

His old green Dodge pickup, the one he used to haul hay and feed to the horses, was moving at a fast clip through the pasture in front of the house. He cursed and closed his eyes, an unconscious reaction as the Dodge narrowly missed a small stand of trees before turning to run alongside the fence leading toward the barns.

"Look at her go!" the driver yelled, and whistled through his teeth as the old truck cleared a dip in the field by sailing neatly over it instead of driving through it.

"Oh, hell," Jesse said, muttering beneath his breath. A long swatch of blonde hair flew out the open window and then was sucked back inside as the truck made a u-turn in the field.

Diamond!

He felt a swift surge of panic, followed by anger. When he'd offered to teach her to drive, she'd laughed in his face and turned him down. If his eyes didn't deceive him, that was Henley sitting beside her in the truck. Jesse stared. By all that's holy, he thought, she's got to him, too. If he hadn't seen it, he never would have believed it. Henley was laughing.

The bus came to a stop as Jesse vaulted from his seat. The driver tossed the bags onto the porch and made a hasty exit. He could tell by the look on Jesse's face that he was none too happy about what he'd seen, and the driver had no intention of staying around for the explosion.

Diamond swerved, missing the trees in the middle of the pasture by inches. She turned the pickup truck back toward the barns and then laughed at the sight of the mare and her colt running with the truck, with only a board fence separating them in the race to the barn.

The bay mare's tail flowed out behind her like a kite as she ran, her mane a rich brown tangle in the wind. She tossed her head and whinnied as if in pure delight from the chase, while her baby followed, determined not to be left behind.

"Watch that dip," Henley shouted.

"What dip?" Diamond yelled, and spit hair from her mouth as it whipped across her face.

"Never mind," he said, grunting as they went slightly

airborne, then landed with a thud on the other side of the shallow ditch.

Diamond laughed again at the look on Henley's face and turned her attention to the business at hand.

"Slow down," Henley shouted again. "The gate is coming up."

"Piece of cake," Diamond said, and sailed through the narrow opening with inches to spare.

For a beginner, she'd been surprisingly adept at driving. Henley would have liked to believe it was solely due to his expertise as a teacher. However, he was honest enough to realize that once Miss Diamond set her mind to something it was her persistence that was responsible for her newly acquired skill. As for the driving, it wasn't perfect, but with only two days of practice under her belt, she was damned good at it.

She came to a skidding halt beneath the trees in front of the house, ground the gears into park, and turned off the ignition.

"Made it," she said, laughing at the expression of surprise on Henley's face. It was obvious he'd been uncertain of the outcome of their ride.

"And I thank the Lord for small favors," he said. He took the key and slipped it into his pocket.

Diamond turned toward the house, intent on teasing Henley into baking some of his brownies, when she saw the man leaning against the porch post. The black denim Levis, red shirt, and wide-brimmed black Stetson were unmistakable. Jesse was back, and from the look on his face he was none too happy about what she'd been doing.

"Uh-oh," she said. "We've been caught."

Henley took one look at his boss's face and made a quick decision.

"So it seems," he said, and escorted her to the house. "Sir. You're home."

That much was obvious, but it was all that Henley could manage considering Jesse's expression and the arms he'd folded across his chest.

"I suppose that you'll be wanting to rest as usual. I've prepared a casserole and some salad. The food is in the refrigerator. Miss Diamond knows. I'll be heading on home now. Have a good evening, sir."

With that, Henley handed the pickup keys to Jesse, got into his own car, and drove away without looking back.

An explanation was on the tip of Diamond's tongue when she looked up at Jesse's face and forgot what she'd been about to say.

That his feelings were hurt was putting it mildly. He was jealous as hell. She'd laughed more with Henley just now than she'd laughed with him since he'd known her. When Henley had handed him the truck keys, he'd had an intense urge to punch his houseman in the face.

It was completely unjustified and unreasonable to expect that Diamond owed him anything other than gratitude for taking her from Cradle Creek. But when he'd seen that look of complete joy on her face and known that another man had put it there, he'd lost all sense of reason.

He stared down at her and started to stuff his hands into his pockets, but found himself wrapping them around her wind-blown hair instead. "Why?" he asked as he tugged gently, urging her up the steps until they were face to face.

Diamond heard the disbelief in his voice but completely misunderstood its origin.

"I didn't think you'd mind me using the truck," she said. "It was all my idea, too, so don't be mad at—"

"Why not me, lady? You let Henley inside your world but you won't let me."

He shook her gently to punctuate his questions, expecting her to stiffen and pull away. But she didn't .

Diamond watched his eyes darken with pain. She couldn't bear the thought of being the one who'd put it there.

"I'm sorry," she said. "Don't be mad at me, Jesse." Her voice faded away into a whisper. "Please . . . don't be mad."

"Oh, my God," Jesse said, and pulled her into his arms. "Mad? I'm not mad, I'm crazy—crazy about you."

The catch in her breath was all it took. He tossed his hat through the open door behind him, lowered his head, and inhaled her sigh. Their lips met and the magic began.

Soft and supple, her mouth responded to the insistent pressure of his own. She came alive beneath his touch, moving against him and with him as if there were a slow but steady magnetic pull between them. He took a step forward, pressing her between his body and the porch post, and then groaned when she moved, letting him slide one leg between hers.

The moan that slipped up her throat and into his mouth sent a line of sweat beading across his forehead.

He thrust his leg forward and rocked it gently against her body, then turned loose of her and reached for the porch post for support when her hands dropped down to caress the bulge behind his zipper.

"Easy . . ."

It was the only warning she was going to get. If Diamond wanted this to stop, she would have to be the one to stop it.

She heard the hesitation in his voice and recognized it for what it was. What happened next was entirely up to her. She made her choice.

"I missed you," she said softly, and began to unsnap his shirt, baring his chest to her touch.

Jesse's eyes narrowed and his nostrils flared. It was all he could manage as her fingers feathered across his belly.

"You sure you want to do this, lady? In about one more heartbeat, what control I have left will be gone."

She answered by pulling his shirt from the waistband of his jeans.

Jesse wrapped his arms around her, tilted her face to his, and swooped, taking what he wanted of this woman's offering. What he wanted was everything. Jesse got what he wanted.

Diamond felt the ground disappear beneath her feet as Jesse lifted her into his arms and carried her inside the house. He kicked the door shut behind him and walked blindly toward the staircase, using instinct to guide him as her hands locked around his neck and her gaze focused entirely on the shape of his mouth.

"I'm going to make love to you," he said.

"I know."

"Is there anything you want to tell me before I completely lose my mind?" His question was no more than a low, husky growl as he looked down at the beauty in his arms.

"Just hurry," she said.

And he did.

A path of their discarded clothing began at the head of the stairs, trailing down the long hallway past her bedroom and through the open door of his own. There was nothing left to remove but their pants and boots by the time he shut his door and tossed her onto the bed.

Diamond's heart was racing, and her limbs were heavy from the wanting. She couldn't move other than to follow him with her gaze as she lay helpless on his bed, waiting. She'd never wanted anyone or anything this much in her life. She'd never allowed herself to care this much for a man. The feeling frightened her. If this was a mistake, she was about to make it. Stopping now was as impossible for her as it would have been for him.

And then he stood naked before her, unashamed of his need as he approached her.

"I don't use any . . . I don't take—"

"I'll protect you," Jesse said, and reached for the drawer of his bedside table to fulfill his promise.

She tried to speak as he knelt above her on the bed and began removing first one of her boots and then the other. And then her body arched beneath his hands as he stripped her of her Levis, leaving nothing between them but a narrow strip of thin white nylon. Then that, too, disappeared.

Breathing became difficult, and his hands shook as he bared her body for his touch. Then he blinked back tears as her eyes closed and she smiled. This woman was made for loving.

His eyes were dark, his movements slow and steady as he lowered himself onto her and then gently into her. She sighed and moved, wrapping her arms around his neck as his whisper feathered across her breasts.

"I'll always take care of you, honey," he said. "I promised."

The fever between them rose. Diamond knew that in moments, she'd never be the same. As his mouth demanded, his hands teased. As her body arched to meet his, she fell under his spell and his body as easily as she breathed.

At first his movement inside her was nothing more than a slow burn that made her limbs weak and her heart race. And then it changed to a spiraling ache as he increased the power and speed. She felt his own need grow as he buried himself deeper and deeper into her in an all-consuming need for completion.

When his quick, intense breaths became harsh gasps for air, she lifted herself to him, wrapped her legs around his waist, and took him with her into the light.

Jesse stared mindlessly up toward the ceiling and tightened his arms around her as she slept toward morning. He remembered the first touch of their bodies as they had joined, and then everything after that was an intense blur of heat and need. He'd never been as swept away by passion in his entire life as he had by this woman.

Diamond moaned in her sleep, and to Jesse it sounded like a sob. He looked down in sudden fright, aware that the woman he held in his arms had become more than a passing fancy. The thought of her pain was unbearable to him, just as was the thought of never loving like this again.

"Ah, God, lady," he whispered. "This wasn't supposed to happen. I wasn't supposed to love you, not like this." He ran his hands gently up and down her arms and then pulled the sheet over them both. "I wasn't supposed to love you . . . but I do."

Only Diamond didn't hear him, and when morning came, Jesse didn't repeat it. He could only stare in wonder as the sunlight coming through his window blazed a path across her hair and brought a myriad of colors to life. And when he ran his fingers through the thick, honey-colored strands, the highlights glittered, like diamonds falling through his hands.

Henley let himself in the back door and started the coffee before he noticed that the food he'd prepared the day before was still untouched. He was walking through the living room on his way upstairs when he spotted the first article of clothing on the steps above. It didn't take him long to see the path of clothes, or to notice that they weren't exclusively Jesse's.

He smiled to himself and then made a hasty but quiet retreat back downstairs. It looked as if his boss had gotten over his anger about the truck. He walked into the kitchen, pulled pen and paper from a drawer, and began to compose a note.

Henley closed the back door quietly behind him, locking them in and himself out. He'd just given himself the day off, and from the look of things in the house, he didn't think anyone was going to mind.

The phone rang in another part of the house. Jesse's answering machine picked up the call. And no matter how loudly Tommy yelled into the phone, no one got on the line.

He slammed it down in disgust, knowing that he'd have to make a trip out to Jesse's ranch if he wanted to accomplish any work today, or else wait until tomorrow.

Tommy rolled off his bed and started to dress when he remembered how withdrawn Jesse had been on the way home. Something told him that pushing Jesse into working on his only day of rest might be a mistake. He yanked his pants back off, plopped down on the bed, and dug in his shirt pocket for the unopened pack of cigarettes.

He'd bought them in Denver, right after Jesse had refused the offer of the buxom Bobbie Lee. It was the first time Tommy could ever remember Jesse completely turning off at the sight of a pretty female fan.

"Damned woman," he muttered as he peeled the wrapper and tapped out the first cigarette he'd held in over a year. He slid in into the corner of his mouth, struck a match, and took the first drag. It was intensely satisfying, he told himself, and well worth the wait. If he had to suffer that blonde bitch in Jesse's life, he wasn't going to do it willingly. A man had to have some pleasures, he thought . . . and besides, everyone dies eventually. How he got there was his business.

Diamond woke slowly and looked down at the head pillowed upon her breast. Strands of Jesse's dark hair lay across her body in stark contrast to her own fair, delicate complexion. His thick black lashes, as straight as his hair, made small, feathery shadows below his eyes as he slept.

She moved once and smiled to herself at the possessive manner with which his fingers tightened their hold upon her arm. Even in his sleep, Jesse wouldn't let her go.

Last night had been unbelievable and inevitable. The attraction that had simmered between them had finally boiled and overflowed into a passion that left her still breathless. She didn't want to face life without this man, though she feared that she would have to. Diamond trusted her own feelings, but not his. Although she knew what had happened between them had been special, she wondered if she'd been the only one to feel the magic.

Unable to resist, she threaded her fingers through hair as dark as a warlock's heart, gently brushing it away from his forehead as she imprinted Jesse's face on her mind.

His high cheekbones framed his strong, shapely nose and gave emphasis to the often stubborn jut of his chin. His hands were slender, the fingers long and supple—true artist's hands. And after the previous night, Diamond had no doubt as to Jesse's mastery of the human anatomy. He'd played her body as gently and skillfully as he played his guitar.

Testing the surface of his skin was addictive. It felt sleek and hard, yet the muscles that rippled beneath her touch were fluid and alive. A faint tan line at his waist teased her to look farther. And when she did, she wished she hadn't. It only made her want him . . . again.

For the last several minutes, Jesse had been watching as she gazed her fill of his body. And when her line of vision dropped below his waist, he closed his eyes and willed his body not to betray him. It was no use. It did, and he succumbed to temptation.

He rolled over and lifted himself onto his elbows, cupped her face in his hands, and looked down at the woman beneath him. Her eyes, as clear and green as spring grass, beckoned him as she bestowed upon him a smile as wide and generous as the mouth that formed it.

"Good morning," he said, and kissed the smile on her face. "If you know something I don't, now's the time to confess."

"Only someone with a guilty conscience needs to make a confession," she said. "I have no guilt; therefore I have nothing to confess." *But I have secrets, Jesse Eagle. And I don't think you're ready to hear them. I don't think you want to hear what's in my heart.*

Jesse watched shadows steal across her face and knew there was a part of herself she was still protecting. His arms tightened around her as he faced the fact that she still didn't trust him. The knowledge hurt him in a way he'd never imagined.

"Don't turn away from me, Diamond. Last night wasn't just an incident. It was a beginning, and the sooner you face that, the better."

Her mouth parted. Words that she intended to say were never born. Jesse took her and what good sense she had left into a place where nothing mattered except his touch and the spiraling heat he created in her.

It was noon before they made it downstairs and found Henley's note. Jesse read enough between the sparse lines to know that Henley had seen the clothes— and where they'd led—and had made as graceful an exit as he knew how.

It was just as well. He didn't want to share Diamond with anyone today. What was between them was too new and fresh.

"You have a message," Diamond said, pointing to the blinking red light on his answering machine.

Jesse played it back and then turned off the machine, unwilling to record any more of the same nonsense from Tommy.

"No, I don't," he said. "That wasn't a message, it was just Tommy having a fit. He can have that without my help, any day."

Diamond laughed.

Jesse smiled at the sound. A toe-tapping song came on the radio. Unable to verbalize the emotion he was feeling, he chose to act on it instead and swung her into a rousing two-step, dancing her around the kitchen and out into the hall as if they were in a wild honky-tonk instead of scuffing up Henley's highly polished floors.

By afternoon they'd run out of food and time. Today

had been a little bit of heaven. Tomorrow was going to be another story. Tomorrow Jesse would be back in the studio, and Diamond would be fielding dirty looks and innuendos from his band.

For the first time since she'd left Cradle Creek, she wished Queen was there. Her big sister would know how to take the starch out of the boys in Jesse's band. She hated the discomfort they made her feel but didn't dare tell Jesse what was going on. It would only cause trouble he couldn't afford.

"You're frowning," Jesse said, wrapping his arms around her. "You know what that means."

She smiled as he bent down for his kiss. "You're gonna have to wipe that frown right off my face, right?"

"You got it, honey," he said. "Come here and take your medicine like a big girl."

"Making love to you isn't medicine, Jesse Eagle. I'd say it's more like a lesson in instant insanity." She returned his kiss and added one for good measure.

His whisper was soft and low as his mouth took license with the curve of her neck and moved down the slope of her breasts.

"Then let's go crazy together, love."

So they did.

7

Henley watched Jesse's sports car pull out of the driveway as he and Diamond headed into Nashville. Although it felt strange to be bidding his employer good-bye as if they were family, he could not ignore Diamond's wide smile and the excitement bubbling within her as she leaned out of the window and waved back at him. He had to return the favor.

It would have been obvious even to a fool that the relationship between Jesse and Diamond had changed. When they touched each other, even discreetly, one could tell it was not enough. The heat between them was tangible. If Henley hadn't become so fond of Diamond, he would have been uncomfortable in their presence. As it was, he felt like a constant Peeping Tom. But however intense the emotion between them, Henley suspected that it would not be enough to stop the inevitable from happening.

Instinct told him that no matter how hard they tried,

they would not bridge the gap between their lives and be happy until Diamond Houston learned how to trust. Henley sighed as he reentered the house. He liked Jesse's lady. He knew that Jesse liked her, too. He hoped that was enough.

Diamond fidgeted as Jesse pulled onto the main road leading into Nashville. The constant touching and smiles between them at his house were addictive, but she knew that if it happened at the studio, in front of Tommy or the band, they would know in an instant that the relationship had changed. And they would laugh or, even worse, make more of the same insulting remarks she'd been hearing. She didn't think she could bear it.

Jesse sensed her fear, and it made him worry. After three miles of sidelong glances and deep sighs, she finally spoke.

"Jesse . . ."

The hesitance in her voice made him swerve the car. The rhythm of his heartbeat skipped and then returned to normal as he told himself not to borrow trouble.

"I don't want you to . . . please don't be so . . ." she began.

He slammed his foot onto the brake and brought the car to a halt at the side of the road. Diamond braced herself against the dashboard. The anger in Jesse's voice surprised her, as did his behavior.

"Dammit, Diamond! Just spit it out. Say what's on your mind and put me out of my misery, okay?"

"What's wrong with you?" she asked. "All I was going

to do was ask you not to . . . touch me so much in front of Tommy or the boys in the band. I don't want them to know that we . . . that things have . . ."

Jesse sighed and buried his face in his hands before sliding them up through his hair. He leaned his head against the back of the seat and closed his eyes. He took two long, steadying breaths before he trusted himself to talk. And then when he moved, it was only to pull her out of her seat and into his arms.

"You scared the hell out of me, lady," he said, trailing kisses along the side of her neck and across her cheek. "I thought you were sorry about yesterday, that you already had regrets and didn't know how to say it."

Diamond buried her face against his neck and inhaled the warm, spicy scent of his cologne.

"The only regret I feel is that I don't know how to handle myself in situations like this. I'm not as practiced in relationships as you are. I don't know how to be casual about the fact that I can't keep my hands off you, or that I panic when I can't hear your voice. I just don't want them to know."

"Thank God," he said. "Because there's nothing casual about the way I feel for you—and to hell with Tommy and the band."

He kissed her gently, lingering longer than necessary on her lower lip. With every tug of his mouth, the heat in her stomach spread.

"You're going to have to trade cars, Jesse," she whispered as he finally relinquished her lips.

"Why, darlin'?" he asked, and gently brushed her hair away from her face and neck.

"Because it's difficult enough just to get myself into this thing and ride. It would be damned near impossible to make love in it."

He smiled, and his eyes glittered as he moved his hands over her body.

"It's not easy, darlin', but it's not impossible," he said, and set out to prove it.

"From the look on Jesse's face, homecoming was goo-ood," Mack said, and slid a slow whistle out from between his teeth as he watched the pair coming through the door into the studio.

"Oh, shut the hell up, Mack," Al said. He wiped down his fiddle and glared at the big guitar player. Mack laughed in his face and then went to get a cup of coffee.

Al was sick and tired of Mack's innuendos about Jesse's woman. As far as he could tell, she was nothing but a lady, and in Al's book, that was all that mattered. Even though she was staying in Jesse's house, she hadn't tried to take advantage of her situation by making a name for herself, nor did he believe that she was some star-struck groupie looking for a free ride.

And the way she sang was proof enough for him that she could write her own ticket in Nashville, given half a chance. The way Al looked at it, that was what Jesse was trying to do—give her that chance. If something else developed between Jesse and his singer, it was no one else's business.

"Mornin', Jesse . . . Miss Houston," Al said. "Everyone's here but Tommy."

Jesse nodded. "He'll show up on his own time. But we don't need him to start recording. He can't sing worth a damn."

Al laughed and then shared Jesse's joke with the rest of Muddy Road while Mack sauntered out from the lounge with a steaming cup of coffee in his hand.

Mack watched until he was certain that Jesse was out of earshot and then headed for Diamond, unwilling to give up on his quest to follow in Jesse's footsteps.

"Hey, baby," Mack said, lowering his voice, "want some coffee? It's good and hot, just the way I like it—if you get my message."

Diamond shivered as Mack's eyes raked her body, lingering on her breasts and then lower, below her belt. Although the blue and white striped slacks and the blue silk blouse she was wearing were not revealing, she felt naked.

"I don't want anything from you, mister," she said softly, unwilling to let Jesse overhear. "Not now, not ever. Not if I had to do *without* for the rest of my life. Do you get *my* message?"

Diamond met Mack's stare and didn't blink as he absorbed her intense anger. And it was Mack who was the first to look away, cursing softly beneath his breath as he downed the coffee and slammed the empty cup into a trash can.

"What's going on?" Jesse asked as he watched Mack stomp away. The expression on Diamond's face was fixed, almost angry.

"Oh, nothing," she said. "Mack just offered me some . . . coffee." She could sense Mack listening but would not give him the satisfaction of tattling. "I told him I didn't want any."

Jesse sensed that he wasn't being told everything, but he was too focused on the session that was about to begin to delve deeper.

"Okay, honey." He reached out and touched her arm gently, wishing he could do more than touch, but he'd promised to be discreet. "I've got a seat waiting for you up there." He gestured to the glassed-in area where the sound engineers were waiting for them to begin recording. "I know you'd rather be singing than watching, but give yourself a chance. It's an education I'd have given anything for when I started trying to make it in the business. I was doing everything wrong before Tommy got hold of me. I'd hate to think of where I'd be today if it weren't for him."

"You'd still be Jesse," she said, and entered the sound booth without looking back.

His dependence on Tommy was the last thing she wanted to hear about. It told her, as nothing else could have, that no matter what happened between herself and Tommy, Jesse could never know how she was being treated by his manager and Mack. She didn't want to put him in the position of having to choose between them and her.

But Diamond's words had started Jesse thinking. And for the first time in his life, he began to realize how much sense they made. Tommy *was* good. In fact, he was one of the best in the business, but he was only as good as Jesse made him. And no one was indispensable, not even a good personal manager. And so the week began.

* * *

"It's a wrap," Jesse said. He was tired, but satisfied that the cuts for his new album were some of the best he'd ever done.

"Sounds good, Jesse, real good," the producer said. "When we're through with the mix, I think you'll have yourselves a winner. In fact, I can smell those Grammys and CMA awards as we speak."

Tommy rolled his neck and rubbed at the ache at the base of his skull as he patted his pocket, needing a cigarette to calm his nerves.

It had taken days to complete the last songs on the album—days in which he'd had to smile and be nice to the tall blonde who hovered just at the edge of his vision. Everywhere he looked, she was there, listening to and watching what went on inside Jesse's world. If he didn't believe the background check he'd had done on her himself, he'd suspect that she was some kind of spy sent by a tabloid to get the inside scoop on Jesse Eagle.

Tommy saw the weariness on Jesse's face and wanted to blame it on sleepless nights with that damned woman instead of the hard work they'd put in on the album. Right now he'd be willing to blame her for anything. He slapped Jesse on the back and grinned. "I told you the stuff you had was good." He'd played a big role in choosing some of the songs to record on the album. "You know me, I can always pick the winners."

"Not always," Jesse said, glancing toward Diamond, who was inside the booth and out of range of their voices. "Sometimes you're way the hell off the mark."

Tommy flushed, suppressing the anger that shot through his gut. Jesse's taunt was nothing more than a reminder that he still had to deal with Diamond Houston. But, he thought, how he dealt with her would be his little secret.

He walked out into the lobby and lit a cigarette, inhaled, and then slowly exhaled, squinting his eyes against the twin spirals of smoke that drifted upward from his nostrils.

"Thought you'd quit," Al said as he walked past, heading for home.

Tommy shrugged and took another pull, relishing the nicotine filtering through his system. He had quit until that woman had come on the scene and shot his nerves all to hell. His relapse was just another thing he could blame on her, and not on the weakness of his own resolve.

Jesse slipped his arm around Diamond's shoulder and hugged her gently. It was the first intimate move he'd made toward her during the entire recording session. It felt good. It felt right. After this, he had no intention of letting her call the shots about their public relationship again. It had been too difficult to be within touching distance of her and not be able to do anything except return her smiles.

"What did you think?" he asked.

"That I have a lot to learn."

"That's what I'm here for," he said as they crossed the lobby and headed toward the exit.

Tommy glared as the pair walked past him. "Don't forget tomorrow night," he yelled. Jesse stopped, and

Tommy got exactly what he'd wanted—Jesse's attention.

"What's tomorrow night?" Jesse asked.

"The Charity Ball. You don't have to perform, just show up and be your natural, smiling self," Tommy said.

"You didn't tell me," Jesse said. The anger was thick in his voice as he glared at his manager. Tommy knew good and well that he hated that kind of affair.

Tommy shrugged. "I have now," he said.

"So get me another ticket and I'll go."

Tommy rocketed out of his chair. He knew what Jesse was angling for and had no intentions of aiding him in his single-minded intent to include Diamond Houston in every facet of his life.

"I can't get another ticket at this late date. It's already planned," he said.

"Then give me yours," Jesse said. "I'm not going without her."

Diamond's heart sank. She knew that she was a bone of contention between these two men, and for the life of her she could think of no way out of the situation other than to disappear. She took one long look at Jesse, remembering the way they laughed and kissed and made love, and decided that disappearing was out of the question.

"Jesse, I don't have to go with—"

He turned that dark, angry stare toward her, and the look on his face silenced what she'd been about to say. She sighed and walked away, leaving the two men alone to finish the argument. She had no stomach for the situation.

"Goddammit, Jesse," Tommy said, flinging his

cigarette into a potted palm. "Have you completely taken leave of your senses? Okay! Granted she's a knockout, but there's a hundred more just like her out there waiting to meet the great Jesse Eagle. And," he continued, holding up his hand to silence whatever Jesse had been about to say, "supposing she *can* sing. I'm the first to admit that she's better than good. That still doesn't mean that every step you take, she has to be in your hip pocket. For the love of God, get a life! And get her out of your fuckin' bed!"

Jesse had never wanted to hit a man as badly as he wanted to punch his manager. Tommy blatantly refused to face what Diamond's presence in his life represented. But common sense overrode Jesse's need for justice, and he settled for a threat instead.

"Don't you ever—and I mean *ever*—speak of her in this way again. She's not just another woman, Tommy. She's special to me, and you damned well know it."

"Special?" Tommy spit to rid himself of the word's taste, ignoring the fact that he was still inside the lobby of the recording studio. "What'd she do that's so special? Come on, man. Let me in on the details. Does she do it with one hand tied behind her—"

Jesse's fist shot out, connecting with Tommy's nose and flattening it against his face. Blood spurted as Tommy slid across the polished floor on the seat of his pants.

"Send the godammed ticket, or make my excuses," Jesse said. "And you open your mouth to me like that again, and you can go find yourself another singer to peddle."

Tommy clasped his hand across his face, closing his eyes against the pain and the sight of fresh blood pouring through his fingers. If he'd had a gun, he would have pulled the trigger and worried about the consequences later. He'd never been so incensed in his entire life. It was just as he'd figured.

All the years that he'd spent building Jesse Eagle into what he was today, and one woman had stepped in and changed everything. He couldn't believe that Jesse had actually threatened to fire him. Even though his contract prohibited it, he was still pissed that it had come to this.

"You bitch," he said softly, watching Diamond through the plate-glass window as Jesse drove past in his car. "I'll get you yet."

Tommy couldn't see that it was all his fault. That if he'd given Diamond Houston half a chance he'd not only have Jesse, but he'd have another client as well that could very well make him the rich man he so desperately wanted to be. At that moment he couldn't see anything but the blood running down onto his favorite shirt.

"Tommy doesn't approve of me," Diamond said as Jesse shoved the car into reverse and drove out of the parking lot.

"He doesn't have to," Jesse said. "He just has to do what I say. It's in his damned contract."

He pulled out into traffic and headed downtown.

"Where are we going?" Diamond asked as she realized that they weren't heading toward Jesse's ranch.

"To find you something to wear to the gala," he said.

"But I thought Tommy couldn't get a ticket," she said. The hard-edged smile he sent her way made her shiver. "He'll get the ticket," Jesse said. "You don't have to worry about anything but finding the right gown. And get that look off your face," he warned. "This isn't the first argument Tommy and I have had, and it won't be the last. He's my manager, not my mother. Sometimes he just . . . forgets, that's all."

Her stomach tightened as Jesse sped through the streets. Something told her that this was only the beginning of trouble, not the end. She knew men. Tommy Thomas was the kind who held grudges, and he had quite a grip on the grudge he was holding against her. Diamond just didn't know what to do to make him turn it loose.

In the end, Diamond chose the dress for the ball. When she'd seen the look in Jesse's eyes as she'd modeled it for him, she knew that this was the one. He'd looked at her as if he were seeing her for the first time—and she wished it had been so.

If Diamond could have taken away the tawdry business of her life before Jesse Eagle came into it, she would have in a minute. If only he'd never seen the pitiful house in which she'd lived, if only he'd never seen the inside of Whitelaw's Bar—but he had. And he'd heard her singing for tips like a beggar on the street corner.

Jesse had seen the look on her face when she'd examined herself in the mirror. This was the one! But when she began to search the dress for the price tag, Jesse bolted from his chair and waved to the saleslady.

"We'll take it," he said.

"It doesn't have a price tag," Diamond whispered. "Shouldn't we ask how much it—"

He smiled once and shook his head twice. "No, darlin'. We shouldn't. It doesn't matter how much. It only matters that it was made for you."

The saleslady gushed and began to write out the sales slip. Diamond shrugged and went to change her clothes. She hadn't known Jesse long, but already she recognized that look on his face. He'd cornered the market on determination.

Diamond smiled as she pulled the gown from its hanger and laid it upon her bed the next afternoon. She had four hours in which to get ready for tonight's affair, and she was going to use every minute to her fullest advantage. She'd warned Henley that she wasn't going to eat and told Jesse to leave her alone. Both were necessary if she was ever going to get into that dress.

Eating would make zipping impossible. And if Jesse tried to help, it would preclude her ever getting dressed. Her excitement surged as she realized that finally she was going to get a chance to see how the other half lived.

She locked her door, stripped off her clothes, and headed for the bathtub. First thing on the list was a long, hot soak in a mountain of bubbles.

"Oh, my!" Henley's exclamation did not do justice to her appearance.

Jesse turned, caught his breath, and swallowed as Diamond walked down the stairs to him.

The sea-green sequins covering the entire surface of her dress caught and reflected the light. Two narrow bands of the same sequins served as straps, but they were only for effect. Her generous curves and the grace of God were all that was holding it up.

A familiar ache tugged in his groin as he watched the movement of her long legs beneath the floor-length skirt, glimpsing just enough skin through the thigh-high slit to make him wish for more. Her matching shoes had three-inch heels that put her at Jesse's eye level as she gained the last step on the stairs. It was too close, and yet not close enough.

He got more than a glimpse of the devils dancing in her eyes and inhaled deeply the scent of her perfume. Unable to resist the bountiful cloud of curls she'd made of her hair, he ran his fingers lightly along a single curl resting just above her breast and wished to hell that they were alone.

"You're beautiful," he said softly.

"So are you," she said, unable to take her eyes from this man.

"Men aren't beautiful," he said. "Maybe good-lookin', but not pretty, darlin'. Around here, calling a man pretty can get you in a whole lot of trouble."

"So you're good-looking, then?"

"Please, Miss Diamond. The last thing his ego needs is bolstering."

Jesse grinned at Henley's teasing remark and winked at Diamond.

"He's just jealous because I've got you and he doesn't."

"No sir," Henley said. "I would say it's more of a . . . relieved state of mind. Remember, I've already experienced Miss Diamond in a way in which I'd never imagined. Personally, it gave me nightmares, but I have recovered."

Diamond smiled, remembering their driving lessons.

"But I corner better than most, don't you think, Henley?"

"I reserve judgment for the day when you receive your driver's license, Miss Diamond," he said. "And do have a good evening, the both of you." He gave them a rare smile as he took his leave with a witty remark: "I won't wait up."

Jesse laughed and Diamond blushed. She felt like Cinderella.

When Henley was gone, Diamond turned and looked again at her Prince Charming.

He'd abandoned his cowboy attire for a black tuxedo, white pleated shirt, and silver-gray cummerbund. But he had retained a bit of his old self. She smiled as she looked down at his shoes. They were black, and shiny, but they were boots. And when he held out his arm and ushered her through the door, he grabbed his trademark black Stetson. Jesse would compromise, but only so far.

"Come on, darlin'," he said. "Let's party."

Jesse escorted her outside, eager to see her reaction to the surprise he had waiting.

"Jesse! A limousine? We're going in a limousine?"

"Yes ma'am," he said, grinning. "And you know what?"

Diamond shook her head. She was past surprises.

"The back seat of this baby has a whole lot of leg room."

Even in the dark, he could see her blush.

Their arrival was marked by a long line of fans standing on either side of the walkway that led into the opulent hotel. Flashbulbs were going off in constant succession as the passengers in the cars ahead of them made their entrance into the face of media, minicams, and adoring fans.

"Oh, my God!"

Diamond's low moan of disbelief made Jesse grab her hand and hold on tight to reassure her.

"It's okay, darlin'," he said. "Just stick with me. It'll be over before you know it. Besides, it won't be like this once we get inside."

And then the driver stopped, and their door opened. Jesse took a deep breath, leaned over and pressed one quick kiss on her lips. "You look fantastic. Give them that million-dollar smile, and don't stop walking."

She nodded, slipped her hand in his, and slid out of the seat.

Flashbulbs went off in their faces, but Jesse just kept on moving and waving, smiling broadly to the huge crowd of people behind the roped-off area who were shouting his name. And then a man carrying a hand mike stepped in front of them and smiled broadly as he interrupted their progress.

"Jesse Eagle! It's the first time I've seen you at an event like this without your famous—or should we say infamous—manager, Tommy Thomas, at your heels. What's the scoop?"

"Hey there, Charlie," Jesse said, trying not to swallow the microphone that the television personality shoved into his face.

Charlie persisted "So, is there a reason why Tommy Thomas is so obviously missing?"

Jesse grinned. "Well now, Charlie, I never did take you for a fool, so why are you asking me such a stupid question? Take a look at her, would you? Don't you think this lady is prettier than old Tommy? I sure do. And I can tell you one thing, she smells better, too."

Charlie laughed. And Jesse escaped simply because another limo had pulled up and unloaded a new set of celebrities.

"Jesse Eagle and guest," Jesse said, handing over the invitations as they entered the doorway leading into the main ballroom. The two envelopes had arrived at the house earlier by special messenger, but without a word of explanation or apology.

Damn him to hell and back anyway, Jesse thought. Tonight was Diamond's night. She was as beautiful as her namesake and a whole lot softer. He didn't know what he wanted more—to show her off, or to take her to bed. Either way, he couldn't lose.

8

It was near the witching hour. The ball was a rousing success, and everyone who was anyone in Nashville was in attendance. Diamond kept imagining she was dreaming, that any minute she'd wake up and see Queenie hovering over her bed, telling her it was time to get up and go to work at Whitelaw's Bar.

"Are you having a good time?" Jesse asked. He'd been watching her face ever since they'd entered the grand ballroom. Her eyes had never been still, and he didn't think he'd ever seen her so animated.

"I feel like Cinderella," she said.

"Much better than that," he teased. "I don't have to go running all over Tennessee hunting for a woman to fit a glass shoe, and you don't have any wicked stepmother hovering in the background, ready to ruin your chances for happiness."

She tried to smile, but instead his teasing comment sent a thread of apprehension through her. She may not have a wicked stepmother, but there *was* Tommy.

"Okay, Prince Charming," she said. "Since I'm not going to turn into a scullery maid at midnight and the limo won't turn into a pumpkin, will you get me something to drink?"

"It will be my pleasure, m'lady," he said, and in front of everyone around them managed a sweeping bow, kissed her hand, and then walked off, laughing good-naturedly at the teasing he took because of it.

Shock, pleasure, and a faint flush swept across her face as Jesse went to fill her order.

A woman wearing gold lamé and what seemed like a ton of diamonds watched from across the room. Her eyes glittered like the dress she was wearing as Jesse Eagle turned and walked away from Diamond. A small, feral smile slid across her lips as she remembered the phone call earlier at her home and the promise that she'd willingly made. She handed her drink to a passing waiter and made her excuses to the people beside her.

"We haven't had the pleasure," she said, digging her long nails into Diamond's arm before sliding them down to grasp her hand in a limp handshake. "I'm Selma Bennett."

Diamond smiled and shook the woman's hand. Before she had a chance to introduce herself, the woman continued.

"And who might you be, my dear? I couldn't help seeing you with Jesse Eagle."

"My name's Diamond—Diamond Houston."

Selma's smile was just above a sneer. "Diamond!

How . . . unique! With a name like that, you've got to be an . . . entertainer."

Diamond knew this woman had not walked across the crowded room to make friends. She'd lingered on the word *entertainer* too long to make it anything but a slur.

"My name *is* Diamond," she said. "My father had a vivid imagination." She didn't feel obligated to add anything else to the explanation.

Selma's mouth thinned. She didn't like people who were born with such obvious assets. And this woman had assets. A beautiful face and body, and a name that matched. She fumed silently as her pale blue eyes swept across Diamond's face. To Selma, it seemed there was no justice in this world.

It had taken Selma over thirty thousand dollars in plastic surgeons' fees and numerous trips to fat farms to get herself to the point she was at now, and God only knew what would happen in the next five years as she aged. Her envy prompted another dig.

"So . . . Diamond . . . what do you do? Besides hang out with Jesse Eagle?"

Diamond wished heartily that Jesse would come back so she could make her excuses without being obviously rude. She had no way of knowing who or what Selma Bennett was, or if she could hurt Jesse's career. Diamond could do nothing other than answer.

"I'm a singer," Diamond said.

Selma's mouth stretched into a wide smile, and then she laughed aloud, causing several people to turn and watch their conversation. Selma was well known in

Nashville, but only for her vicious tongue and the amount of her third ex-husband's alimony payments.

"Oh, my God," Selma said. "Another one. Hell, honey," she said. "This is Nashville. Everyone here's a singer—or sleeping with one."

Her eyes glittered as she watched for Diamond's reaction, hoping her barb had hit home.

"Really? Which one are you?" Diamond asked.

Selma gasped.

Several people around them smiled and turned away so that Selma would not see them laugh. They loved it. Selma Bennett was not a popular person, but she was too rich to ignore and consequently turned up at events such as these.

"Just who do you think you are?" Selma whispered angrily.

"I know who I am and why I'm here," Diamond said quietly, tapping a finger against Selma's gold-covered shoulder. "And don't think that just because you know the names of the people in this room and I don't, that I'm going to be intimidated by the likes of you. Where I come from, someone like you wouldn't last five minutes."

With that, Diamond turned and walked away, moving through the crowd in search of Jesse while her stomach tied itself in knots. She couldn't believe she'd just done that. And to a woman who was wearing more money than Diamond had ever seen in her entire life.

"Hey, honey!" a woman called out.

Diamond turned at the sound of the woman's child-like voice, half expecting to see Selma with an axe in her hand, ready to finish her off. It was a woman. But this time, it was one she recognized.

"Aren't you—?" Diamond never got to finish her question.

The voluptuous blonde with a mountain of curls and a big red smile patted her on the arm and leaned forward.

"Yep," the blonde said. "It's me. But never mind. That's not why I stopped you. I couldn't help overhearing what ol' Selma said to you."

She giggled, and Diamond grinned in spite of the fact that she was actually talking to—

"Don't let people like her get to you," the woman continued. "When I first came to Nashville I was as green as a gourd and twice as useless. Shoot! All I could do was sing and play guitar. People took one look at me—or I should say my body, since they hardly ever got to my face. . . . Anyway, they pretty much ignored me. It took me years to be taken seriously." She gently tapped her fingernail on Diamond's arm. "Don't let what people say about you matter. It's what's inside your heart that counts. And you can take that to the bank, sugar."

With that she winked and walked away on heels almost as high as her hair.

Diamond grinned. In the space of five minutes, she'd just met a real bitch and a real lady.

"There you are," Jesse said as he walked up behind her. "I lost you, darlin'."

"No you didn't," Diamond said as she turned and whispered softly so that no one except Jesse heard what she said. "You'll never lose me."

Jesse's eyes darkened. His mouth slid into a sensuous smile as he set the glasses of champagne onto a table and grabbed her hand instead.

"Something tells me you've been busy while I was gone. Remind me to thank whoever it was that put that glitter in your eyes, honey." He kissed her softly on the lips. "Are you ready to try out that limo's big back seat?"

She nodded.

"Then I think it's time to say goodnight, Diamond."

"Goodnight, Diamond," she repeated dutifully, and then grinned at the look of surprise on his face before he leaned his head back and laughed aloud.

The ride home was long and fruitful.

"You and your lady made the papers," Tommy said as Henley showed him into Jesse's living room the next day. He tossed a clipping into Jesse's lap and looked around. "Where is she? Out spending some more of your money?"

Jesse picked up the clipping, a photo from the entertainment section of the local newspaper, and held it to the light. It had been taken just after their arrival, when they were talking to the talk-show host outside the hotel. Even the grainy, black-and-white snapshot couldn't hide Diamond's beauty or the excitement she'd been feeling. It was there for anyone to see.

Jesse smiled, ignoring Tommy's barbed comment. He figured he'd overlook it, considering the fact that Tommy's left eye was a rich shade of purple and green and his nose was still a bit swollen.

"She takes a real good picture," Jesse said. "It will make album covers easier, I suppose."

Tommy swallowed a curse and started to stuff a

cigarette into his mouth when Henley entered the room and stared at him pointedly.

"Shit!" Tommy muttered, stuffing the cigarette back into the package. Henley didn't allow smoking inside Jesse's house, and it angered Tommy immensely that Jesse let him get away with it. He couldn't understand the relationship that existed between Jesse and his houseman. Sometimes they even acted like friends instead of employer/employee.

Henley's eyebrows rose, but he refrained from comment other than to deliver the message he'd just received from Diamond.

"Miss Diamond will be back within the hour," Henley said. "She told you not to wait supper for her, that she'd eat when she got back."

"I'll wait," Jesse said.

"Yes sir," Henley said. "I'll put the food in the oven to warm." He walked away, giving Tommy one last warning look.

"What's she doing?" Tommy asked.

"I don't know," Jesse said. "She'll probably tell me when she gets back."

"Aren't you afraid that she'll sell what's been going on between you two to the first tabloid that offers her money?"

Jesse glared. Tommy's mind ran on one track, and it had no beginning or end.

"Why should she?" Jesse argued. "She isn't desperate for money. She's got some in the bank. Besides, she's going to have more than she can spend when you get her a recording contract. Have you considered her options?"

Tommy plastered a smile into place and lied through

his teeth. "There are a couple of houses I think might be interested," he said. "All we need to do is get her demo cut, and then I can make my pitch."

Jesse nodded. "I've got that short road trip coming up next month. What is it—six, maybe eight nights out? I don't want to go without her, Tommy. Let's try and get a studio booked beforehand so she can finish it in time to go with me. Okay?"

"You're the boss," Tommy said. "Just leave everything to me."

Jesse nodded. He was so used to Tommy handling all the mundane details of his life that he had no reason to question his about-face. And when Tommy left minutes later, he had no reason to believe that he wouldn't follow through on his orders.

Jesse slapped the mare on the rump to move her over and then poured the bucket of sweet feed into the trough, smiling to himself as she buried her nose in it and began to eat. Her baby danced just out of his reach, nickering nervously as Jesse tried unsuccessfully to coax it toward him.

"One of these days," Jesse warned, and laughed aloud when the foal tossed his head and kicked before making a short run down the fence line.

A big white car turned and started down his driveway. The driver honked and waved as Jesse looked up. Jesse recognized the car but couldn't imagine why Al was there until he saw the passenger door open and Diamond emerge.

He tossed the bucket inside the barn, fastened the gate, and started toward the house.

Al got out of the driver's seat and went to meet him.

"Hey, Jesse," he said. "Me and Rita ran across your lady doing a little shopping. We offered to bring her home and save Henley the trip of going after her."

Jesse smiled. "Thanks, Al. You don't know how much this means to me." He reached out and shook Al's hand.

Al looked at a space just over Jesse's shoulder, embarrassed to be showing emotion in front of another man.

"Yeah, I think I do," Al said. "I remember when me and Rita first met, how much I wanted everyone to like her as much as I did."

Jesse nodded, unable to express how much Al's acceptance of Diamond meant to him. "So, if you were chauffeuring Rita around, where is she?" He looked beyond Al into the empty car.

"Oh, Di took her into the house to show her something, but I don't know what. You know how women are. They buy something new, they got to show everyone in sight." He grinned.

"Di?"

Al grinned again. "Rita did that. You know how she is. She thinks nicknames are cute."

"What's she call you?" Jesse asked, and laughed when Al blushed.

"You don't want to know," Al said. "Come on. I better get Rita out of the house before she starts moving furniture and Henley has a stroke."

Jesse laughed aloud, remembering the last time he'd

had all the members of the band and their families out for a barbecue. Rita had taken it into her head to rearrange the living room furniture and Henley had truly come close to having a seizure. He'd been torn between courtesy for his boss's guests and dismay that a woman was changing his world around to suit herself.

They walked into the house and caught Henley hovering in the hallway just out of sight of the living room, where the women were visiting.

"Saved by the bell," Henley said, and walked away with a dignified air, ignoring the fact that he'd been caught in the act of spying.

"Hey, girl," Al called out. "Come out here. We've got to get on home. The kids should be home from school."

Rita Barkley walked out into the hallway and into her husband's arms, hugging him in spite of the fact that he turned three shades of red when she tugged at his collar to lower his mouth to hers.

"Oh, good Lord," Al said, and grabbed his wife by the arm. "Let's get out of here before you completely ruin what reputation I have left."

"Thanks for the ride home," Diamond called as they went out the door.

They waved and then were gone.

"Nice people," Diamond said. "I think Al's finally beginning to like me."

Jesse looked dumbfounded. "What do you mean, finally? Have the boys been giving you trouble?"

She hadn't meant to bring up the subject of the band members' attitudes toward her. She just shook her head and said, "Let's eat. I'm starved. Henley said you waited."

"I was afraid not to," Jesse teased. "Hell, honey, if I'd eaten too much, what would you have done for sustenance?"

"There's always you," Diamond said.

Suddenly, the last thing he wanted was to sit down at a table full of food. But knowing Diamond, before anything else occurred, that was exactly what he was going to do.

Jesse came out of the shower, expecting to see Diamond in the bedroom waiting for him, but there was nothing but an empty, turned-back bed. He pulled on a pair of Levis, buttoned a couple of buttons just to keep them from sliding down his hips, and walked barefoot through the house, looking for her.

Twice he almost called her name aloud, but something—call it instinct—told him that whatever she was doing, she didn't want him to see.

It was the creak of the swing on his back porch that told him where she was. And when he looked through the screen door, he saw why she'd slipped away without telling him where she'd gone. She was crying.

The hinge protested as the door swung back at Jesse's touch. Her head came up, and the sight of tears running down her face made him sick at heart. He couldn't imagine what had caused this when only hours earlier she'd been so happy and carefree.

"Come here," he said softly, and held out his arms.

She walked into them, wrapped her arms around his waist, and buried her face against his bare chest, mingling tears with the water droplets still present from his shower.

"What's wrong, honey?" he asked. "Did I do something to—"

"No, no, no," she said, and hugged him tighter.

"Then what, Diamond? As God is my witness, you're gonna have to tell me, because I can't stand to see you cry."

He threaded his hands through her hair, relishing the texture of the thick strands falling down her back and across his arms. Her body shook beneath the thin robe she was wearing. Her skin was hot to his touch, almost feverish.

"I'm happy," she said. "And I didn't think I'd ever be . . . not like this."

Jesse gave one long sigh of relief. Women! He'd never understand them, but he damned sure didn't want to live without them, especially this one.

"My God," he said, "you cry like this because you're happy? I don't *ever* want to see you cry when you're sad."

And then a memory surfaced as he remembered the time when he'd first seen her and heard her singing. It was at her father's funeral, and she hadn't been crying at all. A slow but certain understanding of his lady began to surface. Diamond was the kind of woman who buried the deepest hurts inside herself and never let them out. It was only her joy that she was able to share.

Jesse lifted her into his arms and carried her into the house and up the stairs to his bedroom. He laid her on his bed and then watched with satisfaction as the expression on her face changed to one of desire. He leaned forward, splaying his hands across her breasts and caressing them under the satiny fabric of her robe.

"No barriers," Jesse said as he slid the robe off her body and then stepped out of his jeans.

She reached for him, letting her hands follow the curve of his arms and shoulders as he came down to her.

Jesse shuddered as her hands encircled him, and a sweat broke across his forehead. He wanted inside this woman. But wanting and doing were two different things when she had him under her control. An impossible need to stop warred with a constant need to keep moving, and still she would not lessen her hold.

Just when he thought he was going to burst, she rolled out from under him and in one smooth motion settled herself across his legs. He was hard, and ready, and Diamond knew the pleasure he was capable of giving her. But tonight she needed to give something back to the man who'd given her so much and asked nothing in return.

Jesse started to speak, but when she lowered her head toward him, nothing came out of his mouth but a groan. He meant to watch what she was doing, but he couldn't concentrate on anything except the flashes of light going off in his brain. He closed his eyes and reached back for the bedpost as her mouth and hands encircled him.

There was nothing in his world but a heat and a pressure that concentrated into a spiraling need that she'd created. She moved her body up and then impaled herself upon him. Slowly. Completely.

Her muscles contracted around him, and he shuddered and arched. Unable to control himself anymore, he spilled into her and then held her as they slept.

Morning brought them to earth slowly as Jesse kissed her awake. Diamond looked up into the face of love.

"Mornin', honey," Jesse said, and kissed the corner of her mouth.

"Morning to you, too," she said, and cupped his face with her hands, moving her thumbs across dark beard stubble before threading her fingers through his hair. "It's so black it almost looks blue," she said, and rubbed a lock back and forth between her fingers.

"Leftovers of my Cherokee ancestors," Jesse said. "Most of my great-grandfather's family came from Georgia."

"Really? I hadn't thought . . . of course, your name— Eagle." She scanned the dear and familiar face with tears in her eyes.

"Right, love," he said. "Henley might be teaching you how to drive. But I'm the one who taught you how to fly." He lowered his mouth and tasted the tears on her cheeks. "If I can just teach you how to be happy without crying, then I think we'll have it made."

She laughed, but it sounded more like a sob.

"Oh, hell, honey," Jesse said. "I know one way to stop those tears. Get your pretty self out of my bed. I'm going to feed you. That works every time."

She followed willingly. She wasn't sure whether it was because he'd called her "love" or because she couldn't resist the sight of his bare backside walking toward the shower, but she followed.

They were just finishing brunch when Henley came through the door with an armload of groceries.

"Miss Diamond, did you get your message?" he asked as he began unpacking the bags. "I heard the last of it just as I was leaving for town. I supposed you would see the light or I'd have left you a note."

She looked up in surprise and then down at the blinking light on the answering machine.

"No, but I will," she said, and punched the button. Tommy's voice was the last thing she expected to hear.

"Miss Houston, it's Tommy. I've reserved a studio for you day after tomorrow. Unfortunately that's the day Jesse has scheduled for the shoot on his new album cover, so he won't be able to accompany you. However, rest assured that I'll do everything I can to make this as painless as possible. Be ready at eight A.M. I'll send a car." With that, he disconnected, leaving Diamond a little bit nervous and a whole lot excited.

"This is it, darlin'," Jesse said, and hugged her. "This is what I promised you back in Cradle Creek. I'm not going to tell you good luck. I don't think this gambler's daughter wants to hear the word *luck* in the same sentence with *good*."

She laughed and wrapped her arms around his neck. "How right you are," she said. "Besides, there's no such thing as luck, only good fortune."

"Then what should I say?"

"Nothing. Your actions speak louder than words, any day."

"So, you like my actions, do you?" Jesse asked, tightening his grip on her.

"Good Lord," Henley muttered, going back outside to unload the rest of his purchases. "I'm living in the midst of an unending soap opera."

Diamond blushed and Jesse laughed aloud. "I'll go help Henley unload. I can tell by the gleam in your eye that you want to borrow my guitar again."

She smiled. "So?"

"So help yourself. You will anyway, with or without my permission."

Jesse watched her leave and felt as if something tangible had just come between them, then scoffed at himself for being so foolish and so selfish. He had his music. It was only fair that she had hers.

He picked up the phone and dialed Tommy's number. The few words that passed between them were congenial, even pleasant. But Jesse had the strangest sensation as he hung up that Tommy was being too nice. He shook off the feeling, chalking it up to the fact that he just didn't want Diamond out of his sight, and went outside to help Henley.

Diamond ran her fingers across the strings of the old guitar and knew that she'd reconnected with her other self. For a short time she'd lost herself in Jesse. But as dearly as she loved him, she had no intention of losing her own identity by disappearing into Jesse's shadow. She didn't want to be just Jesse Eagle's woman. She loved him, but she wanted her own part of his world . . . the world of music.

9

Tommy was nice, and courteous, and he had even cracked two rather off-color jokes on the way into Nashville just to show her that she was "one of the boys." Diamond wasn't sure whether to be glad or wary. She wasn't certain she could trust him.

The tension of recording the demo was now all-consuming. That Tommy still had to pitch it didn't even come into consideration. It was the first step in a longed-for dream—and it was about to come true.

"All right!" Tommy said. "We're here." He pulled into the parking lot of the studio and stopped. "Get your stuff, girl. We're going to go inside and do it right, you hear me?"

Diamond nodded. His smile and the encouragement in his words were just what she needed. "I hear you," she said, and then stopped him with a touch just before they entered. "Oh, and Tommy . . ."

Tommy looked down at the long, slender fingers wrapped around his arm, half expecting her nails to dig into his flesh. "Thank you."

It was the last thing he expected her to say. He nodded and then stepped aside for her to enter. A small, niggling worry that he suspected was guilt skittered across his consciousness. But Tommy being Tommy, he ignored it. He was all business, and just where he wanted to be—in control.

A motley assortment of musicians lounged around inside the studio. One was tuning his guitar, another absently running through chords on a keyboard. A fiddler was playing softly in a corner of the room, whiling away the time with the instrument tucked beneath his chin.

Diamond smiled as the familiar strains of "Wildwood Flower" hung on the air. She and the fiddler had similar tastes in music.

"Hey, boys!" Tommy shouted. "We're here! This pretty lady is Miss Diamond Houston. You guys introduce yourselves while I get myself a cup of coffee and talk to the engineer. I won't be long," he told Diamond. "Make yourself at home."

The men were as different from the boys in Jesse's band as night was from day. They were friendly but businesslike. And the one man who seemed most likely to flirt was doing it with a modicum of manners. She began to relax.

"I didn't know I was going to have backup," she said, as Tommy came back into the room. "I'd planned to accompany myself and leave it at that. Shouldn't we practice or something before we do the actual recording?"

"Naw," Tommy said, and looked down to brush a scuff off the toe of his boot. "These boys are old hands at stuff like this. You just start out; they'll pick up on you real fast." He winked at her and then walked away with a swagger.

It didn't sound right, but she didn't have enough knowledge to argue. This was all new ground for her. If Jesse trusted Tommy then she would, too.

The band members had been briefed ahead of time. This was going to be easy money. No run-throughs, no discussion about arrangement. Just play. That they could do.

Tommy walked into the sound booth and then stared back through the glass at the tall, elegant woman who was seating herself upon a stool.

The engineer came out and fitted her with a head mike, fiddled with the sound adjustment, and then walked back inside the sound booth. He sat down and adjusted the components on the sound panel, then gave her a thumbs-up sign, indicating that he was ready to begin.

Diamond's hands were sweaty. Her heart raced, and her stomach felt an attack of panic. She closed her eyes, thought of Johnny sitting in the corner of Whitelaw's Bar, and knew it was time to take the gamble.

She tossed her hair back over her shoulder, tucked the heels of her boots in the rungs of the stool, and let her fingers run lightly over the strings of Jesse's guitar. She sat alone in the center of the room, unaware of the men tuning up behind her.

She was unaware that one man had already promised the devil two years of his life for a chance to run his fingers through that mane of honey-gold hair falling down her back.

She was blind to the guitar player who'd stopped in midchord when she'd scooted backward onto the stool, unaware that he was lost in lust at the sight of her perfectly curved backside encased in stone-washed Rockies.

She was also oblivious of the fact that the smile she'd given the man on keyboard had momentarily made him forget his name. She was lost in the music going around in her head.

Tommy tried not to stare at the gentle smile on her face as she fingered the guitar strings. But ignoring the length and slenderness of her legs was impossible, as was the possibility of a friendship. The punch in the nose that she'd given him had done permanent damage to his ego.

If he'd been honest with himself, revenge upon this woman was not his ultimate dream. Tommy was blind to the truth about Diamond, unwilling to admit what he actually felt for her. He didn't really want her out of his life. He wanted her in his bed. But it was never going to happen. As usual, Jesse had gotten to her first.

"What are we doin'?" the fiddler asked.

"Oh . . . right!" Diamond said, and thought for a moment. Then, without looking up from the guitar strings, she answered. "Easy on the keyboards . . . bass guitar, you follow me on the melody." Then she looked up at the fiddler and smiled. "And you, Mr. Fiddle Man, make yours weep. The song is 'I Can't Make You Love Me,' in the key of F."

"But that's not a country song," one of them said. "It's rhythm and blues."

She looked over her shoulder, cocked an eyebrow, and replied, "It's country when I do it."

Tommy grinned. This was perfect.

She began by humming a slow, melodic rendering of the song as they knew it, but in her tempo. Then her fingers picked across a guitar string . . . and another . . . and another . . . and the man on keyboard forgot for a moment that he was supposed to accompany her when she opened her mouth and began to sing.

The song filled the room and their hearts. It was a slow, plaintive admission of a woman's failure to make a man love her the way she wanted. Of how she'd take what he had to offer and have no regrets for tomorrow.

They all stared, lost in the clear, perfect pitch of her voice and the song, drawn into the lyrics by the emotion with which she was singing.

The fiddle player blinked, surprised by an onset of quick tears, and pulled the bow across the strings. The no-big-deal session he'd been expecting had disappeared the moment this lady had opened her mouth. She'd asked him to make his fiddle weep, and instead she'd brought tears to his eyes. As they hovered, hidden behind his closed eyelids, it was all he could do to return the favor.

By the time the song was over, the musicians were grinning. They knew good stuff when they heard it, and this woman was better than good. The engineer in the sound booth held up his hand, letting her voice fade along with the last soulful sound of the fiddler's bow, and then flipped a series of switches on the console before giving them a thumbs-up sign.

She shuddered and dropped her head forward, resting it on the curve of Jesse's guitar. She felt drained, emotionally and physically, although she'd done nothing more than sing a song.

"Oowwee," the guitar player shouted. "Honey, you sure can sing."

"My God, lady, if you need someone to play in your band, you be sure and let me know," the fiddler said, and teasingly tugged at her hair as he walked past to put his instrument away. "I could do with a steady job now and then instead of all this pickup work. My name's on the card."

She looked up and smiled, surprised that it was over, surprised that they were so friendly and demonstrative. She noted that the fiddler's name was Doug Bentin and stuffed his card into her hip pocket. It was a complete turnabout from the way Muddy Road had treated her when she'd sung with Jesse.

"Really?" she asked. "You thought it was good?"

"Yeah, lady . . . really," Doug Bentin said.

She grinned and looked nervously toward Tommy, who was staring at her from inside the booth. She longed to hear the same approval from him.

For a moment their eyes met. Even from this distance Tommy could see the hope on her face and the expectancy hovering at the back of those damned green eyes. He smiled at her, turned his back to the studio, and looked long and hard at the sound man who'd captured the performance on tape.

"Man, you sure can pick 'em," the engineer said. "First Jesse Eagle, now her. I'll run a mix and have the

DAT ready by tomorrow. Want to hear the playback?"

Tommy leaned forward. When they were separated by only a few inches and he was certain that no one would overhear what he was about to say, he answered. "No! I don't want to hear anything. And after we leave, you take that thing and burn it," Tommy said. "You don't ask why. You don't argue. Got it?"

The engineer stared. His mouth dropped, and when it finally closed it was nothing but a grim line. He looked out at the pretty woman with the astounding voice and knew that something dirty was going on. It didn't make him feel particularly good to be a part of it.

"I asked you a question," Tommy said. "Do you want me to repeat it?"

The engineer heard the threat behind the question. He leaned back in his chair and stared down at the floor.

"No, I don't need you to repeat a damned thing," he said.

"That's great," Tommy said, slapping him on the back. "That's the way I like to hear my people talk."

Then he walked out of the booth and up to Diamond, slipped his arm around her waist, and bade the boys in the band good-bye, unaware that the engineer had taken offense at his parting statement.

"I'm not *your people*," the man muttered. He watched the way Tommy Thomas was schmoozing up to the lady and frowned. "You son of a bitch," he said, and began mixing the tracks as if it was going to be picked up. When he was through, he slipped the DAT into a case and looked around, assuring himself that he was still alone. He walked out of the booth and down a long hallway to his office, then knelt in front of his desk.

The small lock on the lower left-hand drawer turned easily when he inserted a key in the keyhole. He slid the case to the back of the drawer and turned the key in the lock again.

Shaking from the intensity of his anger and suddenly in need of fresh air, he took a deep breath and headed for a side exit. If he never saw Tommy Thomas again it would be too soon.

Diamond was shocked at the suddenness with which the session was over and everyone was departing. She supposed it was because the men were only hired by the hour, as was the studio. Tommy had made that part of it perfectly clear on their way into Nashville.

"Let's go grab a bite to eat, and then I'll take you by Jesse's shoot. They should be through soon, and you can catch a ride home with him, okay?"

Diamond didn't know what to think. All she could do was agree. Besides, if he was so willing to take her right back to Jesse, then everything must be on the up and up. She slid into the seat of Tommy's car and buckled her seat belt. This was a whole new world she could hardly wait to explore.

"Don't we need a contract?" she asked. "Between us, I mean?"

Tommy cursed beneath his breath and then flashed her what was supposed to pass for an engaging smile. "We sure do. First time I get a chance, I'll swing by the lawyer's office and get him to draw one up. It'll just be a standard contract, regular fees, that sort of thing. Don't

you worry yourself about a thing. I'll handle everything." He started the car and grinned at her again
before backing out of the parking space. "I always do."

The smile on his face made her shudder. Instinct
kept telling her that she should beware. But for the life
of her, she couldn't see anything to be wary of. Only
Tommy, doing his job. Doing what Jesse wanted.

"Come on, shiny girl," Jesse yelled. "We're going to
be late."

Diamond fussed with her hair and tugged at her
dress. Anything further she did to herself would only
undo what she'd just spent hours trying to achieve. She
opened the door to her room.

"Well?" she asked.

"Oh . . . my . . . God."

Diamond's heart sank. "You told me to look sexy. If
this is all wrong I can change. Better yet, you could go
without me. That's it! You go. I'll stay. Then I won't
have to—"

"You do. It's not. And not a chance in hell."

Diamond grinned. Jesse refuted arguments better
than anyone she knew.

The awards ceremony they were attending was to be
nationally televised. Jesse had given her carte blanche to
pick out something appropriate. From the look on his
face, she had.

Jesse allowed himself one groan. He'd told her to get
a dress for the occasion. Technically, he supposed that
this might be called a dress, since it was one piece and

had armholes and a place where a collar should be. But there was this great expanse of bare skin.

It also had a skirt, several inches of one. For her sake, he could say that the absence of sequins and beads should have given it some modicum of propriety. But the damned thing was red, and an eloquent statement of what a curvaceous body beneath minuscule amounts of red silk looked like.

"Do you like it?" she asked nervously.

He ran a tentative fingertip across her breast. Then his gaze raked her body, taking in the nearly nude pantyhose and the three-inch sling-back red shoes and the masses of long, blonde curls falling all over her face and neck.

"You could say that," he said.

He saw the unabashed need to please shining in her eyes and wished that they weren't going anywhere except to bed. There, he'd be perfectly willing to let her please him all she needed.

"This will be a first for me," he muttered as he escorted her downstairs.

"What will?" she asked. "I thought you'd won about every country award there was to win at least once."

"That's not what I meant," he said. "This is the first time I'm going to be praying I don't win."

"Why?" she asked.

"Because if I have to get up and walk across a stage in front of several hundred people as well as the eyes of the nation, I'm going to be—excuse the pun—hard put not to embarrass myself."

It didn't take Diamond long to get the message.

"Oh, Jesse," she said, batting her eyes in mock flirtation as she tucked her arm beneath his elbow. "You say the sweetest things."

In a crowd where sequins, fringe, and rhinestones were the rule, Diamond Houston stood out in solitary splendor. Her simple attire was the first to catch the eye of the observer. And then when it did, the woman beneath the clothes was seen to be even more spectacular than what she was wearing.

Jesse and Diamond made it through the crowd outside the auditorium, past the mingling throng inside the lobby, and down the long aisle to their assigned seats near the stage. Everything seemed to be going fine until Jesse stopped in the aisle and stepped aside to let Diamond in first.

She looked down into the smiling face of the man next to whom she'd be sitting and wanted to run. Mack Martin looked up, grinned, and took in her attire with one appreciative, sweeping gaze.

She sighed, pasted a smile on her face, and sat down. She should have known that Jesse would be seated with his band. If he was nominated for awards, they were included.

"Glad you're here," Jesse said, letting his hand rest on Diamond's knee as he leaned across to speak to Mack. "I'll have to go backstage midway through the ceremony. You guys look after Diamond for me while I'm gone, okay?"

Mack glanced down at Jesse's hand on her knee and grinned again. "It'll be my pleasure, boss," he said.

"I have to present one of the awards. It's all part of the show, darlin'," he said, squeezing her hand.

She smiled and tried to ignore the knot of dread forming in the pit of her stomach.

Later, after the ceremony was in full swing and Jesse had gone backstage, Diamond shifted in her seat. He had been gone for more than thirty minutes, and Mack had been nothing but courteous. Maybe she'd made too much of the situation. She watched in silent admiration as first one and then another of her favorite singing stars walked onto the stage and accepted an award. Her eyes blurred and her attention wandered as she envisioned herself in their place, smiling brilliantly as she accepted the award for best song . . . or entertainer of the year . . . or—

"Dreamin', darlin'?" Mack asked, leaning toward her in a conspiratorial manner. "Think if you hump the boss enough that one day one of those will be yours?"

She gasped.

She had no intention of dignifying his remark with an answer. Instinct told her that ignoring him would be her best bet. But it was the shock of his surprise attack that caused her reaction.

Tears sprang up and puddled in her clear, green eyes like spring rain on new grass. Her chin quivered once as she bit her lower lip to keep the pain inside where it belonged.

Mack's face fell. Her reaction had been the last thing he'd expected. He'd meant to instill anger, or passion, or even disdain. But he'd never expected her pain to pierce him so deeply. He tried to laugh it off and to look away from what he'd caused, but instead he watched in horror as a single tear finally escaped and rolled down her face.

"Well, God almighty," he said, fishing in his hip pocket. "I didn't mean for you to . . . hell, girl, don't do that. Here." He handed her his handkerchief.

"Why do you keep . . ." She swallowed a sob and looked away. "I love him," she said, blotted her face with the handkerchief he gave her, then wadded it back into his large, beefy palm. "I haven't said that aloud to him, let alone to myself, and here I've gone and told you. Says something for my lack of discretion, doesn't it?"

Mack turned red, slowly, from the neck upward. His mouth dropped at the sincerity on her face.

"You mean you're serious about Jesse? You ain't just here today and gone tomorrow?"

She shrugged. "I'm serious, all right. But I don't know about tomorrow. I'm not even certain about today. Growing up, the only person I counted on was myself. The only certainty was the moment."

Mack stuffed the handkerchief back into his pocket and shuddered. He'd never given much thought to the women who'd come and gone before. In fact, he'd always considered them fair game if they didn't click with Jesse. But the last thing he wanted was to hurt Jesse or ruin what he had with the boys in Muddy Road.

"Look," he said, lowering his voice so no one would overhear. "I'm sorry as hell, Diamond. I just didn't think about you being . . . I mean, I always used to go for the ones who . . ." He cursed softly. "What I'm trying to say is, this won't happen again. I swear. Okay?"

She couldn't look at him; but she heard his panic. And she answered his plea with a nod of her head.

Over an hour later, Jesse was back. A few minutes after that, Jesse Eagle and Muddy Road took the award for best album of the year.

And while Jesse and the band were publicly thanking Tommy for all his diligence, Tommy was hard at work, ruining Diamond's life.

The party was in full swing by the time they arrived. They'd been inside several minutes before their hostess finally made her way over to greet them. Diamond's stomach turned as she stared into the painted, smiling face of Selma Bennett and knew that her instincts had been right all along. She should have stayed home.

"Jesse! So glad you could make it!" Selma gushed, and blew the boys in the band an all-encompassing kiss. "My party wouldn't have been the same without you."

She purposely ignored Diamond's presence, which was exactly how Diamond preferred it, and then Tommy intervened. "Selma, I don't think you've met Jesse's friend. This is Di—"

"We've met," Selma said shortly. Manners made her acknowledge Diamond with a nod.

Jesse didn't miss a nuance of the encounter. He saw Selma smile knowingly at Tommy and then plant a kiss on his cheek as Tommy returned the smile with a wink. And when they walked away, he yanked Tommy by the arm and pulled him aside.

"What's the deal, Tommy? There were half a dozen parties across town. Why did we come to this one when you knew damn good and well that Selma and Diamond hadn't hit it off at the charity gala?"

Tommy pulled away, feigning indignation. "How the hell was I supposed to know anything of the kind? I wasn't there, remember?" He returned Jesse's glare and walked away.

"Let it go," Diamond said. "After all, it didn't amount to anything then, so don't make an issue of it now, okay?" She grasped Jesse by the arm and tugged him toward the buffet. "Besides, what can she do? Forget it. This is your night. You and your band won Best Album. It's time to celebrate."

A photographer stepped in front of them and caught the pair in the midst of their discussion. To the casual observer it would look as if Diamond were coaxing Jesse toward her. And the look of uncertainty on Jesse's face would be interpreted later as looking as if he were being led against his will. The flash went off, and then the man disappeared as quickly as he'd appeared.

But the photographer's presence was not unusual, and Jesse didn't give it a second thought. He was too worried about Diamond. He saw past her wide smile and teasing manner. There was a shadow of panic beneath her laughter. And what made him sick was the fact that it was the same panic he'd seen on her face the day she and her sisters had walked off the hill from the cemetery. It was a panic that said, *My world is falling apart, and I don't know how to fix it.*

Jesse slipped a hand beneath her elbow and began shaking hands and laughing as they made their way across the room. But all the while he was doing one thing, he was thinking another. When he got her home, he was going to love away the uncertainty in Diamond's life or know the reason why.

Henley was waiting in the checkout line, mental ticking off the items in his cart against the list in his head, when the picture on the front page of a tabloid caught his attention.

"Oh, Lord," he muttered, and tossed one into his cart. Jesse would want to see this. And he didn't think his boss was going to be happy when he did.

Less than an hour later, he managed to get Jesse alone long enough to show him the sleazy cover and its slanderous headline: *Has the "Prince" of country music found his "Princess Di"?* In smaller print, it hinted that the woman in Jesse Eagle's life was leading him around by the nose, coaxing him away from a life that had been more than good to him.

"Where do they get off playing with people's lives?" Jesse muttered. He quickly read the article, and then tossed the paper into the trash can.

Henley shrugged. "Is there something you want me to do, sir?"

Jesse shook his head and started to walk away. Then he remembered the way Tommy had insisted they attend Selma's party . . . and this picture had been taken there.

"Yes, Henley. There is one thing. Call Tommy for me, will you? If he's not in his office, just leave him a message."

"Yes sir," Henley said. "And what would you be wanting me to say?"

"Tell him it won't work."

"Excuse me?" Henley said, thinking he hadn't understood the answer.

Jesse turned and glared. "I said, tell him it won't work." There was a bitter twist to his smile as he turned away. "Just tell him, Henley. He'll know what the hell I mean."

Henley's eyebrows rose. He opened his mouth to speak and then shut it quickly, knowing that he had no business interfering in what was going on. He stared down at the tabloid stuffed in the garbage and then began to frown.

He delivered his boss's message.

Two hours later Tommy returned from lunch, satisfied that his day was going great, and slid into the overstuffed chair behind his desk. He tapped a cigarette from the pack, leaned back and put his feet on the desktop, and lit up. After two deep, satisfying drags, he noticed the flashing red light on his answering machine and pushed the button.

He recognized Henley's voice instantly. What totally pissed him off was the fact that Jesse hadn't even called him personally. That the message had been delivered through a third party incensed him highly. And that what he'd instigated was now being ignored made him mad as hell.

His feet came off the desk with a thump. He snubbed out his cigarette and then hurled a stack of papers across the room. The tabloid in question fell to the floor at his feet. He looked down in disgust at the woman pictured in Jesse's arms.

"I'll get rid of you yet."

10

Rain splattered against the windows like angry tears. Flung by the power of the storm front, they ran like miniature waterfalls across the panes, blurring Diamond's vision. She wrapped her arms around herself and shivered, struck suddenly by a chill that had nothing to do with the autumn rain.

Months had passed since her arrival at Jesse's home. In the space of that time she'd fallen under Jesse's spell so completely that she'd let her own dreams simmer unnoticed.

With Tommy's assurance ringing in her ears that he was doing all he could to hasten the record companies' interest in her demo, she'd let everything slide while she'd waited for him to fulfill his promise. But the trust in Tommy was gone. The contract had never appeared, and the constant barrage of journalists that hounded her and Jesse every time they appeared in public was fast becoming impossible to ignore.

Although Jesse had done all he could to shield her from the trash that was published about them, she'd seen enough at his public appearances to know that her presence in his life was making headlines beyond the tabloids.

At the sound of footsteps behind her, she turned away from the window, quick to hide her worries behind a welcoming smile.

"Some rain," Jesse said, and wrapped his arms around her, inhaling the scent of body powder and shampoo from an earlier bath. "It makes me want to cuddle."

She grinned and sank into his embrace. "Everything makes you want to cuddle."

He almost missed the catch in her voice. In fact, he would have overlooked it completely had she not returned his hug so fiercely.

"Are you all right, darlin'?" he asked. "I know the last two months have dragged by for you. But this business is strange. Sometimes things happen for a singer almost overnight, and other times it takes months to get a response from a label. I'm sure Tommy's banging on every door trying to get an answer."

"I'm sure," she echoed.

She knew damn good and well Tommy wasn't doing anything for her. She just hadn't faced what she was going to do about it.

"Come with me," he said. "I have a sure cure for the rainy-day blues."

She leaned back in his arms and frowned. "You can't play doctor now, Jesse. Henley's in the kitchen."

"Darlin'! You always think the worst of me!"

His injured indignation was so badly overdone she had to laugh.

"I only think the truth," she said, laughing up at the devils dancing in his eyes.

"You come with me," he urged. "I'll fix what ails you, I promise."

She obliged. After all, it would distract her. But when he pulled her into his music room instead of taking her to his bed, she turned to him in surprise.

"Sit!" he ordered, pointing to a well-used brown leather couch in the center of the room.

She did so, curling her legs beneath her in anticipation. And when he pulled his guitar from its case and slipped the strap around his neck, she clasped her hands and began to smile.

He went through first one song and then another. Old country songs from Red Foley, Tex Ritter, and Hank Williams.

"I haven't heard those in years," she said, beginning to relax. "My daddy used to whistle 'Red Sails in the Sunset.' He couldn't sing worth a plug nickel, but he sure could whistle," she said.

"I haven't sung them in years, either," he said. "Can't you tell?"

She grinned. "More . . . please."

"You know the first thing I can remember singing?" He let his fingers run lightly through chords as his memories took him back to childhood.

She shook her head.

"Hymns. Hymns and the songs on my mother's old

78s. They were big-band songs . . . you know the stuff. Tommy Dorsey, Glenn Miller, that type of music. I knew the words to 'Amazing Grace' before I knew my alphabet. And I played along on Daddy's guitar every time I heard 'Tuxedo Junction.'"

"Then why country, Jesse? If you were so filled with the other kinds of music growing up, why this?" She looked around at all his trophies and awards, the plaques that were confirmation of his talent and popularity.

"Because for me, country said what the others failed to say." A swath of black hair fell over his forehead as he leaned across his guitar. "Oh, the hymns said plenty, don't get me wrong. But it wasn't what *I* wanted to say, what was in my heart. You know what I mean. I heard the same longing in your voice the first time I heard you sing in Whitelaw's Bar."

He looked into her eyes. "When I heard you singing that day . . . like every other man in that bar, I would have traded a year of my life to be your hero, Diamond. I still would." His hands stilled on the guitar.

"You don't have to trade anything, Jesse Eagle. You already are."

He put down the guitar and stood. She met him halfway. And there on the soft brown leather, Jesse took her to heaven with his hands on her face.

What had started out slow became a race. Lazy, mind-drugging kisses became deep, consuming needs. Clothes fell away as heartbeats accelerated. And when she stood before him clothed in nothing but the truth, he started to shake.

"My God, woman, but you're beautiful," he whispered.

His hands splayed across the heavy ivory globes of her breasts and pressed gently until he felt the nubs harden against his palms. He didn't have to look down to know that his own body had hardened in response.

She moved against him, tilting her head to allow him access to her neck, and moaned softly when his teeth found the wild, pounding pulse at the base of her throat. His tongue slid out, tracing the thin, thready vein, and then he pressed his lips against the lifeblood.

"Mine," he said. The harshness of his voice was evidence of the passion about to overwhelm him. "You're mine."

He pushed her down onto the leather couch, pausing long enough above her so that the expression of desire and fear on her face would be forever etched on his mind. But the need was upon him. He could not wait to ask from what came the fear, and later he would forget that he'd seen it there.

He was hard and throbbing as he paused at the juncture of her thighs. She moved once against him. He felt her warm, wet heat, and then there was nothing else except the knowing of Diamond as he slid inside and she surrounded him.

She sighed, and then cried, and then moved along with him as the ride began.

Lost in the touch of the woman and her body, the eagle took flight and took his mate with him.

Hours later, they lay together in a tangle of arms and legs and listened to the rain until it was no more.

        ◦   ◦   ◦

"Look," Tommy argued. "It'll happen. I promise. I don't know what's going on, but I'll check on it first thing when we get back off this trip."

"Give me a break," Diamond said, lowering her voice to a harsh whisper. "I've been hearing that old excuse for months. You know exactly what's going on. It's what you've spent months engineering. I'm not stupid, Tommy, just fed up. Do me a favor and just shut up."

He was angry that she saw through his every excuse, yet unwilling to admit anything to her that could be held over his head. He held a grudging admiration for the woman, because she had yet to run to Jesse and tell him about their ongoing feud.

Jesse believed everything Tommy told him about the record companies and their hesitance to give Diamond a contract. Jesse also believed that the crazy rumors and the press he was getting regarding his association with Diamond were nothing more than just that—bad press. And if Tommy's conscience pricked him every now and then about all the lies and deceit he was weaving, it wasn't enough to make him stop.

Tommy glared at her. "No one tells me to shut up," he said.

She rolled her eyes. "Oh, God! The ultimate male threat." Her voice was thick with sarcasm. "I *already* told you to shut up. It's obvious you're not going to, but that's another matter entirely and one I have no desire to enforce." She turned and shrugged, unable to resist one last thrust. "Although we both know I could . . . if I so chose."

He was livid. She'd just reminded him that when push came to shove, she could put him on his butt. It was the last straw. He shouted at her just as Jesse walked into the room. "You don't know shit!"

Jesse stopped in the doorway, watched Diamond's face as she sailed past him without a word, and then looked back at Tommy.

Tommy's face paled perceptibly. He hadn't meant to lose his temper. And he certainly hadn't meant for Jesse to overhear him if he did.

"What the hell's going on in here?" Jesse asked. "I leave you two alone for five minutes to take a call, and I come back to this?"

Tommy began to talk. At that, he was a master. "I tried to tell her she has to be patient. I tried to tell her that fame doesn't come packaged for sale at the local Quick Stop. But no! She doesn't believe me. She thinks I'm backpedaling on her, Jesse. And I swear it's not so!"

Jesse stared. Tommy's words rang true. Jesse knew too well how long it took—sometimes forever—before a lucky break would come a singer's way.

He shrugged. "I'll talk to her," Jesse said. "Let yourself out." He started out the door, then stopped and turned. "And don't ever let me hear you curse at her again okay?"

"Sure, Jesse," Tommy said. "You know me. I just lost my temper. I forgot and yelled at her just like I yell at you. I didn't mean anything by it, I swear."

Jesse nodded and grinned. It was true that from time to time, he and Tommy fought like a pair of caged roosters.

"I know," Jesse said. "And I appreciate all you're doing for her, Tommy."

Tommy's eyes narrowed as Jesse left the room. "I don't think that's possible," he muttered.

*   *   *

Launch day arrived. It was Jesse's last trip for the year, and it dawned gray and gloomy. With it came another in the series of arguments that Diamond and Jesse had been having for over a week.

In actuality, Diamond wasn't arguing, and Jesse was only pleading, but it still resulted in the same thing. He had to leave, and she refused to go with him.

"I don't understand," Jesse said. "You can't let a little thing like this stuff get to you," he said, shoving a handful of newspaper clippings beneath her nose. "Hell, darlin', I don't usually even read this stuff, and you've gone and made a damned issue of them."

"You're just not listening, or you would understand," Diamond said. "Half of your fame is your talent, the other half the way your fans respond to you, right?"

He flung the clippings into the air, refusing to answer her with so much as a look.

"You know I'm right. You're just too stubborn to admit it," she said. "Besides, I don't want to go on the road and hang back waiting just to have a minute now and then to ourselves. And if I go, where will I sleep, hunh? You know as well as I do that the tour bus is not fixed up for separate quarters. My presence will only embarrass the boys and make them resentful."

"What about my suggestion to fly with you and let the band travel on the bus?" he argued.

"Right! Separate yourself even more from your fans and the band. That'll really give the papers something to rant about."

She couldn't get the memory out of her mind of all that fan mail Tommy had shown her. Letters upon letters begging Jesse to get back to his roots, to let go of a woman who was only trying to ruin him. Pleading for him to remember what country music and the singers who sang it were all about. They sang of family and values, of love gone wrong, and the roots from whence they came. Many of Jesse Eagle's fans had decided that he'd gone far wrong by moving a woman into his life who was only using him for her own benefit.

Diamond feared that her presence in Jesse's life was ruining everything he'd worked so hard to build.

"Dammit, Diamond, I don't want to leave you," he said, and grabbed her.

The pressure of his embrace was almost frightening. She sensed his indecision. And when he sighed and buried his face in her hair, she knew he'd accepted her terms.

He drew back. For long moments they stared into each other's eyes. Then he cupped her face in his hands, letting his thumbs gently trace the curve of her lower lip.

"I love you, darlin'," he said. "And when I come back, we talk about us, okay?"

His announcement caught her unaware. The implications were plain, and the promise behind his eyes brought tears to her own.

"As God is my witness, Jesse Eagle, I love you, too."

She wrapped her arms around his neck and buried her face against his shirt front. And when they stepped away from each other, she had a sudden urge to shout,

"Wait for me," and to pack and go with him. But she ignored it, as well as the look on his face.

Diamond turned away and went to make the call to Tommy, telling him that Jesse was ready to go. She scoffed at the panic filling her heart as she dialed the number. Nothing was going to happen to Jesse. He was only going on tour with his band. He was going to play his music and sing his songs and come back, tired but happy.

"Come and get him," she said, unwilling to give Tommy time to question her or argue the issue again. It was between her and Jesse, and the decision had been made without Tommy's help.

"Is everyone packed?" Tommy asked.

"We're waiting," she said.

Tommy cursed and hung up the phone. It wasn't until the bus arrived at Jesse's ranch, and he saw the anger on Jesse's face and the pain on hers, that he knew. And for one moment, he regretted what had to be done. But later, he thought, Jesse would thank him for everything.

Diamond watched the bus drive away until there was nothing left but a faint trail of dust hanging in the air.

"Will there be anything you'll be needing, Miss Diamond?" Henley asked. "I don't like the idea of you being alone here."

"I'm fine," she said. "He'll only be gone a week. Before I came, you always had this time free. There's no reason to change anyone's plans because of me. Besides," she said, smiling gently at the worry on his face, "I took care of myself a long time before I knew that you or Jesse ever existed. I can surely manage seven days."

"Still . . ." Something in her manner made him hesitate.

"I don't want to hear any more about it," she said. "Thanks to you I have my driver's license. If I need anything, all I have to do is go get it myself. Go visit your brother and leave me in peace, Joe Henley."

He sighed, nodded, and smiled.

Diamond called out as he walked away. "I'll miss you, Joe. Be careful and be safe."

The warmth her words elicited within him stayed for a long, long time. He was still remembering them when he came back the day before Jesse was due home and found the house empty and everything she'd brought with her gone.

"No, no, no!" Henley couldn't believe what he was seeing. The note was there. *Dear Jesse,* it began. He felt as if he were trespassing as he continued to read, although he knew that if there was a chance of finding her before Jesse returned, he had to take it. *I'll never forget what you did for me, or the love we shared. Saying good-bye is never easy. Seeing you when I said it would have been impossible. Forgive me for my cowardice. Be happy.* It was signed *Diamond.*

The P.S. at the bottom of the page was addressed to Henley. Tears quickened at the corners of his eyes as he read. *I'll miss you, Joe. Take care of Jesse for me. You can pick up Jesse's car at the bus station. I locked his keys inside so you'll have to take the extra set to get in.*

Henley swiped a shaky hand across his face. The note was too organized, the emotion too sparse. There was too much unsaid between the lines. He had a terrible suspicion that Jesse's manager could explain a lot but knew there was no way in hell of that ever happening.

He laid the note back on the kitchen table where he'd found it and went to call a cab. Maybe when he got the car he'd find something inside that would tell him where she'd gone.

"What do you mean, she's gone?"

Seeing the disbelief on Jesse's face was painful. Henley simply shook his head and handed him the note. It had been all he could do to stand firm when Jesse had burst through the front door shouting, "I'm home," and be the only person present to greet him.

Jesse's heart skipped a beat as Henley handed him the note. He read it through twice and still thought it was a joke. "But she was here every time I called except the night before last. I didn't think . . ."

He headed for the stairs, taking them two at a time. He opened the door to her room and then stopped at the doorway, staring blindly at the array of clothing she'd left spread across her bed. It was all there. The green sequined dress, the red minidress she'd worn the night of the awards ceremony, along with everything else he'd ever bought her. She'd left everything behind, including him.

A terrible blackness began to envelop him as acceptance finally dawned. Rage swept through him, coupled with a pain so fierce he couldn't speak. He walked out and slammed the door behind him, then blindly went from room to room, opening doors and slamming them shut.

The music room was last. The guitar she'd borrowed still lay on the couch where she'd left it. He walked inside, picked it up by the neck, and started to shake. Unaware of the tears running down his face, he swung. The guitar splintered against the desk. Over and over, he struck until wood flew and strings broke, along with Jesse's heart.

Henley stood in the hall and tried not to make a sound. He didn't want Jesse to know that he could hear his harsh, choking sobs coming from inside the music room. He didn't want his boss to know that he, too, was crying.

Henley waited and watched. And when there were no more sounds coming from inside, he quietly opened the door and then stared in shock. The room was in shambles, and Jesse was nowhere in sight. The French doors that led out onto the patio were ajar. Henley dashed through but was too late to stop the inevitable. Jesse was gone—and so was his car.

Fear came over him as he looked back at the room and imagined Jesse's state of mind. Driving now would be like playing Russian roulette behind the wheel.

He grabbed the phone and dialed, taking long, deep breaths as he calmed himself enough to be coherent. What he wanted was to rage at the injustice of it all.

Tommy answered the phone and then paled as Henley began to talk. For the first time since his assault on Diamond Houston began, he had regrets. But they weren't for what he'd done to her. They were for the fact that he might just have cut off his nose to spite his face. If Jesse went and wrapped himself around a tree, ending his life and career, where did that leave Tommy?

"Don't worry," he told Henley. "I'll find him. I'll take care of everything. I always do." He patted his pocket for a cigarette as he headed for the door, and then cursed when he remembered he was out. "What the hell," he said to himself. "Who knows? I just might quit again."

It took a week for Jesse to sober up enough to talk. When he did, he wouldn't stop. And the questions he kept asking were making Tommy more nervous by the hour.

"Hell no, I didn't do anything to her!" Tommy yelled. "Why is everything always my fault?" He stood toe to toe with Jesse, aware that if he faltered, Jesse would suspect his duplicity.

"I heard you two fighting more than once, that's why," Jesse said. "And Mack has already confessed to me what he did. The only saving grace he has is that they made their peace before she left."

Jesse spun on his heel and flung his coffee cup across the room. It shattered in bits, leaving a small, damp stain on Tommy's office wall.

"Where are you going?" Tommy asked, panic filling his voice as he watched Jesse heading for the door.

"To find her," he said. "And so help me God, when I do, if I find out you had anything to do with her leaving, I'll kill you myself. Do you understand?"

Tommy spit and cursed, thrusting papers in Jesse's face as he shouted wildly. "You can't leave. You have personal appearances to make. You need to plug your new album. It comes out in less than a week."

"I don't give a damn about that album, or anything else. You want to plug the album, then do it."

"You'll ruin your reputation if you don't show."

"According to you, it's already ruined," Jesse said. Then he walked out and slammed the door behind him.

Tommy cursed until he ran out of words and then slumped down into his chair, burying his head in his hands.

"I'd kill myself, but I'm too damned tired," he muttered. He opened his appointment book, took a deep breath, and began to make the calls. It might take all night, but he was going to get out of this smelling like a rose or his name wasn't Tommy Thomas.

Cradle Creek looked just as it had the day Jesse had first seen it, only colder. And if possible, grayer. He was tired clear down to his bones. He had come back here on instinct. A last-ditch hope had sent him back to the place where he'd found her.

He'd stayed drunk for a week and then searched Nashville for days, with no luck. But he'd known from the first that if she'd left the car at the bus station, she was gone.

Cradle Creek was his last hope. And if he had no luck, it would also be the end of the road. The thought was unacceptable, but probable, and he'd ignored it for days.

He drove up to Whitelaw's Bar and started to park. But when he looked next door to the place where Johnny Houston's ramshackle home had stood and saw nothing but bare, brown earth, he started to shake.

"Oh, God," he said, swallowing his panic.

"Hey, there!"

Jesse looked up. He recognized the owner of the bar from the night he'd heard Diamond sing.

"Whatcha doin' back in this neck of the woods?" Morton Whitelaw asked, and slapped the hood of Jesse's car. "Ain't lost, are you?" He laughed heartily at his own joke.

"What happened to the house?" Jesse asked.

"Oh, that." Morton stepped back and hawked, watching in satisfaction as his spit splattered against Jesse's tire. "Hell, I tore that down for parking space right after I bought it. Didn't want none of them damned Houston women showing back up to plague me. Guess it worked. I ain't seen hide nor hair of any of them since."

Jesse gripped the rim of his steering wheel and willed himself not to come unglued again. He'd just had his question answered, and he'd never even had to ask. She was gone. He leaned back and closed his eyes. She could be anywhere.

Suddenly he put the car into reverse and backed away, eager to put as much distance as possible between himself and Cradle Creek, Tennessee.

He drove toward home with a tear in his soul, and every breath he took widened it just enough to let in the pain.

11

Diamond's feet hurt, but not as much as her heart. She'd known that leaving Jesse wouldn't be easy, but she'd never known it would be this painful. Behind her a man laughed, and she jerked around, expecting to see Jesse's smiling face. But it wasn't him, and the knowledge that she'd never see him smile at her again made the sick feeling inside her deepen. Oh, Diamond knew that sooner or later their paths would cross. She just prayed that it would be later, when she'd learned better how to live with the pain.

Nashville wasn't small, but the circle of people within the country music industry was. Like a large family with roots branching out in all directions, the singers and musicians played out their individual careers until something called them home—whether a tragedy or a celebration—and then they would come together, sharing their common interests in the music they so loved.

The man who had laughed saw Diamond's interest in

him. He tipped his hat and winked, still wearing his smile, and then shrugged and sighed as Diamond walked away.

She blocked out all thoughts of Jesse and ducked her head in reflex to the wind that bit into her cheeks as she turned the street corner. She looked up once to get her bearings and then continued walking, praying that today she'd get an audition.

The month since she'd walked out on Jesse had been without doubt the longest of her life. And the job she'd been so certain she'd get had never materialized. One club after another, one promised audition after another, had come and gone. The lines of girls just like her who came to Nashville to be a star were too long to get through alone. For the first time in her life, Diamond was about to be lost in the crowd. Here she was no different from all the other singers who'd bet their life on a dream.

Although that came as a shock, an even greater shock had come when she'd made the rounds on Music Row and discovered that no one had ever heard of Diamond Houston—or her demo. Oh, they'd heard of Tommy Thomas. Everyone knew the great Jesse Eagle's manager. But Tommy hadn't pitched her demo to any of the houses as he'd claimed.

Her lips twisted into a bitter smile as she passed a storefront window. *It's no more than you deserve*, she told her reflection, refusing to recognize the despair on her face. She had gambled and lost. She had bet the pot on someone else's promises instead of trusting in herself.

She turned away from the window and continued down

the street knowing that she'd never let that happen again. She'd come to Nashville because of a dream. She wasn't ready to give up on that dream—or herself. Not yet.

A sign overhead swung sharply in the wind, squeaking a bit on rusty hinges as Diamond walked past. Its lonesome sound echoed the feelings inside her. She'd never been so alone in her life, but she'd also never been so certain that what she'd done had been right. The last thing she wanted was to endanger Jesse's career. At least now that she was gone, his future would be safe. As for hers . . . She shuddered. Hers was too vague to dwell upon.

The first drops of rain began to fall. Diamond closed her eyes and swallowed, remembering another rainy day and the loving that had come from it. Angry with herself for being so maudlin, she yielded to impulse and ducked into the first shop available to get out of the weather and away from the memories. But it had been a mistake. The shop she entered was a music store. And she wasn't prepared for what she heard.

Lies . . . and lying lovers . . .

"Oh, my God!" Diamond gasped, and leaned against an aisle shelf. It was the song on Jesse's album—their song! She stared blindly at the life-size cutout of Jesse Eagle standing at the end of the aisle and then looked too long at the slow, sexy smile he was wearing on his face. The room began to tilt.

"Are you all right, miss?" a clerk asked, and grabbed her arm as she swayed.

Diamond's face was pale, but the look in her eyes was that of a cornered animal.

"Everywhere I go, you're there," she said, staring at the poster, and then buried her face in her hands.

"Should I call an ambulance?" the clerk asked.

"What? No!" She was shaking as she finally came to her senses enough to realize that someone was speaking to her. "I'm sorry," she mumbled, embarrassed that she'd caused a scene. "I'm just a little bit tired . . . and a whole lot lost."

She took a deep breath and managed a smile to reassure him.

Allen Tillet considered himself quite a ladies' man and had taken this job in the music store for the sole purpose of meeting girls. But his teenage repertoire of tricks and pick-up lines did not include any skills in how to break the ice with women. He watched the tall blonde woman walk away and for the first time in his life wished he were older—and someone else. If he were, he'd help that woman find her way, and how!

Diamond sorted through the display of Jesse's new release, searching for the credits on the tape as well as the CD. She picked up one of each and paid for them, ignoring how much their purchase depleted her precious savings. Her hands shook as she tore away the cellophane, then her eyes scanned the small, almost illegible print in quiet desperation. And when she found the listing of credits for "Lies" and began to read, she gasped, then blanched, then started to smile. The smile turned into a chuckle and then into a laugh.

Allen Tillet shuddered and wondered if he should call the manager. The woman was laughing, but she didn't seem happy at all, not with the tears he saw running down her face.

Diamond dropped her purchases into the trash and then walked out of the store.

Okay, Diamond, she told herself, you've learned a lesson the hard way. You bet your hand on something that wasn't yours. You didn't have a damned thing in writing; all you had was a man's word. Obviously that man doesn't know the meaning of honor.

She smiled once more as she thought of the repercussions he would suffer. And it was no more than he deserved. If she knew Jesse—and she'd bet her life that she did—he was going to be furious with his manager.

The omission of her name on Jesse's album was just the last of a long line of slights she'd suffered at the hands of Tommy Thomas. But no more, she told herself. No more.

Al Barkley knocked on the door and then shivered, pulling his coat collar higher around his neck as he waited for someone to answer. He burst past Henley as the door opened, unwilling to wait for an invitation to enter.

"Mr. Barkley, do come in," Henley said, allowing a slight drawl to surface in his voice as the fiddle player from Jesse's band made a less than proper entrance.

"I gotta talk to Jesse," Al said, shifting from one booted foot to the other.

"He's in the music room," Henley said. "May I take your coat?"

Al shook his head as he started down the hallway.

"I won't be staying long. Thanks anyway, Henley."

Henley nodded and then felt obliged to give Al a parting warning. "He isn't . . . at his best."

Al turned. A look lingered between them, and then Al spoke. "He ain't gonna get any better after I show him this," he said, holding up a cassette and a CD of their new album.

Henley frowned and sighed. It never failed. When something went wrong, all sorts of things followed.

"Hey, Jesse!"

The presence of someone other than Henley was unexpected. Jesse jumped. His heart thumped twice with extra fervor, then calmed as he spun from his stance at the window to stare blankly at the unexpected arrival of his fiddle player.

Al's expression fell. Everything he'd been about to say completely disappeared from his mind. All he could do was stare in shock at the absence of life on Jesse's face.

The joy with which Jesse had lived each day was gone, as was the light in his eyes. Despair had changed the laugh wrinkles at the corners of his eyes into deep lines of worry. Long, sleepless nights and too many skipped meals were evident in his gaunt face.

"What do you want?" Jesse asked.

Al shrugged. There was no easy way to do this. He handed him the cassette and CD.

"Seen these?" Al asked.

Jesse turned away. "No."

"I think you oughta," Al said.

"What the hell for?" Jesse asked. "Tommy's already

called and told me it's riding a bullet toward number one."

The lethargy in Jesse's movements as well as his voice worried Al. What was this news going to do to him?

"I still think you need to see," Al said. "I don't think Tommy told you quite everything. It ain't like you requested, buddy. And for her sake, someone needs to fix it."

It was the word *her* that got his attention. There was only one female in Jesse's life. And as badly as he hated to admit it to himself, although she was no longer present, anything concerning her still concerned him.

"What the hell?" Jesse said.

He took what Al offered and absently turned past the picture of himself. It had been taken when he was a different and happier man. He had no desire to see himself and be reminded of that time . . . or of her.

At first, his glance was desultory, scanning the highlights of each song with casual indifference. And then he straightened. His expression changed to interest, and then to a slow, growing anger.

"The sorry son of a bitch," he said softly.

Al nodded. "I didn't think you was a part of this," he said. "I told the boys this wasn't what you wanted. Even Mack was pissed, and he's still a little sore around the edges where she's concerned."

"Me? A part of this? Is that what they think?" Jesse slumped against the window seat and focused on a bare spot between the area rug and the wall.

Al shrugged. "Well hell, Jesse. At first we didn't know what to think. You ain't never crawled into a hole this deep before."

"I never needed to before," he said. He turned away. He was still sick of himself and the way he came unglued just thinking about her.

"Dammit, Jesse. Ain't there somethin' we can do? Me and Rita feel bad about what happened. Didn't you find any signs of her when you went back to—"

"Not a trace," Jesse said. He held up the tape and CD, his hand shaking with suppressed anger as he waved them in Al's face. "And if this is any indication of what was going on, it's no damned wonder. She probably feels like I stabbed her in the back."

"Oh, hell no, boss!" Al said. "She knew it wasn't you. We all did. Why, when she first came, ol' Tommy said to . . ."

He flushed a deep shade of red, embarrassed by what he'd just admitted as his words trailed off into silence.

"Just what the hell did Tommy say, anyway?" Jesse asked.

Al turned away. "I done said too much as it is. I ain't talkin' anymore. Whatever trouble is between you and Tommy needs to be worked out between you two. You don't need no third party, let alone the whole damn band, interferin'."

Jesse's fury was barely contained. It was the first time in weeks that he'd felt any emotion at all save that of pain. And this was so intense, it was overwhelming. He spun around and flung the cassette and CD across the room, splintering plastic.

"It will be settled," he said.

Al ducked his head. "Well, I'd better be goin'," he said. He started out the door and then stopped and turned. "Jesse?"

Jesse looked up.

"We're all real sorry," Al said. "And the boys said to tell you that if there was anything they could do, just to let them know."

Jesse swallowed. Al and the other men in his band were as close to him as brothers. And like brothers, he got along with some better than others. But when push came to shove, they were, after all, family.

He nodded. "Tell them I said thanks. And if they should happen to hear anything about her . . ."

Al nodded. "It's done."

Henley entered the room just as Al was leaving. He looked at the broken cassette tape and the splintered CD cover and then up at Jesse.

"I'm going out," Jesse said. "I don't know for sure what time I'll be back."

Henley frowned. An argument was on the tip of his tongue when Jesse went on.

"You don't have to worry. I'm not going off just to get drunk as a skunk. Not ever again." The lines around his mouth tightened. "But I *am* going after a skunk. And I won't be back until I find the bastard and skin him alive."

Henley didn't know whether to be glad that Jesse was actually coming out of his shell of indifference, or to be worried about the violence Jesse had just threatened.

He was under no misapprehensions as to which skunk was about to be parted from his skin. It was obvious to him that if there was one in their midst, its name was Tommy.

*   *   *

The door to Tommy's office flew back with a bang. The look of pleased surprise on his face disappeared as he absorbed the expression on Jesse's. He sighed, shoved away the papers on his desk, and tossed his pen on top. This was going to take all the finesse he could muster.

"Start talking," Jesse said.

"About what?"

Jesse inhaled slowly. He counted to three, which did no good, and started over.

"Don't, Tommy. You've spread enough bullshit to cover a football field. Just once, just goddamned once, talk straight."

Tommy stood. "I don't know what in hell you're getting at," he said, "but I know I don't like what you're implying."

Jesse's smile was not friendly. "I don't expect you to like it," he said. "I sure as hell don't like what you did."

Here it comes, Tommy thought. "What am I supposed to have done now?" he asked.

Jesse walked forward, and when he got too close and showed no signs of stopping, Tommy began to back up. When the wall was at his back and Jesse only a breath away, he began to get nervous.

"You son of a bitch," Jesse said, jabbing his forefinger against Tommy's shoulder. "You left her name off that album after I specifically asked you—more than once—to make sure that she got credit for singing the duo."

Tommy began to bluster. "Now you know I did no

such thing. It must have been a printer's error. It's not
the first time we've had a—"

"Shut up," Jesse said. He turned away, knowing he
had to put space between himself and Tommy or else
he'd hurt him. He'd never been so furious in his entire
life. "I don't want to hear it. I don't want to hear anymore lies. I just want you to fix it."

"Well hell, yes," Tommy drawled. "I guess I could do
that. I guess I could have every album on the shelves
recalled. It shouldn't amount to more than several
million dollars in losses, but I guess I can do that. Oh!
And while I'm at it, do you want me to just kiss your ass
and—"

Jesse glared. His fingers curled into fists as his voice
shook with fury. "And while you're at it," Jesse continued,
as if Tommy hadn't even spoken, "I suppose the contract
between you two had all the normal fees and royalties?"

That was when Tommy looked away. His body
language was unmistakable. Jesse took a step forward,
afraid of what was coming next, afraid of what he'd do to
Tommy when he heard it.

"Well, now," Tommy blustered. "That's not my fault
at all," he said, hating himself for the whine he heard in
his own voice. "I kept meaning to pick that contract up
from the lawyer's and get it signed, but I kept forgetting,
what with one thing and then another. You know, we
went on tour and then there was that—"

Jesse exploded. "You mean to tell me that you never
even put her under contract? Are you telling me that you
let a cut go on an album without the singer's signed permission? That you just stiffed her and then ignored her?"

"It wasn't intentional."

"Like hell," Jesse said quietly. "You have twenty-four hours to start channeling Diamond Houston's fair share from the sale of this album into a bank account in her name, or you and I are through."

"You can't fire me!" Tommy yelled.

"I know that. But I can refuse to honor the rest of my commitments for the year. And you can spend the rest of our contract tied up in the courts getting sued along with me for failure to honor—"

Tommy blanched. "You wouldn't!"

"Try me," Jesse said.

It was the lack of emotion in his voice that convinced Tommy he'd crossed the limit of Jesse's patience.

"Okay," he said. "I'll set up the account and make sure that she gets her money. I was going to do that anyway. Goddammit, Jesse. I'm not a thief."

Jesse's look didn't waver. Tommy continued. "And I know you won't believe me, but I swear I had no knowledge of all this. I wouldn't do anything to hurt you, Jesse. Hell! You're like my brother. We're a team, remember?"

"But you hurt her, Tommy. And her leaving almost killed me. Don't you understand, even yet? Damn you to hell, Tommy. I loved her. And for all the good it does me, I still do."

Tommy couldn't watch Jesse leave his office. He knew that it would take a miracle to fix what had happened. The only thing that might work was if he, Tommy Thomas, did the noble thing and found Diamond Houston himself. If he convinced her that everything that happened to her had been inadvertent and then handed her to Jesse on a silver platter. It was the only thing that came to mind . . . and it made him sick.

"Look, honey," the club owner growled, "I've got thirty-three girls just like you already lined up for auditions. I haven't got enough time in the day to listen to half. I'm sorry, but for now there's just no spot for you here." He shrugged at the look of disappointment on the tall blonde's face and added, "But try me again later. You never know."

Diamond pasted a smile on her face, shook his hand, and left, trying not to think about her dwindling savings. Even living in a less than advisable part of town had cost more than she'd imagined, especially since nothing was coming in to replenish her funds.

Winter was here. In less than a month it would be Christmas. She blinked away tears, trying not to think of how lonely she was . . . lonely for Queen and Lucky, afraid that she'd never see them again. How could they contact her when she no longer lived with Jesse? He was their only link with each other, and reconnecting with him was out of the question.

The hole in her life that leaving Jesse had caused was, at times, unbearable. The only way she was able to function at all was simply not to think about him, and that was fast becoming an impossibility. Their single on his new album was into its second week at number one on the country chart. Her bitterness at its success overwhelmed her.

She turned the street corner, intent on heading back to her apartment. The weather was turning ugly and so was her mood. The only thing she could do was get inside and into a better frame of mind. The street on which she normally walked was blockaded. From what she could see, it looked as if someone had driven a car down half a block of storefronts last night.

Muttering beneath her breath at having to go two blocks out of her way to get home, she took a street she'd never walked before. She hadn't gone far when it became all too apparent that she'd definitely walked onto the wild side of Nashville. She stopped and looked behind her, half expecting to see someone step out of a doorway and pull a gun. Shivering, partly from cold and partly from nerves, she increased her stride.

She passed two vacant buildings and was just about to walk past an empty lot when she stopped and stared at a bar of sorts, set off to the far side of the lot. Its back door faced the street in what one could only call a mistake in construction. The marketing strategy of such a blunder was laughable, and it was probably the only establishment in Nashville where she hadn't applied for work. She cursed herself softly as she realized she was even considering the possibility.

She would have to be pretty desperate to walk in there. Then a gust of wind caught her coat and billowed beneath it, sending a chill up her legs and through her backbone. She was just about there.

Before she could talk herself out of the impulse, Diamond found herself hurrying around the building in search of an entrance. She found it!

Dooley's had wasted no money on advertising. The owner had simply painted his name on the door front and eliminated the need for a separate sign altogether. The lettering did nothing for the door or for Dooley's name. The *D* was too large, and someone had not planned well, for there was no room for the s at the end of the name. It had been scribbled on the side of the wall as an afterthought.

Diamond had to grin, and then she realized it was the first time in weeks that she'd genuinely felt like smiling. She grabbed the doorknob and turned. Maybe it was a sign, she thought as she entered, and then instantly rejected the notion. If this place was meant to be a sign, it had to be a sign on the road leading to hell. It was a mess.

Weeks-old smoke hovered in the dusky interior. The place was a carbon copy of Whitelaw's Bar in Cradle Creek. Perfect, she thought. *I'm right back to square one.*

A long, empty bar framed the far end of the room. No more than a dozen tables and mismatched chairs sat between it and the front door. Two customers argued quietly at a table in the corner while a man polished glasses behind the bar. He looked up in surprise at her entrance and then stopped what he was doing and watched in shock as Diamond walked toward him.

Even beneath the long denim duster she was wearing he could see her shape. Her boots were scuffed and her jeans were faded, but they were clean, and he caught a glimpse of a soft blue sweater beneath her coat.

Dooley Hopper stared. He'd seen plenty of beautiful

women in his sixty-three years, but none like her had ever made their way into his place. He rubbed absently at a spot on a glass, and then set it down just to have something to do with his hands. He waited for her to speak, fully expecting her to ask for directions or for change to make a phone call.

Dooley was a hard man and in no mood for nonsense. It had been three years since he'd been able to make ends meet, and if something didn't change for the better soon, he'd meet his end in bankruptcy court.

"My name is Diamond Houston," she said. "I was wondering if you were hiring right now. I need a job."

Dooley swept his hands into the air and looked around at the near-empty bar, fully intending to laugh. He dropped his towel on the counter and leaned forward to tell her to get lost, but the look on her face stopped him cold. He'd wonder later whether it had been her look of expectation or the way she braced herself for the blow to fall, because Dooley Hopper heard himself asking if she had any experience. And when she told him seven years slinging drinks in a place just like this, he heard himself asking her when she could start.

Diamond took a long, shuddering breath. For a moment, she was afraid to relax for fear her legs would give out. But years of hiding her feelings won out. Instead she handed him her coat and asked for a broom.

Dooley took the coat, pointed to a closet, and then watched in fascinated shock as Diamond Houston entered his life.

Before the week was out, word had gotten around

that Dooley Hopper had gone and hired himself a waitress. When the locals stopped laughing at what they were calling "Dooley's folly," they had to satisfy their curiosity and come see for themselves.

It only took one look at the tall, leggy blonde and the braided rope of hair hanging down her back to see why Dooley had lost his mind. And when they saw her generous curves beneath the tight blue jeans and the soft flannel shirt she wore, they began to wonder why Dooley hadn't thought of this years ago. If they were lucky enough to see her smile and watch the lights come on behind those wide green eyes, they went away talking about the woman in Dooley Hopper's bar.

Dooley's recriminations against himself had lasted less than a week. After that, he'd begun to believe that it had been foresight on his part and not fortune that had brought Diamond to him. For the first time in three years, his receipts totaled more than his overhead. For the first time in three years, Dooley had a reason to hope.

And for the first time in the long weeks since Diamond had left Jesse, so did she.

"Now, Diamond," Dooley growled as he tried to weasel out of the corner into which she had backed him. "You're a damned good waitress. Why do you want to go and spoil things? What makes you think you can sing? Had any experience?"

She smiled. And he remembered asking her that same question the day she'd walked into his bar.

"You just let me sing tonight, and I'll prove it," she said.

"But honey, it's Saturday," Dooley argued. "If you bomb, it might turn away the first good run of customers I've had in years." And then he flushed as he realized what he'd just admitted.

"I know it's Saturday. That's why I want to sing. You don't think I'm going to waste myself on Walt and Deever, do you?"

Her gesture toward the two drunks who always occupied the corner table in Dooley's made him smile. He shrugged, knowing when he was licked. Hell, he told himself, she had been calling the shots ever since her arrival. Why stop now?

"Okay," he said. "But don't come crying on my shoulder if they laugh you out of the place."

"I won't," she promised. "But if I start to draw in bigger crowds, I get a raise, okay?"

Dooley stared. And then he laughed and wrapped her in a bear hug. "Girl! You're one for the books, and that's a fact. You make Dooley's famous, and you can name your price."

Diamond clapped her hands and smiled. "I need to take off early."

He rolled his eyes. "Well, hell. I give you an inch, you take a mile."

"No, you don't understand," Diamond said. "I need to go make the rounds of some pawnshops and find myself a good used guitar."

"If that's what you need, go dig in that closet inside my office."

She frowned. "I don't understand."

"I had a band in here once. Damned bunch got into a fight and broke up the place. They couldn't pay damages so I took their instruments instead. Kept meaning to sell them, just never got around to it. I think there's a guitar or two in there, along with a set of drums. Help yourself."

She grinned. "You never cease to amaze me, Dooley."

"I amaze myself sometimes," he said. "Now get. I've got to order extra supplies if I'm gonna have a *live performance* here tonight."

Diamond left him dialing the phone as she headed for his office. She opened the closet with trepidation and then gasped in delight as she pulled a guitar from a dusty case. A Gibson. And from the looks of it, one that had been well loved until the owner had been forced to give it up. She slipped the strap over her shoulder and strummed the strings, then winced. It badly needed tuning. And from the looks of it, restringing too. But that was something that could be fixed.

She left Dooley's office with the guitar in hand and hope in her heart. The guitar wasn't the only thing getting fixed that day. Diamond's life was slowly falling back into order. The ache for Jesse was still there, but there was a tiny bit of hope for the future as well. Maybe there would be a way to reconcile both so that someday she could sleep again without crying.

12

Wind rattled the windows in Diamond's apartment, reminding her that whatever she wore to sing in that night should be warm as well as pretty. She stared at the calendar hanging on the wall and tried not to think about Christmas. It was supposed to be a time of joy and celebration, not a time for regrets.

She stood half-dressed in front of her closet fingering her sparse assortment of clothes and tried not to think of the dresses she'd left behind at Jesse's, or the costly leathers and flashy clothing he'd purchased for their nights out together that she'd refused to take.

But she could never have taken them with her—no matter how beautiful, no matter that they'd been purchased for her. It would have seemed like stealing. Jesse Eagle had given them to a woman who no longer belonged in his world.

Her fingers lingered longest on the first article of clothing she'd bought for herself right after she'd received her money from Queen. It was really too lightweight, but it was the prettiest thing she owned and she wanted to make a good first impression on Dooley and his customers.

Without giving herself time to change her mind, she slipped it from the hanger and tossed it on the ironing board, then lurched from the bare wood to the thin area rug in one leap, unwilling to walk across any more cold flooring than necessary.

She plopped down on the bed, pulled the spread across her feet and legs, and stared at her apartment with resignation. It was so like where she'd lived in Cradle Creek that she hardly noticed the lack of amenities.

It was possible to ignore the permanent rust stains on the bathroom fixtures because she knew they were clean. She'd cleaned them herself. But it wasn't easy to forget that only weeks ago she'd slept on fine sheets and cuddled beneath warm, heavy covers. And she couldn't forget whom she'd cuddled with, or how much she ached to be held by him again.

Diamond leaned back, stared at the multitude of water stains on the ceiling, and tried not to care that the constant flow of heat from the vents could not keep up with the cold drafts filtering through the cracks around the windows. Her stomach growled once in the silence as a rude reminder to herself that she hadn't eaten that day.

"Okay, I'm hungry. Get up and do something about it. Tonight I've got a chance to start over. The last thing I need to do is fall on my face from hunger."

She totally ignored the oddity of talking aloud to herself. As a child, she'd done it for years until Queen had quietly taken her aside and explained that people might think she was strange. The need to do so had slowly disappeared, until she'd made the break from Jesse. And with that break had come the onset of all her old childhood fears. The insecurity of her situation had returned, along with the realization that no matter how long she tried or how far she traveled, she might never fit in.

In the space of five minutes, she heated a can of soup, wrapped a piece of bread around a slice of bologna, and then crawled back into bed to eat her meal. The soup went down in gulps, warming her from the inside out. She chewed mechanically, refusing to think about the wonderful food that Henley always had prepared, and began going over her performance in her mind, but daydreams kept getting in the way.

She was singing, and Jesse walked out from the shadows offstage and took her in his arms. And sometimes she was singing and he came out of the audience and carried her off through the crowd amidst cheers.

Her spoon clinked against the bottom of the bowl, reminding her that she had no time left for daydreams.

"Johnny Houston might have been a fool, but he didn't raise any," she muttered. "There are no such things as white knights wearing cowboys hats. Not in my world."

She climbed out of her warm nest of covers, dumped her dishes into the sink, and put them to soak before hurrying into the bathroom.

With only three hours until her premiere at Dooley's, there was much to be done. She bit her lip and stared at herself in the mirror over the sink. The sadness and regret in her eyes were slowly replaced with a burning determination. She promised herself that when the night was over, Dooley's wouldn't know what had hit it.

"Well, if you don't take the cake," Dooley said, and flopped his ever-present dishcloth over his shoulder as he stepped back to give Diamond a good, long look.

He'd never seen her like this. Her blue jeans and the men's shirts she usually wore to wait tables had been replaced by gray slacks and a pink sweater. The soft fabric clung to her body, and Dooley decided that whether coming or going, Diamond Houston looked fine.

"I'm doing two sets," she said. "One at seven, the other at eleven. I won't take requests, and Dooley—"

"What now?" he asked, grinning at the businesslike manner in which she laid down her rules. But his smile disappeared when he saw pain in her eyes and heard the hesitancy in her voice.

"I don't sing for tips. Not anymore."

"Whatever you say, girl," he said. "Whatever you say. Tonight you're callin' the shots. I done give my word, and Dooley don't go back on his word."

She nodded and turned away to tie on her apron.

"Never mind about that," Dooley said, pretending to be busy at the bar. "Don't go gettin' yourself all messed up before you sing. I went and hired some extra help." The light in her eyes made him add, "Don't get too excited.

If you suck, you're back on the floor slinging drinks to Walt and Deever, and we both know it. Right?"

"Dooley, you're a master of the English language. How can I ever thank you for the kind words of encouragement?"

He squinted and then glared, pulling himself up to his full height of six feet, three inches and hefting his pants over the bulge of his belly.

"Are you makin' sport of me?" he asked.

"Are you doubting me?" she countered.

The standoff was short. Dooley was the first to break, and when he did it was with a loud whoop of laughter.

"Hell, girl, but you're a pistol, and you know it. I woulda liked to have knowed your daddy. I bet he was somethin'."

Diamond smiled. Memories swirled in her head along with the nervous giddiness already in place.

"He was," she said. "And I suspect that he would have liked knowing you, too."

The door banged behind them as a knot of rowdy men blew in.

"Shut the damned door," Dooley yelled. "Was you born in a barn? It's cold out there."

Diamond laughed and headed for his office. In less than an hour she had a show to perform.

"Jesse . . . please," Tommy cajoled. "You've got to show up for this taping, man. It's the 'Nashville Christmas Special,' and we both know it wouldn't be a Nashville special without Jesse Eagle."

Jesse shrugged and then turned his back on his manager. This cold indifference to life was making him miserable, but he couldn't seem to change it. He woke up each morning with nothing to look forward to except going back to bed for more of the same. What had once been a bed full of love that he'd shared with Diamond was now nothing but empty sheets and painful memories.

"I don't *have* to do anything," Jesse said. "But I will, only not for you. I'll do it because it's Christmas, and the boys and their families will be expecting it."

The pain in Jesse's voice and the dark shadows behind his once-laughing eyes made Tommy sick. He'd been living with guilt for so long it had almost taken root.

"Thanks, man," Tommy said, and gave him a rare, man-to-man, roughhouse hug. "I'll call the boys later and tell them to show up tomorrow for the taping. They've all been wondering if we were going to do it. Since families are included, their wives and kids are getting all excited about—"

Tommy bit his lip and wished he could take back what he'd started to say, but it was too late. It would be for families, all right. Only Jesse's dearly beloved would be painfully absent, thanks to him. And Tommy still thought he'd been justified in what he'd done.

He'd been certain that after Diamond Houston was gone, Jesse would pine a while, and then go on to the next woman, just as he had before. Tommy had under-estimated the depth of Jesse's feelings for Diamond. He sighed and looked down at the floor. He didn't like to make mistakes.

"Well," Tommy said, "I'll meet you guys at the set tomorrow. They're taping out at the Opry, sentiment and all that holiday cheer, you know."

Jesse made no further move to communicate, and Tommy gave up and left. Outside he breathed deeply, wincing when the cold air hit his lungs with unexpected force.

"Damn," he muttered. "I'd hate to be on the streets on a day like this." And for one moment, it occurred to him that that could be exactly where Diamond Houston was—on the streets somewhere, and all because of him.

Guilt, regret, and anger sent him scurrying to his car. He didn't want to feel sorry for her. She'd almost ruined everything for him and for Jesse. He didn't want to care about what he'd done . . . but he did. The acknowledgment of his mistake made him spin out as he drove away. But he could have slowed down and saved the rubber on his tires. It was impossible to outrun his conscience.

There was no stage. Diamond had simply asked Dooley to move enough tables around so that she'd have a small clearing against the wall opposite the door. She had no desire to sit within range of the cold air that came inside with each patron of Dooley's. She got enough of drafts in her own apartment.

It hadn't taken the men long to figure out that something new was about to be added to their evening. The bar wasn't full, but it was doing a brisk business. And when the men had seen the new waitress in place, they'd been exceptionally rowdy. They spent half their time pestering Dooley about Diamond's mysterious absence, and the other half trying to make time with the new waitress.

It seemed as if they'd decided to try their best lines out all at once on the new girl, yelling and whistling to get her attention and every now and then giving her a slap on the butt as she hurried by with a tray full of drinks.

Diamond listened from her vantage point in Dooley's office and knew that it was time. She gave herself a last cursory glance in the mirror behind Dooley's cluttered desk. Her hair was in place, her sweater was tucked into her slacks, and her guitar was by the door. There was nothing left to do but walk through it and out into the room.

Suddenly a shaft of fear froze her in place. What if they didn't like her? What if Dooley had been right and she, as he said, sucked? What would she do?

She ignored the fear on her face and gave herself an answer she could live with: She would just do what she had been doing all along. She would get by.

Dooley was the first to see her come out of his office, and that was because he'd been watching for her. He bit his lip and then did something unusual. He poured himself a shot of whiskey and downed it neat.

She didn't look nervous, but he sure as hell was. In the short space of time since Diamond had come to work for him, he'd come to care for her a lot. To him, she was a little bit of every woman who'd lingered in his memory through his sixty-odd years of living. And she was a whole lot of herself—and his friend. He didn't want her to fail.

He started to shout down the noise inside his bar and then saw her motion for him to stop. He sighed and frowned, and his belly growled nervously as he waited for her to make her move.

That she had no microphone didn't seem to faze her in the least. She scooted a bar stool into her makeshift stage area, sat down, slid the pick from beneath the strings, and ran through the chords on her guitar as if she were about to entertain herself and not a room full of people.

Her light fingering on the guitar strings was enough to get the attention of Dooley's patrons. At first there was a stunned silence. And then the catcalls began as first one and then another began yelling out teasing suggestions of what she should be doing with her hands besides running them up and down the neck of that guitar.

The lights were already dimmed from the thick smoke hanging in the air, but Dooley did his part to make this as special for her as he could. He turned off all the floor lights except those on her side of the room and then waited. It was up to her.

Diamond's head dipped, spilling the golden curtain of her hair across her face as she paused for a closer look at the placement of her fingers upon the guitar. She took a slow, deep breath, leaned back, closed her eyes, and opened her mouth.

An old Bruce Springsteen song came rolling into the quiet of the room. Once again, Diamond was taking a song from another genre and making it her own . . . making it country.

The song, "I'm On Fire," had every man in the room convinced that he'd been the one to set it. And as she sang, mesmerizing them with her voice and the sway of her body, she had them fantasizing about how they were now going to go about putting it out.

Dooley's mouth turned up at the corners, and he breathed with relief. "Well, she damn sure don't suck," he muttered. Just looking at the glazed expressions of lust and envy on his customers' faces told him that Dooley's was in for another change. The new waitress he'd hired would have to stay.

He was left with no doubt that Diamond had missed her calling. She had no business slinging drinks when she could sing like that. Real tears were hovering behind those heavy gold lashes, making the green cast of her eyes glow in the subdued lighting. It was then that Dooley had a sudden flash of insight. What he'd seen on her face had been so clear that he knew he couldn't be mistaken.

This woman had known all along she was a singer. She'd taken this job because she needed to eat and because she was running. And she was running from a man, or his name wasn't Dooley Hopper.

Jesse's voice lingered on the last notes of the song. He stared straight into the camera and ended his performance with a farewell that had Tommy fuming.

"Merry Christmas, shiny girl," Jesse said softly. "Wherever you are."

"And that's a wrap," the director said, breathing a sigh of relief that the last song was in the can.

The recording of the "Nashville Christmas Special" was finished. There was nothing left but some editing. He didn't care that Jesse Eagle had inserted a little bit of extra dialogue into his performance. The man was famous enough to do just about whatever he chose. Besides, it would make good press.

Everyone knew about the mystery woman on Jesse's album. No one had made the connection between her and Diamond Houston, the woman who'd recently disappeared from Jesse's life as quietly as she'd come. And the reason was that in Nashville, there was an unending line of women just like Diamond, either waiting to be discovered by an agent or waiting to be loved by a star.

Tommy stood in the corner of the studio and glared, debating whether he should talk to someone in editing and have that last bit of Jesse's performance cut. But something told him that he'd interfered enough. Something, probably self-preservation, told him to like it or lump it. He opted for the latter by stuffing an unlit cigarette into his mouth.

"No smoking on the set," a woman said as she hurried by with a stack of papers in her hands.

Tommy glared and waved the cigarette in her face as she passed to prove it was unlit.

"Damn," he muttered. "Are there no pleasures left to man anymore? Always some busybody trying to mind your business for you."

Tommy didn't see that he did the same to Jesse, because when he did it, it wasn't meddling, it was just part of the job.

The members of Muddy Road were gathering themselves and their families as they began to straggle from the set. Mack slipped up behind Jesse and slid an arm across his shoulder in an unusual gesture of camaraderie.

"Hey, old buddy," Mack said. "We're all going to The Stockyard to get something to eat. Come with us."

"Not hungry, Mack. But thanks anyway," Jesse said.

Mack frowned and tugged at his bushy, graying beard in consternation. "You aren't still pissed at me, are you?" he asked, referring to his earlier confession of how he'd once treated Diamond. It didn't matter that now he was one of her champions. She was gone, and there was nothing anyone seemed able to do to help.

"Not pissed at anyone but myself," Jesse said quietly. "I broke a promise, and I'm having a hell of a time living with myself because of it."

"I don't get it," Mack said. "You didn't hurt her. We all know how crazy you are about her."

"I took her away from her family. And she came with me because I promised to look after her. I promised to help her start a career in country music." The smile on his face never reached his eyes. They were cold, dark, and flat. "All I did was ruin whatever chances she had. I didn't take care of her myself. I trusted others to do what I should have been doing." He turned away. "I have to live with that."

Mack ducked his head. "If you change your mind . . . you know where we'll be."

Al echoed Mack's sentiments as he walked past with Rita and their children.

"Been missing you," Rita said. "I left a message with Henley for you to come to Sunday dinner last week."

"Wouldn't have been good company, honey," Jesse said. He hugged Rita gently and then walked away.

Rita's eyes teared. She turned to Al with a fierce expression on her face. "If I ever get my hands on the person responsible for splitting those two up, I may—"

Tommy walked past, whistling absently on his way to his car. Rita hushed instantly and glared at the man's cocky swagger.

"For two cents I'd—"

"Come on now, honey," Al said, grabbing his wife by the arm. "You don't know for sure, and I ain't having you start a fight in front of the kids."

"Then take them home so they don't see it," she said, and started after Tommy, leaving Al in the middle of the stage at the Grand Ole Opry to do as he pleased.

"Hey, Tommy," Rita yelled.

Tommy spun around and frowned at the expression on Rita Barkley's face. Another damned busybody, he thought.

"Heard anything from Diamond?" she asked, and watched a flush of anger rise from his collar to his hairline.

"No! Why should I? We weren't exactly bosom buddies, if you know what I mean?"

"I know exactly what you mean," she whispered. "And I swear to God, if I find out you had anything to do with her leaving, I'll take you apart myself." She flicked a long red fingernail beneath his chin and let it dig just the least bit into his skin for effect. "Get the message?"

He stepped back and started to shove her hand away in anger when Al caught his wrist and stopped the motion.

"I wouldn't do that if I were you," Al warned. "She's feisty, I'll admit, but she's all mine, Tommy. And I don't take lightly to someone touching her like that." He grinned a bit to take the sting out of his warning. "I'm sure you didn't mean nothin' by it. But it don't hurt to say what you think, right? Saves a lot of misunderstandings later."

Tommy stomped away, unable to do or say anything that would get him out of the hole he'd dug for himself. The only thing he knew was, if Diamond Houston was going to be found, he'd better be the one to do it. That way he'd have first crack at lying his way out of what he'd done. If not, at least he'd have a jump start on getting out of Nashville before Jesse killed him.

Jesse drove up to his house and parked in the carport. He crawled out of his car and then turned and leaned against it, burying his face in his arms as he tried to talk himself into going inside that empty house alone.

The mare nickered in the barn beyond, and the half-grown colt echoed her call. They'd heard him drive up and were hoping for a late-night treat. It wasn't uncommon for him to wander out with a handful of sugar cubes or a carrot or two.

But that night, he couldn't face them. All they did

was bring back memories he was trying to forget. Of the time he'd come home and caught Diamond and Henley in her first driving lesson. It was the first time they'd fought and ended up making love instead. Just the memory made his belly jerk.

He hit the car with the flat of his hand and shouted aloud into the night.

"Damn you, girl! Where did you go? How could you leave what we had?"

But there were no answers for Jesse. Not that night. He walked onto the porch, unlocked the door, and then methodically closed and locked it behind him. His heart told him to head for the bar and drown every ache he had in an amber haze. But instinct halted the thought. He didn't want to start something he couldn't stop. Not again. Not when there was still a chance that he would find her.

Instead, he walked through the dark, empty house and up the stairs, his footsteps echoing loudly in the silence. He paused at the door to her old room, started to open it, and then cursed softly and walked past to his own.

He fell across the bed fully clothed, rolled over on his belly, and then into a ball. There was only so much pain a man could stand without breaking.

Diamond was on a high. It was the first in so long she hardly recognized it. The night had been successful beyond her dreams. The men had loved her singing, and she'd loved performing. It felt like old times, only better.

She hurried up the steps leading to her apartment building and leaned her weight against the front door. It always stuck. Shivering with a combination of cold and nervous excitement, she almost ran up the steps to her second-floor apartment. Humming absently, she jammed the key into the lock and started to turn it when the door swung back at her touch. She gasped, staring in disbelief at the mess in her room. She'd been robbed!

While she'd been gone, someone had broken in and gone through everything she owned. Panic filled her as she realized that whoever had broken into her place could still be inside.

But the thief had obviously been unafraid of detection. He'd overturned everything and then left the light on. It didn't take long to see that there was no one inside.

"Oh God! Oh God! What do I do? You call the police, stupid." She reacted and answered her own question in the space of a heartbeat.

With her legs shaking from shock and the burst of adrenaline still lingering in her system, she willed herself to reach the manager's apartment below without coming undone.

It didn't take long for the Nashville police to show up. They told her that she'd been the third victim in the area to have been robbed that night. They called him a pattern burglar.

Diamond sank down onto the bed and resisted the urge to scream. She didn't care what they called him. He'd invaded her privacy.

"Miss, do you think you could help us make a list

of what was stolen? Microwave . . . television . . . that sort of thing. And if you have any jewelry or—"

Diamond laughed. The sound startled the policeman on duty. He looked up from his notepad and stared.

"I didn't own a microwave or a television. Or jewelry or anything else worth stealing. All he did here was make a mess."

The policeman's eyebrows rose, but he showed no other reaction except to write himself a note.

It was a sobering thought to know that you owned nothing a robber would want to steal. It should have been comforting, but she now realized that anytime someone wanted to get into her apartment, he could. Maybe next time he would wait and take something else. Something she wasn't willing to give . . . herself.

"This is a hell of a note," she said.

Sinking down onto the bed, she buried her face in her hands and started to laugh. The longer she laughed, the more frenetic it became, until the laughter evolved into deep, gut-wrenching sobs.

And then the sea of uniforms parted as a tall, hulking man burst through the doorway, gathered her into a rough embrace, and glared a warning at any cop who dared to stop him. It was Dooley.

"How?" Surprise won out over tears as she began to tremble at his unexpected appearance. But she was thankful beyond words that he'd come.

"Everyone knows everyone's business in this part of town, girl," he said. "You're comin' home with me tonight. Tomorrow we'll come back in the daylight, and when I'm through with this place, won't be a roach able to come inside without a ticket."

"Okay," she said, exhausted from shock and the earlier excitement of the night. What had started out as a high had ended on an additional low to her already messed up life.

13

The house was small and nondescript. There were no outward characteristics that would identify it to a passerby as the house of Dooley Hopper.

But the moment Diamond stepped inside, she knew he must have lived there forever. The walls were covered with old photographs of Dooley with first one famous country singer and then another. Many of the pictures were autographed. Dooley had been holding out on her.

She looked at him, waiting for an explanation.

He shrugged. "Lived in Nashville all my life," he said. "Stands to reason I'd know a few of them beggars, don't it?"

Referring to Red Foley, Patsy Cline, and Tex Ritter as "beggars" made her smile. "I suppose it does," she said, and then shivered.

"Here," Dooley said. "Get over by the fire." He pointed to a gas heater against the wall. "I'll make coffee. It'll warm you up." Then suddenly embarrassed at the change in their relationship, he felt obligated to add, "I ain't got no soup."

Diamond wrapped her arms around his ample waist and hugged him. "I don't want soup," she said. "I just need to sleep."

Surprised but pleased by her unexpected show of affection, Dooley hugged her back. "I'll get you some blankets. It's warmer in here than in my room or I'd tell you to take my bed."

Diamond sank onto the faded sofa and tucked her feet beneath her. "I'm just glad to be here, Dooley. I'll take what I can get." She looked up at his massive frame and then back down at the narrow sofa and grinned. "Besides, I don't think you'd fit."

"I think you're right," he said. "Be right back."

Diamond watched him hurry from the room and then leaned back, closing her eyes against the reality of the moment. But it was no use. When she closed her eyes all she saw was the devastation of the apartment they'd just left . . . and of her life.

She curled herself into a ball and groaned. "Why me, Johnny? Why me?" But her father didn't answer. And even if he'd been able to, there would have been nothing left to say.

At Dooley's insistence, Diamond spent two more days and nights at his place. Her quiet presence wormed its way into his existence so thoroughly that when it finally came time for her to leave, he was reluctant to let her.

But he'd used the time wisely. He'd been to Goodwill

so many times in the past few days that he and the clerk were on a first-name basis. And the manager at Diamond's apartment didn't know whether Dooley was trying to set himself up as her pimp or her bodyguard but had decided not to pursue the issue. Either way, Dooley was too big to argue with.

Anxiety skittered across Dooley's mind as he turned the corner and parked his pickup truck in front of her place. What if he'd overstepped his bounds?

But the memory of her panic and the way she'd collapsed in his arms the night of the robbery was too fresh to forget. He gritted his teeth and cursed beneath his breath. He didn't care what she thought. He needed to know she would be safe, and that was all that mattered.

"We're here," he said unnecessarily, watching her face for signs of panic at having to return to the scene of the crime.

But Diamond just nodded, grabbed her bag of clothing, and slid out the passenger side of the truck.

"Now, you remember I told you I'd fix it so's no one could get in again, right?"

Diamond grinned and nodded once more, wondering what he'd done that was making him so apologetic.

"I can't be havin' my best singer scared out of her wits and lose sleep and such."

"I'm your only singer," Diamond said.

"Yeah, well . . . just the same, it don't hurt to plan ahead."

The steps inside the old building were steep, the stairwell narrow. But Diamond's apprehension at entering her apartment disappeared as they reached the second-floor landing. In plain view of anyone who cared to look were four brand-new, shiny, brass locks imbedded in her door like baubles on a Christmas tree.

"Here," Dooley said, thrusting a ring of carefully marked keys in her hands. "Lock any or all of them you want every time you leave. Just don't forget which ones you lock or you'll have to chop down the door to get in."

"So which ones are locked now?" she asked.

"None," Dooley said, grinning. "It would drive a burglar crazy, right? He'd be lockin' himself out instead of gainin' entry every time he turned a tumbler. Ingenious, hunh?"

"You're ingenious, Dooley. You're also the best friend a woman could have." She threw her arms around his neck and planted a kiss on his cheek.

He blushed and shoved her through the doorway, eager to catch her first reaction to the rest of his surprise.

"Oh, Dooley!"

Except for his labored breathing, her soft, almost nonexistent exclamation was the only sound in the room.

It was still the same two rooms, only now, heavy drapes hung across the drafty windows, faded just the least bit from countless washings but still a cheery cranberry red color and well able to block out the winter's chill.

A thick area rug covered the floor instead of the older, worn one that had been in place when she'd rented the rooms. Its Far East pattern gave a sense of the exotic to the two dingy rooms Diamond called home.

Everything was clean and put back in place, and it looked as if the robbery had never occurred. She turned toward the kitchenette and stared. It was then that the first tears formed. She tried to speak and could only manage another soft "Oh, Dooley."

A brand-new microwave was in place on the minuscule kitchen counter. A thick crockery cup sat alongside a box of tea with a long, curly ribbon wrapped around it.

"Can't be havin' you get any sore throats or nothin'," Dooley said. "Bad for business."

Diamond flew into his arms. "You're right," she whispered. "It would be real bad for business."

Not only that, but the hug she gave him that day was real good for Dooley. It cemented their friendship in a way that the passing of years could never have done. Dooley didn't know it, but Diamond Houston had just given him something that she'd never given to anyone else, not even Jesse. She'd given him her trust.

Tommy gunned the engine of his TransAm, smiling with juvenile satisfaction at the small amount of rubber he'd left on the street in front of the mall. He shifted in his seat, moving the bulge behind his zipper to a more comfortable location, and slid his sunglasses above his forehead as he searched the area for a place to park. It was an affectation to wear sunglasses in the middle of winter in Nashville, but on Tommy it was the norm.

"Damned if it doesn't look like every woman in town is at the mall," he muttered.

Christmas shopping was in full swing. Browsing the stores meant choosing gifts, and choosing gifts meant standing in line to pay, and Tommy hated to stand in line. But he knew that if he didn't do something soon to change Jesse's attitude, he'd be standing in the unemployment line.

He finally found a place to park and walked across the lot to the mall. A sensory smorgasbord overwhelmed him as he entered. The aroma of popcorn wafted through the air, along with the smells of spicy scented candles, warm chocolate from a vendor close to the entryway, and the ever-present cedar and pine so common during the yuletide season.

He inhaled, smiling as an unusual feeling of goodwill swept through him. In that moment, he wished no one ill. And in that same moment, he heard her laugh.

He turned, searching the tide of people coming and going through the mall doors, certain that he knew the owner of that laugh as well as he knew his own name, though uncertain of what he'd do when he located her. He hadn't expected to hear her voice—or hear her laugh. Not here in Nashville. She was supposed to be long gone. She was supposed to be out of his life.

But there was no tall, blonde woman either coming or going that he could see. Tommy wiped a shaky hand across his face and dropped onto a bench to regain his composure.

"It's just my imagination," he said.

A city bus pulled up outside the entrance. The crowd of people waiting to get on parted, allowing the ones on board to descend first. Tommy stood up from the bench, shoving his hands into his pockets to hide their tremble, and cast several furtive glances around the area to convince himself that no one had witnessed his panic.

He turned, intent on regaining the holiday spirit that had driven him into the mall, when the shadow of a woman moved across his peripheral vision. His hands fell limply from his pockets. He stared, slack-jawed and in shock as she walked through the exit, up the bus steps, and out of his sight.

She was tall. A long blonde rope of hair hung down her back in a thick braid. He had not seen her face nor the way she walked. But he knew as sure as his name was Tommy Thomas that he'd just seen a ghost.

The bus door closed. Tommy jerked, realizing that if he was truly about to "find" Diamond Houston, he'd better move. He made a dash for the mall doors and met an influx of shoppers coming inside. As much as he struggled to get through, he could not make it outside in time to stop the bus's departure. All he could do was stand on the street and curse as it pulled away.

Nothing could put a damper on Diamond's spirits that day. She'd taken her entire weekly paycheck from Dooley's and spent it on a new outfit. Tonight was special, and she wanted to look it. Someone had dropped a hint about people "in the business" making a surprise visit to Dooley's to hear her sing. If this was the case she intended to look her best.

The outfit she'd seen in the shop window would make anyone look good. On Diamond it was spectacular. The loose-legged palazzo pants and long-sleeved, form-fitting, low-cut top were winter white. In a fit of genius, the designer had chosen satin, assuring that the thick, rich fabric would hang in perfect folds upon the wearer. A wide belt of gold spandex was the garment's only decoration. Its poinsettia-shaped gilt buckle was nearly as large as Diamond's hand, making her waist look even smaller in comparison.

It had only taken one look at herself in the dressing room mirror for her to make the decision. This was what she'd come looking for. If her talent and this outfit didn't do the job, nothing would.

"Wow, honey," the salesgirl said. "That looks fantastic on you."

"Thanks. It had better," Diamond said, eyeing the price tag. "Shoes," she announced. "Now I need shoes."

The salesgirl made a small circle in the middle of the store and tried not to clap her hands with glee. This was going to be a good commission.

"I've got just the thing," she said. "Let's see if we have them in your size." She began scanning the shelves for gold lamé half-boots.

They did.

Diamond left with the outfit carefully boxed and placed in a large shopping bag that dangled against her knee as she hurried toward the exit to catch the bus. Since leaving Jesse, the MTA had become a vital part of her life, and she had no desire to walk home. Her apartment was on the far side of town and miles from the mall.

On her way outside, she caught a glimpse of herself in the highly polished windows of a candle shop. The woman staring back at her was nothing like the one who'd walked the streets of Nashville months ago, desperate for work. This woman actually smiled back at her. The whimsy with which she saw herself made her laugh aloud.

Unmindful of the admiring glances her laughter drew, she hurried outside to mingle with the crowd awaiting the bus's arrival.

The bus came, and she got on and sat down, waiting for the long, noisy carriage to carry her away. Unaware that she'd been seen. Unaware of the frailty of her safe little world.

Tommy sat in a darkened corner of his house downing the last of his bourbon. He frowned as the amber trickle into his shot glass ended, and then tossed the empty bottle onto the floor.

"It's not my fault," he muttered, swallowing the last drop of liquor down his throat.

After he'd seen her get on the bus, he'd made a run from the mall through the parking lot, intent on only one thing, following the bus until he watched that tall, blonde woman get off. Then and only then would he be certain that he wasn't seeing ghosts. Then and only then could he live with the fact that he truly didn't know where Diamond Houston was. Because if he didn't know, he didn't have to lie to Jesse.

But he panicked and forgot where he'd parked. Sick with frustration, Tommy lashed out at the first object he came in contact with, a radio antenna on the car beside him.

Unfortunately for Tommy, the vehicle's owner witnessed the antenna's demise as it bent beneath Tommy's frustration. Given the owner's rage, it had cost

Tommy a hundred-dollar bill and profuse apologies to get out of the incident.

He'd gone home and crawled into a bottle only to find that there was no room inside in which to hide. And he was still uncertain whether or not it had been Diamond he'd seen.

He picked up the phone and made a call to a local liquor store, then sat back to wait for the arrival of a fresh bottle of booze. He wasn't ready to face reality. Not just yet.

The outfit was a success, and so was Diamond's performance. She'd gone through every request the audience had called for as well as her own routine. Riding high on the enthusiasm with which she was being received, she didn't notice the front door opening in the middle of a song or see the startled expression of the man who'd entered.

Doug Bentin stood for a minute, watching her work the audience alone, then made a decision. He turned around and headed outside, then returned a minute later with his instrument in tow. Winding his way through the tables and their rowdy occupants, he stopped just outside the circle of light within which she sat, and waited to see what she would do next.

"One more for the road," Diamond said in response to a request to sing again. "Only this time, I pick the song."

"You sing it, pretty lady," Doug said as he walked into the light. "I'd be honored if you'd let me play."

Diamond smiled, instantly recognizing the fiddler

who'd played backup when she'd cut her demo. She gratefully laid her guitar aside and motioned for him to step forward.

"How about a real oldie, for old times' sake," Diamond said. "It's a Hank Williams classic. It's one of the first songs I ever learned all the way through. Hang onto your hearts, boys, because 'I'm So Lonesome I Could Cry.'"

The fiddler smiled. The song was perfect for his instrument. He pulled it from the case, drew the bow across the strings just once to find his place, and then nodded, waiting for her to start.

Diamond's voice was like a sigh upon the silence, a whisper into the deepest secrets every man and woman carried inside them. Even the customers at the back of the room were quiet as she carried her listeners into the magic of the melody. The slow, sad rhythm of the old song blended into the late-night hour with perfect harmony as she pulled the listeners into her spell.

Her voice rose with perfect pitch, hanging on the last note of each verse as if it were the last pine needle on a dying tree . . . then drifting softly into the silence as fog drifts through night.

Dooley heard more than the lonesome sound of the fiddle and the sad, melancholy words to the song. If he ever got his hands on the man who had hurt her, he'd wring his damned neck. Diamond *was* lonesome. And there was nothing he could do about it. She had him, and she had her new friends at Dooley's. But someone had hurt her bad. As far as Dooley was concerned, someone should pay.

Doug Bentin took a long, deep breath as he came

back to earth, reminding himself that once again this woman had pulled him into her world with nothing more than the sound of her voice. His hands shook as he lifted the bow from the fiddle and looked up into those wide green eyes of hers.

Diamond stepped back and bowed once, then lifted her hands toward the fiddler so that he would be included in the applause.

The room exploded. Men and women jumped to their feet, clapping and cheering.

"You were great, Miss Houston," Doug said as he followed Diamond into Dooley's office. "I've been expecting to see your name in lights. That demo you cut was damned good." And then he stopped himself and added, "It is Houston, isn't it? I play backup for so many, sometimes I get the names confused."

"You got the name right," she said, and then shrugged. As for the demo, nothing came of it. Maybe I'll be luckier another time."

Doug frowned. "You're kidding! Have you checked to be sure it went to *all* the studios? That was one of the best cuts I've ever sat in on."

Diamond stared. It had never occurred to her to follow up on any of Tommy's actions. After the fiasco with Jesse's album, though, she knew he wasn't to be trusted. Why had she trusted him to keep his word?

Doug couldn't believe it. This business was a strange one, and that was a fact. Sometimes it took more luck than talent to make it.

"Well, like I told you before," he said, "I'd be real proud to play for you on a regular basis. In case you forgot, my name's Doug Bentin. If you ever need a fiddler . . ." He grinned and handed her his card again.

"You made my night, Doug Bentin," she said, tucking his card into her purse. "And if I ever need a fiddler . . ." She cocked an eyebrow and winked.

"What's goin' on in here?" Dooley asked as he barreled his way into his office.

Diamond grinned. "My boss—and my bodyguard," she told Doug. "Dooley, this is Doug Bentin. He's . . . uh . . . played for me before."

Dooley caught the hesitancy of her words and glared, but Doug had nothing to hide, and he stared back.

"There's a man out front who wants to talk to you," Dooley said.

Diamond's nerves jumped, and her eyes widened. This might be it! She tried to catch Dooley's attention, but he was too focused on the fiddler.

"Here goes nothing," she said to herself, and headed out the door, leaving Dooley and Doug to do as they pleased with each other.

"Miss Houston?"

The man's voice was slow and southern. Her name rolled across his tongue forever as she held out her hand. He squeezed her fingers tightly as he pumped it up and down in vigorous fashion.

"You've got yourself quite a little following here," he said, looking around the room at the boisterous crowd still in place.

"It's nice to be appreciated," she said.

He nodded. "Name's Melvin Call. Got myself a club up on the strip that features new singers ever' now and

then. Thought you might be willing to come up sometime between now and New Year's and try your luck."

"Mr. Call, it's real nice to meet you," Diamond said.
"And I know your club. In fact, I was in there about
three months ago looking for work."

Melvin Call flushed. "Well, now, you understand how
it is. There's too damn many dreamers out there expecting to hit it big their first week in Nashville. I got to weed
out the culls before I make my move, don't you know."

Diamond grinned. "Then I take it I've just been
weeded."

He grinned back. "You can take it any way you like,
so long as you come sing for me." He handed her a card.
"Call this number tomorrow, ask for Shirley. She'll give
you a time slot. Don't be late—and don't be a no-show.
Ruins your chances in this town real fast."

Diamond watched him leave and then looked
down at the card in her hand. A smile started at the
corner of her mouth, spreading insistently across her
face as the import of what had just occurred began to
sink in.

"Well?" Dooley said gruffly as he walked up behind
her.

Diamond spun around and threw her arms around
his neck. "We're in," she said. "He wants me to come
sing for him."

"Humpf," Dooley said. "Ain't no 'we' to it. It's you,
and you know it. Now, go on out there and mingle. Let
them men look, but don't let 'em touch. If anyone gets
out of hand, you just—"

"Oh, Dooley," she said. "I've been taking care of

myself longer than I can remember. I don't need a baby-sitter."

"Need somethin'," he muttered as he walked away. "Maybe a new attitude. Gettin' too damn smart for your own good."

She grinned. He was happy for her. Only Dooley chose his own method of showing it. She walked out into the club and did as she'd been told. Diamond had mingling down to an art.

"Here we are. You wait. I'll help you carry the damned thing up the stairs," Dooley said as he climbed out of his pickup truck after parking on the street in front of her apartment.

Diamond rolled her eyes and looked down at the small color TV sitting in the seat beside her. He'd bought it and called it a Christmas present, only Christmas was still a week away.

"Just so's you can watch all them holiday specials," he had said. "You gotta stay up-to-date on the competition. Can't have you missin' out on somethin', can we?"

There was nothing to do but let him help her down from his truck and then watch as he pulled the television from the seat and started toward her apartment, using his stomach as its resting place as he ambled toward the steps.

"Don't just stand there, get the door."

She hastened to obey.

It took Dooley exactly fifteen minutes to hook up the set, complete with rabbit-ear antennae.

"Gonna need cable, too," he said.

"Doo-ley . . ."

The warning was sufficient to shut him up, but only for the moment. Diamond knew that when Dooley got hold of a notion, he went round and round until the thing was accomplished.

"There now," he announced. "It's ready. And I gotta be going. Ain't got all day to stand around and visit. Promised an old buddy I'd stop in. He's been kinda under the weather."

"Tell Walt I said hi," Diamond said, and watched the flush sweep up Dooley's neck. He didn't like people to know he had a soft heart and visiting a sick old man at the homeless shelter definitely fell into the category of "soft."

"Damned woman," he muttered. "Man can't have any secrets."

"Dooley . . ."

"What?"

"Thank you for my Christmas present."

"Oh . . . you're welcome," he said, and slammed the door. "Lock it behind me," he yelled from the other side.

Diamond grinned and did his bidding.

She turned all four locks just because they were there and then twirled in a little circle in response to the small delight of the day.

"Okay. You have a microwave. You have a television. Cook something. Watch something. Make yourself useful."

As usual, her solitary pep talk worked. She dug out a frozen dinner, set the timer, and went to change while her evening meal was nuked through cardboard and cellophane.

Then, dressed in comfortable old sweats, she plopped down in the middle of her bed, curled her feet beneath her, and began flipping channels with the remote control, thinking as she did how much Johnny Houston would have enjoyed what she was doing.

It was the thought of her father, her missing sisters, and the impending holiday that finally ended the spurt of happiness. She dropped the control onto the bed and dug through her meat loaf with little appetite. Loneliness was still her only companion.

The remainder of her food went in the garbage. She tossed her fork in the sink and then turned and faced her existence.

It wasn't what she'd hoped for when she'd left Cradle Creek. Even though she'd given up on love, there was still a chance of professional success. In two days, she would have her first command performance. Just thinking about the opportunity gave her the shivers.

A faint siren's wail came through the newly curtained windows and brought Diamond rudely back to reality in time to hear the last of an announcer's message.

". . . so stay tuned for the annual 'Nashville Christmas Special,' starting in just . . ."

The meat loaf in her stomach did a nosedive as apprehension replaced her daydreams. If a country music special had been taped in Nashville, then it only stood to reason that Jesse Eagle would probably be one of the featured stars.

"Get a grip. It's only television."

But this pep talk did no good. She didn't know if she was ready to face seeing him again, even if it was only on camera.

Diamond crawled out of bed and turned off the lights. If she was going to be able to watch this, she had to do it in the dark where no one could see. There was always the danger that she'd come apart inside, and if she did, she might never get herself back together again. There was always that danger.

14

"*Merry Christmas, shiny girl, wherever you are.*"

The message was an agonizing reminder to Diamond of what she'd lost by leaving Jesse. Listening to his voice and seeing him had been more than she could bear. She shuddered twice, swallowed against the lump of pain in the back of her throat, and willed herself not to scream as Jesse's Christmas wish echoed in her ears.

She'd known that watching the special would be difficult, but she hadn't realized it could be fatal. Her heartbeat had accelerated and then slowed so many times during his performance that she felt faint. She'd gone hot and then cold over and over until her skin felt clammy. It was the first time she realized that heartache was an actual, physical pain.

Blindly she aimed the remote. The screen went black. It was only after burying her face in her hands that she realized her cheeks were wet with tears.

"Jesse."

It was the first time she'd allowed herself to say his name aloud, and as soon as she did, she knew that it had been a mistake. It only made the longing worse.

"Oh, God, how long will this hurt? Why did you let me love him if you knew I couldn't have him? Why, dammit, why?"

Diamond rolled off the bed, stomped across the room, and grabbed her coat and purse. Before she realized what she was doing, she was outside on the street, running toward the phone at the end of the block.

The wind was bitter against her cheeks, freezing the last of her tears as her long legs quickly covered the distance to the booth. With an angry jerk she slammed the door shut behind her, unappreciative of the shelter it provided from the cold. Her mind was not on the weather, it was on the man she'd left behind.

Shaking from the rush of adrenaline that had sent her out into the night, she combed her fingers through her hair and then fumbled with the change in the bottom of her purse, trying to find a quarter to make her call.

Twice she got the coin to the slot, and twice it rolled out of her fingers and onto the floor. She was in tears again by the time it finally fell into place. Frustration, despair, and an aching need to hear his voice kept her attention focused as she punched in the number from memory.

It was only when the phone began to ring that she realized she couldn't go through with it. But still she stared blindly into the darkness, her fingers curled tightly around the receiver, and waited.

She lost count of the number of rings and had almost

gotten herself under control enough to hang up when he answered.

"Hello?"

He sounded disgruntled. It was at once the most wonderful and the most awful thing she could have heard. She gasped loudly, realizing that her impulsive action could ruin what she'd so desperately tried to salvage—his career.

Jesse was in no mood for games. Watching the televised Christmas special had done nothing but remind him of Diamond and of how lonely he was without her. He was mad that the answering machine was off and had ignored the rings until they had gone on for so long. Certain that Tommy would be the only one persistent enough to not hang up, he was surprised by the soft gasp he heard instead.

"Hello? Is anybody there?" he repeated.

Diamond closed her eyes and shuddered as she leaned her forehead against the cold glass. She needed to hang up. She would any time now. But she just wanted to hear his voice, just once more, even if he didn't know it was she. But it hurt to breathe, and she wondered why. As she looked up to stare at her own reflection, she realized that she was crying.

Jesse heard the sob. It was only a small one, insignificant as sobs go. But it was enough to send a chill up his spine. His fingers curled around the receiver as anxiety tied his gut in a knot. A knowing, a certainty filled him as he listened to the soft, almost undetectable flow of tears and willed himself not to join in.

"Diamond . . . honey . . . is that you?"

But there was no answer other than a change in the texture of her crying. His heartbeat accelerated as his mouth went dry. Jesse was so damned scared of saying the wrong thing and losing this tenuous touch he didn't know what to do, yet he was exhilarated by the implications of her call.

"God help me," he muttered softly to himself. "I know it's you, darlin'. And if you can't talk, let me. Just don't hang up . . . okay?"

He held his breath, waiting for a click that never came. Shaking with relief, he leaned against the wall and sighed as he began.

"I don't know what happened to you, but I know it was bad. I swear to God I didn't mean for you to get cheated, baby." He rushed through his apology, frantic that she'd disconnect before he made his point. "But I take full responsibility for what happened to you, because I promised to take care of you and I didn't do it right. All I did was take you to bed and leave the rest of your life up to someone else." His voice shook as he continued. "I'm so sorry that you were hurt. But it can be fixed, shiny girl. Just come home to me. I can fix everything . . . but I can't do it without you." His voice broke and he closed his eyes, breathing deeply as he tried to regain control of himself.

Twice Diamond almost answered. Twice the urge to tell him she understood nearly made her speak, but both times she stopped herself. She caught her breath and then sighed deeply as her tears began to subside. Just hearing his voice was enough for now.

He heard her catch her breath and held his own,

expecting at any moment to hear her speak, praying that she'd tell him where she was. But she said nothing.

"Where are you, baby? My God, Diamond, I've looked everywhere. I nearly went crazy when you left. When I couldn't find you . . ."

She heard the despair in his voice and wished that he were standing beside her so that she could cradle his face in her hands and kiss away his pain. But that would mean a resurrection of the rumors that had nearly ruined him.

She only meant to take a breath, but it ended in a gut-wrenching sob that tore into his soul.

"Diamond. My God! Whatever has happened to you, let me help. Please . . . tell me where you are. I love you, lady. Doesn't that count for anything?"

Still no answer. By this time, Jesse was starting to panic. He sensed she was pulling away, and in desperation he shouted into the phone.

"Goddammit, Diamond, answer me. When I lost you, I lost everything that mattered. Didn't what we shared mean anything to you at all, or am I the only one who cared?"

Oh Jesse, I cared too much. And I'm the one who's lost everything. At least your career is safe.

The ground rumbled beneath Diamond's feet as the night train passing through Nashville rolled under the overpass on which she stood. The noise from the engine was almost deafening, even through the enclosed booth. Then the whistle blew, a long, continuous wail that echoed in Diamond's heart long after the train had passed.

Jesse listened, transfixed by the sound blasting in his ear. It wasn't what he'd expected. He'd expected to hear her voice, or the empty sound of a dead line as she disconnected, but not that. The whistle of the train was a lonely echo of what was inside his heart, an empty cry of despair he'd almost learned to ignore . . . until tonight, and her call.

"Diamond, where the hell are you?"

She jerked, suddenly cognizant of what he must have heard, and slammed the receiver down before she thought. She shuddered, realizing that the connection wasn't the only thing broken. From the pain in her chest, she feared her heart was coming to pieces, too.

Suddenly aware of the loneliness of her location and the darkness that could be hiding anything, or anybody, she shoved the door open and began to run. By the time she reached the front door to her apartment, she was gasping for air. She took the stairs two at a time and hit the door to her apartment with the flat of her hand, slamming it back and then slamming it shut in needless panic.

With shaking fingers she turned all the locks. Then she dumped her coat and purse onto the kitchen table and headed for her bed. Without undressing she crawled beneath the covers, rolled herself into a tight ball, and began to shake. She was inside, but she would never be safe again. Jesse Eagle had stolen her heart, and she didn't know where to find it.

Jesse stared blankly at the receiver in his hand and then flung it across the room with a curse, ignoring the crash it made as it jerked the phone from the table and onto the floor.

She was gone. He shuddered and leaned his head against the wall, willing the bile rising in the back of his throat back where it belonged.

"Oh God, oh God, oh God."

But the harshly whispered prayer did no good. God had already ignored every prayer he'd made for the last few months. Why did he think this time would be any different? He staggered down the hallway toward the front door, uncertain about what he was going to do when he got outside. He only knew that wherever it took him, he would be that much closer to Diamond.

The air was sharp and brought tears to his eyes as he stood at the edge of his porch, staring at the distant lights of Nashville on the night horizon. The long, mournful wail of a train whistle ran with the wind that passed before him. Jesse listened absently and then with quiet intent. He looked at his watch, mentally calculating the time it would take a train to run from Nashville to the crossing below his place. Remembering the train whistle that he'd heard over the phone, he began to smile. It was too obvious to be a coincidence.

"You're still in Nashville, aren't you, girl?"

For the first time in months, there was hope in his heart. What he was thinking was a long shot, but he'd bet the pot on it. Jesse Eagle was about to gamble everything he had on the chance that the woman he loved was still within reach. But this time, he wouldn't make the mistakes he'd made before. This time, when he found her—and he knew that he would—she'd be the one dealing the cards.

o o o

"Oh, hell. I'm here, aren't I? Just pass me the peanuts and shut up."

Twila Hart's grumble was met with a round of good-natured jeers as her friends shoved a snack-laden bowl across the table toward her and then topped her drink for good measure.

Twila hadn't wanted to come to a club that night and watch a bunch of gourd-green singers giving up poor imitations of Garth Brooks and Reba McEntire. Most of the young performers hadn't figured out that they needed their own style, not a good rendition of someone else's. But she'd been reluctantly convinced that getting out would be good for business.

And she did have this new blue suede pantsuit with fringe on the jacket that hung clear to her hips. It had been dynamite on the hanger but had lost something in the translation when she'd put it on, even though she was a trim size 9. However, she was of the opinion that anything that cost eight hundred dollars needed to be seen. Tonight was as good an excuse as any to wear it.

Twila had learned years ago that being a personal manager in a city overrun with them wasn't an easy way to make a living. Every Nashville entertainer who was worth his or her weight in guitar strings already had one.

Twila was overwhelmed daily with the constant influx of newcomers to Nashville who would sell their soul for a shot at stardom. Most of them had some talent, but few had what it would take to succeed in this highly competitive field. She'd had a few good clients but none that had hit star status. There had even been a couple of fabulous flash-in-the-pans and one that was an out-and-out mistake. But, she reminded herself, he'd been great in bed.

She tossed a handful of peanuts into her mouth and chewed as she squinted against a cloud of smoke that drifted across her face. Not for the first time, she wished that she was at home with her bra off and her sweats on, eating pizza and cussing her cat. At forty-four, she was beginning to lose her enthusiasm for the business.

She glanced down at her watch, promising herself that she'd give it an hour and then would get out of there, no matter what kind of teasing she'd get later. She sighed as the lights dimmed. That meant the break was over and another act was getting ready to perform.

A tall, leggy blonde wearing white satin trimmed in gold sauntered onto center stage, calmly ignored the catcalls and whistles that accompanied her entrance, and slipped the strap of her guitar over her shoulder. Twila watched the woman's long, slender fingers run lightly across the strings and noticed that there was little to no fidgeting about her as she stepped up to the mike. The woman gave a toss to the long blonde mane of hair hanging across her shoulder, looked up, and smiled at the audience. Even from here, Twila could see the pure country green of her eyes.

"Good evening, ladies and gentlemen," Diamond said. "My name is Diamond Houston from Cradle Creek, Tennessee—and of late from Dooley's down on Jefferson Street."

The audience erupted into a small round of laughter at Diamond's wry admission of where she'd been singing. Everyone knew that area of town was not choice property, nor did anyone live down there by choice.

"In my line of work, my business and your pleasure are one and the same." She grinned at a couple of men who were sitting down front, trying to get her attention. "And no, I'm not available by the hour. Before you grab for your wallets, I'd better break the news. I'm just a singer."

The audience roared with laughter, appreciating the way the tall blonde made light of what they'd been thinking.

Twila sighed and tried not to roll her eyes in dismay. *Great—a comedienne. She needs to be in Vegas, not Nashville.* She thrust her fingers back into the bowl of nuts and started to dig when the woman's voice rolled across her consciousness and flowed across the room.

Without announcing the song, Diamond began to sing, and the words poured from her lips in easy rhythm. Her fingers rocked across the strings in a slow, gentle beat as the toe of her left boot kept time while she played.

The nuts were forgotten as Twila stared open-mouthed at the depth of tone and clarity of pitch with which this woman sang. It was somewhere between the rhythm of a Negro spiritual and the poignancy of true country sound. It seemed to come up and out of her mouth as easily as she breathed.

Twila forgot that she hadn't wanted to come. She forgot that she'd intended to eat pizza and turn in early. Instead, she sat back in her chair praying that this woman didn't already have an agent and contemplating the best way to introduce herself.

When the performance was over Twila made her way through the throng surrounding the backstage door.

"Miss Houston, you were great!" the club owner said, handing her an envelope with her pay.

"Thanks, Mr. Call. I enjoyed it. You've got a great audience to play to."

Melvin Call grinned. "Call me Melvin," he said. "And speaking of audiences, how would you like to come back—say New Year's Eve?" He saw the shock on her face and grinned again. "Ordinarily I wouldn't be offering, because I'm usually booked up. But one of my singles decided to get himself arrested last night, so my program is now one entertainer short. Are you interested?"

This was important. Diamond knew that such an offer would be a long time in coming again. But everything was happening so fast she wasn't sure how to deal with it. There was only one thing she could think to do, and that was be honest with him about her situation.

"Mr. Call, I'd like nothing better than to take you up on your offer, but I need to be up front with you. I don't know the rules in this business. I don't have a manager or a—"

"Honey, don't ever let them know your weaknesses." Twila Hart grabbed Diamond by the elbow and tugged gently, softening her warning with a smile.

"Hey, Twila," Melvin said. "Didn't know you were out there tonight. Did you hear this little lady sing?"

"She's why I'm not at home eating pizza as we speak," Twila said. "Introduce me, Mel, and be kind."

Diamond was lost. She looked from one to the other,

uncertain of who was in charge. The only thing she knew was that it sure wasn't her.

Melvin grinned. "Diamond, I'd like you to meet Twila Hart. She's been in the music business almost as long as I have."

Twila winced. "I didn't ask for an insult, just an introduction." Then she proceeded to take control of the situation. "Are you really Diamond Houston, or is that a stage name?"

"'Fraid it's real," Diamond said. She held her breath.

Twila rubbed her hands together in glee. She could picture the PR now. A choice name, a beautiful face and body, and, by God, a talent to go with it.

"So," Twila went on, "I couldn't help overhearing you tell Mel that you want a manager."

"Well . . ."

"I'm interested," Twila said. "I'm also honest, and I'm damned good at my job. Ask Mel. Ask anyone in town. They'll tell you the same thing."

It was the word *honest* that sold her. That and the straightforward manner with which Twila had approached her. Diamond took a good, long look at the woman and decided that while Twila Hart could have used a touch-up on graying hair roots and a lighter hand with the makeup, she liked what she saw.

"Great outfit," Diamond said, eyeing the blue suede fringe on Twila's jacket.

"No, honey." Twila pointed to Diamond's white and gold satin. "That's a great outfit. Mine's nice." Giving away nothing of the tension inside her, Twila pressed on. "So . . . what do you say? Are you willing to take a chance on a stranger?" The moment she said it, Twila knew by the look on Diamond's face that somehow she'd stepped on old wounds. But she maintained eye contact and held her breath, waiting for Diamond's answer.

Diamond's stomach turned. A feeling of déjà vu swept through her so quickly she almost staggered. She'd taken a chance on a stranger once before, and it had nearly killed her. But she wasn't ready to call it quits. She took another long look, a deep breath, and held out her hand.

"I think I can take one more chance," Diamond said. "After all, I wasn't a gambler's daughter for nothing. Johnny always said you have to trust your instincts."

"Johnny?" Twila wondered if he was the reason Diamond Houston had turned pale earlier.

"My daddy. He's dead, but a lot of what he taught me isn't. Try as I might, I can't seem to lose my past." Diamond was unaware of the bitterness with which she spoke.

Twila nodded. She had a suspicion that Diamond Houston was trying to lose more than her upbringing. But that was okay with her. As long as she didn't lose that marvelous voice, they were in business.

"Need a ride home?" she asked.

Diamond nodded.

"Good. We can talk details on the way, and while you make me coffee, we can discuss where we go from here." Twila grinned at the look of distrust on Diamond's face. "Don't get cold feet on me now, girl. Because we *will* go on from here—and the only way to go is up."

Diamond grabbed her guitar case, coat, and purse

and was outside before she had time to absorb the implications of what had just happened.

Mack sat in a corner of the club in the darkest part of the room and stared at the woman onstage. His date glared as he sat openmouthed, watching Diamond Houston perform. He'd been so shocked by her appearance onstage that he sat unmoving through the entire performance. By the time she walked offstage, he had come to enough to realize that Jesse would kill to know that Diamond was still in Nashville.

Trying to make excuses to an already furious redhead, he shoved a couple of twenty-dollar bills in her hands and told her to get herself a cab. He was desperate to get backstage and talk to Diamond. Mack could just imagine Jesse's elation when he walked in with his lady on his arm. In some small way, Mack felt obligated to make things right since he'd been one of the reasons things had gone wrong at first.

Mack's date stuffed the money in her bag, made her way out of the club, and didn't look back. He didn't even watch her leave. He was too busy trying to catch Melvin Call's attention to get himself permission to go backstage and talk to Diamond. He caught up with him in the hall, but by then it was too late. Diamond was gone, and all Melvin could tell him was that she'd left with Twila Hart.

"Sorry," Mel said. "I don't need performers' addresses. Only their agents' promises, and warm bodies on the right nights." He started to walk away.

"Damn!" Mack muttered, and kicked the toe of his boot against the bathroom door. All his dreams of returning Diamond to Jesse had just gone up in smoke.

"Hold your horses," a man yelled, believing that Mack's furious kick was directed to the locked bathroom door.

"Hey, Mel," Mack said, and waited for Mel to turn. "How did you get her to sing here? Did she audition, or what?"

Mel grinned and slapped his thigh. "That's right!" he yelled. "I plumb forgot. I don't know where she lives, but I know where she works. Down at Dooley's on Jefferson Street. However," he said, grinning, "I don't know how much longer she'll be working there."

"Why?" Mack asked.

"Because from the look on Twila Hart's face when they left, she'll have that lady signed, sealed, and delivered before morning. She seemed real interested in representing her."

Mack nodded. "I guess I can contact Twila, or maybe—"

"Hell," Melvin added. "I guess I'm getting old. You might also be interested in knowing that she'll be back here on New Year's Eve."

Mack started to grin. "You sorry sonofabitch. I'm damned sure interested, and you know it." He slapped Melvin on the back and left.

Melvin shrugged. It didn't surprise him that men were trying to keep up with Diamond Houston's whereabouts. She was one pretty lady.

* * *

Diamond was nearly home before it dawned on her that she'd performed in an actual, bona fide club, been paid, and possibly gotten herself a manager to boot. She grinned.

Twila saw Diamond's smile as she accelerated, shooting through the intersection just as the yellow light turned red.

By God, Twila thought. *I've gone and got myself a star to shine. And if tonight is any indication of her ability, it isn't going to take all that much polish to do the job.*

"This is it," Diamond said, pointing toward the old, two-story apartment house she called home. "Home cheap home."

Twila laughed aloud. Diamond's wry humor about her situation was delightful. "Looks like the apartment I shared with my first husband." She stopped in front and peered doubtfully through her windshield. "Is it safe, or should I get my gun?"

"No, it's not particularly safe," Diamond said. "I've been robbed once." She shrugged. "Didn't take anything, though—didn't have anything he wanted." She turned and stared at Twila. "Do you really have a gun?"

Twila heard the pain behind the sarcasm in Diamond's voice as she admitted to owning nothing worth stealing. "Hell yes, I've got a gun. I live in a better part of town than this and I've been robbed twice." She grinned. "'Course, I'm probably twice as old as you, so that accounts for the extra robbery, don't you think?"

Diamond grinned back. "Seems like a plausible explanation," she said. "Come on up. As I remember, you said we need to discuss details. And believe me, Twila Hart, I'll dig."

Twila nodded. "Ask away, girl," she said. "I haven't got a thing to hide, and we've got everything to gain." She opened the door and then looked back at Diamond, who was still belted in place. "So, unlock that seat belt and go let me in. This damned suit could get me killed." She pointed at her leather pantsuit and frowned while motioning for Diamond to hurry.

Diamond crawled out of the car and followed Twila Hart's swinging fringe to the front door, let them in with her key, and shut out the boogeyman before he followed them in.

15

Henley entered Jesse's bedroom with five freshly ironed shirts as Jesse exited the bathroom with a towel wrapped around his waist and another that he was using on his hair.

"Your shirts, sir," Henley said, and hung them in the closet, calmly ignoring Jesse's near-nude state and the fact that he was dripping all over the carpet.

"Thanks, Henley," Jesse said. "And I wish to hell you'd can the 'sir' business." He dropped one of the damp towels onto a chair and headed for the dresser. "You always called Diamond by her first name. Why not me?"

Henley's eyebrows rose several inches. To say that he was shocked that Jesse had even mentioned her name was putting it mildly. However, well-trained "man" that he was, he was bound to answer.

"I didn't work for her," Henley said, and then felt compelled to add, "Somehow she just wasn't cut out for the propriety, sir, if you know what I mean."

Henley walked along behind Jesse as he dressed, picking up damp towels from chairs and retrieving lost belts and misplaced boots.

Jesse was so accustomed to Henley picking up after him that he didn't even notice what he was doing until he caught a glimpse of Henley over his shoulder in the vanity mirror and saw the pile of discarded things over his arm.

He walked out of the bathroom, took the towels from Henley and hung them up. "I'm sorry, man. I don't pay you to be my maid. My mother would whack me up the side of the head if she could see me now."

Henley was surprised at the almost good-natured attitude Jesse was exhibiting. It was so like the Jesse of old, before Diamond Houston had come into their lives, that it surprised him. Surely Jesse wasn't getting over her, Henley thought. Surely his feelings for her ran deeper than that. As far as Henley was concerned, Diamond Houston could walk right back in the front door and take up where she left off.

"Then it's a good thing your mother's not here, sir, because you are a pig and we both know it."

Jesse laughed, wadded up a washcloth, and aimed it for Henley's back. It landed with a wet squish and surprised Henley so much he dropped the load of laundry in his arms and turned and stared.

"Is there something you're not telling me, sir?" Henley asked. There had to be a reason for all this good behavior.

Jesse's smile slowly disappeared. He leaned against

the door to his bathroom, and the words that came out of his mouth were shaky.

"She called."

"Miss Diamond—when? Where is she? Is she coming—"

"I don't know. She didn't talk to me," Jesse said.

Henley frowned. This didn't sound good. How could she call and not talk to him? Maybe the strain of the last few months had been too much. Maybe Jesse had gone round the bend.

"Don't frown at me," Jesse said. "I know it sounds crazy, but it's the truth. She called, but she wouldn't talk."

"Then how do you know it was her?" Henley asked. "Maybe you're making too much out of a wrong number."

"Because she was crying."

Strange as it seemed, the answer made sense. "So she called. She could be anywhere," Henley said. "How do you expect to find her?"

"I heard a train."

Henley rolled his eyes and tried not to despair. "Trains run everywhere, sir. There's no way you can tell which train or what city. I'm afraid you're getting your hopes up only to have them knocked down again."

Jesse shook his head. "No! I know I'm right. I heard the train, and then she hung up. I walked outside only minutes later and heard the same whistle as the train took the bend above the crossing below the house. She's in Nashville, Henley. And by God, I'm gonna find her."

Henley shook his head, bent down, and gathered up

the laundry he'd dropped. "I hope you're right, sir. I sincerely hope you're right." He walked away and left Jesse to finish dressing.

Half an hour later, Jesse emerged, surprised to see that Henley was still there.

"Go on home, Henley," Jesse said. "It's New Year's Eve. Take tomorrow off, too. I'll see you next year."

Henley grinned at Jesse's teasing reminder that another year was upon them. "Thank you, sir. I believe I will. If you plan on watching the football games here and have guests in, I've prepared several snacks. They are in the usual places."

"Thanks, Henley."

"Oh!" Henley said, turning as he remembered the message he'd taken while Jesse was in the shower. "I almost forgot. You had a phone call from Mack Martin. He said not to return his call, that he'd see you at the party at the Union Station Hotel."

Jesse nodded, wondering why Mack would call him. In all the years they'd known each other, he could count on one hand the number of times Mack had called.

"Okay," Jesse said. "Did Tommy say whether or not I was supposed to pick him up at his place?"

"I haven't heard from Mr. Thomas in days, sir. I wouldn't know."

Jesse shrugged. "No big deal. I'll just stop by his place on the way."

Henley left, and Jesse went to get his overcoat and keys, eager now that he was dressed to get out of the house and back into society. He'd come to the belief that the more he mingled, the quicker he'd find Diamond, although he knew by all rights they probably wouldn't be mingling in the same circles or he'd already have found her.

The party was one that he and Tommy had planned months ago. The ancient Union train station in downtown Nashville had been renovated several years earlier and was now an elegant but intimate hotel. Jesse had reserved the banquet room for his band and their families as well as some of country music's "important" personages who would be party-hopping in the new year.

He'd left the planning as well as the guest list up to Tommy, but after the revelations of the last few months he was a little apprehensive as to what would emerge. Tommy seemed capable of creating more undercurrents than Jesse would have imagined.

He slid into his car and buckled up, realizing that whatever Tommy'd decided, it was too late to change.

He had left too damned much up to Tommy, he told himself. But no more. He took off down the driveway, leaving a flurry of dead leaves and gravel flying in the air behind him.

Fifteen minutes later he pulled into the parking lot of Tommy's condominium, noting that his manager's car was still in its place. He headed up the steps, expecting to find Tommy pacing the floor and swearing about being kept waiting. He couldn't have been more wrong.

Jesse knocked until his knuckles hurt and then pulled out his keys. Years ago in a fit of camaraderie Tommy had given him a key to his place. Jesse had never used it, but something told him now was the time.

"Dammit," Jesse muttered, squinting in the weak light as he tried to connect the key to the keyhole. It finally slid in place and Jesse breathed a sigh of relief as the key turned easily in the lock.

The door swung back to reveal utter chaos. In that moment Jesse panicked, expecting to walk inside and find Tommy lying dead on the floor, the victim of an assault. But the thought quickly passed as Tommy staggered into the living room, a bottle in one hand, a shot glass in the other. The gray sweats he was wearing looked as if they hadn't been washed in a week. And from the length of his whiskers and the smell of the place, neither had Tommy.

"Tommy?"

He jumped. The empty shot glass slid out of his fingers as he stared blankly at the man blocking the door to his living room. Squinting, he leaned forward and peered through the shadows of the half-lit room. Recognizing his best and only client, he grinned and then mumbled, "Jesse, is that you, ol' buddy? Got a smoke? I been out for days."

Jesse walked inside and quickly slammed the door shut behind him, suspecting that later Tommy wouldn't appreciate any other witnesses to this mess, or his condition.

"What the hell's wrong with you?" Jesse asked, taking the liquor bottle out of Tommy's fingers.

Tommy grinned and tried to slap Jesse's shoulder in a manly fashion, but he missed and would have fallen on his face had Jesse not caught him on the way down.

"Wrong? Nothin's wrong . . . why'd ya ashk? Ain't

nothin' wrong with a man havin' hisse'f a li'l drink . . . is 'ere?" And then he patted the pocketless pants of his sweats and staggered in a small circle as he repeated his earlier request. "You real sure you don' have a smoke?"

Jesse stared. Something was definitely out of kilter here. In all the years he and Tommy had been together, he'd never known him to so completely lose control.

"Nothing's wrong with a little drink, as you call it," Jesse said. "But from the smell of you and this place, you've been at it for days. And—no, I don't have any cigarettes."

Tommy shrugged and frowned, staggering as he wrenched himself from Jesse's touch. "It's not been sho long," he muttered. "Jush since the mall. Didn' spec' that. No sir, didn' spec' that."

"What the hell has a mall got to do with you getting drunk?" Jesse asked.

Tommy raised his arm and aimed his forefinger in the general direction of Jesse's nose. "It's all your fault," Tommy muttered. "If you'd lishened to me . . . she wouldn't have meshed up ever'thin . . . shoulda lef' her where you found her, by God!"

She!

Jesse knew in that moment that Tommy was referring to Diamond. First the call the other night and now this—it was too much to be coincidence. Maybe she'd called Tommy, too. Maybe Tommy knew where she was. Jesse had to know. He grabbed Tommy by the arm, forcing him to listen.

"Where is she? By God, Tommy, if you've known all

this time where she was and didn't tell me, I'll break your neck."

Angry at the insinuation and guilty because part of it was true, Tommy swung at Jesse but missed his target and fell forward onto the carpet instead.

Jesse made a face, unable to believe that this was the same man to whom he'd entrusted his entire career. He poked Tommy's shoulder with the toe of his boot, almost hoping he'd passed out so that, for the time being, the conversation would be at an end. But it was not to be.

Tommy's head lolled on his shoulders as he tried to crawl to his feet. He could feel his stomach roiling and knew that it was time to head for the bathroom.

"Help me up," Tommy begged. "Gonna be sick."

"You make *me* sick," Jesse said, hauling him unceremoniously to his feet. "I asked you a question. Do you know where Diamond Houston is?"

"I don't know nothin'," Tommy mumbled, staggering toward the bathroom. "All I know is . . . she got on a bus. I tried to fin' her. I did, I swear."

Jesse was puzzled. He could make neither head nor tail of Tommy's drunken rambling. "You watched her get on a bus and leave town? I thought you said—"

"No, hell no!" Tommy shouted, and slammed the bathroom door shut just in time.

Jesse frowned and walked away, unwilling to stand in the hallway and listen to Tommy retch.

Minutes later the door opened and Tommy walked out with a wet washcloth pressed over his face, ignoring the drops of water that ran down the front of his sweatshirt in an uneven pattern. He cursed as he accidentally walked into a wall, yanked the washcloth away from his aching, bloodshot eyes, and then jerked back in a nervous reflex as he realized Jesse was still there.

"I asked you a question," Jesse said quietly.

Tommy's stomach turned again. He considered the idea of heading back to the bathroom, but from the look on Jesse's face, there was no time left for procrastination.

"I don' know where the fuck she is," Tommy said, and slapped the wet washcloth across the back of his neck. "My goddamned head aches. I haven't eaten in days. I'm sick, and all you worry 'bout is that bitch."

Jesse slammed Tommy against the wall, and when Tommy would have fallen he propped him up as he glared into his manager's face.

Jesse didn't have to ask again. Tommy could tell that he'd stepped over the line.

"I don't know where she is," Tommy whined, trying unsuccessfully to remove himself from Jesse's grip. "I'm not even sure it was her. All I saw was this tall blonde getting on a city bus out at a mall. Hell, there's a million jus' like 'er out there. I don' know why you don' jus' pick one of them and leave her the hell alone."

"When?" Jesse asked.

Tommy looked away, unable to face him as he answered. "Just before Christmas." He added quickly, before Jesse could punch him for keeping the secret to himself, "But I'm still not sure it was her—that's why I didn't say anything. I didn't want to get your hopes up."

Jesse was so angry he was shaking. But having it out with Tommy when he was in this condition would be like picking on a helpless child.

"What you've never understood," Jesse said, turning away from him, unwilling to let him see his pain, "is that my hopes have never died. I don't want anyone else but her, ever. I'll find her—and when I do, you'd better pray to God she doesn't implicate you in any way. I love her, and I'm going to marry her. If you two can't get along, one of you will have to go. And we both know who that'll be—don't we?"

Jesse walked out of the apartment and into the night, drawing deep, aching gulps of cold air into his lungs to clear away the stench of what he'd left behind. He got into his car, leaned his forehead on the steering wheel, and tried to regain control of his emotions. He couldn't walk into the Union Station Hotel spoiling for a fight.

Then he started the car, turned on the radio for soothing company, and drove away. Only once on his way downtown did he contemplate turning around and going home. And that was when his latest hit came on the radio and he had to listen to a repeat of what had started it all.

"Yessir, country music fans," the disc jockey said, "this is the fifth week in a row that 'Lies' has been at number one. Everyone's been speculating as to who the woman is who's singing with the famous Jesse Eagle. This is the best piece of marketing strategy I've ever heard of. Create a blockbuster hit and then leave the fans guessing as to the identity of the other half of the duo. Well, it takes all kinds, I suppose. So if you think you know who the woman is, give us a call at . . ."

Jesse frowned. This was so far out of hand, he wondered if it would ever be rectified. Diamond's name had been omitted from the album, but Tommy swore it was an oversight. Yet her voice was half of what had sent the song to the top of the charts. His claim that he'd never gotten around to signing her to a contract was bullshit. It was the most unprofessional thing that Jesse had ever heard of, and as far as he was concerned, it bordered on criminal.

Jesse had been asked about the identity of the woman on his song so often during the past few weeks that he'd developed a standard answer for the whole situation. His only response was "ask my manager." He sighed. Maybe that was part of why Tommy was so plastered. Maybe his manager had run out of answers, too.

Diamond's voice was taunting him from the speakers as she sang of lies and broken promises, and his voice came back strong and sure, promising it would never happen again.

"I just hope I get the chance to prove it to you, darlin'," he said, switching off the radio and turning down Broadway as he headed for the party at Union Station.

The party was just beginning as Jesse entered the room. Al and Rita were standing in the doorway, and Rita grabbed his arm as he entered.

"Where have you been, good-lookin'?" she teased. "This is your party and we're stuck here playing host and hostess. And where the heck is Tommy? I thought he'd be early. You know how he is."

"Tommy won't be coming," Jesse said. "It seems he started celebrating a few days early and is a little under the weather."

Al's eyebrows rose, but he wisely refrained from questioning Jesse about the backslide of their manager's manners. From the look on Jesse's face, he knew he wouldn't like the answers.

Rita didn't particularly like Tommy and could not have cared less whether he came.

"You greet your own guests," she said. "I'm goin' to get myself a glass of bubbly."

Jesse kissed Rita on the cheek and apologized to Al, who promptly followed his wife, leaving Jesse alone at the door. Jesse pasted on a smile and began to do his thing as Nashville came to party.

Civic leaders, heads of recording studios, old friends, and a host of country music's finest were mixing and drinking like there was no tomorrow. Jesse watched the champagne flow and the buffet disappear and knew that his party was a success. The only thing that would make the night perfect was if Diamond was by his side, and that wasn't going to happen. At least not tonight.

"Jesse! Darling! There you are! I have someone I want you to meet."

Jesse frowned, mentally cursing Tommy into the next century as he recognized the strident voice of the woman yanking at his arm. He bit his lip, pasted on a smile, and turned to face Selma Bennett in all her silver-sequined glory.

"Selma—I didn't see you arrive. Are you finding

everything you need?" he asked, ever conscious of his role as host. *Damn you, Tommy. I might have known you'd invite this witch.*

"I never have all I need, honey," she laughed, and winked, flirting audaciously with complete disregard for the years that separated them in age.

The urge to laugh aloud was strong. The idea of unveiling this bitch and then crawling into bed with her was ludicrous, but common sense told him that laughing in Selma Bennett's face would do nothing but cause trouble, and Jesse had already had enough of that for the evening.

Selma sighed. The line she'd tossed was sinking fast. Jesse wasn't biting, at least not on her hook.

"As I said, there's someone I want you to meet. She's the daughter of one of my dearest friends and is in town for the holidays. You two would simply be perfect together."

Jesse placed his hand on Selma's elbow and tightened it just enough to make his point. "Thanks, but no thanks," he said. "I'm afraid my heart is already taken, at least for the next hundred years. After that, if your friend's still in town, feel free to look me up."

He managed a smile to soften his refusal, but he may as well have saved himself the effort. Selma turned red. Jesse deduced it was anger, not embarrassment, that prompted it. Her lips thinned and her eyes narrowed.

"Don't tell me you're still pining after that blonde groupie?"

"I've said all I'm going to, Selma. Let it be," Jesse

said, and turned away, wishing she would fall off the face of the earth and take Tommy with her.

But Selma wasn't having any of it. Once she got hold of an idea, she was apt to ruin it by talking it to death.

"You are!" Her laughter was shrill, and there was a high flush of red slashed across her cheeks. "She left you, and you've still got the hots for—"

Jesse spun. His lack of color should have been warning enough for Selma, but she'd always been slow on the uptake. It was the angry hiss of his breath across her face that got her attention.

"Mrs. Bennett, if you're real smart, you'll stop right there. I have no intention of discussing Diamond with you or anyone else like you. My personal life is just that—personal. However, you and your friend enjoy yourselves this evening as my guests. And you'd be well advised to let sleeping dogs lie, before one of them bites you on the ass."

He walked away and didn't look back. He didn't care if she was insulted or just incensed. Either way, he hoped she left and took her friend with her. He yanked his hat from the rack and headed for the door. He needed some air.

"Jesse! Where have you been?" Mack asked, grabbing him by the arm and pulling him into the vestibule.

"Playing host for Tommy while he tosses his cookies."

Mack frowned. "Tommy's sick?"

"Tommy's drunk."

"Good deal," Mack said. "Then that means he's not here."

"What does that have to do with—"

Mack leaned forward as he stared intently into his

boss's face. He could hardly wait to share his news. The idea that Tommy wasn't here to put a damper on things was even better.

"I saw her."

Jesse's stomach turned, and his knees went weak. He knew who Mack meant. As far as his world was concerned, there was only one "her."

"Where?"

"At Melvin Call's club over on the strip. You know the one I mean."

"She was singing there?"

Mack grinned. "Hell yes, she was singing. Man, I never heard anything so sweet in my life. It's even better than on the album."

"What did she say? Where is she? Did she ask about—"

This was where it got sticky. Mack ran his hands through his hair so many times that it bushed just like his beard.

"That's just it—I didn't exactly talk to her. In fact, I'm pretty sure she didn't even see me. Hell, I was so shocked to see her that I just sat and stared. Pissed off my date big time, and it'd taken me an entire month just to get that redhead to go out with me." He grinned for effect, but it was lost on Jesse. Obviously Jesse didn't care what happened to any of Mack's dates.

Filled with frustration, Jesse started to circle Mack as one dog circles another, wanting to tear into him and yank the information out of him, yet knowing that he was going to have to wait and let Mack tell his story his own way.

"And . . ." Jesse urged.

"Oh yeah," Mack said. "So, by the time I came to my senses she was gone."

"No!" Jesse moaned, and leaned against the wall.

"It's not as bad as you think," Mack said. "I found out where she's been working. And I know where she is tonight."

Jesse jerked. The news spiked adrenaline through his system. "Okay, Mack. Talk. I can't take anymore of this suspense. Just tell me where the hell I can find my lady. You can tell me about the redhead later."

"Better yet," Mack said, "I'll show you."

The party was forgotten as they bolted for the front door. In seconds they were in Mack's car and headed for the strip. Jesse was surprised when Mack pulled off the street and turned into a parking lot ringed with security lights that lit up the lot like a night game at a baseball field.

"We're back at Melvin Call's club," Jesse said. "Did she get herself a booking here?"

"No," Mack said. "She works at a place called Dooley's over on Jefferson. When she isn't slinging drinks, she sings there too, as I understand. Tonight she's filling in for a no-show."

Jesse frowned. It sounded like nothing more than a repeat of Whitelaw's Bar back in Cradle Creek.

As soon as Mack parked, Jesse was out and heading for the door. Seconds later he made a complete turn and headed back the way he'd come.

"What's wrong?" Mack asked. "Don't you want to see her?"

"My God, yes," Jesse said, and then braced his arms on the car in front of him as he leaned forward and stared at the distorted reflection of himself in the shiny hood of the BMW. "But what if she doesn't want to see me? What if seeing me just sends her running again? I couldn't handle that, Mack. I still don't know for sure what made her leave me."

Mack nodded. He hadn't considered the ramifications of confrontation. "Maybe it was me," Mack said, facing the guilt of his earlier harassment of Diamond.

"No," Jesse said, and pushed away from the car. "You'd already made your peace with each other. And if I know one thing about that woman, she's not the kind to hold grudges. It was something . . . or someone else. Until I trust her not to run, I don't trust myself to talk to her. Understand?"

Mack nodded and sighed. "I understand . . . but man, don't you even want to see her?"

Jesse's voice shook. The look he gave Mack was desperate. "I'd give a year of my life just to see her face," he said.

"Well, hell," Mack said. "I don't think it'll cost you that much. If you'll come with me, I can fix it so you can see and hear her but she won't see you."

The office in the club was Mel's pride and joy. He'd modeled it after one he'd seen in a Las Vegas gambling casino. The carpeting was plush, the lighting subdued. And the entire west wall was one-way glass. Mel could see out, but no one could see in.

"It's all yours, buddy," Mack said. "Just lock the door so you won't be disturbed. I'm gonna go lose myself in the back of the crowd. She won't see me, I promise."

Jesse nodded, turned the lock, and then walked to the wall, staring intently down into the club below. His stomach muscles tightened as the lights dimmed, a sure sign that an entertainer was about to be announced. He tossed his hat on the chair behind him and then tried to swallow the lump in his throat.

Mel was in rare form, happy with the crowd and pleased with the world in general. He walked onstage, waving to indicate the need for silence, and then whistled loudly between his teeth to get the attention of his customers. It didn't take him long to introduce his next guest. All he had time to say was "Miss Diamond Houston," because the noise of the crowd took him off stage and brought her on.

"Ah, God."

Jesse leaned against the wall as his legs went weak. His hands splayed across the glass as he stared at the woman below. She was thinner than he remembered. And from where he stood, part of her face was in shadow. But it was Diamond. And when she laughed at something one of the customers said, he shook in fury and in shock. How could she be laughing when he'd tried so hard to die? What had he done that was so bad she'd run away and never looked back?

It took everything he had not to walk out of the office and up to that stage, carry her off into the night and to hell with why she'd ever left to begin with. But good sense overcame the urge, and so he watched and died a little in the process.

Rockabilly rhythm and toe-tapping music rocked the

room as Diamond sang. She was dressed all in black. The stage lights caught and sparkled in the rhinestones decorating the neck and shoulder of her shirt; a line of matching glitter ran the long, long length of her black pants. Silver-tipped black boots with small, shiny spurs kept time to the rhythm of the song as her fingers flew across the strings of Dooley's guitar.

> *I walked out that door and I never looked back.*
> *I took everything I needed in a brown paper sack.*
> *Didn't take what he bought, I gave everything back.*
> *All I ever need is in my brown paper sack.*

Jesse listened and stared, unable to tear his gaze away from Diamond. What was worse, the words of her song were nothing more than a reminder of what she'd done to him. She had left him without looking back. And what she owned probably had fit into a sack. Everything else she'd left behind. Of all the things that he'd endured, that had been one of the worst. Leaving what he'd given her was like throwing his love back in his face.

> *Left the love of my life, and that's a little known fact.*
> *But you can't carry love in a brown paper sack.*

Jesse listened to the words, certain that they were part of the secret. But for all the good it did him, she revealed nothing except her talent.

She looked up past the audience, smiling as her fingers strummed across the last chord. She seemed to stare straight into Jesse's eyes.

He jerked back as if the glass had suddenly become electrified. He heard nothing but the hammer of his heartbeat, felt nothing but the pain ripping through his gut, although he knew she couldn't see him.

"Damn you, lady," he whispered. "I need to be whole again, and I can't do it alone. I need you to love me . . . as much as I love you."

But there was no answer from below. She simply blinked and looked away, and the pain of her denial nearly sent him to his knees. His mind knew she couldn't see him, but his heart had forgotten. He buried his face in his hands, and when he could move, he walked away before he did something they'd both regret.

Mack was waiting for him in the parking lot. He could tell from the look on Jesse's face that seeing her had been an endurance test he'd nearly failed.

"You okay?" he asked as Jesse slid into the car.

"No," Jesse said. "But I will be, and so will she when I get her home."

Mack nodded and started the car.

"I owe you," Jesse said quietly.

"No, man," Mack said. "I owed her. I'm just payin' my debts to a lady."

Jesse inhaled deeply and leaned his head against the headrest. "Take me back to Union Station, Mack. We've got a New Year to bring in, and some pretty important resolutions to make."

"You bet," Mack said as he pulled out onto Hillsboro Drive. "And Jesse, when we get back, do you think I've got time to call that redhead? Maybe I can get to her house before the clock strikes twelve."

Jesse laughed. He was glad that some things hadn't changed. Mack couldn't help himself. He had a one-track mind.

"Hell, Mack. It's less than an hour to midnight. Do you honestly think she's sitting at home waiting on you to call?"

Mack shrugged. "I'll never know unless I try."

The assurance with which Mack spoke wiped the laughter from Jesse's face. Mack was right. Unless you tried, you'd already failed. Jesse's lips tightened into a grim line of determination. He wasn't about to give up. Not when he'd just found his reason to live.

"Whatever it takes, I'm comin' after you, girl," he said softly.

"What did you say?" Mack asked as he braked for a red light.

"Nothing," Jesse said. "Just talking to myself."

Mack nodded and accelerated into the new year.

16

"Ten . . . nine . . . eight . . . seven . . . six . . ."

Melvin Call had microphone in hand, counting down the seconds with a brimming glass of champagne as he joined the patrons of his club in ringing in the new year.

"You were great," Twila shouted above the noise as Diamond came offstage.

Diamond nodded her thanks, handed Twila her guitar, and put her hands over her ears, pantomiming her inability to hear or talk due to the racket, then made a dash toward the hallway leading to the club's office.

Twila slipped the guitar into its case and leaned it in the corner by the stage. She was more than a little surprised by Diamond's behavior. By all rights, Diamond Houston should be riding on a high that wouldn't quit. Even if part of it had to do with luck, she'd captured a prime spot in Melvin Call's show on a very special night in Nashville.

It had been bad luck for the entertainer who'd gotten

himself thrown in jail and lost his slot on the program, but it had been the best of fortune for Diamond that she'd been able to substitute. Diamond had gotten the plum job, performed like a seasoned pro, and then walked offstage as if nothing had happened.

"There's something wrong here," Twila said. "And I'm going to find out what."

"Taken' to talkin' to yourself?" Dooley asked, leaning down as he shouted in Twila's ear to be heard over the revelry.

Twila jumped. In spite of the milling crowd, she hadn't expected anyone to approach her from behind, especially Dooley Hopper.

"What are you doing here?" she asked, and then yanked him toward the hall beyond the main room so that they could continue the conversation in relative quiet.

"Caught her act," Dooley said, grinning.

"Who was minding the store at your place?" Twila asked.

"Without her, there isn't one," he said. "And from the sound of things tonight, I'd better go out and get me some new acts. I don't think my girl's gonna be playing joints like mine much longer."

Twila smiled at his possessiveness. "So you thought she was good?"

Dooley snorted. "Hell, I know she's good. It's just that now everyone else is getting the message, too. And it's about damned time. I'm tired of seeing that look on her face. Maybe if she can hit it big, she'll forget whoever it was that put out the light in her eyes."

Twila frowned. She didn't want to consider that her new client might already have personal problems before Twila had time to work through the professional ones.

"What do you mean?" she asked. "What do you know about her personal life, anyway? She hasn't volunteered a thing to me."

"Not a damned thing," Dooley said. "But she was runnin' when I hired her, and I oughta know. When I was younger, I had the same look on my own face more than once."

"Running from what?"

"I don't know for sure," Dooley said. "But I'd bet the lot it was from a man."

"I don't want to hear this," Twila said, fidgeting with an indecently large diamond on her pinky and then yanking at the jacket of her green pantsuit in frustration.

"I don't suppose you do," Dooley said. "And you didn't hear it from me—got that?"

Twila shrugged.

"Where is she, anyway?" Dooley asked.

Twila pointed down the hall. "I was going to check on her. I think she went up there. Probably to get away from the noise. Looked like she had the beginnings of a headache." And then she sighed. "After what you just told me, maybe it was more like a heartache."

Dooley headed in the direction that Twila had indicated, moving through the narrow hall and up the stairs with surprising agility for his age and size. If something was wrong with Diamond, he wanted to know.

Twila watched him go, remembering two days earlier

how excited Diamond had been that Twila was finally going to meet her boss. And Twila remembered thinking as they parked outside the disreputable building that if the boss was anything like the place, he had a lot of improving to do. But she'd had her reasons for wanting to meet Diamond's boss.

First, she wanted to meet the man who'd taken Diamond off the streets and given her a chance to survive in Nashville. Second, she wanted to know how big of a fight she was going to have on her hands when she informed said boss that he was about to be minus an employee, because Twila Hart had big plans for Diamond.

The introduction had been a surprise for them and a shock for Diamond. Diamond had watched in amazement as they'd embraced like the old friends that they were. By the time all was explained, Diamond had learned that once upon a time in Nashville, Dooley Hopper had run with the best.

He'd actually blushed and stammered when Twila informed Diamond that he'd been one of the best backup players in the business and gushed about how he could make a steel guitar cry. When Twila had questioned him about his disappearing act, he'd silenced her simply by holding up his hands and showing her the swollen joints and missing digits.

"What happened?" Twila asked.

"Too many fights and too many years," Dooley said.

It was answer enough.

By the time the "introduction" had ended, Twila had found an old friend and Dooley had faced the fact that

Diamond's days in his employment were swiftly coming to an end.

The noise filtered down to a dull roar as Diamond made her way into Melvin's office. The solitude that greeted her was almost as deafening. It forced her to face the emotions she'd been suppressing.

Her stomach was in knots, her hands sweaty from anxiety as her heart continued to rocket a pulse out of control. But she'd done it! She'd completed a performance that she'd imagined would be impossible. She hadn't been able to concentrate for days, and she'd already faced the fact that the phone call she'd made to Jesse had been a terrible mistake. It had forced her to think about the new year and her future and know that Jesse wasn't in it.

Even now, when her career seemed to be taking a turn for the better, her personal life was killing her by degrees. The only way she'd been able to walk on stage and face the crowd's merriment was to block out every thought and do what she'd done all her life: suffer the pain and ignore the regrets.

As she sang, she had watched the faces in her audience, aware that the tender and sultry looks being exchanged across tables would later result in some late-night loving. It had done nothing but remind her of her own solitary state and what she'd given up. Of all the things she regretted losing with Jesse, it was always the late-night loving that first came to mind.

She didn't even remember her final number or

walking offstage to the sound of wild applause. All she remembered was handing Twila her guitar and running for cover.

"Oh, Lord," she said, pressing shaky hands against her out-of-control heart. "Get a grip. If you can't handle pressure any better than this, you may as well go back to Cradle Creek and beg Morton Whitelaw for your old job back."

Talking to herself did little good this time except to send her toward Melvin's desk in search of a box of tissues. That was when she looked down through the glass wall and realized Melvin could see the entire club area from his office.

Diamond thought back, trying to remember if she'd noticed windows on the wall above the stage, and realized that what she'd first thought was a mirror on the upper deck of the club was in fact Melvin's one-way vision into his world.

"Well, Melvin . . . what other surprises are you hiding?" she asked, looking around the room.

A matching pair of blue and gold striped chairs sat against the wall opposite Melvin's desk. Diamond scanned the shelves above, expecting to see a hidden camera or something similar, when her gaze fell on the object lying in the chair closest the door.

Her heart thumped loudly as she caught her breath and stared. The hat's wide black brim looked too familiar to ignore.

It took three steps to reach the chair, but Diamond thought they were the longest steps she'd ever taken. She lifted the black Stetson from the cushion. It was then that her hands began to shake. She swallowed a moan and blinked rapidly against an onset of tears.

Adjusting the hatband, she gently traced the gold eagle emblem with her fingertips and knew that she could have done so in her sleep. It was that familiar. Lowering her head, she inhaled to catch a faint whiff of the same cologne she'd come to associate with the man who belonged to this hat.

And then realization hit. Wide-eyed, she faced the wall of glass, looked once again at the hat in her hand and then down at the generous view of the stage below. He must have seen her.

"Jesse?"

She clasped the hat to her breasts as her legs gave way.

Dooley found her lying in a heap with the hat beside her.

"Diamond! My God, what happened?"

His anxious shouts went unheard. Diamond's pale face was answer enough for Dooley that something was seriously wrong. Unaware of the hat's importance, he tossed it aside and lifted her from the floor.

Twila met him at the door, took one look at the unconscious woman in his arms, and pushed him back inside.

"Don't let anyone see her like this," she hissed. "It'll be all over town."

Dooley quickly obeyed and laid her on the couch in Melvin's office.

It was only moments, but it seemed forever before Diamond began to move. When the color began to flow back into her pale, cold cheeks, Twila breathed a sigh of relief.

"Honey . . . are you sick? If you need to, I'll get you to the hospital. It's not far," Dooley said.

Diamond shuddered. Dooley was the last person she'd expected to see that night. She might have been able to hide her feelings from Twila. But from Dooley, who'd proven to be more than a friend, it was impossible.

She took one look at the tender concern on his grizzly face and began to cry.

He hauled her from the couch and crushed her against the wall of his chest. "What's wrong? What happened to you?" he asked. His voice rumbled deep in his belly and vibrated against Diamond's ear as he clutched her tightly to him.

"He was here," she said, clutching the front of Dooley's jacket in desperation. "He watched me."

"Oh, hell," Twila muttered. "So there is a *he*. Damn, Dooley, you didn't have to be right."

Dooley glared at Twila and then patted Diamond's shoulders awkwardly. "I'm always right," he said. "I just don't always know it."

Twila sighed as Dooley continued his interrogation.

"Who watched you, honey? Is it someone you're afraid of? Cause if it is, you just tell me who's bothering you and I'll kill the sucker."

"He'd never hurt me," she whispered.

What she wanted was to go to bed and sleep through this lifetime until it was time to start over. She'd gotten as far in this one as she could go alone.

"Girl!" Dooley pulled her away and shook her gently.

"Get hold of yourself and talk to me. I can't help you if you don't talk."

Diamond shuddered and blinked, staring blankly at Dooley and Twila as if coming out of a trance.

"What happened?" she asked.

"I guess you fainted," Dooley said. "I found you over there by the wall."

In that instant she remembered the hat, and began to look around the room for it. When she saw it lying on the floor beside Melvin's desk, she disentangled herself from Dooley and headed for it with single-minded intent.

Puzzled by her odd behavior, Twila and Dooley watched as she picked up the hat, brushed away a speck of lint, and then carefully hung it on the knob of the chair where she'd found it.

"He'll be wanting it back," she said quietly.

"He, who?" Twila asked. And when Diamond didn't answer, she shouted. "Dammit, Diamond, if there's something in your past that's going to hurt your future, I've got to know or we may as well call it quits here and now!"

Dooley glared at Twila. "Don't be so dramatic," he said. "Hell, woman, Nashville's full of secrets. One more ain't gonna sink the ship."

"It's all right," Diamond said. "You can put your worries to rest. My past is just that—past. There's nothing left that can hurt me, at least not any more than it's already done."

"Maybe nothing can, but someone still could. Am I right?" Dooley asked.

Diamond didn't answer, but the look on her face was answer enough.

"Okay," Dooley said. "Enough for now. You come with me. I'm taking you home. You're not spending the night alone."

"I'll be fine," Diamond said. "I'm not sleeping on that lumpy couch again, and you can't because you don't fit. I'll leave with you, but you take me home, okay?"

Dooley frowned. Diamond saw the apprehension in his eyes and suspected he was afraid to say what he was thinking. She sighed, and the sound cut through both Dooley's and Twila's conscience like a sharp wind.

"I'm not going to do anything . . . *desperate*," she said, "so get those looks off your faces. If I were that kind of woman, I'd have slit my wrists six months ago. Heck, you two, I'm just starting to have fun. There's no way I'm going to miss this ride." The sarcasm with which she spoke was not lost on either of them.

Twila sighed with relief. She recognized guts when she saw them, and Diamond Houston seemed to have more than her share.

"Sounds good to me," she said. "Go home. Get some sleep. I'll call you tomorrow."

"I don't have a phone," Diamond reminded her.

"My God!" Twila said. "I can't believe you've put up with that. Everyone has a phone, and you need one too, now more than ever." Twila frowned, then bit her lip. This was as good a time as any to bring up her other decision regarding Diamond. "And another thing, I don't intend to park my car in that god-awful neighborhood any longer. Be ready to go apartment hunting tomorrow. I'll pick you up right after lunch."

"I can't afford to move."

"Yes you can," Dooley said. "I just gave you a raise."

Diamond rolled her eyes.

"You can't give her a raise," Twila said. "She's going to quit."

"I'm not quitting my job," Diamond said. "Besides, Dooley's just getting the club back on its feet."

"Oh, Lord, save me from a soft-hearted woman," Dooley said. "Hell, honey, before you came, Dooley's was just the way I liked it. That's not to say what's happened ain't better . . . it's just a lot more work." Before she could argue, he continued. "You will have to cut back at my place. Can't have you slinging no more drinks to bums like Walt and Deever, but I can still book you as a performer when I want to, can't I?" He turned to Twila. "She can sing for me anytime you don't have her booked somewhere else, and that's that."

Twila thought about it, nodded in agreement, and then added, "I love you dearly, Dooley Hopper. But your club stinks. You put out a bona fide sign and get rid of that damned door with your name peeling off in hunks, and you've got a deal."

"I already did," Dooley said.

Both women stared.

"No big deal," he said shortly. "Just my New Year's resolution. Hell, I been meaning to do it for years anyways. I just finally had the time."

Diamond smiled at the embarrassment on his face. "Take me home, Dooley Hopper. I haven't slept since last year."

He grinned. "That joke's older than you are, girl," he teased, handing her his car keys. "Go get in the truck. It's parked by the fire escape. You can't miss it. I'll be right there."

"I've got to get my guitar first," she said, and left Melvin's office without looking back.

Dooley watched her leave and then made a dash for the chair. Twila had the same idea and beat him to the chair by inches.

"Dammit, let me look," Dooley said, snatching the hat from her hand.

Twila frowned. "Maybe there's a name in the hat-band."

Dooley just shook his head and turned the gold eagle toward the light. "Don't need one," he said. "Just look."

Twila frowned. The emblem seemed familiar. "Where have I seen that?" Understanding came in a flash. "My God," she said. "Does that belong to who I think?"

"It's his, or a damned good copy," Dooley said. "What I want to know is, what's Jesse Eagle got to do with my girl?"

"Maybe she was his before she was yours," Twila said.

Dooley blanched as the implication sank in. "Even so . . . if he cared so damned much, where the hell has he been while she was starving on the streets and looking for work? Where was he when someone broke into her place and scared her half to death? Where was he?"

"Don't ask me," she said. "Ask her." Twila tossed the hat back onto the chair and shook her finger in Dooley's face. "Remember, she's moving tomorrow if I have to move her in with me."

"Fine. All I need is her address. I'm not going to lose her just because she's movin' uptown, and you'd better face that fact," he said, glaring at her.

She grinned. "Listen to us, fighting over her like two dogs worrying a bone. Maybe we should listen to Diamond for a change. What she needs is space, and we can give her that. Now take her home and see that she goes to bed. I've got some calls to make, and I don't think they can wait till tomorrow." She left without a good-bye.

Dooley took a long, last look at the black hat lying on the chair and left, shutting the door behind him.

The new sign in the window was gaudy, but Dooley liked it, and that was all that mattered. A combination of flashing red neon and bright orange bulbs that spelled *Dooley's* had replaced the peeling sign that was painted on his front door.

The old door was in the dump and the new one was in place. Dooley couldn't resist rubbing his hand over the smooth wood before he walked into the club.

Several carpenters were still inside refinishing the old flooring and adding the small stage that he'd decided to install. It was the first of his planned improvements, but not the last. In Dooley's estimation, nothing was too good for Diamond. She'd been the one to bring life back into him and his business, and he'd do whatever it took to keep her in both.

The carpenters looked up when Dooley entered and then went back to their hammering and sanding. Dooley was heading for the bar when he noticed the man sitting at the table in the corner.

"We're not open for business," Dooley said.

Jesse stood. "I didn't come here to drink."

Dooley stopped and stared. His hands curled into fists. It was an instinctive gesture, but one that Jesse didn't miss. This man was too big to argue with . . . and too old to fight.

"Please," Jesse said. "And in private."

Dooley walked toward his office, leaving Jesse to follow if he chose. Jesse entered and closed the door behind him. For a moment, the two men did nothing but stare. Jesse was the first to speak.

"I guess you know who I am," he said.

"Yeah," Dooley said. "I think you're the bastard that broke Diamond's heart."

Jesse blanched. "Then you *do* know her." He dropped into the chair behind him and wiped a shaky hand across his face. "Thank God."

Dooley frowned. This wasn't the reaction he'd expected. Maybe apologies, maybe excuses, but not overwhelming, gut-wrenching relief.

"I know Diamond Houston," Dooley admitted. "But what I don't know is what she is to you."

Jesse stood. "She's my life, man. And I've been looking for her for so long I'd almost given up hope of finding her."

Dooley's jaw dropped. "You didn't dump her?"

Jesse shook his head. "Hell, no. One day she just . . .

she . . ." He swallowed, trying to get out the words that stuck in his throat. "She packed her things while I was gone and disappeared without a trace."

Dooley frowned. "She didn't leave a note or nothin'? That don't sound like my girl." He suspected Jesse Eagle might be lying to cover his own betrayal.

It was hard for Jesse to hear another man claim any kind of relationship to Diamond, although he knew that when Dooley had befriended her, he'd probably saved her sanity, too.

"Oh, she left me a note," Jesse said. "It said, 'Be happy.'"

Then Jesse laughed, and Dooley shuddered. It was the farthest sound from joy he'd ever heard.

"Is she well?" Jesse asked. "She hasn't been sick, has she? She looks thinner, and her eyes seem—"

"She knows you saw her," Dooley said.

Jesse grew still. The look on his face was the proof Dooley'd been waiting to see. If ever a man was in want over a woman, this one was.

"How? I was so damned careful. I was afraid if she saw me that she'd just run again before I found out why."

Dooley pointed to the hat Jesse was wearing. "You need to take better care of that. I found her on the floor in Melvin Call's office with it in her hand."

Jesse stared down at the hat Melvin had returned by special messenger. Dismay overwhelmed him. Everything was only getting worse. "On the floor?"

"Fainted, I guess," Dooley said. "She was lying by the glass wall in Mel's office."

"Oh, Jesus. I can't . . . I didn't mean . . ." Jesse slumped against Dooley's desk. "What the hell am I going to do? I can't live without that woman, and I don't know for sure why she left me." His voice shook. "Do you understand what I'm saying to you? As God is my witness, I'd die for her tomorrow. The last thing I want to do is hurt her. I love her."

"Then that's enough reason for me to tell you that I think she's still in love with you," Dooley said. He jabbed his finger gently in Jesse's chest as he added, "But as God is *my* witness, if you hurt her again, I'll kill you."

Jesse nodded and offered his hand. "Fair enough."

Dooley reached out, wrapped his huge, beefy grip around Jesse's palm, and shook his hand. More than a vow passed between them that day.

"Diamond's gone and got herself a manager. But that's for business. This is personal. I could talk to her myself, if you want to set up a meeting or something," Dooley said. "I can promise you she won't run. I won't let her. I did too much of that myself in my younger days, and I'm here to say it don't solve a thing."

It didn't take Jesse long to decide. "No. As much as I want to see her, for now it's enough to know that she's being taken care of. There are a few more things I need to find out before I confront her and her manager. Who is he, anyway?"

"Ain't a he, it's a she. Twila Hart. Know her?"

Jesse nodded. "Got a good reputation, which is more than I can say for some."

Dooley didn't like what he was hearing. Secrets

didn't do anything but hurt people. "So, what do you need to find out before you talk to Diamond again? What could possibly be so important that you two can't work it out together?"

Jesse shoved his hands in his pockets, debating with himself about how far he could trust this man.

Maybe it was the missing little finger on Dooley's left hand, or the scar below his lower lip that nearly disappeared into his double chin. And maybe it was just the fierce look Dooley got in his eyes whenever Diamond's name was mentioned. Either way, once Jesse found himself talking he couldn't seem to stop.

"I need to find out about the demo she cut for Tommy. Find out if what he told me about the contract they never got around to signing was the truth. See who was really responsible for her name being left off the album. Several times I started to just reveal the whole damn mess and hope the media would help me find her, but I was scared that the fire I would start by revealing the deception might somehow burn her instead."

Dooley's stomach turned. This was uglier than he'd expected. She hadn't just run from love. She'd been on the run from deceit and betrayal.

"I don't like what you're saying," Dooley said. "She made an album with you? How come I don't know nothing about—" Realization suddenly dawned on him. The mystery woman on Jesse Eagle's new album was Diamond!

"Don't even ask," Jesse said. "And as for explaining the mess, if I knew how it happened, I'd be the first one to talk."

Dooley frowned but decided for the moment to give him the benefit of the doubt. "Who's Tommy?" he asked.

Jesse looked away. For a long moment he didn't speak. And then when he did, the guilt was evident on his face.

"My manager. I trusted him. I'm still not sure if I should have."

Dooley cursed. "Well, you keep him away from Diamond. I won't have her hurt again."

"Why do you think I haven't faced her before now? You think I haven't thought the same thing a thousand times? I've got to be sure that when I take her back into my life she'll be safe."

Dooley nodded. "There's one way."

"What?" Jesse asked. "I'm open to suggestions."

"We could just kill the bastard and be done with it."

"Don't tempt me, and don't think I haven't considered it." The expression on Jesse's face was as grim as his voice. "But it wouldn't fix what's already broken, and I'm still not sure how much he's really involved. I need Diamond to tell me. I won't believe anyone else, ever. For now, just take care of her. I'll do the rest. And one more thing. I'm asking that you don't tell anybody about the album until I let you know."

Dooley nodded. "You've got a deal."

Jesse walked away without looking back.

And for the first time since he'd hired her, he faced the fact that Diamond didn't belong—and had never belonged—to him.

17

Twila hung up the phone and stared at the collage of pictures on the wall opposite her desk. But she wasn't focusing on the images, she was lost in thought from what Dooley had just told her.

"So . . . Jesse Eagle. It *was* you," she said.

She dropped her pen, turned off the desk light, and grabbed her purse as she headed for the door. If what Dooley had told her was anywhere close to the truth, the betrayal of Diamond had been carefully finessed. It didn't surprise her. Diamond wouldn't have been the first starry-eyed performer to come to Nashville and make all the wrong choices.

Only this time things were a little bit different. If Jesse was to be believed, someone had been operating for her on his behalf and had simply made no choices at all, leaving her to assume that she'd failed for lack of talent.

Twila fumed. If anyone had talent, it was Diamond

Houston. She just couldn't figure out why Diamond hadn't complained. Most women she knew would have been crying aloud to anyone who'd listen about how they'd been betrayed. And about half of them would already have lawsuits pending. Something else was going on here, and she was determined to find it out.

She turned north toward Jefferson Street with trepidation. The last place she wanted to be was back in that part of town. But it was the only place she was going to get answers.

Diamond was nearly finished packing. Her few belongings fit easily into the six boxes sitting in the middle of her living room floor. She looked around, checking to make sure she'd left nothing behind. When she was certain that everything that mattered had been packed away she dropped down onto the bed with a sigh.

In a strange way, this shabby, two-room apartment on the wrong side of town had become home as Jesse's place had never been. This was where she'd learned that she could depend on herself and survive—where she'd come to terms with the fact that she was never going to get over Jesse, but if she was careful, she just might be able to live without him.

Diamond kicked her toe against the brightly patterned rug beneath the bed and smiled. She could just imagine the expression on Twila's face when she learned she wasn't leaving Dooley's gift behind. The drapes would have to stay, though. Diamond was certain that wherever Twila took her, the windows would already be covered.

A series of sharp knocks on her door sent her running to answer. She didn't have to open it to know that it was Twila, because she could hear her grumbling clear out in the hall.

"About time," Twila said as Diamond opened the door. She looked around and smiled with satisfaction as she realized Diamond was already packed. "Didn't waste any time, did you?" she asked.

"Didn't have any to waste," Diamond said.

Twila grinned. "From the start I knew we were going to get along. I love it when I'm right. Let's go apartment hunting. We can send for this stuff later."

Diamond shrugged into her coat and slung her purse over her shoulder. "After you."

They hadn't gone far when Twila began to talk. It was such a subtle interrogation that at first, Diamond wasn't even aware of it. The questions seemed innocent, natural things that new friends or partners would discuss. But it soon became apparent to Diamond that Twila was in possession of certain information and was determined to get it verified.

"So . . . how long had you been in Nashville when Dooley hired you?" Twila asked.

Diamond shrugged, and what she said wasn't actually a lie. "Not long. Maybe a few weeks."

Twila frowned as she negotiated a turn. "So you came straight from—where was it?—Cradle Creek to Nashville?"

"Almost," Diamond said. *Give or take a few months.*

"Ever sing anyplace else before you started at Dooley's?"

"Not for pay," Diamond said. The album was making a fortune, but not for her. "Back in Cradle Creek, I sang at Whitelaw's Bar for tips. But that was only on weekends. The rest of the time I was slinging drinks to miners who should have spent their pay on something else besides Morton's watered-down booze."

Twila grinned. "You were just paying your dues like every other singer in town before they hit it big. They've either done the same or wound up washing dishes somewhere to keep from starving to death. You were on the right track and didn't even know it, girl."

Diamond returned the smile. "I guess."

"Well, we need to think about cutting a demo, and then I'll start pitching it. I have a feeling it won't take long to get some interesting feedback." Twila held her breath, waiting to see how Diamond would react to her announcement.

Diamond shook her head. "Don't be so sure. I already cut one demo and no one seemed to be—" She caught herself, but it wasn't in time to stop Twila from jumping on the information.

Twila's resolve deepened. What Dooley told her had been right! She was determined to find out as much as she could. "Did you set it up all by yourself?" she asked.

Diamond sighed. There were some things Twila needed to know. After all, she *was* her manager.

"Not entirely," she said.

"Care to tell me who did?"

"Not particularly."

"Dammit! How am I going to help you if you don't talk?" Twila's anger was all-consuming. She slammed on her brakes, pulled off the street into the first parking space available, and then killed the engine. She turned in the seat and fixed a pointed stare on Diamond.

"All right! I've had about enough. Something's wrong, and you and I both know it. You hardly ever laugh when you're not on stage. You passed out holding that damned black hat and then came to as close-mouthed as a nun doing penance. You tell me you cut a demo, but you don't want to tell me what happened to it. That's it, girl. Talk, and I mean now."

"What do you want me to say?" Diamond yelled. "That I was a fool for trusting a man when I should have trusted my instincts instead? That I loved him too much to see past the end of his arms, and that I'm going to pay for that for the rest of my life?"

Tears were streaming down Diamond's face as Twila watched and listened. She was sorry that her outburst had caused Diamond misery, but it was better now than later.

"No, honey," Twila said, reaching out and patting her hand. "But you've got to see I need to know more than you've been willing to tell. Don't you?"

Diamond shuddered. She leaned against the head-rest and covered her face with her hands. "Oh, God. I don't know anything anymore," she said. "All I know is, I'm trying to live without him and I can't find a way."

Twila nodded. "That's why you have me," she said. "Between the two of us, we will. Now, time's wasting. Let's go find you a new place to live. We'll worry about the elusive man in your life later."

Diamond sat silently as Twila chauffeured her across

Nashville. She didn't have the strength to do anything more. Three hours later Twila was on the phone, hiring a mover to bring Diamond's meager belongings to her new home.

"You're going to love it here," Twila said. "It's close to a mall and close to me."

Diamond looked around at the large, airy room and into the adjoining kitchen, wiggled her toes in the soft blue carpeting, and then ran her fingers lightly along the heavy white drapes. "It's fine," she said. "But I'm not real crazy about the carpet in the bedroom. I think I'll put down the rug Dooley gave me instead."

Twila rolled her eyes. "I don't care what you do with that thing, as long as it's out of sight. In the bedroom will be fine. No one will see it except you." Then she grinned. "And, knowing men as I do, if one makes it that far, he won't be looking at the floor coverings. He'll be looking at you."

The smile disappeared from Diamond's face. There was only one man she wanted in her bed, and that was about as likely to happen as world peace.

Twila bit her lip, wishing she could take back what she'd said, but as usual it was too late. "So, now that we have you settled, let's go to dinner. My treat. We'll celebrate your new place, your new life . . ." Some instinct made her add, ". . . and old memories. Especially the ones worth keeping."

Diamond smiled through tears. "Thanks for understanding," she said. "Where are we going? How do I dress?"

"Dress up or down. Where we're going, it won't matter. Ever been to The Stockyards?"

"No. I thought we were going to eat, not sell cattle."

Twila laughed. "Your stuff will be here in about an hour. When you've gotten changed, give me a call and I'll pick you up. And you better be good and hungry. They put out a spread there you wouldn't believe."

"I don't have a phone," Diamond reminded her.

"You do now," Twila said, handing her a small, black, cellular model with the antenna already extended. "Your own will be installed tomorrow. Use mine for now, and just bring it with you tonight."

Diamond grinned. "You never give up, do you?"

"No. And for your sake, you'd do well to remember that."

Twila left, and Diamond settled down in her new apartment to wait for her boxes to arrive.

She stared down at the phone in her lap, lightly touched the keys that would have dialed Jesse's number, and then quickly set it aside before she could follow through on her impulse. There was no place for old love in her new life.

"I've got to get you out of my mind. Going back wouldn't solve anything. It would simply be a replay of everything that went wrong," Diamond whispered as she traced and retraced the number at his home.

But Jesse was nowhere around to hear or question the conviction of her vow to herself. And Diamond would soon learn the difference between saying and doing.

∘   ∘   ∘

"Wow!"

There was nothing left for Diamond to say as they were escorted to their table. The Stockyard was everything Twila had promised and more. It was an eclectic mix of antique and elegant, of fine linen and old floors, of new patrons and old company. What had once been the offices of cattle buyers from all over the country were now unique, intimate dining rooms. The owners had managed to retain enough of the old charm and had added enough of the new for comfort and convenience.

The courses were as plentiful as the servings, and Diamond leaned back with a smile on her face as she rubbed her midriff and politely refused the dessert tray that was offered.

"I would have been full if I'd quit on the first course," Diamond said, remembering the thick, hearty vegetable-beef soup. "But no—I made a pig of myself and finished it off as well as the salad that came next, and then the steak and vegetables. It was too much—and so good."

Twila grinned. "Sometimes we need to pamper ourselves. If you don't know that, you'll learn."

"Being pampered was the last thing on my mind when I was growing up," Diamond said. "Staying ahead of the bill collectors and social workers was more like it."

Twila's eyebrows rose a fraction. But it was the only indication of her surprise that Diamond had actually volunteered something about her earlier life.

"So, did you move around a lot when you were growing up?"

Diamond nodded. "About four or five times a year

until I was, oh, maybe eight or nine. That was when Johnny landed in Cradle Creek. I don't know whether he just ran out of money, got tired of moving, or actually got an attack of conscience for dragging us over half the country."

"Johnny?"

"My father. We never called him anything else. He was always Johnny. I don't know why, he just was." Diamond tried hard not to think about the last time she'd seen him, and the white pine casket, and the rough clods of dirt that had shattered on impact when the gravediggers had begun covering it up.

"I hate to keep asking, but I don't know any other way to get answers." Twila smiled to lessen the inquisitive turn their conversation had taken. "Who's the 'we' you keep talking about?"

Diamond smiled. "My sisters. There were three of us. I was the middle child, although I can honestly say I never felt left out. There was never enough to go around, so we were all in the same boat."

"What about your mother? You never mention her."

Diamond looked down at the napkin in her lap and then back up at Twila without flinching. "I barely remember her. She walked out on Johnny when Lucky and I were just babies. Queen raised all of us, including herself."

Twila grinned. "Queen? Diamond? Lucky? What's the deal?"

Diamond shrugged. "Johnny was a gambler by profession. He couldn't have done any other kind of work and survive. But he did have a particular love for cards.

And he did—in his own way—love us. I guess he thought it was only fitting that he combine the two."

"You took after your—after Johnny, didn't you?"

Diamond gawked. She was so thunderstruck by Twila's calm assumption that she had a difficult time finding the words to answer her. "Lord, no!" she finally said. "Why would you think something like that?"

Twila shrugged. "It just seemed obvious. Johnny gambled with money, you're gambling for fame. I don't see much difference."

Diamond was silent for so long, Twila feared she'd offended her. But in fact, it was just the opposite. When she finally looked up, the smile on her face was one Twila would have given a year off her life to have captured and slapped on an album cover. Her green eyes were shining, and they set off that beautiful face of hers to perfection. Her smile was wide and easy, as if she'd been loved too long and set loose to rest.

"You know what, Twila Hart? You're right, and I never knew it. It's a strange sort of comfort to know that I brought a part of Johnny with me after all."

"When you get rich and famous, you can go back and thumb your nose at the lot," Twila said. "All those bill collectors and social workers and such."

"I won't ever be going back to Cradle Creek," Diamond said. "Johnny's dead, and my sisters are gone. All I can hope for is that someday we'll find each other again. For now, just knowing they love me is enough."

Before she inadvertently opened up another painful subject, Twila decided to call for the check. It was time to go home.

They were on their way out the door when a woman's cry stopped them in place and sent Diamond whirling around with a look of panic on her face.

"Oh, my God! Al! It's Di!"

Rita Barkley made a dash for the tall blonde going out the door. The woman's soft, brown-suede pantsuit was tailored to fit her tall frame and much more elegant than the denim she usually wore, but Rita would have known her anywhere. She clamped a hand on Diamond's elbow and held on for dear life.

"Diamond, honey! Where have you been? We've looked all over Nashville for you."

Diamond's heart sank. Of all the people to see, this was close to the worst. Rita had been a friend, and explaining in front of the curious bystanders was going to be impossible.

"Introduce me, Diamond," Twila said.

Diamond wanted to run. This kept getting worse. "Twila Hart, I'd like you to meet Rita Barkley and her husband, Al. Rita, this is Twila Hart, my new manager."

Twila nodded in greeting, recognizing Al as one of the members of Jesse Eagle's band, Muddy Road.

Rita threw her arms around Diamond and began to cry. "I don't know whether I'm happy or sad," she said. "But I do know someone who's going to—"

"Don't!"

Diamond's sharp cry stopped her and froze everyone in place as they watched the distress sweeping across her face.

"We need to talk," Rita said, refusing to give up on the fact that she'd just found the woman Jesse had lost.

"Rita, don't push your nose into places it don't belong," Al warned. Then he couldn't help himself from hugging Diamond gently. "We miss you, girl. *All* of us."

Diamond shook her head and blinked back tears. "I miss you too, all of *you*."

Twila knew that the reunion had staggered Diamond. She could see Diamond's panic spreading, but Rita Barkley was obviously not to be dissuaded.

"When you disappeared Jesse nearly went crazy," Rita said. "We couldn't find him for more than a week— and then when we did, we almost wished we hadn't looked. I thought he was going to lose his mind. Why didn't you call? What happened?"

Diamond moaned and buried her face in her hands. She couldn't bear to think of the pain she'd caused him. Twila pulled her outside, away from the people in the foyer. They were entirely too interested in the conversation.

As Twila expected, Rita and Al followed. They made it down the steep column of steps, and then Twila pulled Diamond into the shadows, away from prying eyes. Falling apart in a public place made bad press.

Diamond knew what she was about to do was only going to cause more pain, but she couldn't stop herself. "Is Jesse all right?" she asked, and then turned away in embarrassment as a sob burned her throat. It hurt even to say his name.

Al nodded as he slipped an arm around her shoulders. "Good enough, honey," he said. "In fact, ever since New Year's Eve, he's been close to his old self again."

Diamond laughed, and the sound split the silence of

the night. Twila shuddered. She remembered too well Diamond's reaction to the fact that Jesse had seen her performance at Melvin Call's club.

"And how's . . . is everyone else all right?" Diamond asked.

Twila felt there was more than common courtesy behind the question. From the expression on Al's face, she knew she was right.

"Everyone is about as you'd expect," Al said. "Mack's still chasin' women, and Tommy . . . well, Tommy's the same, too. And honey, we was all real sorry about the mess with the album. No one was madder than Jesse. Him and Tommy had a hell of a fight."

Diamond turned away. It was just as she feared. Nothing had changed.

"It's cold," Rita said, and shivered in the January wind. "Come back to our place. We can talk."

Diamond shook her head. "Thanks, but no. Enough's been said as it is."

Rita panicked. "Where do you live? How can I find you again? You know that Jesse will—"

"Don't tell him," Diamond begged. "Please, Rita, if you were ever my friend, don't tell him you saw me." Her chin quivered, and she bit the inside of her lip to keep from crying. "I don't have the strength to leave again."

"That's just it," Rita said. "I don't know why you left in the first place. He'd have done anything for you, and you know it."

"There's a lot you don't know. But take my word for it, I did what was right, and there's no going back."

Rita began to cry. "I don't understand. But I'll do as you ask. Only for Pete's sake, call me sometime."

Diamond turned away without answering and hurried toward Twila's car. Twila followed, afraid that if she didn't, Diamond might never stop running.

She got her inside the car and started the engine, shivering from cold as the heater kicked in and slowly began to warm the car's interior.

"Nothing like a little music to soothe the old nerves," Twila said, and punched a button on the console. It was probably the worst move she'd ever made in her life.

Jesse Eagle's voice came through the speakers in a soft, coaxing tone as he pled for forgiveness and another chance. The voice of the woman who answered, singing her reply in clear tones, echoed inside the car's small interior. And then the announcer's voice interrupted.

"And that, country music fans, was the title song and the biggest hit from Jesse Eagle's new album, *Lies*."

"Oh, God," Diamond said, and buried her face in her hands. It was the last straw. She began to cry.

Twila stared. It was all she could do. Something Al had said only moments earlier began to click. Something about the mess with the album, and how mad Jesse had been. She gasped and shut off the radio. In the silence that engulfed them, there was nothing but the sound of Diamond's soft sobs and Twila's swift intake of breath. Dooley hadn't told her everything.

"It's you! You're the mystery woman on Jesse Eagle's album, aren't you?"

Diamond shuddered and wiped her face with her hands, futiley trying to gain control of her emotions. All she could do was stare blindly out into the darkness and wish that she could start over, beginning with the night Jesse had walked into their house in Cradle Creek and taken her away.

Twila persisted. "Why? What happened?"

Diamond's answer shocked and silenced her. "Ask Tommy Thomas," she said. "He was the one who was supposed to be taking care of my career."

About fifteen blocks later, when Twila could talk without cursing, she said, "And don't think I won't."

Diamond shrugged. Too much had happened, and she was too tired to care.

Twila had done some checking, mostly on the quiet, and it had paid off. She was holding some of the most explosive information in the industry and had no intention of letting it ruin any more of Diamond Houston's life.

She parked her car in the lot of the recording studio and got out. Had anyone cared to notice, her stride toward the door was warning enough that she was about to go into battle. She hit the glass entry with the flat of her hand and grimaced with satisfaction as it popped sharply against the inside wall.

The receptionist looked up, startled at the sudden noise, and frowned.

"May I help you?" she asked.

Twila slipped out her card and leaned forward across the desk. "I'm here to see Larry Tudor."

The receptionist looked at the card and then back up at the woman. "Ms. Hart? Do you have an appointment?"

"No," Twila said. "But I don't think it's going to matter. I want to speak to the studio manager—now."

"I'm sorry, but you have to have an appointment. I'd be happy—"

"You'll be a lot happier if I don't have to shout," Twila said, smiling coldly. "Now please pick up the phone and ask Larry if he's willing to talk to me. Tell him it's about Diamond Houston's demo."

The receptionist frowned and did as she was asked, hoping that Larry would come out and deal with the woman himself. Aggressive women were beyond her expertise.

Mere seconds passed before the door flew open and Larry Tudor came bursting through. He half expected to be facing a swarm of lawyers and a couple of cops. That he saw only one angry woman was nothing if not a relief.

"Ms. Hart? Twila Hart? I've heard of you. It's a pleasure to meet you."

"I hope you'll think so after our conversation. Is there somewhere we can talk?"

Larry quickly complied, and less than an hour later Twila emerged with the missing digital copy of Diamond's demo safely stuffed in the depths of her purse. She wasn't sure what it was going to take, but if it took her a lifetime, she was going to make Tommy Thomas pay.

Larry Tudor would go home that night a relieved and lighthearted man, satisfied that his part in something ugly had ended in a most satisfying manner.

Twila headed for Dooley's to get Diamond. They had a layout to shoot and no time to waste. Twila was a woman on a mission.

"Put down that tray," she yelled as she entered the club. "Go wash your face and comb your hair, woman. You're going to have your picture taken." And then she grinned impishly at the shocked expressions on Diamond's and Dooley's faces.

"Why?" Diamond asked.

"Because I need them," Twila said. "Don't argue with your manager. It's a futile waste of breath."

But Diamond stuck her ground. She was new at the game, but not so naive she didn't know what was going on.

"I can't afford to have professional portraits done," she said, then glared at Dooley before he could open his mouth. He grinned and then turned away, willing to admit defeat.

"I'm footing the bill," Twila said, and then added, "but only for now. I'll reimburse myself when you make your first million."

Diamond rolled her eyes. "You've both taken leave of your senses. I may be green when it comes to this business, but I know this isn't normal protocol. What's the deal, Twila? Don't try and tell me you pay for all your clients' promotions before they've even got a foot in the door."

Twila's eyes turned cold. "No, I don't normally do this much," she said. "But I also don't normally come across such illegal, back-stabbing behavior from one of my own. Most of the kids who come to Nashville have a dream, and few ever see it come true. But I'd like to think it's because of a true lack of talent or not enough luck. I'd like to think that what happened to you was the exception rather than the rule."

Diamond turned away, embarrassed by Twila's

generosity, and in some way feeling guilty that she'd been unable to prevent what had happened.

"Okay. So today I take pictures. What do we do tomorrow?"

Twila laughed. Dooley pulled Diamond off her feet and danced her around the floor, laughing uproariously at her cheeky response to Twila's statement.

"We give 'em hell, honey. We give 'em hell," Twila said.

18

The early-morning sun slid through the half-open blinds on Jesse's bedroom windows, casting light across his back and legs as he slept. Muscles across his shoulders and down his arms twitched as he reached out in his dream toward a woman who wasn't there.

Outside, the wind whistled through the trees as a reminder that winter still existed beyond the warmth of his house. But Jesse was unaware of his uncovered state or the weather. He was dreaming of a woman with long blonde hair and wide green eyes who sang like an angel and made love with unequaled passion.

The strident summons of the telephone beside his bed brought Jesse into reality with a jerk. He rolled and grabbed for the receiver, and his unused voice came out in a growl as he answered.

"Hello?"

"Hey, Jesse! It's me! Tommy. I've got some papers you need to sign as well as a few items we need to clear up. Have you got time to come in, or do you want me to come out?"

"You come out."

Tommy rolled his eyes and mouthed a curse Jesse didn't hear. "No problem," he answered, lying through his teeth about the inconvenience of having to drive out of the city on a cold, blustery day. "I'll see you shortly."

"Give me an hour," Jesse said. "You woke me up." He hung up before Tommy had time to argue.

Tommy uttered the curse he'd been thinking as the call disconnected in his ear. Patting his pockets, he cursed again as he realized he'd forgotten to buy cigarettes. The thought of facing Jesse weakened his resolve to quit, and he made a mental note to buy a pack on his way out of town.

He knew there was no use prolonging this meeting. He'd been dreading it ever since he'd sobered up enough to remember what had happened between them on New Year's Eve. The passing of weeks since had not alleviated the weight of guilt.

Tommy gathered the papers he intended to take, including the special folder he'd pulled earlier from his files, and headed for the door. Since he had an hour to kill, there was no reason not to treat himself to a hearty breakfast. Ham, biscuits, and red-eye gravy sounded too good to pass up, and he knew just the place to get all three.

Henley opened the door to Jesse's room carrying a tray of hot coffee and biscuits still warm from the oven.

"I knew you were awake," Henley said. "I heard the phone, but you answered it before I could get to it."

Jesse swiped his hand across his face and sat up in bed. "What's this?" he muttered, waving at the tray in Henley's hands. "I'm not sick. Why breakfast in bed?"

"Why not?" Henley asked, and waited for Jesse to pull up the covers before he lowered the tray.

In spite of his bad temper and the rude awakening he'd suffered, Jesse grinned. It was impossible to argue with a man like Joe Henley.

"Why not, indeed, Henley." His face creased into a wide, almost boyish grin as he reached for the tray. "Just make damn sure you don't let this get around."

"Of course not, sir," Henley said, allowing himself a small smile. "Will there be anything else?"

"Tommy's on his way out with some papers. But he won't be staying for lunch." Jesse grinned. "Mainly because I didn't ask him."

"Good," Henley said, then had the grace to blush. "I mean—"

Jesse grinned again. "Don't make it worse by trying to explain yourself," he said. "Believe me, I understand. I don't know why, but Tommy has an awful time winning friends. He's a lot better at making enemies."

Henley left Jesse to his breakfast before he could make another faux pas regarding his employer's business associates.

Jesse lifted the heavy crockery mug and gratefully inhaled the coffee aroma, allowing its essence to tantalize his senses before taking a sip. He remembered how Diamond had raced for the coffee pot each morning, unwilling to communicate until she'd had that first cup. He tried to smile at the memory, but it wasn't worth the effort. All he could manage was a long, deep swallow that was too hot for comfort.

Tommy knocked. Expecting Jesse to answer, he instinctively took a step backward. When the door swung open, Tommy was so happy to see Henley that he overdid his welcome.

"Henley! How ya' been doin', old buddy?"

From the look on Henley's face, it would have been obvious to a fool that Tommy was not one of Henley's buddies.

"Mr. Eagle is waiting for you in the music room," Henley said, and walked away, leaving Tommy to close the door behind him and make his own way to Jesse. Henley could hardly bear to look at the man he considered responsible for Diamond's departure.

There was no way to make this easier, and Tommy knew it. He hitched up his pants, stuffed his Stetson tighter onto his head, and headed down the hall. The heels of his boots clicked forcefully against the shiny wood floor, announcing his arrival in staccato time.

Jesse was on the window seat, the guitar resting in his lap as he picked across the strings and hummed softly to himself. The sunlight coming through the mullioned windowpanes ricocheted off the instrument's metal plates and into Tommy's eyes as he walked into the room, momentarily blinding him to the frown that Jesse wore at the interruption. By the time Tommy's vision had cleared, so had Jesse's expression.

"Hard at it, I see," Tommy said. "It sounded good, Jess. Maybe it'll be your next big hit."

Jesse shrugged. "Just fiddlin' around," he said. "It needs a lot of work."

The encounter was strained. Their curt formality did not ease the way for anything further, and so for several moments the two men simply looked at one another, remembering their last meeting. Tommy fidgeted as Jesse stared. Finally, it was Tommy who broke the silence.

"I have something you'll be interested in seeing," he said, handing Jesse a thick manila folder.

Jesse laid aside his guitar and opened the folder. It didn't take him long to realize that Tommy had finally followed through on one of his requests regarding Diamond Houston. It was the account Jesse had ordered him to open and the record of deposits made to it on a regular basis.

"Looks good, doesn't it?" Tommy said.

Jesse nodded. "Yes, Tommy, it really does," he said. "But the question still remains, how do you propose to distribute it? It's one thing for Diamond to be accumulating all this. It's another to be able to spend it."

Tommy flushed. "I've been thinking about hiring a private detective. What do you think?"

Jesse frowned. "I would have thought a lot more of it if you'd mentioned it sooner—say, several months ago." He stood, placed the folder on the seat behind him, and walked to his desk. "What was it you needed me to sign?" he asked.

Tommy stared. He'd expected more of a reaction

from Jesse than this. Gut instinct told him that Jesse was holding something back.

"Uh . . . just these endorsements," he said, and flipped open the proper pages for Jesse's signature. He paced as Jesse read and signed the papers. Finally, his curiosity got the better of him. "So . . . what do you think we should do? About Diamond, I mean."

Jesse signed on the last page and handed the stack of papers back to Tommy.

"Nothing."

It wasn't what Tommy had expected him to say. But hope sprang in him as he asked, "Does this mean you've come to your senses about her?"

Jesse grinned, and the hair stood on the back of Tommy's neck. "I never lost my senses, buddy," Jesse said. "I just lost my woman."

Tommy began to get nervous. This quiet man with the cool, calm demeanor wasn't the Jesse who'd ranted and raved and then withdrawn from the human race.

"Yeah, I know . . . and I'm real sorry about that," Tommy said. "But you know, maybe someday she'll turn up and—"

"Maybe she will," Jesse said. "Maybe she will. I'll be in touch, Tommy. Let yourself out, will you? I'm kinda anxious to get back to this melody before I lose it."

"Yeah . . . sure! Don't want that old creative genius of yours to get away, do we?"

But Tommy got no answer from Jesse other than a slow, almost secretive smile. In response he felt a wrench in his gut that stayed with him long after he'd left Jesse's house.

After Tommy left Jesse didn't pick up his guitar but made a phone call instead.

"Hey, buddy, it's me, Jesse. Long time no see." Jesse traced a pattern on the desktop as he listened to the man's smalltalk. Finally he interrupted him. "Say—remember that favor you owe me? Well I'm callin' it in. I want you to call this number and invite Diamond Houston to perform. I know you've never heard her name, but whether you realize it or not, you've heard her sing. Don't ask questions, just do me this favor. You won't regret it, I promise."

He gave the man Twila's number and then disconnected, stared off into space for a long moment before picking up his guitar, all the while telling himself that he wasn't meddling, he was just fixing what Tommy had broken—and fulfilling a promise.

"Twila Hart?"

Twila looked up from the stack of papers on her desk and stared straight into a cocky grin and more hair than a man had a right to have.

"Yes, I'm Twila Hart."

"Good," the young man said. "Sign here, please."

Twila signed on the dotted line, accepted a large brown envelope, and then watched the man with more than passing interest. He couldn't have been more than twenty-one, if that, and he had a terrific body, blue eyes that didn't miss a thing, and a glorious mane of wavy black hair.

"What's your name?" she asked.

"Quint, ma'am," he said, and smiled as he leaned across her desk to give her a closer look at how blue his eyes truly were.

My God . . . dimples, too. "So, Quint, when you're not delivering packages, what do you do? I don't suppose you're a singer?" Twila could just picture what women would do at the sight of this man on stage.

"No, ma'am, I don't sing. But I sure can make the women sing—for joy, if you know what I mean." He grinned wider. "I don't suppose you'd be interested?"

"I don't suppose," Twila said, unable to hide a grin of her own. "I don't go to bed with men who call me 'ma'am.'" She laughed aloud at the look of dismay crossing his face. "Just for future reference, sonny, you might try substituting the word *lady*, or possibly *honey*. It would cover any span of years in a woman's life without calling attention to the lack of your own."

"Yes, ma'am," Quint said, and then blushed as he realized he'd done it again. "I mean—"

"Never mind," Twila said, and began digging in her purse for a tip.

"Forget the money . . . honey," Quint said, quickly regaining his swagger. "Your advice was worth more than any tip. You take it easy now, you hear?"

Twila laughed as the messenger disappeared. It was the first real break in an otherwise gloomy day. Remembering the envelope, she tore into it, absently flipping through the pages and then frowning as she realized their implications.

"Well I'll be . . ." The enclosed letter said it all.

Ms. Hart . . . I don't know you except by reputation.

Diamond Houston has every reason not to trust another living soul, but I know for a fact that she trusts you. That's all the reason I need. I'm asking you to see this gets where it belongs. Suffice to say that I will explain more later. It is enough to know that someone is taking care of my lady.

There was no signature. But none was needed. Twila couldn't believe what she was seeing. She picked up the phone, dialed, and when she received an answer, asked for the bank's bookkeeping department. After giving the teller the correct information, she had all the verification she needed.

"Well, well, Diamond girl," Twila said to herself. "It seems you're not as hard-up as you thought. And whatever happened between you and Jesse Eagle, it looks like he's trying to do the right thing by you."

Twila stared into space. She had a suspicion that things were about to go their way. And when the phone rang and the caller identified himself, she knew it.

Diamond stuffed the broom back into the closet and tossed her apron on the counter. The glare from Dooley's newly installed sign outside came through the window, mirroring an orange and red reflection in the beads of water drying on top of the freshly washed bar, giving the old, scarred top an oddly elegant look.

"I'm leaving," she yelled, and then waited for Dooley to come barreling out of the storage room. She didn't have long to wait.

"You're through already?" Dooley asked, grunting as

he squeezed through the door with a case of whiskey in his arms.

Diamond nodded. "I had to hurry. Twila called. She's picking me up."

"What for?" Dooley asked.

She shrugged. "I have no idea, but she seemed excited. I don't know whether to go with the flow or get nervous. All this is still a little bit too much to believe."

"Believe it," Dooley said. "I always knew you were good."

Diamond grinned. "You did not. I believe I remember you telling me that if I sucked, I would be back waiting tables."

"That's beside the point," Dooley said.

He set down the whiskey and dusted his hands on the seat of his pants. Then he rubbed a hand across the small of his back and groaned.

"I'm gettin' too old for this," he muttered. "I need my head examined for even gettin' out of bed."

Diamond reached out, brushed the dust from his shirt, and wiped a smudge of dirt from his chin with the ball of her thumb.

"The only thing you need is a bath, Dooley Hopper."

The gentleness of her touch tugged at his conscience. It was all he could do not to tell her that the man she loved had come to see him. He struggled against the urge to tell her how much Jesse Eagle seemed to care, and how much he seemed to be suffering. But he'd promised, and Dooley kept his promises.

Dooley caught her hand as it slid off his face, and he pulled her toward him.

Diamond blinked in surprise as his huge hands cupped her cheeks, gentle beyond belief in spite of their size.

"You're real special to me, girl," he said. "I wouldn't hurt you for the world. I haven't let myself care about another single soul in too many years to remember."

She blushed. "Why, Dooley! Is this a proposal?" she teased. But the serious expression in his eyes ended the jest.

"If I was thirty years younger, hell yes!" he said. "As it is, it's just a fact, nothing more."

Diamond surprised him as well as herself when she walked into his arms. The hug between them was swift but certain. And when she stepped away, each ignored the sheen of tears in the other's eyes.

"So this is what you do when customers are scarce," Twila said as she came in the door. "Dooley, you're too old to be fooling around with the help. Besides, I thought I told you to fire her."

"I'm not help," Diamond said. "I'm family, and decent people don't fire family. Besides, the waitress called in and said she'd be late. I was just helping out."

Twila frowned, knowing that Diamond was going to do as she pleased with Dooley. They were too close to part company just because her career was taking off.

"Well, hell," Dooley growled, lifting himself from the barstool and ambling behind the counter, eager to put some space between himself and the two women. He'd already exposed more of his feelings than he'd intended, so he grabbed his towel and began shining shot glasses that were already gleaming, unwilling to admit how much her words had pleased him.

"Too many damn women in the place," he muttered without looking up. "Can't you two find somewhere else to gab?"

"We're already gone," Twila said. "Have fun, you old goat. I know we will."

"What are you gonna do?" Dooley asked, in spite of his determination to remain uninvolved.

"Diamond is going shopping and then going to practice, because tonight she will be performing at the Bluebird." Twila grinned, enjoying the reactions to her announcement.

Dooley whooped. "Oooweee! How did you manage that, Twila Hart? I would have thought that was down the road a piece."

She raised her eyebrows. "I have my connections," she said, ignoring the fact that the connections were Diamond's instead of hers. "Mind you, it's only the early show, but it's still the Bluebird."

Dooley grinned. "This calls for a drink." He turned up a shot glass and started to pour.

"None for me, thanks," Twila said. "I'm driving."

"None for me, thanks," Diamond echoed, trying to still the adrenaline that had burst through her body. "I'm flying."

It was an exaggeration, but it fit her excitement. If her manager was to be believed, she was about to perform at the most famous stepping-off spot in Nashville for country singers. At one time or another, everyone who was anyone in the business had performed there.

And it was still considered a coup to walk into the place unannounced and be allowed to sing.

"What will I wear?" Diamond asked.

"The universal female question. Get out of my place and do your woman stuff somewheres else," Dooley said.

He tried to hide a smile behind his gruff complaint, but it was no use. It was so unusual to see Diamond relaxed and happy he couldn't suppress it. But the smile died on his face as they disappeared. If Diamond was to start singing in places like that, it would only be a matter of time before she and Jesse met again. He hated to consider the possibilities of what might occur when they did.

Darkness came early, bringing the night people of Nashville to life. It was evident from the amount of traffic that some of them were coming to the Bluebird Cafe.

"Maybe we should'a bought the red outfit," Twila grumbled as she pulled off Hillsboro Drive and into the small parking lot in front of the club, giving Diamond's tight black jeans and long sleeved black shirt a last look. She shrugged and smiled as Diamond made a face. The clothes were a perfect contrast to her long blonde hair and green eyes, and they both knew it.

"It's so small!" Diamond said, referring to the club and the insignificant sign outside.

Twila grinned. "You think it looks small now, wait until you get inside. It's one small room that might hold a hundred people if everyone held their breath. It's got maybe five barstools at a bar shorter than my bed, and a tiny kitchen in the back. Add a couple of bathrooms, one pay phone on the wall in the hall, some old church pews for the overflow—and you've got the Bluebird."

"And it's that important?"

Twila nodded. "It's that important. The Bluebird's reputation sort of outgrew its size, but the owners chose not to relocate. Probably the smartest move they could have made. Tennesseeans are big on tradition."

Diamond shivered with anticipation and looked around the lot. "I hope Doug's not late. I really want him to play with me, especially on a couple of particular songs."

Twila frowned. "I don't know this Doug Bentin, so I hope you know what you're doing. You wouldn't want to mess up this big break by having some half-bit fiddle player accompany you."

"Believe me," Diamond said. "He's not half-bit. He's great. Besides, we've played together several times before."

"Really?" Twila said. The more she learned about Diamond, the more she realized that this lady had more experience in the business than she'd first imagined.

Diamond nodded. "Once at Dooley's, but that was after I'd cut the—" She never finished her sentence. It still hurt to think of those times . . . and of Jesse. "Come on," she said. "Let's go inside and get set up. I don't want to keep the customers waiting."

Twila followed Diamond's hasty exit from the car. There was nothing more she could tell her without revealing the role Jesse had played in this booking. Even though Diamond didn't know it, Jesse Eagle was back in her life in a very big way. And for whatever reasons he had, Twila was willing to keep it to herself until Jesse changed the rules.

"Come on in here," the cook said, grinning to himself as he opened the back exit to the Bluebird to admit the tall man in the big black hat. "You've been here several times, Jesse. But I can't say that I ever remember you comin' in the back door."

"Keep it down, will you?" Jesse asked, and yanked off his hat before someone spotted it and his presence was revealed. He stepped into the tiny kitchen and peered through the small horizontal opening between it and the dining area, assuring himself that he'd have ample view of the performance when it took place.

It didn't take him long to spot the three men sitting at a table toward the back of the crowded room. Jesse smiled. They were here, just as he'd asked. Although she didn't know it, the rest was up to Diamond. All she had to do was be herself and sing like an angel. If those men were as smart as they claimed to be, they'd take it from there.

"Want a drink?" the cook asked.

Jesse shook his head. "No, but thanks. All I want is to remain unseen. Think you can manage that?"

"Hell, yes," the cook said. "No one gets in here but me. Ain't no room, anyways. You just stand here to the side of the pass-through and you'll be able to see what you want without being seen." Then he grinned. "I just sure would like to know what's so special about tonight."

Jesse returned the smile. "One of these days you will, I promise. For now, it's enough that you're about to witness a little Nashville history in the making."

"I don't get it."

"I know," Jesse said. "But down the road, you will."

It was all he could say without revealing his plans. But if everything went accordingly, within weeks the world would know who the mystery woman was who'd sung with him on the album, Diamond would have the recognition she deserved, and he'd have the love of his life back in his arms.

"Ooowee." The cook whistled under his breath at the sight of the woman dressed in black who'd just entered the club. "That's one fine-looking woman."

Jesse shuddered, wiped his hands on the back of his Levis, and then stuffed them into his pockets. He tried to concentrate on the smell of hot grease and hamburgers cooking or he'd lose control and walk into that room, toss Diamond over his shoulder, and carry her off into the night, to hell with explanations and excuses.

"God give me strength," he whispered as he watched her step up onto the tiny stage and adjust the microphone to her height.

"If you got her in bed, you'd need it," the cook said, grinning.

Jesse frowned as a man stepped onstage, kissed Diamond lightly on the cheek, and then took a fiddle from its case. He knew the greeting was nothing more than friendly, but it had still been hard to watch. He wondered how many other men had befriended his lady and wished them all to hell on a one-way bus.

The audience grew silent as Diamond stepped up to the mike.

"This man beside me who's teasing his fiddle strings is Doug Bentin—in my opinion, one of the best musicians in Nashville. And I'm Diamond Houston, from up north, a place called Cradle Creek. I'm sure you've never heard of it; I can't even say for sure it's on the map. But it's there—and once, so was I."

Jesse inhaled slowly and closed his eyes, letting the sound of her voice flow over him, praying that it would ease the pain in his chest. If it didn't he feared he would die, and he hated to think his life would end in the kitchen of the Bluebird Cafe.

She began to sing. The accompanying sound of Doug's fiddle was a powerful addition to her pure, clear voice. And when he knew that she was lost in her music, unaware of the crowd to whom she was singing, he stepped out of the shadows and looked. He didn't hear anything or feel the heat from the grill at his back. All he could do was watch her mouth forming the words of the songs, her hands on the guitar, and the way her body moved to the music—and remember that once, she'd done the same for him.

"Man, you were right," Shorty said as he and his two business partners walked with Jesse to his car. "And you know what? The strangest thing was that I'd swear I've heard her before. You know how I am—I can't remember names to save my soul, but I never forget a voice."

Jesse grinned. It was just as he'd hoped, and the three men who'd listened to Diamond's performance only moments earlier wielded enough power in the music industry to do just as they pleased.

"I'm always right," Jesse told them, and laughed at their hoots in response to him.

"Talk about an ego," Shorty said.

Jesse corrected him. "It's not ego. It's the power of positive thinking."

They paused beside their car and waited for Jesse to let the other shoe drop. They'd been in the business too long to think that all he'd wanted from them was to listen to another singer, no matter how good she was.

"So, what's the scoop, Jesse?" Shorty asked.

"What's the biggest mystery running in Nashville?" Jesse asked.

"Who Selma Bennett's next husband will be," Shorty replied, and grinned at the appreciative round of laughter that followed his statement.

"Besides that," Jesse said.

Shorty became quiet. He turned and stared at the back door of the Bluebird and then back at Jesse. "Who's the mystery woman that sang on your album?"

Jesse just grinned.

"Shit! Are you telling me what I think you're telling me?"

"I didn't tell you a thing," Jesse said. "But I need for you boys to do a little talking for me. I want Diamond Houston to be invited to sing at the Grand Ole Opry. This is the date and the time." He handed them a slip of paper.

"Hell, Jesse. You know the rules. A performer doesn't just show up unannounced and unknown. They've got to have some recognition—maybe a hit song—or have a lot of air time. You know the drill."

"How much more recognition do you need, Shorty? Being part of a duo on a number-one song isn't enough? Getting that same song nominated for a Grammy as best song of the year, and having said song played daily across the nation, wouldn't do it for you?"

Shorty looked at his two friends for approval. They nodded.

"The catch is, you can't let on what you know," Jesse said. "I want it to be a surprise for everyone. Think of the coup you can claim when you three admit to knowing her identity long before the rest of the world."

"It's a deal," Shorty said. "I'll give Tommy a call when I get the details worked out."

"No!" Jesse's exclamation caught them all by surprise. "For this to work, you have to leave him out of it. Do we have a deal?"

It didn't take them long to read between the lines. What happened between Jesse and his manager was nothing to them. But being in on the revelation was an appealing idea.

"You've got yourself a deal, and on your terms. I'll be in touch," Shorty said.

Jesse watched them leave and then leaned against his car and buried his face in his hands, unable to believe he'd pulled this off.

I'm getting as backhanded as Tommy, he told himself.

He drove out of Nashville with a smile on his face.

For the first time since he had come home and found her gone, his world was about to get back on track.

Then a thought occurred to him. He made a U-turn in the middle of the deserted, two-lane road and headed back into town.

19

Diamond waved good-bye to Twila, shifted the heavy guitar case to the other hand, and let herself into her apartment. Tonight had been a milestone in her budding career, and she knew it. Twila had been on pins and needles through the entire event, and more than once Diamond had seen her fidgeting nervously as she looked around the room, gauging the reactions of the audience. What she hadn't seen was Twila's eyes widen in shock at the sight of the three men sitting against the east wall of the club. It was just as well. If Diamond had known the power the men held in the country music business, she might have blown the entire performance.

But as exciting as tonight had been, Diamond couldn't bring herself to rejoice. She locked the door behind her, set the guitar in the closet, made one turn through the kitchen, opened the refrigerator door, and tried to convince herself to eat. She had everything going for her and wanted only what she couldn't have.

She slammed the refrigerator shut, wincing as the glass jars and bottles in the door rattled against one another. Her gaze strayed, as it had more than once during the past few weeks, to the white princess phone sitting quietly on the table beside her sofa.

Yet she knew calling him again would be a mistake. Hearing the pain in his voice wouldn't do a thing except remind her of her own.

She walked into her bedroom, dropped to her knees beside the dresser, and opened the bottom drawer. They lay just where she'd tossed them when she'd moved—all the clippings, fan mail, and tabloid articles concerning her and Jesse.

And they taunted her, just as they had since the day Tommy had stuffed them into her hands and shouted in her face that she was ruining Jesse Eagle's life and career.

Some of the newspaper clippings were beginning to turn a bit yellow. The envelopes containing the angry fan mail were wrinkled and smudged from handling. But Diamond knew that if she dared, she could pull them out and still feel the same sensation of shock she'd felt on the day of their arrival.

How could anything so small cause so much pain? she wondered, fingering the stack of paper. And how could she have let someone else's words mean more to her than Jesse's?

The ache in the back of her throat swelled into a sob. With one swift shove, she slammed the drawer shut, buried her face in her hands, and let the tears come.

There was no consolation in the knowledge that if she

could have done it over again, she would have stayed and fought for what—and who—belonged to her.

Twila parked her car. Still riding on the high from Diamond's performance at the Bluebird, she missed the fact that the security light above her apartment door was out. She locked the car then slung her purse over her shoulder as she started walking, her door key dangling from her fingers. She didn't see or hear the man until he stepped out of the shadows in front of her apartment and stood between her and safety.

"Twila Hart?"

Twila jumped, grabbed for her purse, and fumbled in its depths for the can of mace she always carried. She'd known it was only a matter of time before the law of averages caught up with her and she became a crime statistic. Her breath caught on a sob as she yanked out a ballpoint pen instead of the cylinder of mace and aimed it toward the man.

"Don't come any closer or I'll—"

"What? Mark me off your Christmas list?"

The humor in his voice slowed the rapid thud of her heart. If she weren't mistaken, she knew the owner of that voice.

"Oh, Lord," she said, slumping against the wall. "You scared me half to death, you fool."

Jesse sighed. All he could do right these days was the wrong thing.

"I'm really sorry, Ms. Hart," he said. "But I needed to talk to you—without witnesses. May I come in?"

She slapped the door key in his hand. "You open it," she said. "I'm still shaking too much to hit the keyhole."

"I'm pretty nervous myself," he said. "When I saw you yank out that ballpoint, I thought my days were numbered."

"Shut up and open the door."

Jesse did as he was ordered. Twila pushed past him, flipped on the lights, tossed her purse on the sofa and flung her ballpoint across the room in a last fit of wasted adrenaline. She tossed her coat across the back of a chair and, when she was certain she could talk without screaming, turned to face her uninvited guest.

He leaned against the door, unwilling to come any farther into her home without invitation.

"Oh, for Pete's sake," Twila said. "Have a seat."

But Jesse just pushed himself away from the door, shoved his hands into his pants pockets, and walked toward the window overlooking Nashville, giving her nothing but a very enticing view of his backside.

"We've never been formally introduced," Twila said, appreciatively eyeing how well the western-style suit he was wearing fit his tall body.

"And it's been my misfortune," Jesse said as he turned and extended his hand.

Twila's heart skipped a beat as their hands touched. The pain he was suffering was palpable, and in spite of her intentions to remain aloof, she winced at the chill on his skin. A muscle twitched at the corner of his mouth, and his dark eyes were bright. Too bright for the mood. She suspected they housed a constant sheen of tears.

"Let's cut to the chase," she said. "You're here for a reason. I want to hear it."

Jesse nodded. He wiped his hands across his face, inhaled slowly, and then began to talk. "First, I just need to hear how she's doing."

Twila snorted. "As all right as a person can be who's been cut and hung out to dry. What the hell did you do to her?"

His groan gave Twila second thoughts about the culpability of the man standing before her. From the look on his face, he was in just as much pain as Diamond.

"Oh, God, I don't know," Jesse said, dropping into the chair behind him. He stared down at the floor as he tried to find the best way to continue without making a total fool of himself. "I've spent the better part of the last few months trying to find out."

"I don't get it," Twila said. "Either you cheated her or you didn't."

Jesse exhaled slowly. It was strange what kind of pain mere words could inflict. Having someone say aloud what had happened to the woman he loved was agony.

"What I did do was leave the business end of her life up to . . . up to someone I trusted. For that, I claim guilt. What I didn't do was cheat *on* her. I loved her . . . love her. When I came home and found her gone, I nearly went crazy."

Twila frowned. "So are you saying that your—"

Jesse interrupted. "I'm not saying anything. Not until I can talk to Diamond and hear from her lips exactly what happened to her to make her leave me like that."

"Okay," Twila said. "I admire loyalty, even the misplaced kind. So this is the deal: We don't point fingers— just yet. I'll go along with that. But what do we do?"

"Prepare for the revelation, Twila Hart. Prepare for the revelation."

He began to explain, and as he did, the expressions on her face ran from disbelief to shock to unadulterated pleasure. This was one performance she couldn't wait to see.

"Oh, Dooley, I still can't believe it."

The awe in Diamond's voice was as real as the smile on her face. Dooley hugged her closer, an unconscious gesture that was a reflection of his fear of losing her.

"I can," he said. "I always knew you had what it took, honey. Playing the Grand Ole Opry had to come soon. I'm really proud of you."

Diamond shivered in spite of her excitement. Something, a subconscious warning, told her that this wasn't a step, it was a leap. It was the fulfillment of the promise Jesse had made to her and her sisters the day he'd taken her from Cradle Creek. And it was going to happen without him. Overwhelming sadness threatened to ruin the thrill.

"I need you to be there for me, Dooley. I will expect you to attend, even if you have to shut down the club, at least this one night."

"Honey, I'd sell the damned place if I had to. I wouldn't miss this for the world." Sympathy made him add, "Everyone will be there, don't you worry."

He disappeared into his office, unwilling to look into her eyes and face that ever-present, lost expression.

Diamond nodded, thinking of Twila . . . and maybe Doug Bentin, who had become such a good friend. It never occurred to her to search farther into her past for others who might provide the moral support she so desperately needed. She'd spent too many months trying to put that same past behind her.

She'd also lost more sleep than she could afford, trying to decipher the mystery of Jesse's appearance at Melvin Call's club. For weeks afterward she'd imagined the phone ringing and Jesse on the other end of the line pleading for her return. She'd dreaded it to the point of actual illness, and then, when it hadn't happened, had lost sleep trying to figure out why not. The only conclusion she could come up with was that she'd hurt the relationship and him too badly to fix. He didn't want her anymore, and she had to live with that.

The club was quiet now that Dooley had gone into his office. It was too early in the morning for even Walt and Deever to make an appearance. Diamond walked around, absently admiring the changes that had taken place since her first day on the job. She *and* the derelict building had taken on new life.

She walked up the two steps onto Dooley's new stage and looked out across the room, squinting through the shadowy haze and imagining the tables crowded and the noise level that could be heard on a busy Saturday night. Although she'd often wished for fancier surroundings, Diamond knew that when it came time to leave Dooley's for good, she was going to miss the place and the security of knowing that she had always been accepted and loved there.

She heard Dooley's stereo come alive behind the closed door of his office and smiled, knowing that he'd finally forced himself to drag out the books. Of all the chores associated with his business, bookkeeping made Dooley crazy, and he always put it off until it was almost too late to decipher it.

Unwilling to leave this haven of comfort, she lingered onstage, brushed at a smudge of dust on her Levis, and unrolled the cuffs of her long-sleeved blue shirt as she eyed the newly installed ceiling lights. Minutes later, confident that she could walk onto the street and face strangers without humiliating herself by crying, she bowed to the absent audience like a child playing make-believe. It was her own personal farewell to Dooley's.

She was about to step off the stage when she heard it. The song, and the truth of what had started and ended it all. "Lies."

Diamond closed her eyes and inhaled sharply against the pain in her heart. The melody drifted faintly into the room and through her soul, and before she knew it, she heard herself singing along.

But the smiles and lies of a lying lover
go hand in hand like kisses and wine . . .

Her body swayed to the melody, her voice a whisper as the words cut deep. Unable to face even an imaginary audience, she closed her eyes as she sang along.

The words were so faint, at first Dooley imagined they were from the stero behind his desk. And then he listened more closely, and as he did, he knew that he was hearing what could only be called the unveiling of a secret. He laid down his pen, pushed back his chair, and walked quietly to the door, careful not to open it too much and alert Diamond to the fact that she was being overheard.

. . . like the fool I am, can't get you out of my mind.

And when her voice ended with a sob and a sigh, Dooley quietly closed the door and leaned his head against the aged wood, wishing himself a younger man. But the thought left as quickly as it came. His time was over, but Diamond's was just beginning. He would give his life to see that hers was finally happy.

"Sir," Henley said, entering the music room with a portable phone. "You have a call."

The interruption was a blessing. Although Jesse had disconnected the phone in the music room in hopes of being able to work, he'd still been unable to concentrate. All he could think about was the upcoming performance at the Grand Ole Opry. In less than a week he'd know whether or not he had a future with Diamond. Without his lady, his life was hardly worth living.

Jesse took the phone and smiled at the exuberance of the man on the other end of the line.

"Whoa, Mack. Slow down," Jesse said. "Yes, you heard right. And by the way, just as a matter of interest, who told you? I was planning on calling all the boys in the band tomorrow and getting together to have a little practice session."

"Oh, shoot," Mack said. "I forget . . . one of the boys . . . I think it was Al. Yeah! That's it! It was Al. He said Rita came home from the beauty shop and told him that—"

Jesse started to laugh. Leave it to a woman! And then his smile disappeared. If he had his way, he'd be doing just that—leaving the rest of his life to one certain woman.

"Never mind," Jesse said. "I guess it doesn't matter. It would have been common knowledge soon enough. You know how the music industry is; you can't keep anything a secret for long."

"I don't know about that," Mack said. "We've done pretty darn good keeping a certain secret of our own."

Jesse debated with himself about telling Mack the truth. As it was, he didn't have to tell much, since Mack and the band seemed to have guessed most of it already.

"About the Grand Ole Opry performance," Jesse began. "You guys should know that I—"

"And it's about time," Mack said. "Does Tommy know she's gonna be there?"

Jesse's stomach turned. This was too much, too soon. If everyone suspected what was happening, then it was entirely possible that Diamond would get word of it and fail to show. What if she ran again, and this time out of Nashville for good? Then he sighed and faced the fact that if she did, he had to accept what she'd been trying to tell him all along. She didn't want anything more to do with a man who stole, even if all *he'd* taken was her heart and her trust.

"No, Tommy doesn't know yet. But if you guys do, it's only a matter of—"

Jesse looked out the window toward the driveway and rolled his eyes at the sight of the car pulling into his yard.

"Speak of the devil," he told Mack. "I'll have to call you later with a practice schedule. Our manager has just arrived."

"I don't envy you," Mack said, and hung up.

But Jesse was past caring whose feelings got hurt and

who stepped on whose toes. All he wanted was Diamond back in his life. He laid down the phone and went to meet Tommy.

"I'll get it," Jesse said as Henley started for the door. "And Henley, no interruptions until Tommy leaves. No calls, no nothing, okay?"

Henley nodded. "If you need me, sir, I'll be in the kitchen."

Jesse grinned, remembering the fury with which Henley had received the news about Diamond and the ill-fated album. Jesse had been slightly shocked by the fact that Henley had suggested "terminating" their manager, and he'd never been completely certain that Henley had only meant on paper.

The knock was vehement. Jesse masked a smile as he opened the door to a very angry man.

"Just when the hell were you going to tell me?" Tommy yelled, and shoved his way inside the house.

Jesse closed the door and walked past Tommy toward the living room. "Come on in, Tommy. Care for a drink?"

"Hell no, I don't want a drink!" Just the mention of the word still made his stomach turn. "What I want are answers."

"And you'll probably get them," Jesse said, "as soon as I hear the questions. Where do you want to start?"

Tommy fumed and slammed his hat down on the table as he paced the floor.

"I had to hear it from another agent. My own people couldn't even tell me the truth. It had to come from an outsider. How the hell do you think I felt?"

Jesse's eyes narrowed and his fingers curled into fists,

but he put them behind his back and answered as calmly as possible.

"I don't know how you felt, Tommy. But I know what I felt when I came home and found Diamond gone. I don't intend to go through that or anything remotely like it again."

"It's not the same thing!" Tommy yelled.

"But it could be, if the wrong person got hold of my plan and broke the news early," Jesse said.

Tommy's eyebrows arched and his mouth dropped open. A faint sheen of perspiration popped across his lip, and a flush of red swept across both cheeks. The implications of what Jesse had just said were beginning to take hold. It was the first time he realized that there was more to Jesse Eagle's appearance on the Grand Ole Opry than a surprise performance. If he understood Jesse correctly, he was going to go public with the mystery woman's identity.

"My God! You know where she is, don't you?"

Jesse let the question go unanswered. It was verification enough for Tommy, who felt sick to his stomach. He wondered what she'd told him and tried to figure out how he was going to explain away his part in the debacle.

"Well, I don't care what she's told you. It's not the truth! I would never do anything to hurt you, and that's a fact you can't deny. Don't stand there and try to make me say otherwise." Tommy was nearly screaming. Spittle ran from a corner of his mouth as he banged the desk with his fist.

"I know you wouldn't hurt *me*," Jesse said. "I never in my life thought that for a moment, buddy."

The censure in Jesse's voice was enough to quiet Tommy's anger. He wilted in premature relief.

"And I haven't talked to her—not yet, so I can't tell you what, if anything, she's going to tell me. If there's nothing to tell, you have nothing to fear. Right?"

Oh, God! "Right!" Tommy said, dropping into the chair behind him. "So, what's the plan? What do you want me to do? I can get media coverage for the unannounced performance of Jesse Eagle. I can get you a full-page spread in—"

"I want you to do nothing," Jesse said. "Absolutely nothing. This time, I'm calling the shots. And if I find out that you've ignored my orders, you can just pack your bags and start looking for a place to hide. Do you hear me?"

Tommy shivered at the ominous tone in Jesse's voice and slid a smile in place. "You don't have to threaten me, buddy. You know me—I'd never hurt you, remember?"

"But if you hurt the ones I love, you hurt me, too. Understand?"

Tommy nodded. "Understood." He fidgeted with the crease in his pants as he considered his options, and then another thought occurred. "What songs are you going to sing? Some of the cuts from the album?"

"I thought we'd do the number-one song, since it's been nominated for a Grammy. Sort of a pre-premiere performance. What do you think?" Jesse asked.

"You can't sing a duo alone."

"I don't intend to," Jesse said, and then smiled.

Tommy shuddered and felt his bowels rumble. "She's agreed to sing with you? After all that's happened?"

Jesse frowned and turned away. "There's the rub. She'll be there, but she doesn't know we will. If my luck holds, she'll sing with me when the time comes. If not—"

Tommy shot from the chair. "You can't take a chance like that. If it blows up in your face, you'll look like a fool. What will happen to your career if she doesn't comply and you have to stand up there trying to sing alone? Everyone's going to think she's angry, and then they're going to start speculating as to why. Before you know it, the whole industry will be blaming you for what happened."

Jesse shrugged. "It's no more than I deserve," he said quietly. "Besides, I don't care. If I lose her, I don't give a damn about my career. You may as well face that now."

"Oh, Lord." But Tommy's muttered prayer wasn't enough, and he knew it. It would take more than God to get him out of this mess.

Diamond stood in front of her closet, staring at the array of costumes she'd collected since her performing days had begun. Rhinestones and sequins winked back at her, catching and reflecting the light from the overhead bulb as she sifted through the hangers. But nothing seemed right.

Granted, she could hide behind flash and glamour and give her usual performance. But tight and flashy wasn't what she needed. Diamond needed an affirmation of her talent, and she wanted it to come from the heart of her listeners, not from admiration for her face and body.

"Are you about dressed?" Twila yelled from the living room.

"Nearly," Diamond answered, despite the fact that she had on nothing but panties.

An instinct sent her digging into the back of the closet. And when she came to the hanger for which she'd been searching, she slipped the garments off and laid them on the bed, then stepped back and stared.

They were exactly what she'd been searching for. Now if she could only get past Twila's objections, she'd have it made. If she dawdled until there was no time to waste, Twila would have to agree.

Slowly, as if performing a ritual, she turned to the mirror, stared at herself long and hard, and when she was satisfied with what she saw in her eyes, began getting dressed. Thirty minutes later she exited her bedroom and waited for Twila's wrath to fall. It never came.

"Well!"

It was the only thing Twila had to say about Diamond's outfit. And when their gazes met, an understanding passed between the two women. Twila sensed that whether Diamond knew it or not, her choice of clothing would make more of an impact than if she had been dripping in the real thing—her namesakes.

"Let's get a move on," Twila said. "We can't leave it too long or we'll get caught in the traffic around Opryland."

"I'm ready when you are," Diamond said. "Just let me get my coat and my guitar."

"Don't forget your makeup," Twila said.

"What I need is in my purse," Diamond said.

"My God. I carry more than that just to get ready for bed. You make me sick," Twila said, knowing full well that Diamond would pay no attention to her grumbling.

"Tonight it's just me," Diamond said. "What they see is what they get."

They're going to see a whole lot more than they've been led to expect, Twila thought as she started the car. *The fans who attend the Opry tonight will see history in the making.*

"I'll be there," Twila reminded her. "And probably your friend Doug Bentin, and Dooley. Lord, don't forget Dooley Hopper! He'll probably make such a pest of himself they'll throw him out."

Diamond listened and nodded but didn't bother answering. There was no need. Diamond knew Twila was talking to her so that she wouldn't do so much thinking and make herself unduly nervous. But it was too late for that. Diamond was already as nervous as she was going to get—and as sad as she'd ever been in her life. This was, to date, the most important event in her life, and she didn't have one single family member or loved one with whom to share it. She shivered and pulled her coat tighter.

"Cold?" Twila asked, and flipped the heater to a higher setting.

Diamond nodded. It was an easier answer than admitting that a ghost had just walked across her conscience. The only thing was, she didn't know if it was Jesse's or Johnny's ghost who'd reminded her that she was alone by choice, not fate.

20

It was not what she'd expected. A little of the magic was missing, and she knew that it was because the magic came from the entertainers, and most of them had not yet arrived. The stage and auditorium were still empty.

Diamond stood on stage, her toes even with the edge, and stared up in amazement at the heavy burgundy curtain above her head that would later come down and separate her from the audience. She shivered with anticipation and looked up into the vacant balcony and then down into the rows and rows of seats on the main floor, trying to imagine what it would look like full of people. Definitely nothing like Dooley's.

An engineer above the balcony was checking the lighting, and he ran a slide-show test of the half-hourly sponsors of the Grand Ole Opry across the big screen above the doorway of the red barn backdrop. Their familiar names made her smile.

She'd grown up listening to the radio and AM 650's WSM broadcast of the Opry every Friday and Saturday night. But never in her wildest dreams had she imagined that she'd be standing on stage in front of that famous red barn, awaiting her maiden performance on the show.

She turned and walked toward the center of the stage until she came to a dark circle of wood set in the middle of the floor. She walked around it, testing its boundary to make certain lightning wouldn't strike, and then took a breath and stepped inside. She closed her eyes and let her head fall back as she tried to imagine the footsteps of the famous who'd been there before her.

"Know what you're standin' on?" Dooley asked, surprising her with his presence and his touch.

Diamond opened her eyes and smiled. "I'm so glad you're here," she said, and then looked down. "Of course I do. I wouldn't be worth my salt if I didn't. This is a piece of the stage from the old Ryman Auditorium where the Opry used to be held. Right?"

Dooley grinned. "Right! A whole lifetime ago, before you were even born, country stars were leaving their footsteps on that piece of wood. Think of 'em! Patsy Cline, Hank Williams, even Johnny Cash. It's enough to give you the chills." He patted her arm and wiggled his eyebrows. "Feel any ghosts?"

Diamond shook her head and tried not to think of ghosts. If there were any beside her, they belonged to Jesse, or maybe her father. Those were the ghosts in *her* life.

"I'm glad you came to share tonight with me," she said.

"Honey, I wouldn't have missed this for the world," Dooley said. "Are you nervous?"

She nodded.

"Good! That means you'll be fine. Doesn't pay to be too cocky. I'll be right back there, rootin' you on. All you have to do is remember that even though you don't know who's out there," he motioned toward the audience, "you can count on who's behind you."

He pointed toward the chairs on stage in front of the red barn backdrop where the honored guests and family members of the performers were privileged to sit and watch the Opry. With only a fake fence and the stage instruments of various bands separating them from the performers, they had a better than average view of everything going on.

"I can always count on you," Diamond said. "Wish me luck."

"You won't need it," he said. "Just do what you always do. You're the best."

He slipped his arm around her shoulder and together they walked offstage to where Twila was conferring with the announcer regarding Diamond's introduction.

The curtain came down as the audience began to pour in. Diamond could hear people twittering in nervous excitement as they found their allotted seats, and she began to smell the popcorn as it burst into life, filling the hoppers for later sale. In no time at all, a heady combination of anticipation and excitement overcame her, and she knew that for whatever reasons, tonight was going to be magic.

*   *   *

Jesse paced nervously, bumping into first one and then another of his band members as they remained secluded in their room beyond the main staging area at the Grand Ole Opry. For this plan to work, they could not mingle with the other performers as they would normally have done, and it seemed to make them all a little jumpy.

"For God's sake, Jesse, either sit down or slow down. You're makin' me seasick."

Al's good-natured grumbling was echoed by others in the band, but none begrudged him his anxiety. They all knew what this night meant to Jesse. In a way, it meant their future, too.

To a man, none doubted his claim that if he lost his lady because of this business, he wanted out of it fast. If he left, that meant they would have to start over, and no one wanted that.

"Sorry," Jesse muttered, and stepped in front of the full-length mirror again. He adjusted his hat, yanked at the sleeves of his long-sleeved white shirt, retied his string tie, and then shined his belt buckle with his coat sleeve, making certain that his appearance would pass muster.

Mack brushed some lint from the shoulder of Jesse's black suit coat and then patted him roughly on the back.

"You're gonna be fine, buddy," he said. "I don't know what you're worryin' about. You know that lady better than me, and I'd bet my life she won't let you down."

"She has the right," Jesse said. "I let her down so far it nearly killed us both."

"That's in the past, Jesse. Tonight is a brand-new start. Don't mess it up by harping on what was. Be ready for what is. Okay?"

"My God, Mack. You're makin' me nervous. When did you become a philosopher?"

Mack grinned. "Remember that redhead from New Year's Eve? Well, she *was* home. And you know what else? She's college-educated, and pretty to boot. I just might be thinkin' of settlin' down myself . . . one of these days." Then he blushed as Al walked by and hooted derisively. "Well, I didn't say for sure—I just said I was thinkin' about it."

Jesse grinned. The tension of the moment was broken, and he settled down to await the unveiling of Diamond Houston.

"Ladies and gentlemen," the announcer's voice echoed through the auditorium. "You're in for a real treat tonight. There's a bright new star shining over Nashville. And I can guarantee that she's going to shine far and wide in her career. If you'll let her, she'll take you on a ride you'll never forget. Let's give a big Opry welcome for Miss Diamond Houston, of Cradle Creek, Tennessee."

The round of applause sounded friendly. But it wasn't rousing, and Jesse knew it. He stood offstage right to where Diamond would enter and waited in the shadows for her appearance.

He'd been a performer there too many times not to hear the difference in the audience's welcome. It wasn't normal for a near-unknown to appear on the Opry, but in true country-music fashion, they were generously giving her the benefit of doubt.

She sauntered onstage as if she'd done the same a thousand times before, giving away nothing of her anxiety. Her hair was full around her face, loose and flowing as it moved in opposite sway to her body.

The stage lights caught the sheen of her green satin shirt, and a separate spotlight seemed to follow the length of those long, jean-clad legs as they propelled Diamond toward the microphone. Her breasts pushed against the satin and bounced slightly with every step she took. A wide belt accentuated her tiny waist and slender, almost boyishly slim hips, and her old but very polished boots added to her elegant height.

Yet she was woman personified. No sequins, no rhinestones, no flash and flutter. Just a blonde with a guitar and a smile that would melt icicles off a pump handle in the dead of winter.

She'd heard a lot of the patter with which other entertainers would start their performance, but she opted once again to be different. Thanks to the announcer, the fans now knew her name. It was up to her to show them why she was there.

She leaned over, unconsciously giving the audience a very enticing view of her backside as she picked up her guitar, and then faced them once again as she slid the strap over her shoulder. Her fingers ran across the strings, and then, unexpectedly, she assaulted the audience with sound and emotion. The song burst forth from her lips, and instantly her listeners were ensnared in the words of the story as Diamond took an old Hank Williams song and made it her own.

She went through her performance in a daze, hardly aware of the surprised smiles and then the enraptured faces of the audience who'd found a new singer to adore.

And then the old standard was over.

As the audience clapped loudly in appreciation of her obvious talent, she smiled and bowed, trying to calm her racing heart enough to be able to perform her last number. The song that would finish her performance was one that she'd written more than five years earlier. It had been written at a time in her life when she'd believed she would never escape Whitclaw's Bar or Cradle Creek. Even recalling the words made her teary.

The smile disappeared from her face as she took a long, slow breath and found the right chord on the guitar. The words that then came out painted an image of her life as Johnny Houston's daughter.

Little girl running, little girl lost,
gambler's daughter hidin' from the names they toss.
Never understanding that the rules don't change,
'cause if you don't fit in, you can never play the game.

Jesse gripped the edge of the curtain and leaned his forehead against the thick folds as the words of her song enveloped him. This was almost too much to absorb. To hear this now and know firsthand the pain that had caused its birth made what he'd planned next nearly impossible. But it was already set up, and he was too far in to back out now.

The audience gave Diamond a rousing round of applause as she ended her performance with a broad smile and a wave of her hand. She slid the guitar from around her neck, set it upright behind her on a stand, and took another bow before starting offstage.

Twila was standing behind the announcer, beaming proudly, as the shouts from the audience and the announcer's encouraging wave sent Diamond back to center stage for another call.

She didn't see the men quickly taking their places in the band section behind her. She didn't hear the audience's gasp of surprise as first one and then another of them were recognized. She was still riding on the tails of her successful performance.

But the smile died on her face as the first strains of the melody filled the stage behind her. She froze in place, afraid to turn around as Al Barkley's fiddle began the first notes of the song that had nearly ruined her life.

And then Jesse's voice rang out, strong and sure, and she buried her face in her hands as the audience gasped with surprise when he walked onstage toward Diamond Houston.

Don't tell me lies, just say you love me.
Don't try so hard to make me believe.
It's not too late if you really mean it,
but you can't stay just to watch me grieve.

Tension hung in the air. Even the audience sensed the drama of the moment. Diamond shuddered, aware of Mack's deep voice behind her quietly urging her on.

She dropped her hands, unaware of the tears running down her face, and turned. For one long, heart-stopping moment she stood face to face with the man who'd stolen her heart and her sanity. And then Al repeated the notes that were her cue to join in.

She saw the pain, and the doubt, and the love on Jesse's face and knew that by the grace of God she'd been given a second chance. She wasn't going to blow it again. She tilted her head, opened her mouth, and began to sing.

But the smiles and lies of a lying lover
go hand in hand like kisses and wine.
I've had my share of one or the other.
But like the fool I am, can't get you out of my mind.

The audience went wild. They knew what they'd just heard: the voice of the woman who was on the hit song with Jesse Eagle.

Jesse couldn't finish the song for the tears in his eyes and the lump in his throat. Diamond could see the question on his face and the love in his eyes. She sighed and smiled. She'd had the answers all along and had never known it.

She opened her arms and he walked into them. His black hat fell onto the floor behind him as he wrapped her in a tight embrace and buried his face against her neck.

The fans went crazy. The announcer quickly cut to commercial, aware that his radio audience was in the dark as to what was occurring here. It would be the next morning before the papers informed the world that that night, on the stage of the Grand Ole Opry, Jesse Eagle had lost his heart to a woman from Tennessee—and had found her again.

"My God," Jesse whispered, running his hands across her shoulders and then back to touch her face over and over, as if to assure himself that he wasn't dreaming. "Why did you leave me, darlin'? What did I do to you to make you run so far and hide so long?" He could barely speak through his thick sobs.

Diamond threw her arms around his neck, plastering herself so tightly against him that she could feel his heartbeat against her breasts.

"It wasn't you . . . it wasn't you," she sobbed. "Leaving was the hardest thing I've ever done in my life, and I'm sorry. There were so many things happening at once I . . . just didn't understand." She shuddered, buried her face beneath his chin, and then inhaled the scent of his cologne and began to cry all over again.

The curtain came down, leaving the frenzied audience with a final glimpse of the tall, dark man and the elegant blonde in blue jeans who were lost in each other's arms.

"Shit," Tommy said quietly. He debated whether to run now or wait for the axe to fall.

Diamond and Jesse were ushered offstage as the stage crew quickly went about setting up for the next half-hour. She looked once toward the place where she knew Dooley was sitting and smiled through her tears as she saw him give her a wide grin and a thumbs-up. It would be much later before she learned that he and Jesse had already met.

"Get ready, darlin'," Jesse said, smiling through tears. "Here comes the band."

Diamond turned and was instantly engulfed. She was tossed from Mack to Al to Dave and the others and then back again, as they each welcomed her back into the family.

"Enough," Jesse said. "Don't maul my lady. Go home and maul your own women."

"Mine would punch out my lights for tryin' and then yours for suggestin' it," Al drawled. "I think I'll just go home, period. It's a lot safer." He grinned at Diamond, tugged a lock of her hair, and then embarrassed himself when his voice cracked with emotion. "Don't you go and leave on us, you hear, girl? I'm too old to go through anything like this again."

"I'm not going anywhere."

Her voice shook as Jesse's hand slid up her back and came to rest at the nape of her neck. His fingers kept stroking and testing and feeling, as if he couldn't assure himself too many times that she was really there.

"Promise?" he whispered behind her ear.

She turned in his arms, and as he kissed her for the first time in more months than she cared to count, she knew she was home.

"Promise," she said when she could breathe and focus enough to think. Then she looked over Jesse's shoulder into the eyes of the man who'd started the mess. Tommy was watching them with an almost fatalistic look on his face, as if he were simply waiting for her to point her finger and shout, "Aha!"

Jesse felt her withdrawal, and when he turned around

to see who'd caused this reaction, he stepped between them without thinking, unconsciously protecting Diamond from any more harm.

Tommy nodded. "Diamond, you sounded real good. How have you been?"

She didn't answer. Her lips thinned and her hands fairly itched to slap him until he couldn't see, but instead she did nothing.

Jesse inhaled sharply. This was what he'd feared. He could almost taste the antagonism between them. And just as he was about to speak, Diamond slid her arm beneath Jesse's elbow, leaned her head on his shoulder, and hugged him. She wanted to reassure him that whatever needed to be said, she could do it herself.

"Probably better than you can imagine," she said quietly.

Tommy's eyes opened wide. For the first time since she'd walked offstage, he began to hope.

"I don't expect you to believe me," Tommy said, "but I'm glad. Really glad. Jesse's happiness means a lot to me, and if it's you that makes him happy, then that makes me happy, too."

Diamond smiled, looked up at Jesse and the worry on his face, and back at Tommy and the fear in his.

"All I've ever wanted is Jesse's happiness, too, Tommy. I guess now we have to believe each other, right?"

Tommy shivered at the warning in her eyes and knew that no matter what, he'd never cross this woman again.

"That's great, then," Tommy said. "Say! I've just had the best idea. You know, Jesse goes on tour later this year. What if you were the opening act? You'd be able to travel together, and it couldn't hurt your career any to sing nightly with Jesse Eagle and Muddy Road. Want me to set it up?"

Twila Hart came hustling through the crowd of people surrounding them, and it was then that Diamond knew that in one small way, she *would* have her revenge.

"That sounds just fine, Tommy. But you'll have to talk to my manager." She pointed to Twila behind him.

Tommy's face fell. Now that all had been revealed and he'd not been quartered and hung, he'd begun considering the fact that Diamond Houston just might make someone a whole lot of money. Obviously, it wouldn't be him, and he had only himself to thank.

He turned, and the smile on his face disappeared. *Twila Hart! The hellcat from Texas. The bitch who says no and means it.*

"Twila!" Tommy said, trying to regain his composure and failing miserably as Twila glared down at him. He hated women who were taller than he, and that was a fact.

"Tommy." Her tone of voice was just as judgmental as the look in her eyes, and Tommy knew that Diamond *had* told someone what had happened. Unfortunately, it was a woman who already hated his guts.

"I understand you're representing our girl here," he said.

"She's not your anything, Tommy Thomas. And don't you ever forget that I know it," she said under her breath. "Why, yes I do," she said loudly, clapped her hand across his shoulder, and led him away. "Let's talk business."

Jesse frowned. He knew there had to be more to this than what he'd heard, but it was time to put the past behind them and take the rest of the world on trust—at least for the time being. When Diamond was ready, if ever, she'd tell him what he needed to know. Until then, he'd thank God for the chance to love her.

"Will you come home with me?" Jesse asked.

Diamond knew in that moment that her world would be all right.

"It's been a long time," she said softly.

Jesse cupped her face, kissed the tears from her cheeks, and wrapped her in his arms. "You have no idea, darlin'," he said. "You have no idea."

A mixture of nerves and need were making Jesse crazy. The long drive home had resulted in Diamond just looking at him while he did all the talking. He was about to run out of conversation and was down to a growing ache he couldn't ignore.

"The colt has really grown," Jesse said as they turned into the driveway and parked inside the garage. "You won't believe it's the same spindly-legged little—"

"Jesse, take me to bed," she whispered. "I've been alone too long and tired of crying myself to sleep. Tonight, I don't intend to sleep. I just want to be loved."

"Oh, God," he said, and pulled her across the seat and into his arms. "I've been afraid to tell you how desperate I am to hold you. I didn't want to rush you, but I knew that if I didn't get those damned clothes off you and get inside you soon, it was gonna be too late."

The impact of his words was enough to set off a hunger inside her that had nothing to do with food. She shivered and traced the line of his lips with the tip of her fingernail, smiling at the response her touch elicited.

"Come with me, darlin'," Jesse whispered. He pulled her across the seat and out his side of the car.

Hand in hand, they walked into the darkened house, stopping every few feet to touch or to kiss or to wipe an errant tear from one or the other's cheek. Just when they'd started upstairs, a small white slip of paper taped to the corner post of the staircase caught their eyes.

"What in—" Jesse pulled it off the post and tilted it toward the faint glow of the night light.

> *Welcome home, Miss Diamond.*
>
> *I heard the program tonight. I will be conspicuously absent for the next two days. The answering machine is on. The refrigerator is full. The bed is empty.*
>
> > *My sincerest regards,*
> > *Henley.*

Jesse laughed, crumpled the note, and had started to toss it when he looked up at Diamond. Tears were running down her face.

"Honey! What's wrong? Please God, you're not having second thoughts?" The pain in Jesse's voice was thick.

"It's not that," Diamond said. "It was the note. I really am home . . . aren't I?"

"My God!" Jesse lifted her off her feet and into his arms. "You still have no idea, do you?"

He nuzzled her hair as he carried her upstairs, unable to take his lips from her face or his hands from her body. He laid her in the middle of his bed and then stretched out beside her.

"Wherever you are is home for me, lady. Without you, I have nothing, I want nothing." He leaned forward until their foreheads were touching and then lost himself in her wide, green gaze. "I'm asking . . . I'm begging . . . I'm not going to let you out of my bed until you promise me."

"Promise what, Jesse Eagle?" Diamond said as she slid her arms around his neck.

"To marry me."

"I do."

Jesse grinned. "You're supposed to save those words for the ceremony," he said.

"I'm not saving anything," she said. "I'm down to 'use it or lose it.' What'll it be?"

Jesse rolled over on his back and started yanking off his boots and unsnapping snaps. Then Diamond gave a sob and a sigh as Jesse pulled her into his arms.

A long time later, Diamond heard Jesse whisper just before she finally fell asleep.

"Welcome home, shiny girl. Welcome home."

Epilogue

Jesse buttoned the last button on his red flannel shirt and tucked its tail into his jeans. Diamond was already downstairs; he could hear Henley's deep voice and her laughter in response to something he'd said. Jesse inhaled, caught the faint aroma of fresh coffee and the strong, outdoorsy scent of the evergreens Diamond had draped all over the house in honor of the coming holidays. It was two weeks until Christmas.

He bent down until he could see himself clearly in the mirror on Diamond's dresser and gave his hair a casual swipe with her brush. This Christmas would definitely be better than the last, although Jesse knew that Diamond, on occasion, still quietly grieved the loss of her sisters.

Jesse hurried down the hall, eager to get in on the morning routine. Nowadays, it seemed that he didn't want to miss a thing. The door to his left was ajar as he headed for the stairs. Unable to resist, he stepped inside, looking around as he often did at the neat, convenient office Diamond had made of what had once been her bedroom.

It was complete with a three-line phone system, a separate desk for Twila when she came out to conduct business, and cabinet upon cabinet filled with an extensive collection of old country music albums as well as a growing number of Diamond's own works. Already, songs that she'd co-written with Doug Bentin had been recorded by other artists, and one was heading to the top of the charts like a speeding bullet. Not only was his lady becoming a favorite singer, she was gaining quite a reputation as a songwriter.

Everything was perfectly coordinated, right down to the wood paneling—except for the rug on the floor. It was worn in one spot and faded in two. It was cranberry red with a gaudy, Far Eastern pattern that had nothing to do with the rest of the room, and it was Diamond's proudest possession.

He laughed to himself, remembering the look of shock on Henley's face when they'd moved Dooley Hopper's gift into this house. Only Henley's devotion to Diamond had silenced what would have been massive disapproval. He'd simply chosen to ignore it.

Yet within weeks, the oddest thing had begun to take place. Dooley's frequent visits to Diamond had resulted in a strange but growing friendship between him and Joe Henley. The two men had become the best of friends.

Jesse stepped out of her office, closed the door, and headed for the kitchen. He had a sudden need for his lady, a good-morning kiss, and a cup of coffee, and in exactly that order.

Diamond looked out the kitchen window, saw the puffs of smoke from the mail carrier's exhaust as it condensed in the cold winter air, and headed for the hall closet to get her coat.

"I'm going to get the mail," she told Henley, and disappeared before he could voice his disapproval.

Although she was barely two months pregnant, Henley and Jesse both behaved as if she would break. She sighed, pulling on her coat as she shut the front door behind her. If they didn't lighten up it was going to be a long seven months.

Her boots crunched in the thin crust of snow that had fallen two days earlier. She inhaled, enjoying the breath of cold, fresh air she took into her lungs, and looked up at the sky with a smile. It might be cold, but the sky was clear, and after Cradle Creek and the constant pall of coal dust, she'd never complain about the weather again.

The mailbox door yielded to the firm yank she gave it, sending thin shards of icicles flying. Wishing she'd brought her gloves, she grabbed the thick stack of envelopes and had begun to flip through them when a cold gust of wind changed her mind. She began to stuff them inside the daily paper for safe-keeping until she could get inside to read in comfort and warmth.

But the handwriting on two of the letters caught her attention. Her heart slammed against her rib cage with sudden force, and she shivered, afraid to believe . . . afraid to hope.

"Oh . . . please . . . let it be," she said, tearing into the first envelope. With shaking hands, she pulled out the pages, opened them, and began to read.

Tears came swiftly. When they hit her cheeks, they froze, reminding her once again of her exposure to the cold. Quickly she stuffed the papers back inside their envelope and tore into the second one.

Jesse heard her scream. He was out of the house and off the porch before she had begun to run, scattering letters and papers along behind her like breadcrumbs. Uncertain whether to laugh or cry, she flew into Jesse's arms.

The terror that had sent him out of the house was subsiding, simply because she kept laughing and waving the mail beneath his nose. He wondered if pregnant women did this often. If they did, he wasn't certain he could survive many more frights like this one.

"Honey, are you all right?" He cupped her face, touched the traces of tears that still remained, and looked around anxiously, afraid that some unseen presence had caused her pain.

"Oh, my God!" She kept repeating the words, over and over, and then in a fit of joy she threw her arms around his neck and began to cry. "They're coming! They're coming!"

"Who?" Jesse said, trying to ignore the mail she was trampling beneath her boots as he returned her hug. It was all he could do. "Who's coming, darlin'? Don't you think you should get inside? It's too cold for you out here, and I don't think you should be dancing around like this in the snow, especially in your condition. If you want to dance, come inside. I'll dance with you there."

Diamond started to laugh and began retrieving the mail she'd dropped.

"I don't want to dance, you goose. My sisters— they're coming for Christmas. And they said they're bringing surprises."

Overwhelming relief spread a wide grin across his face as he nuzzled against the warm spot below her coat collar.

"That's fantastic, lady. But you get yourself inside—

right now!" he said. "Go tell Henley to expect God knows how many more. He'll be in a constant panic not knowing the head count, but who cares? Besides, we have a little surprise of our own for them, don't we, darlin'?"

Diamond covered his hand with her own, and the joy in her eyes as she looked up at him would remain forever in his heart.

"I'm on my way." She looked across the yard and then smiled apologetically at him. "I hope I didn't miss any letters."

"I'll check," he said, grinning. "Do as I asked—please."

Jesse watched her long legs flying as they cleared the porch steps. He winced when she jumped and then sighed in relief when the door slammed shut behind her.

"My God," he muttered as he began to retrace her steps to the mailbox, "I will not survive these next seven months."

Moments later Diamond stood at the window and watched Jesse's dark head and broad shoulders as he walked up the path. Once in a while his red shirt would disappear as he bent down to retrieve another piece of mail, and then when she could see it and him again, she would smile through tears of joy.

The scents of cinnamon and fresh-baked bread wrapped around her, a comforting reminder that she was home where she belonged. She leaned her forehead against the cold panes of glass and remembered what a gamble she'd taken by leaving Cradle Creek with a total stranger. Then she smiled, thinking that Johnny would have loved the hand fate had dealt her. It was a winner!

She saw that Jesse had started home and went to the door to meet him.

If you enjoyed *Diamond*, take a gamble with the other daughters in the Gambler's Daughters Trilogy, *Queen* and *Lucky*.

Coming soon from HarperMonogram

AVAILABLE NOW

HIGHLAND LOVE SONG by Constance O'Banyon
From the bestselling author of *Forever My Love* comes a sweeping and mesmerizing continuation of the DeWinter legacy begun in *Song of the Nightingale.* In this story, set against the splendor of nineteenth-century Scotland, innocent Lady Arrian DeWinter is abducted by Lord Warrick Glencarin, laird of Clan Drummond—the man of her dreams and the deadly enemy of her fiancé.

MY OWN TRUE LOVE by Susan Sizemore
A captivating time-travel romance from the author of *Wings of the Storm.* When Sara Dayny received a silver ring set with a citrine stone, she had no idea that it was magical. But by some quirk of fate she was transferred to early nineteenth-century London and found a brooding and bitter man who needed her love.

ANOTHER LIFE by Doreen Owens Malek
Award-winning author Doreen Owens Malek takes a steamy look behind the scenes of daytime television in this fast-paced romantic thriller. Budding young attorney Juliet Mason is frustrated with her job and pressured by a boyfriend she doesn't want to marry. Then she gets assigned to defend handsome leading actor Tim Canfield, who may be the most wonderful man she's ever met—or the most dangerous.

SHADOWS IN THE WIND by Carolyn Lampman
The enthralling story of the Cantrell family continues in Book II of the Cheyenne Trilogy. When Stephanie awakened on Cole Cantrell's ranch, she had no idea who she was. The only clues to her identity were a mysterious note and an intricate gold wedding band. Feeling responsible for her, Cole insisted she stay with him until her memory returned. But as love blossomed between them, could they escape the shadows of the past?

DIAMOND by Sharon Sala
Book I of the Gambler's Daughters Trilogy. Diamond Houston has always dreamed of becoming a country and western singer. After her father's death, she follows her heart and her instincts to Nashville with legendary country star, Jesse Eagle. There she learns that even for a life of show biz, she must gamble with her soul.

KILEY'S STORM by Suzanne Elizabeth
Daniella "Dannie" Storm thought she had enough trouble on her hands when her father found gold in the local creek and everyone in Shady Gulch, Colorado began to fight over it. But when Marshal Jake Kiley rode into town to settle the matter, she realized that her problems had only just begun—especially her strong attraction to him.

COMING NEXT MONTH

CHEYENNE AMBER by Catherine Anderson

From the bestselling author of the Comanche Trilogy and *Coming Up Roses* comes a dramatic western set in the Colorado Territory. Under normal circumstances, Laura Cheney would never have fallen in love with a rough-edged tracker. But when her infant son was kidnapped by Comancheros, she had no choice but to hire Deke Sheridan. "*Cheyenne Amber* is vivid, unforgettable, and thoroughly marvelous."—Elizabeth Lowell

MOMENTS by Georgia Bockoven

A heartwarming new novel from the author of *A Marriage of Convenience* and *The Way It Should Have Been*. Elizabeth and Amado Montoyas' happy marriage is short-lived when he inexplicably begins to pull away from her. Hurt and bewildered, she turns to Michael Logan, a man Amado thinks of as a son. Now Elizabeth is torn between two men she loves—and hiding a secret that could destroy her world forever.

TRAITOROUS HEARTS by Susan Kay Law

As the American Revolution erupted around them, Elizabeth "Bennie" Jones, the patriotic daughter of a colonial tavern owner, and Jon Leighton, a British soldier, fell desperately in love, in spite of their differences. But when Jon began to question the loyalties of her family, Bennie was torn between duty and family, honor and passion.

THE VOW by Mary Spencer

A medieval love story of a damsel in distress and her questionable knight in shining armor. Beautiful Lady Margot le Brun, the daughter of a well-landed lord, had loved Sir Eric Stavelot, a famed knight of the realm, ever since she was a child and was determined to marry him. But Eric would have none of her, fearing that secrets regarding his birth would ultimately destroy them.

MANTRAP by Louise Titchener

When Sally Dunphy's ex-boyfriend kills himself, she is convinced that there was foul play involved. She teams up with a gorgeous police detective, Duke Spikowski, and discovers suspicious goings-on surprisingly close to home. An exciting, new romantic suspense from the bestselling author of *Homebody*.

GHOSTLY ENCHANTMENT by Angie Ray

With a touch of magic, a dash of humor, and a lot of romance, an enchanting ghost story about a proper miss, her nerdy fiancé, and a debonair ghost. When Margaret Westbourne met Phillip Eglinton, she never realized a man could be so exciting, so dashing, and so . . . dead. For the first time, Margaret began to question whether she should listen to her heart and look for love instead of marrying dull, insect-loving Bernard.

Harper Monogram The Mark of Distinctive Women's Fiction